INTO THE CURRENT

INTO
THE
CURRENT

JARED YOUNG

Edited by Bethany Gibson.
Cover and page design by Julie Scriver with Jared Young.
Cover image: "Morning Sun" (detail), copyright © 2014 by titoslack (iStock.com).
Printed in Canada.
10 9 8 7 6 5 4 3 2 1

Library and Archives Canada Cataloguing in Publication

Young, Jared, 1979-, author
Into the current / Jared Young.

Issued in print and electronic formats.
ISBN 978-0-86492-889-4 (paperback).--ISBN 978-0-86492-930-3 (epub).--
ISBN 978-0-86492-931-0 (mobi)

I. Title.

PS8647.O62475I55 2016   C813'.6   C2016-902434-2
                                            C2016-902435-0

We acknowledge the generous support of the Government of Canada,
the Canada Council for the Arts, and the Government of New Brunswick.

Goose Lane Editions
500 Beaverbrook Court, Suite 330
Fredericton, New Brunswick
CANADA   E3B 5X4
www.gooselane.com

For the women I am so lucky to have in my life.

We possess nothing certainly except the past.
—Evelyn Waugh, *Brideshead Revisited*

Time is our element, not a mistaken invader.
—John Updike, *Rabbit Redux*

As long as you can blame *me*, none of what
happened is *your fault*, is it?
—Rick Flag, *Suicide Squad* #23, written
by John Ostrander & Kim Yale

–0–

Hello, my love.

I suppose I really ought to explain.

Hours ago (years, maybe; seconds, possibly) I was napping happily in the twenty-third row of a Siam Airways jetliner shooting through the stratosphere between Bangkok and Tokyo.

The plane was all in one piece, at this point, and everyone inside was calmly doing what people usually do during long cross-continent flights: the fortyish Thai fellow in the seat beside me was asleep, head thrown back as if in villainous laughter, snoring in clicks and pops; the Japanese mother and son sitting in front of me were snoozing, too, cocked heads interlocked, just a tangle of fine black hair visible between the seats; across the aisle the Scandinavian girl in yoga pants was sitting all statuesque, eyes pressed shut, ears plugged by earphones, listening to music on her mobile phone and politely eluding the American dude sitting beside her, who, after spending the entire taxi and takeoff attempting small talk (attempting it poorly, too: all first-person pronouns), eventually got the hint and passed the next hours paging angrily through his ragged paperback copy of *The Beach* and ordering round after round of tomato juice from the tiny Filipino flight attendant, Ireneo, who earlier in the flight had offered me a cup of ice to press against my still-swollen black eye, and who, as I dozed, was somewhere up ahead pouring drinks and distributing cellophane-wrapped sugar cookies.

And me, yes, right in the middle of it all, napping happily, my sweater bunched up behind my head, my collection of *Suicide Squad* comics stacked neatly on the tray table, my aching brain soothed by the lullaby drone of jet engines sucking, igniting, exhaling.

All was well.

All was calm.

And then—

The plane quivered and swayed and dipped and settled.

My ears popped, and from the hundred other passengers in the cabin there came a harmony of gasps, moans, whimpers, wails, and hissing inhalations. But there was a pleasant dissonance to that single note, like the wheeze of a warming-up orchestra, and because I'm an experienced flyer, not prone to panic over some minor spasm of turbulence, I ignored it all, kept my eyes closed, kept sweetly dreaming.

A soft single note rang throughout the cabin: the seat belt light coming on.

But there was another note, too. Far off, faint, but slowly rising, definitely there, definitely the sound of—what? Something familiar, something mundane, something that was completely out of place here at ten thousand feet. Maybe a teakettle gathering its breath and getting ready to scream?

And then, like a gaggle of waterfowl frightened by a gunshot, the stack of comics on my tray table exploded into flight. Paper wings flapped madly in my face; stapled spines karate-chopped the bridge of my nose. My hands swatted spastically in front of my face, and through the kinetoscopic blink of my fingers I saw my comics dart away (in a V-shape, I swear!) into the bright blue crack in the fuselage above my head.

But.

Well.

That's not *totally* accurate.

You see, my love, as the plane went through its silent pre-explosion paroxysms, I wasn't really "napping happily." Neither napping, nor happy. My eyes were closed, my arms were folded, but I was only *feigning* sleep. The truth is (sorry, this is going to be awkward for you to hear) I was in the midst of a grand sexual daydream about a girl I knew back in high school.

Her name was Erin Seeley. She was a biathlete with a svelte boy's body padded in the proper girlish places. She had the jaundiced complexion and acute features of a figure from a Victorian faerie painting, and I loved her the way that teenage boys love teenage girls: with desperate stupidity, with pathetic hope. How stunned I was by the very potential of her! She sang, she played guitar. She headlined every high school talent show with acoustic covers of Smashing Pumpkins songs. She was smart, too: in English class she made reference to books that no one had ever heard of, that many of us suspected she had fabricated altogether (*Love in the Time of Cholera*? It sounds so fake). Mysterious, also: she was always absent from school to attend Olympic time trials and fundraising dinners with famous amateur athletes. She won every essay contest sponsored by the local clubs and community associations. She was flown across the country to hold private audience with minor politicians and activist celebrities. Yes, Erin Seeley lived a portentous sort of life, and every girl I've met since has suffered in comparison.

The point?

The point is, in the teenage caste system, at the age of fifteen, I looked up at Erin Seeley from my disadvantageous position as the new kid in town, recently arrived under dubious circumstances, physically underdeveloped, poorly dressed, socially clumsy, an academic underachiever and hierarchical nobody, and, as I admired her from a distance, she became totemic to me, and remained such, and *remains* such, even here, even *now*, almost a decade since I last laid eyes on her. To be with a girl like Erin Seeley is to be cured of your meaninglessness, absolved of your crimes, proven *worthy*; a perfect girl, in wanting you, can make you perfect, too. And so, when I am feeling ill, or bored, or depressed, or must otherwise pass time in a half-conscious meditative state (while jogging, while commuting to work, while searching for sleep on a long pan-oceanic flight), my thoughts often drift to her.

I'll imagine running into her at random. At a party, in a restaurant, on the street — doesn't matter. We'll chat and laugh and reminisce about those long-ago high school days. I am no longer a doughy-faced teenage wallflower, and she senses the change in me. A current of attraction arcs and crackles between us. So we sneak away from the party/restaurant/wherever and share a tender kiss; later, at her apartment, she drapes newspaper on the floor and cuts my hair and afterwards strips off her shirt to shake out the bristles (we're already this comfortable with each other); after that, while I'm above her, thrusting, she urges me to go "faster!" and pulls the discarded T-shirt over her face like an executioner's mask (she's into this sort of debauchery, I happily discover); months later, we rent a small studio apartment in Paris and make love on cloudy afternoons in that casual, half-drunk, European way (beautifully lit in gauzy yellows, scored by a solo piccolo); months after that, in New York City, drunk and dizzy from the bass beat of a dance club, we conduct Romanesque experiments with third and fourth and fifth parties (in this fantasy world, I've been doing a lot of abdominal crunches, a lot of shoulder presses, drinking a lot of protein shakes). We spend the following years travelling the world together, Erin and I, from the slums of Mumbai to the sidewalk cafés of Buenos Aires, and our cross-continent plane trips have become so prosaic, so tedious, that to pass the time we cuddle beneath the coarse airline blanket, and she uses her tiny fist to coax from me quiet orgasms while around us the other passengers doze—

—but, no, no, you've got it all wrong. It's not *just* about sex. Didn't you see those connective plot devices, that clever symbolism, that, uh ... *catharsis*? There's a narrative logic to these fantasies, I swear!

Okay, sure—maybe I linger in the most salacious moments. And sure, yes, all that stuff about haircuts and Mumbai slums and gauzy Parisian afternoons is thrown in to make my filthy imaginings seem less filthy (boys will do that, you know: give boring context to their illicit urges to make them seem well-intentioned). I will, however, defend my lechery in this particular case, because my fantasy of Erin Seeley was no functionless act of perversion. There was purpose in my perversion. As I sat there in my narrow seat, eyes closed, listening to the phlegmatic growl of the engines, I was in excruciating physical pain. Each little jitter of turbulence electrified my skeleton. Every shallow half-breath expanded my lungs against quills of hot pain growing from my ribs. Every infinitesimal movement abraded a sensitive cluster of nerves, pebbles of broken glass grinding in sockets, nettles twisting and turning in bone marrow.

Two days before I boarded the plane, I was in a street fight beneath the Phrom Phong Skytrain station in downtown Bangkok. A vicious brawl. A real knock-down, drag-out type of thing. Lead pipes, brass knuckles, stilettos, switchblades. I barely escaped with my life—

Ah, hell, I've completely lost the capacity to lie, up here.

It wasn't really a fight.

Fight implies some degree of mutual participation. What happened two days ago was really more of a *beating*. The truth is, I was *mercilessly beaten* beneath the Phrom Phong Skytrain station, and I conjured that well-used daydream of Erin to distract myself from the lingering physical agony. Like I said, a functional act of perversion. What better salve for my broken hand than to sweep it lovingly over the swells and declines I remember so well from my long-ago classroom observations. What better way to drown out the caterwauling of my swelled brain than with the sound of Erin's arrhythmic breaths building to climax—

But why am I telling you all this? *You*, in particular? If anyone should be spared the specifics of my lecherous delusions, it's you, my love. So I'll skip over what Erin was doing when the *Suicide Squad* comics exploded into my face (hint: it involves the flexibility she learned as an amateur athlete) and will instead point out that the memories of her from which I built that soothing bit of pornography were the *very last memories* I remembered in the traditional, fragmented, fleeting, blurry-movie-screen manner—

What was I—?

Yes, right.

I was telling you about the crack in the fuselage.

It was, oh, about three feet long, six inches wide. Big enough to frighten to life all the napkins and newspapers and magazines and jackets and hats and plastic wrappers and plastic cups and mobile phones and laptops loose in the cabin, send them all spinning in accelerating arcs, clattering against the walls and seats and overhead bins, which unlatched and puked out a torrent of purses and coats and bubble-wrapped folk art from Chatuchak Market. Teakwood portraits of Buddha cartwheeled over our heads. Elephant carvings rattled against our skulls. Colourful silk scarves swam like eels around our ankles. Ice-cold air blew in our faces. Tendrils of fog spread across the ceiling.

And, then—oh, poor Ireneo.

The intruding atmosphere sucked her up. She fell against the cabin ceiling as if gravity had switched its polarity. Her body sealed the breach, and for a moment she just *hung* there, limbs flailing, hands reaching. The roar dimmed, the soothing white noise of normal pan-Pacific air travel resumed. I had the strange sensation of being suspended myself, as if I were looking down on her, and thought to myself: maybe this is it? Maybe we'll pass the rest of the five-hour flight watching her scramble like a pinned beetle against the vaulted ceiling? My eyes met hers and I saw that she was not yet in a panic, not yet in pain, rather calmly considering this strange new circumstance of physics.

But then her mouth tightened. Her eyebrows lifted. Not an expression of surprise, no. Her hair was yanked back and then her purple Siam Airways blouse stretched and strained. Plastic buttons, subject to the gravity her contortions were enabling, clattered to the floor. Her name tag landed near my foot: *Ireneo Funes, Siam Airways*. There rose the slurping sound of milkshake dregs sucked through a straw, and behind it an urgent, rising whistle—

With a riflecrack, Ireneo disappeared.

The ribbon of sky, now a bellowing blue mouth, had swallowed her whole.

The plane tilted, my face was thrown against the porthole window, and I watched the right-side wing, propelled by a flaming nacelle trailing black smoke, make a break for Okinawa. Now wingless (the other coward abandoned us, too) the plane began to plummet. I was stomach-punched, lifted in my seat, hips pinched by the twisted seat belt. Looking down the length of the cabin, I could see that the immutable machine that had carried us with such confidence into the sky had adopted a disturbing aspect of liquidity; the fuselage wrinkled in oncoming waves, a reflection of itself in rippling water. The secret of all solid stuff, that it's just a bunch of tiny particles rubbing together, was revealed in the bending and bowing and oscillation of once-straight lines, and, unable to bear the embarrassment of it, panels in the floor and wall began to flee, bolts popped like bullets, a whole volley of them fired up through the ceiling and pierced some vital structural vein that split the cabin on a lengthwise hinge as if it were a cadaver cracked open for autopsy. Flamelets of black hair flickered madly above the seats.

Next to me, the fortyish Thai fellow was still gape-mouthed, now shrieking, but the sound of his shriek was the roaring nothing-sound of jet engines in the throes of death. The Scandinavian girl across the aisle was still statuesque, still snubbing her seatmate, but her eyes were open, her hands were clutched to the armrests, her mobile phone was jouncing over her head like the hand of an eager, answer-bearing student, tethered still to her ears by the little plastic buds, but then one popped loose, then the other, and the whole thing helicoptered away. Beside her, the American dude jerked in his chair. Everyone jerked in their chairs. I jerked in my chair, and the wild wobble and yaw of the plane scrambled my senses: I saw the screech of shearing metal, heard the stink of jet fuel, smelled the vivid blue hues of sky. My innards took it poorly, too: the saliva in my mouth evaporated instantly, leaving my tongue a husk, my throat a bundle of straw.

We fell.

We fell and fell and fell and I floated weightless, two inches above my seat, tethered by my sturdy seat belt. The terrible speed contracted my stomach into a hard little muscle the size of a quarter and, like a collapsing star, drew towards it all my other organs—the whole heavy mass, the whole wet mush of kidney and liver and lung, pressed against my anus from the inside; it felt like being turned inside out.

What does one think in a moment like this? To be honest, few thoughts of mortality or transience crossed my mind.

No euphoria, no dread. No thoughts of family and friends. No deductive analysis of the previous week's events and how they seemed (especially now) a conspiracy to get me aboard this stupid, doomed plane. Even as it's happening, you can't quite believe it's happening; it looks so much less real than it looks in movies; a plane can't *really* be made of this fragile, crumbly stuff. A small part of me was certain that this was nothing more than a weird waking nightmare, a fever dream, a hallucination induced by all those painkillers I swallowed in the departures lounge bathroom before boarding, and that if I could just blink my eyes at the right speed, in the right sequence of short and long dashes, I'd awaken to find myself still sitting in the Sala Daeng Police Station, or still splayed on the sidewalk beneath the Phrom Phong Skytrain station, or still at Bumrungrad Hospital, uncomfortably folded up in the armchair next to Carrie's bed, or maybe still standing at the Cambodian border, staring down that cycloptic scam-artist—

—and then another deafening *pop*, a tremendous whiplash shock, like we'd struck some solid barrier. My head ping-ponged between the tray table and headrest. Stars burst, fires worked. I blinked open my prickly eyes to see, where the front of the plane had been, a serene view of planet earth's horizon.

The plane had broken in half.

The crack was no longer a crack, it was a vista, a panorama.

The plane was no longer a plane, it was a hollowed-out missile hurtling earthward, wilting flowerlike.

FTANG!

Far ahead of me, a row of seats blasted into the atmosphere. Three chairs and the passengers sitting in them, detached, ejected, flung aside, plunging, gone.

FTANG!

One row closer, another three-seat section peeled free, another trio of passengers lifted into the sky, hands reaching high like rollercoaster aficionados cresting the first big drop, faint shrieks truncated.

My instinct was to escape, so I reached for the buckle of my seat belt, made to flip it open, but noticed then that my Thai companion was gone, his seat belt unbuckled, straps unstrapped and whipping around, so instead of opening the buckle I slipped my fingers beneath the belt and held on, as they say, *for dear life.*

FTANG!

The metal tracks that ran the length of the cabin, upon which the seats were mounted, curled up from the floor in elegant swoops and spirals and beckoned like tentacles.

FTANG!

Across the aisle, the stoic Scandinavian and her American pursuer were gone. Where they once sat, an empty square of floor.

In front of me, above the headrests, sneakered stick-legs kicked at the sky. The Japanese boy wasn't wearing his seat belt, and his mother, with her immense motherly strength, was holding him there, playing tug-of-war with the heavens, and just when it seemed that she'd locked her grip, that she was going to save him, *FTANG!*, they were both gone, just like that, and all that lay before me was horrible height and blinding brightness, until—

FTANG!

An invisible hand plucked me from the chaos.

The three seats in my row exploded from their steel

moorings and I was shockingly immersed in white nothingness, somersaulting, spinning, twirling, hurtling, clutching
the armrests, a kaleidoscopic collage of blues and browns and
greens, the ocean below, above, below, bright sky to my left,
the ocean, the ocean, the ocean, the sky, the ocean, the seat
belt straps on either side whipping and snapping as if desperate, like me, to gain purchase on the edge of any precipice,
then more ocean, more sky, and, looming beneath my feet,
the wingless shaft of the jumbo jet cracked open like an egg,
leaking strands of mechanical yolk.

Something soft struck me in the face (a woman's purse,
these lonely months of contemplation have revealed),
something hard rattled against my arm (a fist-sized curve of
plastic that was once part of the plane's interior wall), and then
a split-second glimpse of a curious thing: one of my *Suicide
Squad* comics, still wrapped in its protective polybag, tucked
between the armrest of my seat and the cushion, pinched there
and held tight through all the spinning, twirling, etc. — but
as soon as I noticed it, fingers of wind shook it loose and it
darted away to catch up with the rest of the flock, and that's
when, suddenly —

Everything slowed down.

The downdrafts pushing me earthward were curtly extinguished. The somersaulting became a gentle glide. The
smudge of green/blue/brown coalesced to form this serene
topographic view.

And then it all stopped.

The plane, the flames, the smoke, the clouds, the wind, the
waves, the rotation of the earth, the nuclear boil of the sun,
the slow spin of the galaxy, the expansion of the universe — it

all just stopped, and, as it was minutes earlier, while I was dreaming of Erin Seeley's busy fist, the world and everything in it was peaceful.

Yes, everything has stopped, everything is frozen in place, and I've been left stranded up here in the sky.

But that, my love, isn't even the weird part.

Oh, no.

Not even close.

A NOVEL BY
JARED YOUNG

INTO
THE
CURRENT

PART I

DRAG THE SUNLIT SEA

−1−

My Throne faces northeast, ten thousand feet or so above the ocean. Below me, spread flat over most of the eastern horizon, is the Japanese archipelago and, somewhere on Kyushu's coastal shoulder, my erstwhile destination: Fukuoka Airport. On the western horizon there is an illusion of breadth that I suppose is the eastern shore of China. To the northwest, the ripped-paper edge of South Korea. I can see just a small section of it, though, because there is cloud cover in that direction. If the clouds were moving, they'd perhaps float past and offer me a clear view of the entire peninsula, but, of course, the clouds aren't moving. They are, like everything else, stationary. Stuck, paused. Way down beneath me, fishing trawlers and cargo ships sit among the parallel perforations in the ocean's surface like little musical notes on an infinite staff. And up here, all around me, hung like ornaments in the sky, are the remains of the plane. All that formerly vital stuff: jagged fragments of iron-lined eggshell that were once pieces of the fuselage; balled-up wads of used tissue that were once the papery marrow that insulated it. Hanging near the detached left wing (suspended upright like a shark's fin) is a murder of sheared-away turboprop blades, raised and crossed like the swords of warring samurai. Past that, a darting school of flat aluminum panels. Turbines and hydraulics and curled strips of shredded tire and bundles of wire and copulating oxygen-mask octopi and cloud-like accumulations of personal effects (to the southwest, a flock of newspapers and magazines; to the southeast, a pack of shoes migrating towards Australia; migrating, but, you know, not actually *moving*—a dioramic suggestion of migration).

And besides all that inorganic dross, the passengers, too.

There are no faces close enough for me to see, but a few hundred feet below me, to the west, a human body in a sky-diver's spread-eagle pose is silhouetted against the ocean, and, a few hundred feet above me, in the same direction, another human shape, this one tucked in a cannonball—a man, woman, child? White, Thai? I don't know (but I *do* know that they're barefoot; their pink soles are pointed right at me). For a while, I called out to these folks. I thought perhaps they were still conscious, like I am, but there has so far been no response. They don't move; they don't make noise. I can only assume that they're frozen in place like everything else. Just inanimate things, now. Just more wreckage.

I am alone. There is just me, Daniel Solomon.

Let me state, for the record, that I was/am, at the moment of Time's cessation, twenty-three years old, 5 feet 8.5 inches tall, which is precisely the median height for my age, and 147 pounds, which is within the range of my optimal weight according to the body mass index (*optimal*, in this case, a synonym for normal, common, standard, regular, etc.).

What other details shall I record for you, my love?

I'm pasty without being pale, pink without being tan.

I show off a few protruding ribs, but not enough to look gaunt. I'm not skinny, not fat. My body is a generic textbook illustration of the human body. If I were to commit a crime, the police artist's sketch would be a stick-figure, or the symbol from a men's room door, or Da Vinci's Vitruvian Man (minus the magnificent hair). And this face! My nose, my mouth — how can I describe them? They are simply a nose and mouth, too plain to deserve any exotic qualifiers like Roman, piggish, hawkish, hooked, humped, oft-broken, pouty, pursed, pinched. I have eyes that waver, depending on the light, between brown and dull green. I have dun-coloured hair that is neither long nor short, rather inscrutably mid-length, betrothed to no popular fashion, cut that way (probably on purpose) by the person who put me on this plane.

My surname, Solomon (the name of a king!) might imply that I carry within me the whole rich history of the Jewish faith. But Solomon, in my case, is derivative of Solovski, the Slavic name carried across the ocean by my Russian forebears and immediately abandoned in favour of something they thought would be more advantageous in the WASPy new world. Ha! If only I *were* Jewish — then at least there would be some hefty historical block to fill the empty slot where, in others, an *identity* is found.

I do feel sort of kingly, though, perched up here, looking out across this interrupted commonwealth. Among all these commoners, I am special. Time exists, now, only for me. Or maybe *within* me. Under normal circumstances, Time passes and iron rusts, bread moulds, water evaporates — atoms, at their own selfish whims, intermingle, transfer energy, ruin everything. But up here, where Time has taken a vacation, a barrier has been erected between these particles; they can't speak to each other, they can't touch each other, they can't fall out of their rank and file. Without Time to prod them along, these atoms can't scatter. The universal process of decay has somehow been suspended.

But somehow I am breathing. My heart is beating. I can shift myself from one sitting position to another. I can unbuckle my seat belt, stand up in my chair, stretch. I can speak aloud, like I'm doing right now, and send waves of vibrating particles through the air. I can form deep thoughts about matters of quantum reality (I think, therefore I am), and each of these events occurs as part of a sequence, divided by a measurable instance of Time.

But how to measure those immeasurable stretches? After moving to Thailand, where the changes in season were invisible, I found myself unable to account for the passing of months; no fall, no winter, no spring, just an endless summer marked by torrential or slightly-less-than-torrential periods of rainfall. Twice I lived through those climatic changes and still couldn't make sense of it: I thought July was February! Being up here is like that: time is somehow still passing for me, but not for everyone/everything else, so there is no variation to distinguish one nanosecond from the hundred billion others. The sun is just sitting there. We're not moving around it anymore. The blissful disintegration of the plane might have occurred seconds ago, or weeks, or maybe *decades*.

But, like I said, this breaking of Time's Arrow isn't the weird part. It's just context for the *real* weirdness. My physical predicament is preposterous, sure, but it could very well be the result of some heretofore undiscovered principle of quantum mechanics, and could then be explained by some miles-long formula filled with numbers and letters and Greek characters and square roots and parentheses within parentheses within parentheses. But the other thing that has happened to me—

——there's no noun or verb that can accurately describe it.

I suppose I'll just have to show you.

Are you ready?

"*Iz dvukh zol vybi—vbyi, vbyi… uhhh, vbyi*rayut *men'sheye*," my grandmother says. I'm sitting beside her bed, in her wheelchair, gripping the grey rubber rims on each wheel and pacing back and forth in short thrusts and retreats.

The clock on the wall reads 2:02 p.m.

"It's a famous old Russian saying," she continues. "Which means that when all the choices are bad, you, uhhh … you choose the one that is …"

I'm watching her knobby finger turn circles, conducting an invisible orchestra, searching for the elusive final notes of the cadenza. My grandmother's remaining vitality, learned during her laborious farmhand childhood and effortlessly maintained into her seventh decade, is now concentrated in the circling finger struggling to reel in the second half of that fleeing phrase.

"You know—the one that … *hurts* the least."

Her finger curls into a fist, her lips go flat, she shakes her head. *Oh, hell, I give up,* is the sum of these gestures.

She lives, now, in the Sunnyside Adventist Care Home, a one-storey tan-brick building crouched low, abashed, behind the fast food restaurants and car dealerships of Regina's commercial outskirts. Eight months of tenure have earned her the least cramped and least sad of all the sad, cramped rooms; at the very end of the easternmost L, with a window facing west onto the parking lot of a convenience store, where in summer teens too young for nightclubs park with their high beams blazing, shedding plastic wrappers, tossing empty cans, spilling quaking bass from their expensive car stereos; another window looks north onto the square patch of dirt-choked grass referred to (satirically, I think) as *the garden*, where the same teenagers go to piss and smoke weed out of sight.

My grandmother was a gardener, once upon a time; her fingernails were always clipped short and tamped with dark dirt. Dirt and sometimes paint. She was, in secret, a painter. But her only hobbies, now, are sleep and stillness. She was once a champion chatter, too, able to clinch a telephone receiver between her shoulder and cheek while she rolled perogies and scrubbed linens in the sink, but she speaks now, when she speaks at all, mostly in non sequiturs, mostly to the ceiling tiles. *She's just not herself*, my mother had warned me, but the literality of that diagnosis didn't strike me until I saw her. The same way a growing infant can seem an entirely new organism after a few months, the elderly can lose, in that same span, an inverse measure of essence and heft. Barely a hundred pounds is left of her, yet she is sunk deep into the soft mattress as if she weighs a thousand. Her face, once a finely sculpted and symmetrical whole of bone and cartilage and flesh, is now a loose heap: nose and brow and cheeks and chin wadded together, a likeness built from chewed chewing gum and putty and translucent gauze. A death mask. Yes, it really does appear as if she has been torn down and rebuilt from scratch like that; haphazardly, lazily.

She says, *"Budet kuzovok*... you know, like a seed?"

"Sure, yeah—" I begin, but a yawn blocks my throat. I'm exhausted, right now. Marti called again last night, and no matter how cold and curt my answers, she kept asking questions, kept tolerating my intolerance. It was almost three in the morning before I finally got her to hang up, and, once again, her parting words were some nonsense about how she'd forgiven me, which, frankly, justified all the coldness and curtness I'd earlier hurled her way and should have given me reason to sleep peacefully. But I didn't. I slept in fits and starts. And now I can't stop yawning in my poor grandmother's face.

She looks around. "I had a cup of tea sitting here—where did it go? It was right there. In a green cup. It was a green cup of tea, with... above, it was like the sky. You know? It was like water, with the waves and the... you know."

I roll myself backwards and scan the room.

"I don't see a cup, Grandma."

She tries to lift her head. "Did she take it? I know she takes my things. Go and look in her drawer, see if my tea is in there. It's in there, I can see the lines. See it? It's making that same shape as tea makes."

I roll myself to the small bureau on the far wall, extract each drawer and stick my nose inside and tell her: "No, nothing in here."

"She probably drank it, the goddamn *bitch*."

Wow, she really delivered that one, didn't she? Her mouth seems familiar with profanity. A false familiarity created by the three minor strokes that have razed the nerve cells in her aging brain? Or is this simply a lifting of the veil—has she always been a secret swearer that same way she'd been a secret painter?

Who knows. She certainly doesn't. She has forgotten her whole human self, right down to the very foundational grains of genetic knowledge passed down through umpteen steppe-dwelling generations. Dementia the mortar, her skull the pestle, and in the grinding pressure an entire lifetime of memories has been reduced to dust. The doctors boast about her robust health (with these sturdy joints and meaty heart she could live to ninety, they say) but it's no comfort to hear that her physical form marches on without the rest of her. She possesses a body but no recollection of where it has been, what it has done. Her consciousness is now at the whim of synaptic breakers switched on and off by clotted blood blowing recklessly through the narrow vessels in her brain. I can see it happening: her eyes turn smoky, parboiled; the whites dim, the pupils darken.

"My cup of tea—what did you do to it? Did you steal it?"

Right now, my mother might stroke her mother's parchment hand and say something soothing like "don't worry, it's okay, no one stole your tea," but such calming corrective statements are not second nature to me as they are, after months of vigil, to my mom. Instead, when my grandmother goes off on her tangents, I just nod in agreement and laugh as if she's joking.

"It's dark, now," she says.

"What?" I say.

"Come on, let's go, we're leaving." Her eyes go wide. "*Yes*, right now, *hurry*!"

"What?"

"It's okay. He's drunk, he's asleep. He won't hear a thing."

I nod. I laugh.

Are you picking up on this, my love?

Oh, come on, it's so *obvious*!

The verbatim dialogue?

The impossible detail?

"Pacing back and forth in short thrusts and retreats ... Watching her knobby finger turn circles ... The clock on the wall reads 2:02 p.m." You think I'm picking out these bits from memory? Dumb, half-blurry fraudster memory?

No, my love, I'm *looking right at it.*

Don't you find it the least bit suspicious that I'm describing it all in the *present tense*?

The extraordinary thing about this particular memory is that *it's not a memory*. It's not playing out, as memories do, on some candescent movie screen in the darkness of my conscious mind. No, I am *there*! I am physically *there*, right *there*, sitting next to my grandmother!

Right *here*, sitting next to my grandmother!

I've torn through the caul of consciousness, reversed some irreversible law of space-time, and am *right now* strapped into my long-lost twenty-one-year-old body! I'm wearing myself like a suit of armour, each of my five senses slipped into immaculately tailored apertures. Eyes, ears, tongue, nose... each is wearing this earlier iteration of itself! I'm not "remembering" my grandmother. I'm *here* with her!

I can see, as if my twenty-one-year-old corneas are contact lenses worn over my present pair, every tiny detail of her face, each individual hatch-mark wrinkle in her sunken cheeks, in the bunched-up skin beneath her chin.

I can see, pinned to the wall above her bed, the collage of family photos my mother has hung: myself, my mother, my grandmother, her parents, her younger sister, Masha.

I can see, on the bedside table, the little porcelain figurine, a baby horse curled up and catnapping on a plinth of polished grass, that belonged to my grandmother when she was young, which she gave to me when I was a kid, and which I have now returned to her in hopes of beautifying her desolate room.

I can taste the sweet residue, dark and sticky and bitter, of the Coke I chugged a minute (or two years) ago.

I can hear, behind me, the buzz and tick of a trapped bumblebee throwing itself against the closed window, and above it, the soft hiss of the ventilator and a susurrus of voices conferring in the hallway.

I can smell my grandmother's elderly skin, eighty-six years of dust and ointment and food accumulated and absorbed and in these last hours expelled, as if the human body, in its final days, exhales its aggregate experience from each microscopic pore.

No, I'm not *remembering* this. The verb *remember*, in describing this peculiar phenomenon, isn't accurate. No verb is accurate. No noun, either. This is no metaphysical reconstruction of my grandmother's room at Sunnyside in May of 2003, this *is* my grandmother's room at Sunnyside, this *is* May 2003.

I am *here*!

I have travelled through time (two years, two hundred sixty-seven days, four hours, and twenty-three minutes into the past) and space (four thousand miles in a general north-easterly direction), and am sitting next to my grandmother as she tells me:

"I'm grabbing your hand, and, oh, hell, stop, leave that behind— yes, *that*, you don't need that, Masha, come with me."

When I try to move my hands, they remain motionless. My consciousness has travelled back here, my senses have stowed away (illegally, incomprehensibly), but my Free Will has been left behind. My muscles obey only the invisible commands programmed in the long-ago moment:

I shift in the wheelchair seat to alleviate the numbness in my left buttock.

I tap my heel against the folded-out footpad.

I pull at the waist of my jeans, hike them up to cover the band of bare skin exposed by the slipping elastic waist of my boxer shorts.

The sound of my grandmother's failing voice, abraded by age, is as crystal clear as the phlegmatic growl of grinding-apart glass and steel and plastic just minutes ago inside the plane.

"It's such an easy thing to do. Look how easy it is. You just — there we go, like this."

I nod: pulling tendons in my neck, twin twinges in each shoulder, a ghostly tick in the base of my skull; quondam hydraulic processes mindlessly performed but not my own—they belonged to me, once, but not anymore.

I laugh: an echo flung forward three years without dissipating.

For some strange reason I am thinking of:

The hot tropical sun.

The sound of the ocean.

My grandmother says:

"Oh, it's so hot! Even from far away. We're so far away and it's still so hot! Can you feel how hot it is? I can feel it on my skin."

Oh, here it comes, my nostrils draw air, my lips peel apart, my chest compresses and presses up from my throat a column of air that is carved by my tongue and teeth into the sound of myself saying:

"ARE YOU TOO HOT, GRANDMA!? DO YOU WANT ME TO TAKE OFF THE BLANKET!?"

Good God! Did you hear that? My voice, here, isn't merely a wave of pressure trapped inside my cochlea, I'm not hearing it as an external stimulus; it occurs as a deafening roar inside my head, even louder than the naked bawling of the jet engines; it's the loudest sound I've ever heard; it's vibrating in my eardrums, but travelling in the wrong direction, out of my head, out through my ears.

"I say to you, he's asleep, he's drunk, I promise—he won't feel a thing."

"I THINK YOU'RE JUST HAVING A BAD DREAM."

"Yes, you're right. Don't look, Masha. This is just a bad dream. You'll wake up soon, and it will all be over."

She stops herself. One of those breakers in her brain just switched on. See? In her eyes? The smoke has blown clear, the dimness has turned silver. Her pupils are hollow again, permeable. She looks at me and smiles and, with a surprising display of agility, reaches over and picks up the little porcelain horse. Just that minor bit of movement (the lifting of her shoulder, the turning of her neck, the clamping mechanism of her fingers) seems supernaturally athletic. I'm stunned by it.

I feel a peaceful clarity. Like drawing in a cold draft of spring air, like the normalizing sigh after a bout of deep laughter. A skipped beat.

"Oh, hello," she says.

Her voice sounds just like her real voice.

With a beatific grin, she adds: "It was on purpose, you know. And I'm only sorry that I'm not sorry."

But just as quickly as this gracefulness possesses her, it absconds, and she sinks back into the mattress (even deeper, now). Her eyes go up to the ceiling, still searching for the secret cipher hidden in the perforated panels. Her head rocks from side to side, she's politely saying no, she's listening to some great old song with a quick snare in the backbeat. Her pale tongue drags itself from one cracked corner of her mouth to the other.

And then she's gone.

Dead, I mean.

That porcelain bauble is still in her hand, though; the little foal's painted-on eyes peek through her knuckles. My eyes focus on it, then flit away, then whiz around the room, ocular muscles twitching with epileptic speed, barely a fraction of a second focused on one thing before moving on to another. I'm getting dizzy. Not me, there. Me, *here*, inside me-there. It's the typical wandering attention of the conscious mind, but, for me, as a passenger inside myself, it's chaos. It's just like (or *will be* just like, or *was* just like) the frightening wobble of turbulence that announced the cracking open and shredding apart and plunging away of the jet. I've learned to bear it, though, the same way you learn to bear water in your nose while you're swimming.

Some memories (like this one, for example) feel clearer than others; the glove into which my senses fit is sometimes thin like gossamer, other times thick as an oven mitt. But lucidity isn't dependent on my age. We can go right back to the very beginning. Watch this:

Here I am, wrapped in a blanket, cradled in the crook of an arm. My focus gropes and grasps but can't quite find the right depth. The world is a grey haze, a foggy maritime afternoon; mountainous shapes merge and separate in the distance; my ears are filled to overflowing with a booming clatter, crashing waves, far-off thunder. One mountain looms close, a cliff-face of crags and creases and ridges and white grassy plains above. The wind carries acrid bursts of garlic and sage and the earthy chemical smoke of instant coffee. This is my great-grandfather, my grandmother's father. The Russian. He came across the Atlantic on an Estonian cargo ship shortly after the clock of history was reset to welcome the new century. Even with my week-old nose I can smell him: the thin mountain air of Verdansk, goat manure and lea flowers and the grease he stroked on wagon axles when he was ten and just learning to shoulder the immensity of his present and future life. His enormous, distorted, planet-like visage fills my narrow field of vision, and while I recognize him behind these baby-goggles, and recognize the elements of his human face (a mouth, a nose, eyes, bushy eyebrows), I am terrified. The ticklish broil of tears rises in my sinuses. My little lips jitter. Let's get out of here. Let's go somewhere a little more pleasant, like, say—

Kyle Sutendra's house party in the twelfth grade, where I'm sitting at the top of the stairs, making out with Marti Barrett.

Kissing! Transcendent! How easy to forget what a charge two poking tongues can generate! She was sitting here on the top step, waiting to use the bathroom, but clearly waiting for me, and when I sat down beside her there was nothing to say, our eyes met for only a millisecond before our wide-open mouths, with a clockwise quarter-turn, locked together, and now we have released our tongues to do that strange disco dance where they're seeking simultaneously to collide and elude (so glad I chewed that curled worm of toothpaste, swallowed that capful of mouthwash, drank all that coppery tap water out of my cupped hands and rinsed the vomit from my mouth).

Her tongue is so soft, so *sharp*. Knifelike it runs across the edge of mine like it's a sharpening stone, then curls back, touches the roof of my mouth, the back of my front teeth. Mine follows, clumsy, eager, a half-step behind. But no ceasing this epic, furious kiss. No coming up for air. Ever.

I could stay here forever, you know. But there is so much more to share with you, so much more to explain.

See?

I told you it was weird.

I also told you that no verb or noun is accurate in describing this phenomenon, and for a long time (or perhaps just a short time) I believed that to be true. But I was wrong. There *is* a term to describe this flashing-by of life's major and minor movements. A common saying, a popular idiom:

Your life flashes before your eyes.

It's more than just a turn of phrase, though. You read about it all the time: climbers who fall off cliffs, soldiers staring down the barrel of an enemy rifle, motorists who turn away from oncoming traffic at the very last second—they all tell stories of Time slowing down, lost memories coming vibrantly to life in front of their eyes, visits from sweet old grandmas and childhood pets and teenage crushes.

So it seems, trapped ten thousand feet above the surface of the frozen-solid world, that my life is flashing before my eyes—but not quite in the manner one might expect from those euphoric accounts of near-death experiences.

Most significantly, I am in control. I can manipulate my movement in and out of my memories. I can choose when and where to go, how long to stay. I can skip forward and back between events and sensations like tracks on playlist. The entire archive of my past experience is accessible; this nameless talent denies me nothing. I can go anywhere within myself, but when I do, as you saw, I give up physical control to my past self and must follow along as he (me) bumbles his (my) way through life. An observer, but nothing more.

Sure, some moments, in reliving them, feel backwards and wrong. Doorways appear on opposite walls, seasons switch from fall to spring, one person is swapped with another. Deeper searches have revealed that certain dramas occur out of sequence and can't possibly be linked by the causes and effects I have so meticulously diagrammed in my head. Grand moments that have served throughout my lifetime as self-explicatory anecdotes play out as alternate-universe adaptations — the memories of a complete stranger. And there are skits and sketches that seem not to exist in this archive, and must, therefore, have *never happened*. But that's to be expected, isn't it? It's common knowledge that we're all unreliable narrators.

Outside of this magical recollection, I have little influence over the corporeal. What can I do, here in the "real world"? I can push the button on the armrest and recline my chair; I can lift my legs and sit sideways with my feet hanging over the arm of the seat; I can lift the flap of fabric behind my head and listen to the crackle of ripping Velcro (and do, some-times, for hours: a real, brand-new sound!). I can spit into the

PART I

ocean. I can weep. And yet I haven't felt the urge to urinate or defecate. Which, I suppose, makes sense, since I'm not eating or drinking. But it raises an interesting question: how come I'm not hungry or thirsty? I seemingly have no need for sustenance other than the recycled vitamins and nutrients I pick up second-hand in the past (I think often of food and have revisited some great feasts). Yet I have tried holding my breath, to the familiar effect of becoming light-headed and hot-faced until finally I gulp down a painful rhombus of oxygen. Seventy-nine seconds is so far my record, which doesn't suggest any magical new lung capacity or chemical restructuring of the atmosphere. I need air but not food. Funny, huh?

While my circulation and respiration continue as normal, other physical systems lag behind. My left hip, where I fell against the pavement: still a gorgeous nebula of yellow and green and grey. This welt on my forehead is still raised like a Braille character. My knuckles are still gouged, the scraped-out pits filled with crusty caulking. My old wounds aren't healing! The same pattern of blots and blemishes like imperishable watermarks beneath the surface of my skin. A few months (weeks?) ago I picked at one of the half-formed scabs on my elbow and a flake of it came off. A tiny red dot of blood appeared. I wiped it away, but it blossomed again. For days I observed it, wiping it away and watching it regenerate, until it occurred to me that the protective fibrous stuff *wasn't growing back!* The flaky scab I had nonchalantly flicked into oblivion was one-of-a-kind! I might be very, very, very, very slowly bleeding to death!

You're hurt, too, I know. You have your own wounds to

48

nurse: a separation, a tear, a sprain, a compression. Would it make you feel better, maybe distract you a bit from your own injuries, to see how I got mine? I'd really rather not re-experience the *whole* painful occasion—but if it would help you better understand why we can't be together right now, I'd be willing to go back a few days and drop into my body right after it percussed the Sukhumvit sidewalk, causing this much-celebrated hip-bruise and canonical elbow-scrape.

Sound good?

Okay, let's go.

One.

Two.

Th—

Oh no, fuck, I'm not ready, I came in too early—

Here comes the *ground*—

****!

This is, this is—

—*this*, I think, is a close-up view of the sidewalk.

Stars! You really do see them.

Agkch!

Fttt!

More punches and kicks to my forehead and neck and ears while I'm on the ground, fluttering my hands in poor impression of defence, and then—oh, right, *these* guys! I forgot about these guys, these three beefy Brits pulling the blond guy away from me. But, even as they do, fat forearms looped through his armpits and around his neck, he strains towards me, exhaling furiously, spitting through his clenched teeth. I can see, in his fist, the strap of an orange- and white-striped traveller's backpack; he has torn it right off my back, and as he's swallowed up by that tangle of sunburnt limbs, the front flap opens and ejects a pair of balled-up socks and a tube of moisturizer. I draw a breath to complain, to cry *thief,* but instead I recede into a greyish fog of half-consciousness. A surge of spilling blood plugs both nostrils, but I can still smell the fecal stink of durian fruit; there must have been a vendor parked here beneath Phrom Phong station, on the very tract of sidewalk where I'm now crumpled, now sprawling, now propped on my elbows and trying to unite the vibrating planes of vision clubbed out of synchronous orbit by the blond guy's fists. I gain my feet and shuffle, half-hunched, into the nearby alley, past the congregation of evening commuters and strollers and street people stopped in their tracks by my puppyish whelps. I sit down hard against the crumbling stone wall. Here I am partially hidden from view by a shuttered-up vendor cart. I spit a gelatinous, leech-like clot of blood into my cupped hands. I tip my palms and watch the thing slither to the edge of my fingers, cling at the tips for a brave moment, then fall against the pavement with a wet slap.

I think to myself: so much blood, this last week.

And then I pass out—

—and now I wake up.

(No, not quite the right word.)

—and now I am *revived*, and in these first milliseconds of consciousness I know only naked fluorescent light and mortal bodily pain. I'm still freshly bloodied, still spouting pimples of blood from the apertures punched in my face by the cement sidewalk. My bottom lip is swollen almost to bursting, pulling with unusual weight on the corners of my mouth, like there's a double-A battery sewn inside of it. Taste that? That copper-taste, that sandy substance? It's the enamel debris of a chipped incisor.

After the fight (sorry, right: the *merciless beating*), the police arrived pretty quickly. Two street cops screeched up on motorcycles and were directed by onlookers to where I had collapsed in the alley. They lifted me by the arms and carried me rather indelicately to the curb, where an ambulance was just then pulling up. Not an ambulance, actually, but a *songthaew*-style truck decked out to look like an ambulance; the sort of bad prop you might see in a low-budget movie. The attendants, in their vaguely nautical all-white uniforms, offered a few fleeting dabs and wipes. As they led me to the rear doors of the *songthaew* and helped me inside, I scanned the crowd. But I couldn't see the blond guy. He was gone.

As I sit here, I'm yet too drowsy to report accurately on my route through the city. All I know is that instead of racing up Sukhumvit towards Samitivej Hospital, we curled off on an unfamiliar side-*soi* and ended up in some secret pocket of Bangkok that I've never seen before. Luckily, the building had an English translation above the Thai name:

Sala Daeng Police Station.

This white room is furnished only with a table and stools, and decorated only with a single, wrinkled poster bearing bold statements in Thai script overlaying a police photo of a highway accident: an upside-down car and, spilling out the smashed passenger window, an amoebic cluster of blown-up pixels, red and brown, from which emerges a human hand, palm up. Similar pictures appear every day on the front pages of Thai newspapers, always digitally obscured and somehow more gruesome for it. Cigarette packages carry government-mandated portraits of throat cancer victims posing with their chins proudly lifted.

Two hours have passed since the beating. Another ten hours will pass before I'm escorted to the airport by the man with the missing tooth.

Finally, voices. The door opens. I'm joined by a chubby Thai of indeterminate age and authority. He's wearing a polo shirt, black jeans, rubber flip-flops, and it's not clear if he's a police officer or government official (or a taxi driver, or street hustler). He wears, too, the pre-emptive wide smile of someone about to deliver bad news. Behind him, a younger fellow in pinstripe slacks and a pink tie, a button missing from his tailored blazer, an incisor missing from his otherwise impeccable mouth. He stays standing while the chubby guy sits down across from me.

"You feel hurt?" he asks.

"I don't feel great," I say. "I think my hand is broken."

"Why you make a fight this man?"

"I didn't fight. He came from behind, from the stairs. I didn't even see him."

"You know him?"

"No, never seen him before."

"A stranger make fight with you? How come?"

"He stole my backpack. I was mugged."

The slatted windows are tilted open. Beams of heat blow through them. Outside, palm leaves sway. The guy standing by the door is either taking notes on his cellphone or bored and texting with a friend.

"I should maybe go to the hospital," I say.

"We can take to hospital soon, okay?"

"Okay."

"But have a problem first."

He lays my passport on the table between us. I don't remember handing it over (though my divine hindsight reveals that, in my post-pummelling daze, I flipped it out of my pocket into the hands of a kneeling paramedic). He opens it to the page with my solemn portrait.

"This your?" he asks.

"Yes, that's me."

He leafs through my passport. The back pages are stiff with Cambodian visa stickers. On each of them my name is misspelled in a different way. Daniel Soloman. Daneil Solomon. Danial Salmon. Denial Solowar. The chubby Thai finds what he's looking for, lays the passport flat on the table in front of me, stabs a finger at an entry stamp from late last year.

"You come."

"Yes."

He flips the page and balances his fat finger on the subsequent exit stamp.

"You go."

"Yes."

On the facing page, another entry stamp. His finger bounces over to it.

"You come back."

"Yes."

This is the precise moment that panic begins to tickle the base of my spine. Through conscious effort, the chubby Thai swallows his smile and does his best impression of a frown.

"Sixty day!" he says.

I nod.

"Sixty day!" he repeats, mustering what sternness he can. He shakes his head. "Cannot!"

"Cannot what?" I ask, playing ignorant.

My head is a sucking void of oxygen. My hip screams. My hand has turned invisible. These physical obfuscations press me deeper into disadvantage, while the chubby Thai repeats:

"Sixty day too much! *Kow jai mai?*"

He glares. He sneers. He squints as if through smoke. But he is incapable, like most Thais, of sustaining an interrogatory mood and quickly lets that smile return (not a vindictive smile, but not without a small bit of condescension spelled out in the vertical lines of his dry lips). He says: "Sixty day too much! Cannot come back!"

An unformed breath waits in the chamber of my mouth to be fired back, but I can find no reasonable, aerodynamic phrase with which to give it shape. This sluggishness: an effect, maybe, of my concussed brain. "But..." I take the passport, open it to display the stamps and signatures documenting two years of completely legal (so far as I know) border runs. Mimicking his pidgin English to be clearly understood, I tell him:

"Can stay. Have stamp. See?"

I show him the dates of my most recent return, just two weeks ago, initialled and approved by the border guards at Aranyaprathet. "Have stamp to come back. *Can* stay. Sixty more days, *na*?"

He smiles.

"No real," he says.

"Real," I say.

"No real," he says, almost laughing.

I stab the open passport with my finger. "Real, real, *real*."

He shakes his head. The edge of his jaw vibrates. Is that sympathy in his eyes? Or are his eyeballs perspiring like this from the building-up pressure of holding back laughter? I appeal to the younger fellow: he's still thumbing his cellphone.

"Real visa! Real real!" I say to him.

The younger fellow looks up from his phone, gestures to my passport with a flick of his chin, and says (that hissing undertone you hear is air whispering through his tooth-hole): "Cambodia visa not like this... not real visa." And back he goes to his composition.

I've built up such equity in my boldness, this last year and a half in Bangkok. I've felt a prince, a king, a conqueror, and what better time than now to exert my *farang*'s entitled severity—the same severity with which the Chinese and Indians and Portuguese throughout history have forced capitulation in their Siamese hosts. "I'll buy a real one, then."

The chubby Thai's eyes go wide and he coughs out the guffaw he's been struggling to suppress.

"*Tow lai, na khrup?*" I ask. *How much?*

He's really laughing, now. Genuine, stomach-deep laughter.

"*Tow lai, tow lai?*"

The chubby Thai looks over his shoulder to his toothless friend, then to the closed door, and the way his chair creaks when he shifts his weight seems a surreptitious message passed to whoever is on the other side. When he turns back, he's shaking his head. He holds up his palms and shakes them like a blackjack dealer leaving a table. "No more come back, come back, come back again." He gazes up at the ceiling, searching for words and, unable to find them, launches into a firecracker burst of Thai, the only piece of which I catch is *mai dai*, which means, literally, *no can do*. All this, still with that stupid smile on his face.

"*Dai,*" I say. "*Dai, dai!* Can!"

He shakes his head. "Right now, in one day, you go from Thailand. After that, cannot come back *ever*."

Does it seem like I got what was coming to me? Like my undiplomatic behaviour earned me this unfortunate diplomatic outcome? That's simply how Thailand works, my love; there's no statute or regulation that won't bend under the weight of a few notes of currency. It was bad luck that on this occasion the country's prevalent ethical flexibility worked against me; sixteen weeks earlier, the ruling government was overthrown by the military in a bloodless (and rather *fun*) coup, and the, uh, *interpretive* visa rules that had so far allowed me to live and work in the country for almost a year were now being rigidly (if randomly) enforced. So I suppose I should have known better.

The deportation order was immediately filed and fast-tracked (the toothless guy, I later learned, was an immigration agent), and I was held in custody until the following morning so I that I'd have no time to contact a lawyer or contrive a plan to delay the process. They gave me just time enough to return to my apartment and pack up what little I could (some clothes, my computer, my *Suicide Squad* comics) and then escorted me directly to the airport. I suspect they wanted to make an example of me. And I can't blame them. I've seen the spring-break insurgency that American college kids in their board shorts and bikinis bootleg across the Pacific—all fists and vomit and remorselessness. They mistook me, I think, for a Yankee anarchist. As a result, I ended up on this doomed flight, and now I'm adrift in limbo, remembering the memories of how I got here.

But I'll admit, it's getting lonely up here. This abundance of empty space is pressing upon me; claustrophobia and agoraphobia and acrophobia have mended together to become an all-encompassing fear of *everything*. That's why I'm so happy to be able to talk to you. That's why I'm so eager to explain why I'm up here and not down there with you. It's important that you know I'm not the sort of person who would just disappear like this. It's important that you know *me*. This might be our only chance. What luck, then, that with my newfound omnipotence, this ability to flash my life before my eyes, I can describe it to you exactly as it happened!

Yes, let me map out the succession of reprisals and repatriations that led me aboard this blown-up plane. Let me take you back to when I was a baby, and I can show you how I was first hollowed out. Or back to the junior high schoolyard, where you can hear Justin Sloan's voice calling out to me through the winter air, "Hey, faggot!" Or to Marti Barrett's closet, where, beneath piles of laundry, she keeps a detailed record of her duplicity.

But the truth is we don't have to go much further back than, oh, eighteen months ago. Yes, crossing the Cambodian border—that's when things *really* started to go wrong. I didn't know it, but I was in Thailand for only a few months before the machinery of my expulsion began to fall into place: the one-eyed con man grabbed me, the military deposed the prime minister, the blond guy beat me bloody, and the whole time, conscious or not, *she* was urging me towards this seat on the stupid exploding plane.

You want to know how I ended up here?

Let's start with Carrie Franklin.

It's her fault, and I can prove it.

−2−

I'm on the bus, speeding for the Cambodian border, six tires singing contralto on the hollow asphalt, big ol' steel haunches straddling both lanes of the highway, ripping past pickup trucks stacked to capacity with shrivelled old women and shirtless young men, thundering past motorcycle-drawn carts farting along the edge of the road, blustering past child farmers leading columns of sickly livestock with lazy waves of leather switches — all they can see, as we overtake them, is a blurry mural of spike-haired cartoon characters karate-punching starburst patterns, sexy anime girls in frog costumes playing beach volleyball, a grinning Mickey Mouse wearing a bandolier and a holding a smoking AK-47, coiled Chinese dragons breathing purple fire, and the blue-skinned Hindu monkey-god Hanuman locked in battle with an airbrushed likeness of Hugh Jackman as Wolverine. As this ten-year-old Japanese girl's sugar-induced nightmare flies across the countryside, I'm sore and nervous and trapped in a vapour of broken sleep. With my forehead against the cold glass, I catch photographic impressions of the onlookers as we whip past: their expressions are impenetrable; they're not even disdainful, not even annoyed; they could care less about this bus disturbing their calm, monochromatic morning with its rocketing fluorescence.

I've been in Thailand for only fifty-nine days. I have eight thousand baht left in the bank, enough, at current market prices, according to current spending trends, to keep me viable as a bon vivant expatriate for another two weeks. Three, if I curb my habit for banana roti, iced coffee, and the VIP theatres where they massage your feet while you laze in a leather recliner. First, though, I must purchase another thirty days of citizenship by hopping back and forth over the invisible line that separates the Kingdom of Siam from the former Khmer Empire. The bus is half-full with what I will come to recognize as a pretty typical crew of visa-runners. Mostly lone white guys like me and a handful of backpackers: mulletted Spaniards, flushed Brits, bronzed Germans, snoozing Americans, jittery Koreans, a cornrowed Swede. Our guide makes his way up the aisle, collecting passports and photographs. He's young, bespectacled, carries himself with the semi-detached benevolence of a summer camp counsellor and wears a lanyard that declares him a tour guide for the Sun-Thai Tourist Expedition Company, even though the service we've hired to ferry us over the border and back again is called Easy Visa Run, and the storefront on Sukhumvit Road from which the bus departed was called Virtue Immigration Service Bangkok (and the receipt from my credit card payment is from a company called Sanuk Massage). Everyone hands over their vital documents with such casual acquiescence; isn't it a cardinal rule of international travel to never give up your passport? This, right now, is my very first visa run, so I plunge ahead, hoping that by pretending to know what I'm doing, I might accidentally know what I'm doing.

The guide reaches me, and, mimicking the others, I open my passport to show him the two small photographs tucked between the pages. He snatches it up and shuffles it into the colourful deck he's collected. I watch where he slots it, just in case this is some kind of magic trick and I have to pick it out later. Across the aisle, the cornrowed Swede gives up her passport, and, a row ahead, the napping American girl is nudged awake. She lifts the brim of her baseball cap with the tip of her finger (this is how I know she's American), sighs at the imposition, and proceeds, to the rattling rhythm of loose change and nail polish bottles and plastic sheaths of pills, to dig through her oversized traveller's backpack, flamboyantly striped in orange and white like some nautical emergency pouch, in search of her travel documents. She catches me watching, and for a moment our eyes are joined, locked, but I quickly look away and—

—our mouths are joined, locked, and inside the hollow space between them I follow her lead through a rousing bout of skilful tonguework, ballestras and lunges, ripostes and feints and flicks, a parry and moulinet, double and triple-trompemonts. This, interspersed with brief reprieves: our mouths undock and linger centimetres apart, heavy gusts of heat, tongues now sharp and delicate tools, wet little scalpels cutting through clenched lips to layers of clenched teeth, fine brushes painting each other's lips and faces and necks and ears, now duelling again, and our mouths twist shut, hiss, clamp, airlock re-engaged and—

—the bus brakes engage, calipers clamp shut, we hiss to a stop at a roadside checkpoint on the outskirts of Aranyprathet. Our guide, with the stack of passports pressed between his hands, sprints to a nearby cement building. While he's away, we're boarded by a pair of teenaged soldiers, who pace up and down the aisle in search of stowaways or smugglers or, more likely, something less tangible: our respect. When our guide reappears, he returns our passports to us with crisp new visa stickers stuck inside.

Ten minutes pass. Now we're at the border.

Safety in numbers, security in skin pigment; as we spill off the bus, I huddle close to my companions as they follow our guide across a stone bridge that spans the kind of garbage-choked gully where dead bodies can remain undiscovered for years and years. We join the larger crowd that is filing towards the customs building; mostly older Thai men and women in sun visors and big square sunglasses, there to run the tables at the Poipet casino. At the arrivals counter, we flash our dubious travel documents and, a few skittish and sweaty moments later, are freed to pass through the triple-pronged stone archway and into the furious Cambodian sun.

Poipet is a Wild West movie set. A single street, all camera-facing facade. The main thoroughfare opens into a muddy cul-de-sac lined on all sides by storefronts that reveal, upon closer inspection, nothing for sale, no services on offer, just greyness and shadow behind the iron grilles. The only splashes of colour are sponsored; every parasol and awning and banner and poster bears the white-ribbon cursive of Coke or the bicolour bouncy ball of Pepsi. All around me are iterations of the same skinny guy in silky button-down and flip-flops; he's either sitting stoically, or staring off into the middle-distance, or in the midst of fierce negotiation with some twin antagonist, or pushing/pulling a wooden handcart the size of a compact car. Hardly any women, just these guys. And little kids. Little kids everywhere. And I mean *little*. Not wily preteens, not precocious ten-year-olds. These kids are five, six, seven. As soon as we step out of the customs building, they're at our feet, adorable pet-store puppies with treacherous eyes. These whiz kids, they know their languages: "*Khrup mek, poot Thai*, spick Englitz?" They know their exchange rates, too. "One dollar! Fifty baht! Five hundred riel!"

Backpackers hoof through this scene with their heads down, making scientific study of the slimy mud beneath their flip-flops. You'd think they'd be paying closer attention to this magnificent poverty; it's why they come to places like this, isn't it? To witness the grimy malady of the Third World first-hand? No, they just press through it all with their breath held and ears plugged with earphones. Not that I blame them. Imagine if you had to acknowledge every call from every tout, show concern for every orphaned child. It would take you weeks, in a place like this, to travel twenty yards—

Ow!

—something just hit me in the forehead.

Oh, yes, *her*: this filthy little thing in the sundress, jogging alongside me. I have acquired a valet. She's holding a parasol

63

over my head, twiggy ochre arms outstretched, not quite tall enough to keep the tines of the umbrella from tapping a Morse warning against my temple.

"Hello!" she says.

Acceleration, evasion, neglect—they all fail as deterrents. What am I supposed to do? Shoo her away? Throw stones until she gives up? I've heard people say that: to throw stones. How many years as an expat does it take build up such a nacre on your soul? I'm eager to find out, but, for now, I concede.

I ask her: "What's your name?"

She says something that doesn't sound anything like a name.

"What's your name?"

Gibberish.

"What?"

Farther up the road, I can see our guide leading the group towards the casino, where a buffet lunch of tepid seafood and beige curries awaits us. But a bus passes between us and I lose sight of them. My little assistant smiles and repeats herself: "Cold Coca-Cola, one dollar!" The words roll off her tongue with such chirpy precision that I mistake them again for some choppy Khmer dialect.

"Sorry, I don't understand."

Now she's pointing off into the heat-hazy distance. "Beer, one dollar!"

This I understand. "Maybe later," I tell her.

My junior aide and I get only twenty yards farther into the dreary dominion of ancient Angkor before we're intercepted by—

This guy! The lid of his left eye is rolled up over the lashes to expose a crenulated band of red interior tissue; below, a crescent of milky eyeball with a milkier core that is focused on mine. "Can wait here!" he tells me. "Waiting for tourist is here. Bus come soon." Clipped to the pocket of his golf shirt is a plastic badge: *Cambodia Tourist Association*.

He's shooing me towards a fenced-in area where a troop of khaki- and bandana-clad tourists sit back to front, rearranging items in their backpacks and grooming themselves baboon-like by picking flecks of dried mud from their socks. I turn to see, fifty yards up the road, the Spanish mullet and ginger mop and bleached-blond braids disappear into the crowd along with our guide. I point towards them. "I'm with them," I say. "With the tour."

This guy ignores me. His hand is on my shoulder, I can feel the stony calluses on the tip of each finger. "You wait here first—bus come, five minute."

Then he turns on the little girl, still dutifully at my side, and barks at her in Khmer. Whatever he says causes her umbrella to list to the side. She yowls a long single syllable that emulates the sharp, chevron shape of her angry brow, and scowls, as only little girls can, with the heart-rending fury of a million exploding suns. I reach into my pocket to give her a few bills, but the guy stops me. "Cannot pay," he tells me. "Illegal. Use for drugs. For gangster. Cannot."

My valet, defiant, sensing the nearness of her financial reward, approaches me with an upturned pink palm, the webbed lines creased with dirt, but the guy kicks out his leg, kicks her hand away, barks at her. It's all gibberish to me, this fissured and fricative sparring, but it's obvious, as my former assistant jabs her closed umbrella like an epée, that she's levelling some unpleasant threats. At us both. I shrivel at the thought of being a villain (my disfigured new friend is so much better suited to it!) but this guy, he's unfazed, he lunges at her with a cocked fist and the little girl retreats into the crowd, prancing on her bare feet.

I'm just about to follow him into the corral when a hand grips my forearm and pulls me away. I turn. Baseball cap, silver earrings: the American girl from the bus.

"Never mind this guy," she says. "Follow me."

We kiss, and kiss, and kiss, and she doesn't seem to mind my hand following the topography of her flank, fingers strumming ribs, sometimes threatening equatorial breach, but lingering, mostly, near the elevated areas of her naked chest, the excellent mounds of flesh tight-knit to her hard breastplate; I clasp one in my hand, gather the loose silken mass into a hard little bulge, squeeze harder than I otherwise might as I follow the subtly coded instructions transferred by the pace of her breathing, then release it, let it settle, and place my whole hand overtop it so that the hard pink knot at its centre brushes the polestar cluster of nerves in the middle of my palm (imagine the thickness and force of the ocean at its deepest point, and imagine that powerful part of the ocean boiled off, turned to steam, and the steam collected in a glass jar, thickened with sugar and fresh cream and a fine powder of ivory and opal, and then this miraculous substance, not liquid or solid or air, all of those things and none of them, is poured into your open hand: this is what it's like for a man to hold a woman's breast). Her hands are busy, too. Roaming, gripping my forearms, probing my shorn temples, my trimmed bangs. She pulls back, examines my face, and brushes the dust of snipped hair-ends from under my eye. "Your hair looks really good," she says. "If I do say so myself." A little dry kiss on the spot she just touched, then my nose, then it's back to the lips. Her inquisitive fingers have disappeared and now (oh, hello!) have reappeared in the waistband of my shorts, snouting their way into that hot and clamorous place—

I do what she says, I follow her through the crowd, through the hot clamour of clownish horns and antique combustion engines. When we reach the far side of the muddy plaza, she spins on her heels, and, walking backwards ahead of me, wags her finger and says: "Watch yourself."

"He had a badge ... I thought—"

"*Everyone* has badges."

"They're not, like, cops or anything?"

"Cops? Here?"

She spins back around, resumes her strut. "It happened to me before, that's how I know it's a scam. I was stuck there, like, an hour, and I was, like, what *is* this?" The silver hoops in her earlobes dangle in preposterous conflict with the frazzled hairs radiating loose from the upswept wave of hair tucked under her hat and the sweat-yellowed, stretched-out collar of her Death Cab for Cutie T-shirt. "They keep you there until there's enough people to fill a bus, then they drive you to the bus station, which is, like, two blocks away, but you'd never know it, the roundabout way they go. It was totally the same guy, too, with the half-an-eye or whatever."

"Yeah, Blofeld, the funny eye."

"*So* creepy."

"Did you just save my life?"

"Oh, yeah. They were going to human traffic you, for sure."

I follow her to an open-air café, where she settles in a plastic chair and seems only mildly surprised to see me standing there. Her baseball cap is tipped so low over her eyes that, to make eye contact with me, she tips her head perilously back, exposing her throat, stares at me down the bridge of her nose. "The rest of the group is up there, at the casino," she says, pointing. "They'll be there for, like, an hour or so. You'll want to avoid the food, though. The food is definitely *not* awesome. Cold curries and river-fish and mysterious red meat that is *definitely* not beef. You're welcome to hang out here if you want. Have you ever had Angkor beer? It's shitty, but it won't give you gastro."

"Sure," I say. "Thanks."

It seems so innocent, us meeting like this.

She says, "I'm Carrie."

I say: "Daniel."

She holds out her hand for me to shake, and I grip her fingers like they're the butt of a gun and notice immediately that the climate and topography of her hands is wrong, it's reversed, the pads and palms are dry and raw like the shell of a temperate nut, the knuckles and tendons on top are moist and soft and quite obviously cared for with expensive aloes and exfoliating scrubs. I shake her hand twice, quickly, twitchily, like I'm trying to shake beads of water off it, and then, wanting to correct for this quickness, I let go too slowly and a hundred thousand false inferences are exchanged in that half-second of unnecessary lingering contact.

Sure, yeah, *of course* I'm attracted to her. Look at her: plump lips unnaturally pink, hair dirty-blond with dyed-blond streaks, dark lashes further darkened (even today, on this jaunt to the war-torn wilderness); beautiful, yes, a real stunner, sure, even though it's the sort of stunning beauty you often see in fast food commercials and department store catalogues. She'd need a gap in her teeth or a hump on her nose to be the sort of chick who could coerce a flotilla.

(Oh, definitely, yes, all this erotic analysis in the first minutes; it's simply what we do, we sensitive boys, we timid gentlemen, we fantasists; from glimpses of hair [just *hair*, just a lock, just a single blond sparkle flagging around a corner after its proprietor] we'll quit our jobs, we'll sell our electronics, we'll abandon our mothers, we'll emigrate to other countries, other planets, other dimensions—and that's just *hair*! Think how bad it can be with a face, with a body, with *acquaintance*. Just think how bad I still have it with Erin Seeley, and that was half a decade ago!)

Per Carrie's instructions, I order two lukewarm cans of Angkor from the vendor and we sit together watching the multitudes stream in and out of Poipet.

"Thanks for that, back there," I say. "I booked my seat online, and the website doesn't tell you much, except to show up with your passport, photos, and a couple thousand baht. All those guys back there look like the bad guys from a Rambo movie. I don't know what I was thinking. You just get into this totally acquiescent space. Some guy tells you, *go here*, so you go there."

"They weren't going to murder you and sell your organs. It's a two dollar ticket, and they save, like, forty cents in gas if they only travel when the bus is full."

"It's not that. It's more like what it represents."

Carrie laughs. "Are you upset that you were rescued by a girl?"

"No. I'm just upset that I wasn't able to make it a hundred yards into the country before getting ripped off."

"Honestly, it looks dangerous, it looks completely war-torn, but you have to do something profoundly stupid to get in trouble here."

"You say that, but, trust me, if anyone got snatched by organ-harvesters, it'd be me. I'm that one-in-a-million type of guy."

"Oh, really?" she says, and the arch of her eyebrows, as much as any human gesture can, has achieved sentience, because it knows, independent of her own self-awareness, how cute and charming and coy it is.

She laughs, takes a long slug from her can of Angkor, then slurps up the dregs of beer from the channel around the can's edge.

Christ, I'm freezing! The wind, out here in the schoolyard, is thin and sharp and slices its way between the cells of my twelve-year-old body. I'm no longer whole, just a bunch of bunched-up particles separated by the cutting wind. My nostrils feel five feet wide. Smell that? Oooh, the semi-bitter floral fragrance of pine resin and frozen earth: the wintertime boreal forest. It's recess, right now, and I'm drinking from the can of Coke I bought from the vending machine in the laundromat across the street.

I'm approached by these cigarette-smoking miscreants, Justin Sloan and Dave Brewster and *this* girl, what's her name (Dana, I think), and they have a request: Gimme a sip of that Coke? Justin Sloan is testing the limits of my obedience. I don't realize it right now, but what I do next will map the path that brings me here to you.

I obey.

I pass the can to his held-out hand. Holding it up to his face, he peers at the skinny circumferential canal around the lip: a curving segment of brown syrup is trapped there.

"Jesus," he says. "Take your fucking friends with you!"

He blows a nicotine-stinking burst that catches the droplets of Coke in the can's circular ditch and sprays them up my nose and into my eyes. He laughs (they all kind of laugh, but he *really* laughs), tips the can against his cracked lips, drinks, then, with a flourish, staring right at me, he noisily sucks up the residue around the spout.

"See? Take your friends with you. No one ever teach you that, fag?"

Delicately, faggily, I drink from my warm can of Angkor. Carrie is saying:

"My boyfriend and I live up in Nichida Thani, north of the city, sort of on the way to the old airport. It's a very weird neighbourhood — like someone took a shovel and scooped up some random American suburb and just dropped it into the middle of the poorest neighbourhood you've ever seen. All these beautiful villas and condo buildings, all these rich housewives riding around in golf carts, all the streets lined with palm trees like Beverly Hills. But as soon as you pass through the gates, right away it's dirt roads covered in garbage, chickens running around, stray dogs — a whole shantytown. You're on a patio at the Starbucks, watching these private school kids learning to row on this man-made canal, and you walk twenty feet and suddenly you're in the middle of the worst poverty you can think of. And no one thinks twice about it."

A small girl in a Toronto Raptors T-shirt tromps by with her hand open, muttering in Khmer, bare legs speckled to mid-calf with bright brown mud, too glassy-eyed to notice that we're purposefully not noticing her. She doesn't stop, goes right past us, into the street, and the melodious drone of her voice is obscured by Carrie's:

"To be honest, though, I really *like* having a swimming pool, and I *like* sitting on the patio at Starbucks, so I'm culpable in the weirdness of it. Which is why, when I tell people where we live, I always make a point to describe all that other stuff, because I feel, like, guilty or whatever for enjoying it so much."

Another sip from her can of beer, another slurp. She's looking off into the street, now, at the slow column of traffic, the vehicles that are barely vehicles and the people who don't quite seem like real people, even sadder for how the sun lights it all so beautifully.

Getting rescued by this particular girl is a crueller twist of fate than you might think, my love. Among the rules I have imposed upon myself for this exotic self-seeking journey is to avoid the opposite sex at all costs. Not as a vow of chastity (though the chastity part is a real killer) or as some ill-considered expression of misogyny. Quite the opposite. It was to maintain my focus and clear-headedness and keep the powerful electromagnetic forces generated by the female body and brain from interfering with the orientation of my own body/brain compass. But already I can feel the needle trembling (oh, the column of ligaments on the back of her knee as she uncrosses and crosses her legs!); so, as we sit together, I make an effort to be callous in my observations and snide in my assumptions: she's a wannabe bohemian from a well-to-do big-city family, sensibly pursuing a major in communications, with a minor in art history that she can cite later in life to prove that she's enlightened; or an aspiring middle-class suburbanite afraid to admit her domestic aspirations to the idealistic inner self she's trying to appease with this international meandering; or a prepubescent wallflower grown happily, if clumsily, into her womanly body, and capable, only after a bit too much wine, only when the lights are dimmed, of exploring the shallow limits of her wantonness.

(She is actually none of these things.)

"Where do you live?" she asks.

"In Banglamphu, close to the big wat there."

"Near Khao San Road?"

"Sort of."

The sound *ugh!* slips out of her mouth, and she immediately regrets it; I can tell by the way she dips her chin and shrugs a deep shrug like she's trying to hide between her shoulder blades. She's not wrong, though — *ugh!* is an accurate way to describe Khao San, the backpacker ghetto where local culture meets the basest Western expectations of it. The streets are filled with hungover gap-year kids still chalk-skinned from last night's foam party, bus-tour hustlers wrangling the slowest and sickest sightseers from the herd, prostitutes doing impressions of prostitutes in a satirical "You want make boom-boom?" dialect. The all-night thumping music and piercing fluorescent light is enough, after these first months, to make me afraid that some terrible navigational miscalculation has been made, that the angle of my ascent was crooked by a few degrees, that it should have been Buenos Aires or Turkmenistan or Kinshasa instead, somewhere less infected by the very things, in choosing Bangkok, I was hoping to avoid: transience, shallowness, and most importantly, the lack of those invaluable tectonic forces that might pulverize this shapeless mass known to friends and relatives as Daniel Solomon and reveal within it something distinct and different and worthwhile.

I say: "If I could afford to live anywhere else, believe me, I would."

"I shouldn't talk, living up where we live," Carrie amends. "I'd love to be closer to downtown, off Sukhumvit or Si Lom. We have friends on Si Lom, and their apartment looks out on Lumphini Park, and it's like being in some million-dollar place in Manhattan, looking out on Central Park. Big windows, high ceilings. If I could live anywhere—like, *anywhere* in the world, I'd live there."

"What does your boyfriend do?" I ask.

"He's a teacher. He teaches at ISB. That's why we live up in Nichida. That's *how* we're able to live there—the school totally pays for everything."

"You're a teacher, too?"

"No, no. He was recruited right out of college at this job fair, and we were dating, and we'd always wanted to travel together, so it was just sort of ... perfect."

She spits out those last two syllables like she's trying to blow flecks of chewed skin from her lips, and I can't yet tell if it's a swell of passion for her present condition, that she's just so happy how things have worked out, or the opposite (it takes me six months, but don't worry, I figure out which).

"I *do* have a job, though," she continues. "I work a few days a week for this company—it's like an academic coaching service. Tutoring, mostly. Elementary school kids, high school kids, people applying for MBA programs overseas. It's all under the table, I get paid in cash, so that's why I have to come here every month to get my visa renewed."

Carrie finishes her beer and once again runs her pursed lips in a quick crescent moon around the perimeter of the can. It's a nervous habit, I'll come to learn; a tic that fills the time while she thinks of what to say next.

"You know, if you're looking for work, you should give me your email. I'll put you in touch with P'Milk, who runs the place. It's called Admissions America."

"Sure, that would be great."

Funny, these small moments that alter one's trajectory. Dumb little decisions: turn left, turn right. Spontaneous statements; cursory commitments. I suppose if they kick you onto a different course, they're not really that small, but they certainly seem that way in the moment they occur: just some vague promise to put someone in touch with someone else, whatever, no big deal. Then, before you know it, you find yourself sitting in—

An office:

Plaster walls painted to look like ancient rock, big window looking out onto the Chao Phraya, fancy fogged-glass door with ornate engraved lintel of a grinning Buddhistic chorus. High-back leather chairs, a spongy carpet of red and gold and fractals. It's a converted boardroom, technically, but mine and mine alone. And I've earned it, these past six months at Admissions America. With each successful application of my newfound skill in piecing together whole human lives from seemingly inane narrative bits, I have graduated from sharing the noisy rec room with the grade-school tutors to this elegant, extravagant space of my own.

"Is like, um—I have many times make a decision to, um—"

The fellow right now sitting across from me, hemming and hawing, making greasy snow-angel palmprints as he nervously caresses the polished surface of the table, is one of my clients, Benjaporn Worapivut (but you can call him Benz). We're discussing his leadership experience, his strengths/weaknesses, his hopes/regrets, his professional aspirations, his family background, and he tells me, in broken English, about his job, about his father, about eating chicken and rice at a streetside café (he won't shut up about the chicken and rice). He tells me about riding the city bus to school, about a flood, about his daughter, about his car, which is, of course, a Mercedes-Benz E320 (he is, in this one respect at least, living up to the high expectations he set for himself by adopting that name at the age of twelve). As he talks, I transcribe, listen, nod.

"There is one time I do this, um—for making better end-line process—"

This is my job: I help students like Benz prepare their applications for Ivy League schools in the United States; I fill out their registration forms; I write, from scratch, their personal essays, reference letters, and resumes; I carefully plant verb tense errors and grammatical turnabouts to allay suspicion; I write scripts for phone interviews and groom my mild-mannered students to mimic, in their performances, the boisterousness and self-determination so valued by American schools and so disesteemed by the Thai ego. But this is my *real* job: I conduct interviews and pan the sluice of memory in search of shiny bits hidden in the sediment; I superheat them and hammer them together; I fashion them into something distinct, something *meaningful*; I build narratives that assert a case, prove an argument (that's why I'm so good at this, my love—months and months of practice).

"Very many important people think, yes, this is good—"

Benz's first application packages are due at Stanford and Wharton in less than a week, and so far, all I have to work with to begin composing his essays are a few random anecdotes and a collection of mistranslated platitudes. The alchemy I perform requires the exact substance Benz is holding back: the truth. All these details about late-night meals with his father, about the plastic plates and pink napkins, about the hum of the streetlights—when you start remembering the memory instead of the event, that's when you get into trouble, that's when you lose your sense of what's consequential and what isn't.

"And, um—they say to me, this is good." He has apparently reached the denouement, and smiles at me hopefully: "So it's like that."

A knock at the door saves him. Carrie peers inside. "Sorry to interrupt. Can I talk to you for second?"

I excuse myself and duck out into the hallway.

"Are you busy this afternoon?" she asks.

"That's a trick question," I say. "Tell me what you want first, then I'll tell you if I'm busy."

"I need someone to take a couple of my students at 4:30? It's the twins, Internet and Email, and they're super easygoing, I swear. You just have to give them their pages and they'll read quietly for the whole hour. I know it's Friday, and I hate to ask, but I'm moving to a new apartment, and I was supposed to do it this weekend, but I just found out that I can get the keys early, which means if I can get up to Nichida Thani this afternoon and get all my stuff out of our old place, then I don't have to see Chad tomorrow and deal with all the awkwardness."

News of Carrie's breakup reached me a few days ago. I've never met her boyfriend, just know his name (*Chad Billings*, who I can only assume comes equipped with a proton-rifle, fully articulated elbows and knees, and has that notch in his left heel so you can mount him on various attack vehicles [sold separately]), but it's not hard to imagine the progression of events that led him to decide that Bangkok was better experienced without the hindrance of an American girl and her American self-assuredness and American sexual hang-ups. Maybe she'll tell me all about it sometime.

"No problem," I say.

"For real?"

"Of course, yeah."

"Thank you *so* much. I'll buy you a million drinks at Churchill's."

"All at once?"

"I'll make you a punch card with a million squares, and each of those squares will be a drink that I'll buy you, I promise, thank you!" She's already backing away down the hallway, now turns around, calls over her shoulder: "I'll text you when I'm back this evening. I'll cry on your shoulder and all that." Her hair flags around the corner.

I'm not doing her this small favour because she's beautiful, or because I feel sorry for her, or because I'm hoping to take advantage of her gratitude. The fact is, I owe her. She's the reason I'm sitting here in this majestic lavender- and sandalwood-scented thirtieth-floor office, listening to poor Benz's cryptic autobiographical dry-heaving, living this charmed life in a faraway foreign country, and not back in my father's basement. Without her intervention, my self-seeking sojourn might otherwise have ended shortly after that last trip to the Cambodian border: I would have frittered away my last few baht on deep-fried chicken skin, and milk tea, and knock-off Nike shoes, and maybe, just to say that I'd done it, just to smuggle home a bit of that sinister carnal contraband, a single sad dance-club hand-job from some gorgeous upcountry girl forced into servitude by the poor performance of rice on the commodity exchange (but, no, my love, I'm really not that kind of guy [but perhaps, given the chance, I would act like one]). But instead Carrie did what she promised: she passed my name along to P'Milk and Rob Sangran, the half-siblings who run Admissions America, and it was the semi-regular writing and editing work they provided (and the generous cheques that ensued) that allowed me to escape from the wretched gecko-infested Khao San crash pad to a condo building in the decadent concrete corridor of Sukhumvit Soi 26.

I could tell you everything I loved about this fantastic new life of mine, everything that made me feel special, worthy, but I've always hated travelogues and their attempts to make romantic all our common differences of culture. Paradise isn't alien or exotic or extrinsic. No, no, no: likeness and familiarity and recurrence are the best part. You go to a foreign country, and *of course* the food tastes different, *of course* the architecture is grand, *of course* the distinctions of class are distorted (the poor so desperately poor, the rich so preposterously rich!). But how wonderfully eerie it is, on the other side of the world, to find oneself in a 7-Eleven just like the 7-Elevens back home, and to find, on the same bleacher-style wire rack, the same candy bar that was a staple of one's childhood diet; slightly smaller, maybe, and perhaps there's a strange taste to the nougat, but nonetheless a wonder to find that familiar item and go through the familiar ritual of obtaining it: picking through a handful of change, pouring it into the open palms of a teenage cashier in an ill-fitting smock. And then you step outside and you're almost trampled by a passing elephant. An elephant. An eight-foot high jungle beast with a hide like triple-knit burlap chain mail, with a bicycle reflector dangling over its massive haunches, just padding along the narrow sidewalk like all the other pedestrians, led by a shirtless thug flogging bundles of sugarcane at two hundred baht a pop ... this elephant cuts you off without even a trumpeted *sorry* or wheezy *'scuse me*. That's all. Just another elephant. *Yawn*. Whatever.

That's how you know you've arrived in Paradise: because the mundane has become amazing, the amazing mundane. The trick is to never not be conscious of how preposterous your day-to-day routine has become. You wake up, you shower, you commute to your white-collar job, you eat dinner, you go to sleep, and the next day, when you repeat it all, it still feels brand new:

I wake up in my apartment, in arctic cold (my air conditioner hums its chilly lullaby all through the night), and the air is so thin that I don't need to contract a single sleepy muscle, I simply levitate out of bed and hover, ankles loose, toes dangling, into the bathroom. I open the door and the hot held breath of tropical morning exhales in my face. Ah, the rainy season's ancient pheromones! I keep the bathroom window open all night just so I can partake in this great daily whiff. I shower and brush my teeth in this redolent sauna, then get dressed in the still-Siberian main room, then step outside into the amazing unfiltered heat (hot, cold, hot, cold—terrific for circulation). Even at this early hour the sun is torrid. Instantly my glands begin to weep. Within minutes, ticklish tears of sweat are falling down my back and inside my thighs. I call over a motorcycle taxi (lifting my leg over the back of the seat feels like a medal-winning feat of anaerobic exercise) and here I go, zipping to the end of the *soi*, into to the heart of Krung Thep city.

On my way to the office, I catch my reflection in a shop window: brown leather Prada shoulder bag, tortoiseshell Versace shades, an oversized Omega that jangles like an ammunition belt on my wrist. Did you see inside my closet when I was getting dressed earlier? More clothes than I have ever owned! An embarrassment of designer jeans! Belts of all conceivable leathers and fabrics! Each shirt in five different colours! Paradise is rich in such commodities! These rainbow arrays cost me the same as a single stupid shirt/belt/watch back in the Old World. So why not indulge? Who would have thought that Daniel Solomon, footwear philistine, former wearer of vulgar runners and economy loafers, would someday be a collector of shoes? But look! The fancy racks on the floor of my closet boast sneakers and high-tops and wing-tips and oxfords and soccer cleats and hiking boots and army boots and flip-flops and canvas slip-ons and old-school Velcro-strappers. I have it all!

To the mall! In through the sliding doors I go, from the shimmering asphalt plains to the temperate commercial steppe, from concrete to smooth tile, in my slapping plastic flip-flops. I hit a wall of cold. My sunglasses fog over. I ride the escalators to the top floor, up to the Gourmet Loft Mega Café, where I pay three American dollars for lunch: crispy roast duck on a dome of steamed rice with a zigzag drizzle of sweet jus and a carrot shaved into the shape of a tulip bulb. I eat in front of the towering windows that look down onto traffic-choked Sukhumvit; above it the concrete terrace where embedded fountain nozzles blast loops and sprays of water in choreographed patterns; above that the Siam Skytrain station, perched on the tracks like a sleeping steel cicada. Asphalt, concrete, steel, glass: architectural castes, in ascending order. Even here, in the midst of a simple weekday lunch, my daily life now bears the fanciful patina of a science fiction story.

Where to this weekend? Down to the islands, maybe? Throw some trunks and a paperback into a gym bag, flag a cab and flee to the airport, slap cash on the counter for a fifty-dollar ticket to Samui and queue with the confused tourists on the rain-slick tarmac, nap through a bumpy airborne half-hour (perhaps with some help from Erin Seeley), disembark and sprint for the doors and let the nearest tuk-tuk driver take me to his cousin's place near the beach, where I can trade more paper baht for a beachside hut and spend Saturday sleeping and reading and eating and listening to the ocean wheeze and drag and wheeze and drag and for a while watch the geckos in their death-sleep on the ceiling? Or maybe I'll just stay in the city. Maybe just an after-work beer with my fine colleagues from Admissions America: P'Milk and P'Nai and Nong Kit and Rob Sangran and sometimes Carrie, too. Maybe just a reclusive night at home, eating nori seaweed chips, drinking Ovaltine, watching pirated DVDs, in bed by eleven. Or maybe out for a night on the town—

In knife-sharp wingtips and ratty jeans, Rob Sangran and I swagger to the front of the line outside the new dance club XIII, and when we arrive at the nexus of pressing bodies shimmying to get through the eye of the needle, we're greeted in a fanfare of back-slaps and hand-clasps and one-armed hetero half-hugs. Rob Sangran knows these bouncers from another place (you know, that place on Ratchadamri that was there before the other place), and they know me through him. I'm drunk on sake, sated on sashimi, horny on self-restraint (I've become a teetotalling onanist), and the deafening drum and bass is like a fine icy mist on the inside of our skin as we soar through the doors and all the pretty heads turn to watch us alight. Is it just my imagination, or does the crowd on the dance floor part before us when the DJ (another friend of Rob Sangran's) waves us over to commiserate over slow jams and trance tracks? A sunset-coloured cocktail comes to me with the compliments of the bartender. A caramel-coloured cocktease comes to me with compliments on my clever T-shirt. A disco-coloured rap anthem comes down from the rafters, and with every cocky verse my hands are cleverly contemplating the tenderness beneath her T-shirt.

On Sundays I glide over the churning beige waters of the Chao Phraya in a river-taxi, up and down, from Sathorn to Banglamphu and back again, sometimes reading a paperback, sometimes scanning a week-old Western newspaper, sometimes, like today, just admiring the skyline, which from this offshore perspective suggests, in both its grandeur and decay, the otherworldly anime metropolis I hoped Bangkok would be. We chop through the current, past the Grand Palace, all twinkling pinpoint pagodas and dragon-scale gables, a digitally enhanced postcard photograph propped up in front of the hazy grey horizon. In the distance is the golden dome of State Tower, and, farther to the northeast, portending the coming apocalypse, monoliths of scaffolding in tattered loincloths. As Sundays stack upon Sundays, as nautical miles are strung together, I feel the city becoming more and more my own.

Quite the storybook ending, isn't it? Our hero has finally found what he's been looking for. The elusive circumstance/object/phenomenon discovered. The void satisfactorily filled. But Paradise is found so that it may be lost. That's the original human narrative. I am living (kind of) proof: cradle-bound, floating over the abyss. The truth is, though I felt quite indebted to Carrie, that verb, *owe*, implies an intimacy that in the ensuing ten months was absent between us; we were simply colleagues; we sometimes chatted in the hallways; we sometimes had drinks after work with our coworkers; we sometimes exchanged little inside jokes about bathtubs of ice and missing kidneys. But, with the exception of our meet-cute in the mucky boulevards of Poipet, I had kept my promise to myself, I deflected magnetic waves and kept my orientation true; we spent no time alone together and settled into our roles as minor acquaintances.

But remember, my love: even though she was the reason I was able to stay, she was also the reason I was kicked out.

Yes, my amazing new life was going great. Until—

—her inquisitive fingers finish their hard work, and I'm naked, and she's naked, too. No more shorts, no more socks. No more thin layers of this and that getting in the way. Just skin, skin, skin. Warm and hot and soft and hard and prickly and smooth and slippery. She rearranges herself in sneaky slo-mo shiftings, and now, somehow, I'm on my back, and she's on her back, on top of me, her feet planted on the outside of my legs, ass seated flat on my pelvic plane, spine against my sternum. We're stacked, her head is thrown back on my clavicle, shoulder tucked under my chin, the full weight of her upper body pleasantly compressing the air from my chest.

"We probably shouldn't..."
"No..."

"We shouldn't finish it."
"It's just the dregs. We *have to* finish it."
"That's the logic of an alcoholic."
"Nah, it's just logic."

Churchill's is unusually quiet tonight. We fill our cups with the last half-inch of whiskey, top them up with soda water, watch the noxious mixture foam up, lose its vigour, and go dead flat; the urine-yellow drink tastes about as good as it looks, but it doesn't matter, we're not here tonight to explore new epicurean frontiers, we're here, just the two of us, to get drunk and commiserate. I thought perhaps Carrie was joking about crying on my shoulder, but twice already her eyes have brimmed up with tears, and earlier, standing at the bar waiting for our bottle, she responded to some bad joke about her ex-boyfriend (the one about proton-rifles and reticulated limbs) by giving me an affectionate little head-butt on the upper arm.

She takes a squeamish sip and says:

"We met at a party, but it was a while before we hooked up. We saw each other sometimes, at other parties and out for drinks and whatever, and we flirted with each other, but we didn't hook up until this trip we took to Daytona Beach. Me with my friends, him with his friends. We ran into them there, purely by chance, and it was, like, oh, hey, *those* guys, what a coincidence, and we hung out with them all weekend. And that's when we first hooked up. He was a teacher, he worked with kids, and I used to go watch him coach soccer after school, and he's cheering these kids on and high-fiving them, and he had this great way of talking to them that wasn't parental or condescending, more like he was their friend, a cool older brother. And you could see how much they loved him. The little boys all vying for his attention, the little girls lining up to give him hugs. How could I not love him, too? That kind of thing, it's lame, I know, but seeing a guy so comfortable around kids, it's, like, *wow!* It does something to you. It's that maternal, primal thing: these little alarms go off inside your body, all this old machinery that's there to help you find a suitable mate, and here's this guy, he meets all that invisible criteria, you don't just *know* it, you *feel* it. We were only dating for about six months before he got the job offer at ISB, and it seemed at first like that would be it, that was the end, he was going to leave and we would break up. We liked each other, but it was just so early, everything still felt … *unsteady*. Still, I wanted him to *want* me to come. And he must have picked up on that, because one night he's, like: 'Why don't you come with me?' And of course, looking back now, he was obviously just saying it to be nice, I should have been, like: 'No, no, I can't.' But instead I was, like: 'Really? Should I?' And now—"

The music drifting in wisps through the background of our conversation suddenly stops, and the whole place, which is usually booming with turgid English voices and clattering glassware, goes dead quiet. Only now do I realize that we're the only patrons; it's just us and the Thai bartender, who is standing at the window, staring outside, speaking with severity into his cellphone. Maybe he's breaking up with someone, too.

"— now I wish I could travel back in time and see the look on his face at that exact moment — like, really *examine* it, because I think I was just so *giddy* with the idea of going away with him that I didn't see it. His heart probably dropped out of his chest. He probably suddenly felt like he was going to puke. But, stupid me, I believe what I want to believe, I'm making these grand plans, telling my friends, telling my family, and all of a sudden he turns all aloof, which should have been my first clue, but I just said to myself, he's stressed out about moving, he'll get over it, everything will be back to normal when we get there. It's funny how deluded you can be. I'm not retarded, I can see it clearly now, but back then I was just, like, *blind*. I don't know. So, we move here and he just turns into this total *dick*, barely talks to me, won't even *kiss* me. Like a completely different person all of a sudden. And now I'm thinking back and I'm, like, *how* did I *not know* something was wrong? We had sex maybe... *twice* after we arrived here. And the excuses you make! Oh, it's jet lag. Oh, it's culture shock. Oh, it's just this new job, it's stressing him out. And then when he started to go out all the time, I was so happy that he was making friends and meeting new people and thinking that maybe this vibrant new social life will help him adjust, get him back to his old self. And of course it turns out that the new people he's meeting are these asshole wannabe-player types who cruise Soi Cowboy every weekend like it's some big hilarious joke and that he's adjusting really well to this new lifestyle of fucking all these whores —"

She makes tremendous use of the word *whore*, which, with her Midwestern accent, she expels like a whooping cough.

"—and I don't mean 'whore,' like, in a descriptive way, I mean, *literally*, whores, prostitutes, hookers. So I know it's my fault for being so stupid, but, like, on the other hand, here's this *one* moment, he's not thinking, he asks me to go with him and I say yes, and even though me going with him is the last thing on earth he wants because, I don't know, he's searching for the call or whatever, he actually lets me *pack my bags* and *borrow money* from my sister to buy this crazy-expensive plane ticket. He *lets me do it*. We move into this apartment, we set up this … like, *life* together. We buy dishes. He lists me as his *spouse* to get me health insurance through the school. I just don't understand why he didn't say anything. To not hurt my feelings? If he would have said, 'You know, probably you shouldn't come with me,' I would have been heartbroken, but nowhere near as broken up as I was when he says to me, after we've been here for five months, 'I'm moving out.' That's all he said. 'I'm moving out.' Not even the courtesy of the old it's-not-you-it's-me, or the we're-growing-apart … none of that lip service, just a big *fuck you*, I'm moving out, good luck here in this foreign country, nice knowing you."

It occurs to me to tell her all about Marti, about the similar circumstances that compelled me to cross the ocean, but I'm not quite drunk enough to reckon my approach, and, besides, there's nothing I dislike more than one-upmanship.

"The worst part," she says, "is that all of the regret and sadness he feels isn't for me, for hurting me, for bringing me all the way over here and then abandoning me, it's for himself, that he has to go through this, that the price he has to pay to live forever on Pleasure Island is to go through this very painful thing of breaking up with me."

Why does she look so different, right now? Why does she sound so different? She's playing brave, but she's hurt, she's staggering. Beautiful girls like Carrie seem by their very nature to be indestructible, impenetrable, unflappable, aloof as cats, and, like cats, able to land feetfirst and unharmed from the highest heights.

But now—

Yes, that's what was missing before: fragility; a capacity to be harmed. She's showing it to me, now. Consciously, I suspect. It's like boarding the Skytrain during rush hour: you're pushed forward by shoulders and elbows and knees and sometimes a forearm in the middle of your back, and the harder you fight to go in the other direction, the more heavily the crowd presses upon you. Resistance produces nothing but more resistance, so you let yourself be carried along. Tonight, all these small circumstances of fate (move-in dates, small favours, conspiring military officials) are shouldering and elbowing and kneeing me forward.

Carrie says: "I have this urge to do something drastic. Like I have to mark the occasion, like I can't bear to be my same old self anymore. I want to get a tattoo. Or burn all my clothes and buy a whole new wardrobe. Or cut all my hair off."

"Don't cut your hair," I say. "I like your hair."

In other places, in other circumstances, this might have sounded too much like a come-on, but in this strange solitude, the world beyond our small table having fallen away, it seems even more earnest than I intended.

She says: "*Your* hair is so long compared to when we first met."

"I haven't been able to get a decent haircut to save my life. Have you seen the weird Japanese catalogues they make you pick from at the hairdresser? It's like a topiary garden. It's like, pick between looking like you're wearing a swan on your head, or like a character from *Dragon Ball*."

"I used to cut hair, you know."

"Really?"

With her lips hovering over the edge of her cup, she says, with utter seriousness: "I was a hairdresser back home. For two years. Really. I brought my whole kit with me. I could totally cut your hair."

"Sure," I say.

"Like, *right now,* if you wanted."

"We probably shouldn't…"

"No…"

She's tapping the ball of her foot on the piano-key metatarsals of mine; her toes, surprisingly dexterous, grip the tips of mine, wrap them up in a toe-fist; with my other foot I pinch her Achilles between my big toe and index toe; she rubs the arch of her instep against my ankle, working slow circles around the little knob of bone there; and so on, and so on, until she breathes into my ear:

"—but I want you to fuck me."

Oh, the supernatural brawn of that word! A single-syllable incantation that erases memory, corrodes self-awareness, melts away caution, obliterates all sensibilities, and remakes the world as a bed-sized realm in which such things as restraint

92

have never existed. Who can say whose fault this is? We succumb in equal time to the power of that word; by speaking it aloud she has set it free from the corked bottle where it was safely stored as a far-off fantasy notion, an abstraction instead of an act; but now it's real—that tricky little witch, that clever conjurer, she made it real, and I might love her for it.

Carrie is pushing open the door to her apartment, and the dark room is exhaling a heady girl-smell, rose petals, coconut lotions, sandalwood incense, vanilla creams, jasmine somethingoranother, papaya-scented this-and-that, the stinging alcohol twinge of makeup-remover, boiled noodles and bedsheet musk and burnt hair. The apartment's laid out identical to mine, identical to all the affordable crash pads in the city: a single room, like a hotel room, with the front door flanked by bathroom and kitchenette, living space flanked by bed and desk, sliding glass door open to a narrow balcony. The walls are bare, but the floor is cluttered with precise little piles. Books and folders and papers flush against the baseboard, a copse of tubes and bottles and pump-action dispensers, balled-up socks stacked like grocery store oranges. A sea anemone made up of bras has committed suicide on the knob of the closet door.

"It's sad, I know." Carrie kicks her flip-flops into the corner. "I keep meaning to go to Suan Lum to get some decorations or something, but..."

In my shorts pocket, my phone begins to vibrate. I let it plead until it runs out of breath and goes still.

"Do you want a beer or something? I have Singha. Or Tiger."

"Yeah. Singha."

From the small fridge under the counter, Carrie produces a cold bottle and hands it to me. Grip the cold neck, twist the cap's teeth into the soft skin of my palm, and, just when it seems they might puncture the flesh, the cap gives way, grinding glass, the aperture smokes, and I take a long, self-conscious draft, the way beer-lovers in commercials do —

(*Siiiiip.* Oh, that's lovely! — never a more drinkable beer brewed than wonderful, watery Singha!)

— and while she spreads sheets of the *Bangkok Post* on the tile floor, I inspect the photographs tucked into the frame of the mirror above her desk. Most feature her and her friends from home, though they all look so much alike, these fit Midwestern girls, that I have trouble picking her out among them. Even their wide smiles seem, by adaptation, a common phenotype of the same genus. Here they are, clockwise from the upper left corner: standing shoulder to shoulder, posed poolside in bathing suits; in a dark gymnasium in prom dresses; at a wedding in matching bridesmaids' gowns; in a classroom, dressed casually; on a green field in numbered uniforms, blond hair flattened back with headbands; at a nightclub in wispy tops that expose slender teardrop shoulders and the shallow slopes of small breasts. On her bedside table: a scattering of hoop earrings and bobby pins, a bottle of moisturizing hand lotion, one of those night-market lamps with the tall rectangular fixtures, a plastic snap-case for a retainer or mouthguard (the latter, it will turn out; a lifelong tooth-grinder, this girl).

"How is it that you're this professional hairdresser?" I ask.

"I don't know," Carrie laughs. She's squatting over the laid-out newspaper and unveils, from a rather impressive folding leather case, her tools: stainless steel scissors, a long notched razor, combs and clips. "Just one of those things that happened."

My phone rings again, a nagging child, and I discipline it by reaching into my pocket and switching off the ringer.

Carrie leads me into the bathroom, tells me to lean over the sink, positions my head beneath the tap, execution-style, and runs water over my skull. She speaks loudly so that I can hear her through the gush: "After high school, all my friends were staying close to home, working or whatever, so I decided to stick around, too. It was a lark, I just needed a job. *Any* job. My aunt was a hairdresser, and I worked at her salon. Sweeping floors and washing hair, at first, but, you know, you pick things up along the way, the girls their offered to train me. Just one of those things — you make this random decision and you're carried along by the current."

I speak loudly, too, with water in a narrow column at the end of my nose and two streams streaming off at each corner of my mouth: "I had the opposite thing. I stuck around, but all my friends left, went off to school. I wasn't a hairdresser, though. I was a security guard."

"That's, like, the boy version of hairdresser. We had the same gender-determined destinies." She guides my head out of the sink with a protective hand on my occipital lump. "Why did you stay? For a girl?"

"Of course."

"Why does anyone go anywhere or do anything?"

"True."

From my pocket, another vibrato entreaty.

"You might as well just answer that," she says.

Annoyance. I pull it out, check the display. It's Rob Sangran. As were the two previous calls. I wipe the wet hair away from my ear and listen: "Yeah? What?"

Rob: "Dude!"

"Yeah."

"Where are you?"

"I'm—" I consider a lie and settle for an obfuscation. "Getting my hair cut."

"Really? Fuck... I thought they shut everything down."

"For what?"

"You didn't hear?"

"Hear what?"

"Oh my *God*, dude! There was a coup. The army took over. They rolled up in fucking *tanks*, man. They're out there *right now*."

"Out where?"

"Everywhere. In the streets. Twenty minutes ago I was on Prakanong and a fucking *tank* rolled by. It was amazing. And then this army jeep goes by, and there's a dude in the back with a megaphone telling everyone in the street to go home and stay home, they're enforcing a curfew, everything is shutting down."

I go to the window, press my face against it, shield my eyes from the reflection of Carrie's various lamps. "I don't see anything out there."

"Turn on the TV, you don't believe me. All the local stations are off the air. BBC News is blacked out. So is CNN.

It's the beginning of the workday back home. Been getting all sorts of emails from family and friends asking what the fuck is going on."

Carrie mouths the words: "What's going on?"

I tell Rob I'll call him back and disconnect. I tell Carrie to turn on the television. We flip through the channels on her tiny set: the local stations are blacked out and the foreign news channels are broadcasting static. Only one station is still alive, looping stock footage of His Majesty the King: jumpy sixteen-millimetre clips in which He visits labourers in a rice field, and they're *wai*-ing so deep they're practically flat on their stomachs, practically surrendering; He's got His camera hanging around His neck, and He's going down the line, gently touching the tops of their heads (the tops are all they're offering). "Same footage they play during the anthem at the movie theatre," Carrie says. She flips open her laptop and balances it on her knees. The *Bangkok Post* webpage won't load, but we get through to BBC and CBC and MSNBC, and above the fold they're all reporting the same story, scant of detail, starkly suggestive: with the prime minister of Thailand in New York to attend the United Nations General Assembly, military forces have secured control of the capital city, Bangkok, and declared the current government dissolved.

All the sites offer different versions of the same image, as if all their photographers are shooting shoulder to shoulder: two tanks with their barrels crossed, and beyond, through a spiked iron gate, the lights of the Government House.

"Do you think it's safe to go outside?"

"Why do you want to go outside?" she says.

"Rob said there was a curfew."

"A curfew means you stay indoors."

"I know, but—"

This quaking sensation—it isn't quite panic, but perhaps the initial stages of it; I'm an animal that has never fought or fled, and whichever internal apparatus of my endocrine system is responsible for such responses is unpractised; my cells and glands and tissue are flooded with contradicting hormonal messages; I'm anxious and excited and uneasy and afraid and flush with nervous energy. "Should we, like, knock on a few doors, talk to your neighbours, find out what's happening? Should we call P'Milk?"

"What are they going to know that we don't know? I think we know everything there is to know."

"But this is crazy, right?"

"Yeah. But, no. It doesn't seem crazy out there."

I go to the window, but nothing about the view from Carrie's third-floor apartment suggests unrest, civil or military or otherwise: the *soi* below is empty, just flat asphalt turned yellow by the streetlights; beyond, the skyline of hotels and office towers are sleepily conscious, like hosts and hostesses waiting for the last lingering guests to leave. No tanks, though. No helicopters, no neon-green tracer fire.

"It's so quiet. Nothing's happening. Creepy, right?"

"You're right," she says, and makes a charade of looking panicked. "They're coming for us. They're probably in the building *right now*."

I mimic her googly-eyed pantomime: "I think I can hear them!"

"We should probably hide."

"We should probably go to the embassy."

"Yeah. They probably have helicopters on the roof. We can escape in one."

For a while we sit in silence on the edge of her bed, cycling through TV channels, refreshing news websites. For twenty minutes, nothing changes: the same looping footage, the same two sentences of disobliging copy. Finally, Carrie stands up and points me to the newsprint tapestry so meticulously laid out on the floor and the chair she earlier set up in the middle of it.

"You still want to cut my hair?"

"I'm actively trying to distract you, now. All this flipping through channels is going to trigger my epilepsy."

"You have epilepsy?"

"If I said I did, would that give you something else to focus on?"

"If you have a seizure I will definitely focus on your epilepsy."

"I'm glad to hear that," she says, and throws me a towel. "Put that on. I have to rinse your hair again."

"You don't really have epilepsy, right?"

Carrie laughs. "Oh my *God*," she says. "Just come here." I follow her into the bathroom. There's a comb and pair of strange scissors with notched teeth tucked into the back pocket of her jeans. I bow my head into the sink, and before she turns on the water, she says: "Relax. What else are we going to do right now?"

"I want you to fuck me."

"How do you want me to fuck you?"

Oh, that word! Just saying it sets my guts to throbbing.

She reaches down with her right hand to clutch and stroke; overhand, underhand, knob-grip fractal manoeuvres like she's changing gears down a slow residential street, and while she does, she turns her head and speaks softly against my cheek:

"Like this," she says. "Just like this."

Our sticky hot skin is glued together with sweat — my stomach, her back; every little movement pulls pleasantly. Our chests, stacked, rise doubly high and sink together. We're like this for a while, waiting for the next thing to happen. With her face turned towards mine, her mouth is level with my eyes; she has seventy-nine vertical ridges on her lower lip. If I stretch my neck, I can bite the underside of her chin, so I do.

First gear, fifth gear, second gear, reverse.

"Do it," she says.

"Yeah," I say.

"Do you have a condom …?"

Condom is the antonym of *fuck*, and, spoken aloud, has the reverse effect; heaving oceans evaporate, our skin goes dry, her weight suddenly makes me breathless in the bad way.

"No, shit, I don't. Sorry."

She sighs. Frustrated, or flustered with lust? I can't tell.

"What are we going to do?" she says.

"I don't know."

"We probably shouldn't."

"You're right."

"We should stop—"

I should stop, turn around, get the hell out of here, make some excuse about the traffic, or food poisoning, or an emergency trip to the border to correct some issue of citizenship, but as soon as I walk into the café she spots me. She's sitting at a table near in the back, dressed down in shorts and flip-flops, hair swept modestly back. Even her oversized Chanel sunglasses with the inlaid mother-of-pearl insignia, which usually give her the countenance of an heiress or movie star playing incognito, seem, today, utilitarian.

Three weeks, now, since Carrie and I spent the night together, and except for an uncoordinated exchange the following morning, we haven't spoken. In the light of day, in the absence of danger, the fine tempo we'd tapped our feet to the previous night developed a fatal arrhythmia. We were left bedridden and blundering; interrupting each other; talking over each other; thinking and saying and implying all the exact wrong things. It started, actually, in those awful minutes of lucidity that immediately succeed ejaculation (remember, please, that men do that—they get all coherent and fair-minded after their incoherence pays dividends).

It must be a mutual feeling, though, because in the proceeding three weeks we did an excellent job of avoiding each other. There was only that one afternoon, travelling in opposite directions on the escalator in the lobby of the building, when we acknowledged each other with casual nods (in my sudden panic I added a military salute to mine), and that other morning when she ran into Rob Sangran and me as we were waiting in line for a sweet milk tea. But only in the last two days have there been a few phone calls (unanswered), a few text messages (unresponded to), and now this meeting, arranged the old-fashioned way, with a note posted to my office door that said: *call me please thank you.*

Three weeks, too, since the coup, and already the international news networks are bored with this latest Thai revolution. Rightly so: the promise of violence went unfulfilled. No one was considerate enough to throw a brick through a storefront window or tie a T-shirt around their face. Even the BBC is yawning at the poised and practical installation of a democratic government. We're not even making the scrolling ticker at the bottom of the screen anymore; we're not even worth a short expository sentence. Before I took the Skytrain here to Happy Café, I was biding my time back at the office, scrolling and scanning the unpunctuated lower-case accounts of long-time expats refused entry at the border because of the sequential tourist visas pasted in their passports. These are guys (always guys, never gals) who have lived in Thailand for years, who own property, who run businesses. What hope do I have if guys like this are getting busted? Visa-run operations, allegedly, aren't answering their phones. English teaching outfits, reportedly, are falling apart. I've been pestering Rob Sangran for news (he's half-Thai, half-Irish and seems like an equable source), but he knows only what I know: rumour neutered and sewed up and pumped full of hormones and repackaged as sexy fact. "You might have to marry a nice Thai girl," he said to me, and there was something gut-wrenching in the way he seemed not at all to be joking.

Carrie is thumbing away at her phone and doesn't look up until I'm standing right over her. "Hi," she says, with a wide smile that I mistake, then (now), for zealousness, and which I now (here) see is stretched on her face against her will, fish-hooked at one end by sympathy and at the other by contrition. A cup of iced coffee is sweating on a pink napkin; she hasn't touched it; it's still full to the rim, ice cubes reduced to floating pebbles. All these clues, but I'm too bloated with hot oxygen to see them. I'm repelled and attracted with equal force and torque. I'm thinking: how can I remove this yoke without becoming, in her mythology, the villain? How can I extract myself from this? How can this extraction be accomplished with, perhaps, a return trip between her sheets, where I can easily (be) convince(d) closure is hiding? ·

"What's up?" I ask.

"Oh, nothing much," she says, but she stretches that last syllable, lets it die on the tip of her tongue, and I know that something *is* going on.

"Haven't seen you in a while," I say, pre-emptively address-ing (rather cleverly, I think) the matter at hand. "Did you change your schedule at work? I thought maybe you were out of town, down in Koh Phangan or something. Weren't you planning that? Or was it Koh Chang?"

Bless her heart, Carrie doesn't waste any time with small talk, doesn't wind herself up with any conversational calis-thenics, doesn't need to test her vocal register before making this announcement, which she has been composing for days.

"I'm pregnant," she says.

"I'm pregnant," she says.

There's that touch of bratty confidence that swells some-times to the surface of her voice; there's that suppressed smirk, showing through her veneer of sincerity, peeking out at me from the dimpled corners of her mouth; there's that artificial sophistication, the folded fingers and stretched-wide shoulders and sideways tilt of her chin, the impersonation of profundity. She's enjoying this—this turning of the tables, this surprising plot twist, this earth-shattering I-told-you-so. She's getting, like always, the spoiled brat, exactly what she wants.

"I'm pregnant," she says.

There's that numinous, luminous sincerity that every so often appears, by some rare convergence of photonic emissions, like the aurora borealis, to reveal shimmering in the night sky all her goodness and kindness and fairness. Her mouth is bowed, but not in satisfaction. This is a smile, not a smirk; a sad smile emitting a billion kilojoules of sympathetic energy. And this sideways tilt of her chin? It's just an aerodynamic adjustment as we're hurled forward towards our deaths, now and forever tethered together by the intermingling of our reproductive cells and the little pink cake they will bake.

"I'm pregnant," she says.

Oh, there goes my pumped-up muscle, hot oxygen farting out through the holes poked by those jagged consonants; the cleaving *P*, grapple-gun *R*, coathook double-*N*s, switchblade *T*. The lever controlling my nervous system clicks through ten temperate settings and engages at "flaccidity." This chair, now, is too deep for my withered carcass. I can barely see over the top of the table to make eye contact with Carrie, who won't stop smiling/smirking at me with that bratty confidence/luminous sincerity.

"I'm pregnant," she says.

There are two other patrons, two rows behind us, sitting across from each other at a table for four. I can see them over Carrie's shoulder. A girl with her back to me. A guy with an adenoidal stutter, hunched low with his fingers knit over his nose and mouth, like a surgeon's mask. At the counter the coffee shop girl in her rayon golf shirt fires up the hundred-horsepower blender and annihilates a pitcher of ice cubes, banana, condensed milk, and sugar water; even from here I can smell the motor's electrostatic halitosis. Beside me, the café windows show the frond-lined pathway between the building and a flaking stone wall erected to block the sights and sounds of traffic; the narrow apertures are filled with light and shadow, cars passing in illusory reverse motion; on the cement squares of the walkway, a paint-stroke of viscera that was once a gecko, trod upon weeks ago and washed away by the monsoon rains. The coffee shop girl calls out in Thai, and the patron stands to fetch his drink and spins his gonads right into the corner of the chair. He plays it cool, though, and only lets the vocoid half of *whoa!* slip through his lips before stifling it and sidling past. In the meantime, a hundred cars have flickered past on the other side of the head-high barrier, a hundred ants have crossed the ravine to wherever it is they're going.

See? Life goes on. This pronouncement is no big deal.

"The last couple weeks, I've been feeling really weird, and I missed my period, and I'm usually very punctual when it comes to that sort of thing, and so I got a pregnancy test, and I thought of calling you *before* I took it, but I thought that would be silly, because what if it was nothing? But, anyways, it turns out it's *not* nothing, it's *some*thing. It's—" she laughs here, the way you laugh at a joke told at your expense, to diffuse the power of it "—a *baby*." She picks up her iced coffee, touches the sweating glass to her bottom lip, then puts it back down and wipes the condensation off her fingers with the pink napkin. "My first instinct was, like, oh my God, *no way*, so I bought another test, and another one, and... well, I haven't been to the doctor yet, but we didn't, you know, *use* anything, so it's looking pretty certain. So, yeah, that's it. I'm pregnant. There, I said it. I'm pregnant. I'm pregnant. And now we have to figure out what we're going to do."

"What are we going to do?" she sighs, and her breath rolls in rivulets down the channels between my ribs.

"I don't know," I say, and my breath makes the invisible hairs on the back of her neck flutter.

"We probably shouldn't."

"You're right."

"We should stop—"

But her hand continues its priming, cocking, fuse-sparking.

But we're already in the penultimate position.

But the angle is right, I'm aimed at the bullseye, no manual guidance now required, just a flex, a clench, a spasm, a twitch. My cock tick-tocks to the click of my heartbeat, and on each downward tick, a daub of warm wetness like a kiss on the forehead.

Okay, here we go, a little push.

Nestled, now, all happily curled up among soft linens, head on the pillow, ready for bed.

This is probably enough.

No, she flexes her legs.

Now cautiously poking in to check things out, ask if anyone's home, make sure everything's okay.

I wedge my heels against the mattress.

She lifts her heels and settles her weight.

Nnnnhh—

All this hot viscous tension spills like melted wax, floods the room, rises up to swallow us. We move like we're underwater, deliberate, decelerated, like we're giants. We strain and urge and writhe, fingers claw, flat palms paw.

We *fuck*, and our fucking will change everything.

—3—

What?

No, I'm fine.

Fine, fine, fine. Totally fine. I'm okay, now.

No, I wasn't crying about *that*.

It was something else entirely.

Give me a minute—

Shhnnnnf.

Shnf—

I haven't wept like that in a long time. Not even in the last few weeks/months/decades, when in each dark second it seemed I *should* be weeping. By the way, did you hear that strange sonic effect? In this dead, unmoving air, my sobs seemed to echo. A pitiful sort of reverberation, don't you think, like a lonely voice in an empty room? Here is my theory: those jittery particles that are in perpetual erratic motion have stopped along with everything else and formed a sort of flat wall against which sound ricochets. This would also explain the thickness of the air, the sense I have of under-water resistance.

Anyways, no, I wasn't sobbing from loneliness (though I'm still a bit lonely) or fear (though I'm afraid) or regret (my feelings on the matter of Carrie and me sleeping together are, for obvious reasons, somewhat complicated). I was sobbing for my lost comic books: that precious run of *Suicide Squad*, which, among all this avionic rubble, has disappeared. I've spent days looking for them, measuring each speck of dust on the horizon and hoping I might recognize a pinprick of purple or yellow from a front cover, a vague molecular impression of stacked panels from an interior page. But so far nothing—just the same boring landscape.

No, no, it's not that they're valuable. I mean, they aren't mint condition books (even *near-mint*, with clean corners and original staples, they'd be worth less than a dollar). They don't even hold any special nostalgic value; I read them, sure, when I was a kid, but they were never my favourites. I brought them with me because they seemed accessories essential to my trot across the globe. Artefacts of, oh, I don't know, the tempo of living I was hoping to recover by running away to another country. You know: the uncomplicated, guiltless lethargy of being sprawled on the floor on a Sunday afternoon. You see, before these hanging ruins, before the sky, before the Kingdom of Siam, before adulthood and all its stupid responsibilities, it was the floor—

—the floor is my domain. Carpet and tile and linoleum and polished hardwood. I rule over it all. I can paddle myself from one end of the kitchen to another, collecting dust on my fleecy bum; with my fingernail I scratch pictures in sticky spills matted dark with the fur peeled from the bottom of socks. In the bathroom, when I miss the toilet, my fragrant pee pools in the grooves of rhomboid tiles, and I'm right down there, on my knees and elbows, studying its distribution, damming channels with the corner of a tissue-square. I am intimate with the underside of things; I see things that others can't: the gummy accumulation of crumbs pushed deep into the seam of the dining room table's prosthetic leaf, visible only from below; the tumbleweed dust-bunnies and lone coins and wadded-up grocery store receipts and tabs from aluminum cans that have colonized the arid landscape of the inch-high space beneath the couch. I lie stomach-down on the carpet, reading comics, drinking Coke-flavoured slushes, and where my shirt rides up, my skin feels like a falling-asleep limb. When I pick up my elbows, they're red and impressed with the curlicue pattern of the carpet's whiskers—

Ah, but I don't want my *Suicide Squad* comics back to indulge in such sentimentality. I don't want them back to read them and add a fresh sensation to my stalled memory banks. No, I've resigned myself to the fact that all those books and films and songs, all of humanity's eloquent self-expressions, are lost to me; because I've never read or seen or heard them, I will never read or see or hear them. They might as well have never been created.

Those comics … it's something different.

And when I say "those comics" I really mean just *one* of them. Issue #23. Forget all the others. When I talk about scanning the wreckage for "a pinprick of purple or yellow,"

I'm referring specifically to the cover of issue #23, which features two bipedal robots blasting purple plasma rays, and, in the foreground, Bronze Tiger and Vixen leaping away from the explosion in full grand jeté. The story inside is called "Weird War Tales," and it's all about how the squad (which, by the way, is a crack team of reformed super-villains and ne'er-do-wells who operate under the direction of a secret government branch run by a sassy, no-nonsense black woman with cornrow hair and powerful calves) splits up to confront coincident alien invasions in Russia and Australia.

But, no, the story isn't the thing, either.

Funny to think that just yesterday (yesterday, in the traditional accounting of quantum time), while packing up my stuff, I almost left them behind. Not that I was in the most perceptive frame of mind; the man with the missing tooth was standing in the doorway of my apartment, checking and double-checking his watch while I rushed from drawer to cupboard to shelf trying to cram as much crap as possible into the single bag I was allowed to bring with me. My designer jeans and tailored shirts; my sneakers and high-tops and oxfords; my collection of pirated DVDs from Pantip Plaza; my scroll paintings and decorative wooden bowls and wicker balls—I had to leave it all behind. And my comics, too. Almost. A final mental audit revealed my error, and I scrambled, as the missing-tooth man regarded his watch and clicked his tongue, to find them and fold them gently into a pair of jeans, which I placed in the centre of my bag, safe on all sides from the blunt-force trauma of pan-Pacific transport.

But then, in line at the airport, I panicked. I couldn't bear be separated from my comics, so I opened my suitcase, pulled them out, and clutched them to my chest as I carried them through the security gate. On the plane, as the great machine roared and rose, I held them in my lap. When the plane levelled and the seat-belt light was extinguished, I lowered my tray and arranged them in a stack. And from there, you know how it goes—blah, blah, blah, into the sky like a gaggle of geese.

Yes, they are important. In the midst of this bizarre captivity, those comic books might be the only chance I have to escape. If I could just get my hands on them, I could prove to you, irrefutably, that I never wanted our time together to end like this—that, even though I'm way up here in the sky, thousands of miles away, I haven't left you behind.

Would it help if I showed you how I got here in the first place?

Not *here*, as in *way up here in the sky*.

I mean here, as in this *hemisphere*, this *continent*, this *time zone*.

It was all pretty typical, if you must know:

I turned twenty-one and, like many twenty one year-olds, decided to embark on a period of exile and self-denial, to search for the call. Why not? I had nothing to lose. In the half-decade since the end of high school, when all things briefly seem possible, I had accomplished nothing, I had made no progress—I *was* nothing. And then, for the second time in my life, I was deserted by the only person who should have been responsible for *not* deserting me, and whoever I had hoped to be, whatever I had meant to accomplish—it all turned from solid matter into gas, and I was left, as before, with a bowel-twisting pocket of nothingness in the middle of me.

But though I knew exactly *how* I'd been hollowed out and precisely *who* had performed the hollowing, I couldn't articulate the shape of it any more clearly than I could look inside myself and tell you the colour of my pancreas or the length of my small intestine. It didn't possess the common contours of drugs and alcohol; I tested those things out, as everyone does, and found them rather unpleasant (I have a hard enough time regulating my baser instincts; why would I purposefully loosen my grip on the controls?). It wasn't the shape of sex, hetero or homo, though the former does well to make me feel in the moments leading up to it (not during, not after) like I am living an upper-case version of MALE LIFE. It wasn't a pyramidal gap that might be filled by money or success, nor the inverted teardrop shape of adrenaline and danger, nor even a fist-sized emptiness easily plugged up by selflessness and sainthood. Neither, sad to say, was it a soul-shaped hole where the love and company of family and friends snugly fit. So I thought: why not search for it elsewhere? Perhaps *elsewhere* itself was the elusive circumstance/object/phenomenon I was seeking? A voice rose up from the deepest place inside me, not the soul, not the toes, but that functionless nether-pocket on the interior side of the perineum, and it said: *go somewhere, go anywhere, go away from this place to any place that isn't this place!* And how easy it was to take my body's advice! How easy it was to run away, with no bonds shackling me to the country of my birth! Not a career, not an education. Not my mother, who had banished me at the age of thirteen to live with my father, and not my father, who had embraced me in exile, I sometimes suspected, only to spite her. Not the girl who had recently entrapped and abandoned me. Not my few childhood friends, who had left me behind in pursuit of cooler people and places; not my grandmother, who had recently passed away. Not a single reason for me to stay, so, with the modest sum my grandmother left me, I purchased a plane ticket for Bangkok, Thailand, and set out to live the life of a castaway: I would build from driftwood and coconut husks and palm fronds a brand new version of myself.

But why Bangkok? Why not Paris or Sydney or Hong Kong?

Because Paris was too expensive, Sydney too familiar, Hong Kong too toweringly urban. The sensual Latin life of South America has never much appealed to me (it seems to be a particularly feminine fetish), and though I thought it might fluoresce the few remaining cells of my Russian heritage, the shady daily life of Moscow was too intimidating. Japan was intimidating in the opposite way: the brightness, the cleanliness, the incessant stimulation of each and every sensual nerve. I chose Bangkok not because it was economical or extravagant, familiar or exotic, plebeian or provocative, but because it was the median point between all of those things — the perfect place for Daniel Solomon, who was himself equidistant from all matters of import and therefore defined by none of them.

And for almost an entire year I had this perfect place all to myself. I was once again a worthwhile human creature, present in the world, visible, material, transmuted back into solid matter by the equatorial climate. I had found the thing that fit comfortably into the nullity. I felt it with as much certainty as a decade earlier I'd felt the hot interior fission of puberty. And then I met Carrie, and we committed our sin of omission (restraint, discretion, chastity, judiciousness — we failed to perform any of these acts), which, along with whatever cheap manufacturing processes and failed safety protocols caused the plane to crack apart, led to my aerial captivity.

Yes, so, there you go, that's how I got here.

But that doesn't mean I *should* be here. That doesn't mean I *deserve* to be here. It might seem like I'm spitting out a bunch of alibis and excuses and explanations, but I don't want you to think of me as some kind of coward who can't face up to catastrophe. Quite the opposite. I've been facing catastrophe my entire life. And I don't mean this most recent aviation-related catastrophe (though you can add it to the list). I don't even mean the catastrophic mistake I made with Carrie. None of that stuff would have happened if I hadn't been sent searching for solace in the first place. Inasmuch the whole sum of my human experience since birth (which you may very well get the entire breadth of as I work backwards like this) has brought me here, *she* brought me here, too.

No, not Carrie. The *other* one.

Oh, yes, I know — I should have learned my lesson. Escaping to Thailand was supposed to be the lesson. But I guess it's true what they say about being fooled once or twice or three times; eventually it's your own fault. It's true, too, about hindsight — it's so much easier to see all the connective threads and paths of causation when you reverse-engineer your life like this.

How could I have possibly known, without these amazing powers of retrospect, that when I met her at the age of sixteen, Marti Barrett was going to ruin my life?

—4—

"Remember when I missed my period that one time, and we got all paranoid? Every morning you were, like, *is it here yet, do you feel bloated, are you crampy?* And we tried to ignore it, pretend it wasn't happening, but, just for fun, even though it seemed impossible, we started making lists of baby names?"

I'd forgotten Marti's voice: this high-pitched vibrato, this cartoon singsong, this half-nasal/half-throaty chirp; she sounds like a precocious little kid with bronchitis.

"I found them the other day, in one of my notebooks. We made top-ten lists. Do you remember your top names? Ripley, for a girl. And Zeus, for a boy. Remember that? Imagine if we had a son named Zeus. Seriously, Daniel—did you feel disappointed when my period finally came? I didn't. Not really. I don't think the world was ready for little Zeus Solomon."

I say: "Yeah, I guess not."

This telephone has been suction-cupped to my sweaty ear for almost an hour. I'm in the basement bedroom of my father's house, this stale-stinking, dark and damp, barren and bare-boned underground apartment, and I'm crashed lengthwise on this crumb-sprinkled corduroy couch, my attention divided between Marti's droning voice and the droning TV.

"He'd be three years old, now," she says. "If he really existed. Crazy, right?"

I say: "Yeah, I guess."

I'm tired. So tired. Working as a security guard doesn't require any real physical effort, all I do is sit on my little stool and flirt with the cute girls in their mall-bought business slacks and mannish glasses as they sign in for job interviews with the PR practices and investment groups and marketing firms and insurance bureaus and communications agencies in the office tower above. But still, after every shift, I'm exhausted like this. Not with exertion, but rather a sort of spiritual lethargy; tired from the inside out. The boredom, the stillness, the sameness—it leeches the vigour out of your muscles and leaves your body feeling like you've spent eight hours running stairs or hauling couches or laying shingles. I've managed to wrestle free of my uniform shirt and vest but lost momentum at the unbuckling of my belt, so I'm still entrapped from the waist down in my starchy black work slacks with the yellow double stripe. I tried to pry off my boots, but they were too tight, so I thought: ah, fuck it. *Ah, fuck it* was my first thought, too, when the phone began its anodic bleating, but I can't stand the eerie silence that succeeds an unacknowledged alarm (hazard of the job), so I picked it up, and, sure enough, it was Marti. Again.

"Remember I'd read to you from my mom's romance novels?" she says. "I don't think I've ever laughed so hard. I was thinking of that because I was thinking of how much I liked the name Claire, and I think I read it in one of those books. What was that one part? Oh, oh, oh, that one part about 'his fleshy horn'—how did it go? She's kissing the forehead of his red helmet, or something. I was laughing so hard I couldn't breathe, remember, and I almost panicked, it was like I was drowning. You know, I pretended like it was a joke, but I knew where the all dirty parts were because I'd read them all. I'd steal them from my mom's room and hide them under my mattress, you know, like boys do with porno magazines, and—my God, the ideas I had about sex! Wow. Those books, it's all ear-biting and nipple-tweaking and all this straight-up masochistic stuff. It's all *powerful chests* and *strong buttocks*."

She laughs at her own joke, and in the quiet seconds that follow I can hear music playing faintly behind her.

"Sounds like you're at a club," I say.

"No it doesn't," she says. "Russell has a few people over, that's all."

After we moved out of our apartment six months ago, we each ended up back with our parents: she with her mother, I with my father. But while I've adapted to life down here in the basement suite (biologically, I mean: my skin has turned bluish from the dim light, my armpits have begun to emit the same odour as the moist patch of carpet by the bathroom door, and in the thick underground silence I have developed the capacity to sleep for sixteen hours at a stretch) Marti couldn't bear to live for too long under her mother's roof (or thumb). On a previous late-night call she told me how they fought constantly: about Marti's eating habits, her stormy moods, her epic showers, her obsessive-compulsive laundering of sheets and pillowcases. Marti moved out after a few weeks—into the spare room of a townhouse rented by some of her colleagues. *Male* colleagues, but this didn't bother me as much as I wanted it to. Russell, Martin, John—all she has ever shared about them is their names, which are so common and dreary that I'm able to imagine them as a bunch of sexless brotherly types who self-identify as gentleman and wear fedoras and read fat fantasy novels on the bus (I'd have it worse if they were named Colton or Julian or Javier). In this manner I've been able to detach myself from her. Only apathy remains. She can pretend to need me all she wants. I don't believe her. Even when she says:

"I found that list of names," Marti says, "and the next night I had a dream that we had a baby together. This tiny, tiny little baby—like, tinier than normal. It was the size of a kitten. Even smaller, actually. We were carrying it around in the palms of our hands and showing it to people like it was—I don't know, like something we scooped out of the sand. And we had little blankets for it, and little jumpers, and a little toque, and it was totally normal. And at night we had to do this thing—we slept with our bellies together, squeezing the baby between them, because that's how you were supposed to do it in this weird world of small babies. It didn't suffocate or anything, it was safe there, and we stayed up all night, face to face, talking and talking because we were so excited about having this tiny little baby."

The program I'm half-watching on TV is a compilation of extreme video clips: a dune buggy somersaults through a chain-link fence into crowded racetrack bleachers, a woman has her arm swallowed by an alligator at a Florida theme park, a Taiwanese hostage-taker is drop-kicked by a quick-thinking court stenographer. The clips are shown over and over, edited together like a music video, but the song only has a chorus, that outrageous three seconds of bystander-slapping/jaw-snapping/head-cracking, and it's repeated in spasmodic slow motion and blown-out blurry pixels and sped-up triple-takes. The food I'm eating is a submarine sandwich that I picked up from the most convenient convenience store on my way home from the bus stop. You poke holes in the plastic condom-sheath and put it in the microwave: this turns the cheese into a salty paste and the bread into an edible sponge.

"Did I tell you that I'm going back to school?" Marti says. "In the spring, hopefully. To the college here in Westborough. They have a really great nursing program, which, you know, is something I've been thinking about for a while. But I was reading about this social work program, where you can become a counsellor, and I think I might do that instead. I'd be good at that, don't you think? Being a social worker."

My dad's footsteps creak across the ceiling; it must be midnight; his fussy bladder keeps a more accurate record of space-time than any atomic clock in the world. It seems impossible, as I lie here in a state of semi-undress, sick with fatigue, probing the groove between my cheek and gums to remove this sticky mortar of quasi-bread, alone and lonely and doubly depressed over how comfortable that loneliness now feels, that in two short months I'll quit my job, leave my dad looking for a new basement tenant, collect my *Suicide Squad* comics and other essential worldly belongings in a duffel bag, and leave this place, never (apparently) to return.

"Hello?" Marti says. "You there? I'm sorry, do I sound all fucked? I feel all fucked."

"Are you drunk?" I ask.

"I'm not drunk. Do I sound drunk? No, I'm just retarded. Sorry. I was out late, and—"

"Are you high?"

"Not 'high'. You're such a *squaaare, maan*. Not *high*, but—yeah, I'm coming down."

"From what?"

"I'm not telling you, Mr. Judgmental, Mr. Squaaaare."

"I'm not judging. You can live your life however you want."

All her false gaiety fades: "Are you mad at me?"

"Why would I be mad at you?"

"For calling so late?"

"It's not late for me. I just got home from work. It's fine."

But it *is* late, and it's *not* fine. I dread these late-night calls, the forced familiarity with which she tries to win back my faith and attention, but for some reason I can't quite tell her directly. Instead, I breathe glacial cold air back through the phone.

"Are you sure?"

"Yes, it's fine," I say (glacially, coldly).

So strange to be interacting like this with a person who was—for four years, almost a whole fifth of your life—the other half of you. Strange, because it's like talking to yourself. But even though they are, materially, the same person they used to be—same voice, same face, same body—everything you adored about them, that magical internal quality that in the depths of infatuation you can only call "amazingness" or "perfection" or "a certain *something*" has dematerialized, their veins are dry of it, and you wonder, did I ever really love this person, or was it some delusion, some trick of the light, some false memory? And when the pace of their shivering and sniffling picks up and is joined by a wobbly murmur and is interrupted by a rising succession of hitched breaths, you surprise yourself with how little sympathy you feel for this person who, once upon a time, was the split atom at the centre of your thermonuclear compassion.

"I feel dumb for calling you," she says. "I know you don't want to talk to me. I can tell." Whatever crystalline flakes have been flushed through her bloodstream are starting now to dissolve, and, along with them, her chemically enhanced sprightliness. "But it's, like, *so, so, so* good to talk to someone who knows me, and *you* know me, you're, like, the only person who really *knows* me."

I feel myself paying attention, now. This fragile Marti, this hurting Marti, this helpless Marti—this is *my* Marti.

She says: "I never lied to you, you know."

A purr of empty telephonic air. Onscreen, a fat tourist is gored (and gored, and gored, and gored) through the thigh in the streets of Pamplona (guitar screech!). I swallow the last rubbery nub of my "sandwich." I swallow a big, satisfying yawn. I swallow my urge to acknowledge her last statement, and so she moves on:

"Sorry. I'm just tired. Tired and a bit wasted. I shouldn't be calling you this late. What is it, there? Two in the morning? Seriously, I don't know what I was thinking. I had that weird baby dream, and it was so *real*, it was like time travel, it was like I was back there. Remember how much our apartment reeked? Remember we left that half-eaten Christmas turkey out on the balcony until, like, the middle of February? Remember how fucked up all the carpet got from candle wax? I miss it sometimes. I get homesick for it."

She wants a sweet answer, I can tell. She's fishing for an *I miss it, too* or a *we had some great times together, didn't we?* But instead, I don't know why, I say the last thing she wants to hear: "Was it really that great?"

That was a real body-shot. That one rattled her kidneys. She's reeling away from the receiver when she says: "You can choose to remember it however you want. I choose to remember it another way."

On TV, a skateboarder alights testicle-first on a steep stairwell railing, freezes there, then rises up, splay-legged, arms flapping, an ascending angel. But it's just a tease; the editors reeled it back so they could smash his balls again. And again. Again, again.

Marti is all business, now: "Anyways, I'm sorry for calling. I gotta go … it's almost four in the morning, here, and I'm supposed to work the early shift tomorrow. I have to drink about a gallon of water and get some sleep. I'm sorry for calling." And then, after a short beat: "I'm not sorry, actually. I don't have to be sorry. I know you think I'm pathetic, but I'm not. I'm being generous to you. I'm making an effort to still be nice to you. I'm sorry if you find that annoying. But I love you, and I forgive you."

Perhaps I'm distracted by all the physical trauma, or maybe my focused aloofness has turned me deaf, but I don't seem to hear what she just said, and so the last words I speak to her are:

"Well—have a good day at work."

The last words she speaks to me are:

"Hey, remember how we could never figure out who said *I love you* first?" Silence, and she says, "I know it was you. If you can remember at least *one* thing correctly, remember that."

Marti and I are lying naked on top of the sheets, post-coitus, peeled off each other and letting the confectionary mist kicked up by our slapping skin drift out the open window. Our communal smell: it's its own thing, a whole, not a sum, not a bouquet, not a perfume of intermingled individual odours. It smells like *us*. And it's been like that since we started our alchemical experiments in that shabby hotel room all those years and all those orgasms ago. I'm intoxicated by it, and not in the poetic sense. It's a stimulant, like weed, like booze, and with each inhalation, like that first or second toke, like that third or fourth cocktail, I feel a peaceful tightening of reality.

"I wrote it all down, you know. I can *prove* that you said it first."

"If you did," I say, "you wrote it down wrong, because it was *you*, I'm a million percent sure."

Marti rolls off the mattress; the springs groan; she pads across the laundry-strewn floor, crouches in front of the closet, and, duck-footed, rustles through the rubble. "You're going to feel so stupid."

I am conscious, even in these meaningless domestic moments, of how changed I am by her. I am no longer Daniel Solomon; I am Daniel Solomon, sex object, lounging naked in the sheets; later, in the kitchen, washing dishes, I will be Daniel Solomon, king of domiciliary affairs; after that, walking to class, impervious to the judgments of the people who pass me on the street, the dudes and chicks and disdainful adults, I am Daniel Solomon, the Great Love of Marti Barrett's Life. She is proof of my goodness, and every moment that I'm with her, I am the best version of myself it's possible to be.

We've spent the last ten minutes debating first impressions and who liked who first. Our recollections of courtship differ; in these parallel realities, we are each the crusher and crushee, each the prize and pursuer, each the alpha and underdog. I have no proof to support my version other than the circumstantial details cherry-picked from my memory. But my Marti is a vehement diarist. Or was, until recently. She has given it up in the last year—I don't know why. In our early days as enthusiasts of each other, though, she was still keeping a record of her daily moods and domestic affairs and public relations and so has proof of this alternate dimension in which it was an effort for her to win my heart, and not, as I remember it, a gradual weakening of her better sense through my strategic campaign of posturing and maundering.

"Here, ha! Here it is," Marti says and holds up a small book bound in puffy plastic and locked shut by a cheap and penetrable tin mechanism. She holds her free hand fig-leaf-style over her pubic mound as she bounces back into bed—this weird modesty when just seconds ago she had been urging: *fuck me harder.*

She's always so worried, you know, that her breasts are too small, that her hips are too narrow, that the tomboyish figure she brought with her into puberty is, six years later, still not exaggerated and engorged enough to make her anything more than superficially cute to the boys and men whose attentions, she can already see, are drawn by biological impulse to the hovering round globes and cello-curves of her luckily mutated peers. As hard as I try to convince her, I don't think she believes there's anything sexy about her sylphic body. But there is: the alikeness of her body to mine, along with its minor enhancements, the apertures and flanges and whatnot, makes it even more magical and mysterious. Even her short, boyish hairstyle enhances the femininity of her features: her delicate nose, her thin, calligraphic lips.

She flips through pages and finds the passage she's looking for.

"Okay, listen to this," she says, and starts reading:

"I've been feeling really alone lately even though I'm around people all day at school and at home. But at the same time I feel depressed when I'm around people. Which is why I want to be alone all the time. It's a paradox. I say things and then I feel stupid for saying them and then I'll go off by myself for a while and stew over it. Which I know is a really unhealthy way to live my life but I can't help it. I sometimes feel like I'm going to lose all my friends. Or else like they don't really like me in the first place and they hang out with me out of pity. I know that's not true. But that doesn't stop me from constantly worrying about it. I was so busy feeling sorry for myself today that I completely forgot that I was supposed to work at five-thirty and ended up being late for work. I had to run all the way from Northlands. I showed up all out of breath and—"

Marti pauses, pinches her eyes, brings the page right up to her nose:

"I don't know what this word is. Sizzle? Mmmm. Trazz, razzle—oh, *frazzled*."

She continues:

"—I showed up all out of breath and *frazzled*. I was so angry at myself. I almost started crying in the back room when I was changing into my work clothes. But I got myself together and stopped feeling so sorry for myself which I think has been becoming a problem lately. I was counting my float and of course Mr. Stelkic comes by and introduces me to this new guy working there who I recognized was a boy from school and I'm sure I looked like a complete weirdo with sweat stains and my face all red and in the worst mood. Sometimes I can't believe my bad luck."

"This is Marti," Mr. Stelkic says, stressing the first vowel the way a police officer might over-pronounce an obvious pseudonym. He's the shift manager here at the grocery store and executes his minor administrative duties with a militaristic flourish.

"Hey," I say to her.

Just a perfunctory glance from the girl behind the checkout counter as she ejects quarters from her fist with little thrusts of her thumb. Her cheeks are still flushed from when she burst in from the cold just a few minutes ago: a blur of whirling backpack straps and blond hair, a beam of damp atmosphere radiating from the pinched interchange of muscle between her eyebrows.

"Hey," she says.

I immediately calculate statistical likelihoods down to microscopic millionths: a woven friendship bracelet on her right wrist; a single thin braid drawn back from her temple and looped over her left ear; a gold loop punched into the flushed apical curve of that same ear. The diktat: a year older than me, elfin-cute, unlikely to be single, but, even *if* single, so far beyond my reach that I'm embarrassed even to be privately contemplating her singleness/unsingleness. I fear that this girl possesses an instinctive knowledge of the local food chain and my low place within it. Within seconds, I resent her. I resent that I like her. I resent liking a girl so easily, within seconds of laying eyes on her. Too many girls, already. Too many girls after whom, from a distance, I lust. Too many girls with whom, in my fantasy fugues, I carry on affairs, and who, in the waking world, prove to be cruel amnesiacs. My fantasies are never sexual, though (well, *rarely* sexual [okay, let's say *half* of them are sexual]). They're rescue fantasies, mostly. Reveries of being stolid and stoic and dependable, of being kind and considerate and thoughtful beyond a girl's wildest expectations. For me, wanting a girlfriend is less about needing someone than it is about being needed. I pray every night that I might be worthy of a girl's needfulness, and somehow, despite the fact that the look this girl gives me as she pours quarters into the change drawer suggests that my birth sixteen years ago is the root cause of her life's aggravation, I sense that it's an act, that she needs something, someone, and that, despite the poor mathematical odds, I could be (or become) the thing she needs.

Of all those too many girls, yes, she could be the one who chooses me, and, as I follow Mr. Stelkic to the produce department to help him uncrate navel oranges and baby carrots, I am dizzy with thinking about it. I want her to be mine in that trivial, cursory, earth-shattering, life-changing way that, in innocent youth, you believe another human being can become yours.

That was the first time Marti and I met.

Back in bed, two years later, cheap notebook paper flickering while Marti whispers sentence fragments under her breath, scanning pages, searching for the next verse. When she finds it her voice blooms back to full colour:

"Tonight was a slow night and I spent most of it sort of spaced out, daydreaming, and thinking. In the course of all this thinking I actually became completely sickened with myself and my attitude lately. I decided (realized) that my depression is self-inflicted. I've turned into someone I don't want to be. After work I walked home with Daniel, who is that new boy in the stockroom. I hung out outside for a while after I closed my till and I smoked two cigarettes that I bought from Valerie. I wasn't necessarily waiting for him but not necessarily *not* waiting for him. He left from the front door and would have walked right past me so I yelled at him to get his attention and immediately felt like a dork—"

"Hey," someone yells.

Fat flakes are coasting down from the not-quite-black sky, turning transparent when they pass through the orbs of light that surround the stooping heads of streetlights. They become visible again when they stick to my black work slacks, which are still flecked, after this evening's shift, with bits of onion skin and walnut dust. My footsteps in the snow are making a sound like celery stalks sliced by knives. I'm almost to the street when I hear the voice again, this time louder, this time aimed decidedly at the back of my head: *"Hey!"*

I turn and look back.

The cute cashier girl is sitting on the edge of the concrete ramp that descends from the loading door, knees pulled to her chest, arms folded and hidden between her stomach and legs ... hidden except for the two fingertips peeking from the cuff of her jacket, holding a half-smoked cigarette down by her hip. She seems almost to be glowing: a bit of that fluorescent indoor light still clings to her. "Hey," I say back.

"You walking home?" she says.

"Yeah, it's not far. Near St. Joe's."

"It's cold."

"I know," I say. The dead space at the end of the statement seems to demand some exclamatory finish, so I shrug. Not a subtle shrug but a sort of quick twitch of my shoulders; a shrug that seems, in the milliseconds before muscle contraction, a terrific demonstration of my dispassion towards the cold, and, in the milliseconds that follow, a childish bit of bluster.

Silence.

Marti pops her bottom lip and nods thoughtfully. Her two fingertips, magically disembodied, float up to meet her puckered lips; the cherry blinkers and she blows out quills and pinions of smoke that in their spiralling intricacy are completely different than the regular clouds of steam that she breathes.

More silence.

Words! Speak *words*! I push my hands wrist-deep into my pockets; I look behind me as if I've just heard someone call my name; I force a shallow cough so that I can turn my chin into my shoulder; I remove a hand from my pocket and scratch the back of my neck with my elbow skyward, in the manner of a Howard Chaykin drawing. My instinct is to turn and dash into the street. I can feel my centre of gravity swinging left and drawing my waist and knees with it; I can hear the rubber heels of my sneakers tamping powder as they pivot towards the street. But I stop myself. Oh, glory, some saboteur impulse pushes a pin into the grinding gears of my getaway! So close! I almost walked away and left her behind, but instead I keep my feet planted, I contain my instinct for flight, I finally swallow the blockage in my throat and ask: "You working tomorrow?"

"Naw. You?"

"Yeah."

"That sucks."

"Why?"

"It's, like, Friday and whatever. I don't know."

Her turn to shrug, though she manages it with a bit more grace, she holds it for longer, and there's something in it, too,

I see now—it's something of a sloppy parry, like mine. "Are you going to Kyle's on Saturday?"

"Yeah, me and Jimmy are going. Are you?"

"Yeah."

Marti stands and tosses her cigarette into the snow, brushes the crystal dust from her butt. "Where do you live?" she asks.

"This place called Woodcrest Circle. It's off Finlayson. Near St. Joe's."

"I live on Sissons Court."

From our mutual knowledge of local geography we know that we're travelling in the same general direction, and without another word we set off together towards the Frame Lake bike trail where, two months from now, we'll huddle on a lakeside bench, we'll kiss, and with my hand beneath her jacket I'll feel the hardness of her nipples through the slippery silver cup of her bra, and I'll smell, with the full strength of my inhaling lungs, with my nose just millimetres from the soft surface of her neck, the gentle bouquet of nicotine and shampoo and perfume that, right now, as we walk shoulder to shoulder, raises an agonizing bubble of hope in my chest.

That bubble of hope is yet unpopped, still crowding the inside of my ribcage as, weeks later, I walk up this muddy hill, stepping in a ciphered sequence of duck feet and tiptoes to avoid rivulets and ridges and puddles, up to this big house blaring through its open windows the wails and whiny guitars of the Offspring, which sounds, to my seventeen-year-old ears, like the fanfare of the Four Horsemen, because, really, where can music go after the Offspring, what could the future possibly hold; this feels, already, like the peak of things; like everything that will follow is postscript.

I am walking up the hill with Jimmy Boychuk. I am carrying a backpack full of beer bottles that we've poached from Jimmy's father's garage. I am wearing the coolest shoes I own (suede Vans, powder blue), and these are the coolest jeans I own (huge, barely held up by my skinny hips, swimming around my legs like a skirt, inseams torn and stitched back together with safety pins so that the cuffs flare like bell-bottoms), and this is the coolest shirt I own (white with a black-and-white print of Jack Nicholson leering through a chopped-up bathroom door), and this is the coolest hat I own (a Blue Jays cap turned backwards), and I am wearing the coolest accessory I own (a puka-shell necklace purchased in Florida while I was visiting my mother the previous spring). Each of these elements, in ideal astrological alignment, forebodes consequence. I am, right now, the coolest iteration of myself it's possible to assemble and am endowed, because of it, with an unfamiliar sense of courage.

In through the front door, where, thrillingly, there are unfamiliar kids: a black kid, a kid with a goatee, a goth moderate who has neutralized his dyed-black hair and eyebrow ring with a plaid button-up and neon-trimmed high-tops. Into the Sutendra's suburban palace, where the Offspring has given away to Collective Soul and a bedlam of voices. They always get it wrong in movies: no one dances at house parties; there's no wildness, no dance-club histrionics, no beer-chugging contests with red plastic cups, no high-fiving football captains dry-humping drunk sluts against hallway walls hung with family photos.

No, not here.

Here the beer is in bottles and cans, all of it hunted and gathered from the fridges and cabinets of parents, the liquor poured into plastic pop bottles in refutable ounces and sneaked away in plain sight. None of the booze or beer has spilled yet, but the whole place nonetheless smells of spilled beer and booze. There's Russ Matonabee and Crystal Kelemen's older brother sitting cross-legged on the carpeted floor, playing *GoldenEye*, snipers in the stack, while an audience hails and heckles, and, right behind them, Jody Brule holds court from his place at the end of the couch, all three hundred pounds of him bound up in the denim jacket that is the only jacket he ever wears, telling Missy Stevens and her friend about running his uncle's four-wheeler off the end of the Walsh Lake dock and trying to hoist it out by throwing tow-chains over a tree branch and how his cousin was almost crushed when the limb snapped and crashed through the dock. And there's Kyle Sutendra sitting presidential in the dining room, vetoing a motion to hotbox the upstairs bathroom, okaying a request to make nachos in the oven, all the while winning his seventh consecutive hand of asshole and punishing the losers with fines they pay in swallows of alcohol. Through the patio doors behind him are dark impressions of smokers in silent conversation, all coolly holding their cigarettes down low, pinching them at the filter instead of nestling them between knuckles, sucking with a flourish to emphasize or interrupt or agree or disagree. And there she is: the new girl from the grocery store; the girl who walked home with me the other night. I see her and she sees me and I look away and she looks away and I look back and she catches me looking back so I lift my beer bottle and swing it in a pendulous tick-tock to say hello and she lifts a palm and smiles and turns back to her conversation.

Later, drunker, I'm saying: "This one time Jimmy was so tanked I had to carry him home, like literally, because he was all *bleaaaaaah*, I'm carrying him like *this*... and I get to his place, and I go in the back door and take him down the stairs, and his limbs are flailing like *blam, bang, blam* against the walls, I can barely keep him upright, but I eventually get him into his room and into bed, and I'm thinking we totally got away with it, but then I hear footsteps on the stairs, and I'm like, *oh shit!*, there's nowhere to hide, the closet is all full of crap, so I'm about to shimmy under the bed, but under the bed is full of crap, too, so I just sort of crouch down behind the dresser, which is basically right in plain view, but I stay really still, and I hear Jimmy's mom come in, who, by the way, already hates me because every time Jimmy gets in trouble for going through his dad's porn collection he blames it on me—"

Marti laughs. *"Gross."*

"—and I'm just *baaaarely* hiding, and she goes right up to the bed and starts shaking Jimmy, saying 'James? *James?!*' and I can practically see the wrinkles in the corners of her eyes, all

DRAG THE SUNLIT SEA

she has to do is look to five degrees to her left, I'm *right there*, but she's too busy bitching him out, she doesn't even see me."

"Oh my *God*," Marti says, and closes her eyes and bows her head and collapses towards me and softly touches my shoulder with the tawny tips of her smoker's fingers, as if this story, which is a semi-fictional first-person interpretation of a story belonging to someone else entirely, is simply too much for her to bear, too funny, too suspenseful, she can't remain upright, she has to keep her balance with this little half-second touch, and that half-second turns out to be the best half-second of my life.

This, the first of our seventy-nine thousand nine-hundred thirty-two kisses.

Marti's saliva tastes just like I imagined it would: slightly of cigarettes, sweet from soda, a candy musk that negates the lemony tinge of puked-up Jamaican rum still clinging to my tonsils. How easy this turns out to be! She apparently wants me as much as I want her. All of my initial suppositions about her availability and willingness were inaccurate, and, for the first time ever, for the *only* time ever, one of my obsessively imagined fantasy scenarios is occurring beat by beat in the material world. Marti Barrett is in my arms and all opened up like a pollinating flower.

Back we go, onto the floor, legs still hanging over the top step, visible from below as a quartet of knees and twitching socked feet. My shirt is pulled up and I can feel the furry carpet prickling my back. Her shirt is pulled up, too, but not by the friction of writhing together on the hallway floor, rather by my hands, made suddenly brave by the alcoholic fumes transmitted between our open mouths.

A female voice from the bottom of the stairs: "Oh my *God*!"

A male voice: "Nice!"

But we keep going. No ceasing this epic, furious kiss. No coming up for air. Ever.

Kissing! Transcendent!

In the following days, I'm athrob with my new status as *boyfriend*, all these suspicions of a secret grand self alive inside me now authenticated by her kisses. I am a valuable commodity (to one person, at least). I have been cured, finally, of my worthlessness, and my bathroom-mirror twin gives me a big congratulatory grin each time I see him.

There's much to tell of the following few weeks. The plotline of our courtship is a canto of a thousand stanzas, with essay-length footnotes for each spoken word, a hundred-page bibliography listing books and movies and albums that provide the necessary context. That first month, that first beautiful month, Marti's mother works evenings and I lie to my father about covering shifts for sick stock boys so I can ride my bike to her house; we sit on the living room couch and kiss and grope, and I lick her nipples until the clumsy movement of my tongue induces ticklish convulsions and bursts of apologetic laughter, and she goes down on me with such skill that it makes me sick to think she likely learned how with some other boy; I ask her about the small scar on her breast, which appears to me, during my sloppy sessions, as a crater the shape of a sickle moon, and she tells me about how her uncle's dog, a bull mastiff, jumped on her when she was twelve; we skip school, one afternoon, and watch a movie at my house — I make her a bagel, but she doesn't like marmalade or honey or cream cheese, and so she eats it plain (we're learning each other in these small portions); she reveals her bizarre arboreal streak, incessantly suggesting woody strolls and picnics (oh, the picnics!), which she composes with same specificity of vision she'll later apply to our first night as lovers — she wants to make love under a tree, she tells me, she wants to graze in long grass and eat soft French cheeses; at the end of the year, we go to graduation together, and with all the bittersweet observances made, childhood now forever behind us, we slow-dance in a casual clutch, and when that song by No Doubt comes on, that one that was so big that year, she's overwhelmed by the magnitude of the moment (we're only seventeen: life still has magnitude) and she pulls me out of the gymnasium into the foyer, where she cries for a while on my shoulder and tells me that it's nothing, it's fine, just hormones.

I wish I could show you all those moments in vigorous detail. But there's no time. Succinctness is a virtue in first-person stories like this. You'll come to learn, my love, that this is the great tragedy of human life: no other person will ever fully understand what it is to be *you*; they'll only ever know the abridged, desaturated, second-hand versions of our most important stories.

"Tell me the story of why you moved here with your dad," Marti says.

We've been together almost a month, now. We see each other almost every day, and on the days we don't see each other, we talk on the phone while hiding in locked bathrooms so that we can drown out indictable verbs with the whoosh of running water. This is what we're doing right now (who knows what my father thinks I'm up to, all these secret evening sessions behind closed bathroom doors).

"Is it weird that I live with my dad?"

"No, not at all," she says. "It's just that I have lots of friends with divorced parents, and they all live with their moms. I live with my mom. It's, like, the default. So it feels like maybe there's a story about why you don't. But you don't have to tell me if you don't want to. I'm just curious."

But of course I want to tell her. I have steeped for so long in my own curiousness about her that her curiosity about me is exhilarating. Her questions are more thrilling than sex; each of them is like a tender little touch, stroke, squeeze, or knead. So I tell her: "It's not much of a story. My mom just decided that it would be better for me to live somewhere else. I was kind of a difficult kid, I guess. No, actually, that's not true. I don't think I was very difficult. I think *she* found me difficult. For whatever reason."

"Were you hyper? Were you on Ritalin? Did you burn things?"

"No, nothing like that." The long pause in which I contemplate how to explain myself is so obviously a long pause in which I'm contemplating how to explain myself that I have to begin by saying: "I'm thinking about how to explain it."

"Really, you don't have to tell me—"

"It wasn't some big, dramatic thing. It just happened. My mom thought it would be good for me to come live with Dad—good for me, good for my dad, good for her. She was pretty young when I was born and never had the chance to be on her own, to figure out who she was and what she wanted to do, and she needed some time and space to do that. She wanted a new start, and she wanted *me* to have a new start. You know? We both needed a new start."

It's the first time I've said any of this out loud, and I'm disheartened to find that the logic of it, which makes perfect sense inside my head, is corroded by the outside air. Spoken aloud (to Marti, especially, whose curiosity I want to reward with the absolute truth) it all comes out sounding like lame excuses and justifications. I try to amend: "But it's more than that, too. Maybe I was a bit difficult. I mean, I *was* difficult. I *did* need a new start. I was having a hard time at school. I was going to be held back a year. Not because of grades or anything, but for other reasons. It wasn't exactly a healthy environment for me, and I guess that's what made it difficult. What made *me* difficult."

Marti saves me from my circuitous, hollow logic by asking: "Where's your mom now?"

"She moved to Toronto last year. She lives in this big condo building downtown. It's cool. You can see SkyDome from the living room window. And there's a movie theatre in the lobby. You can take the elevator right down to it; you don't even have to put on shoes."

"Do you see her a lot?"

"Yeah."

But this isn't true, either. I've only been to see her once since she moved east—all my breaks at school have coincided with some conference in San Diego, or Las Vegas, or Miami. It's so thrilling to be asked these questions, I can't bear for my answers to be misleading, so I amend once again:

"Actually, I haven't seen her since last summer. She travels a lot. It's hard to connect. But she'll come down in the spring, probably."

"Will I get to meet her?" Marti asks.

"Of course," I say, and it only becomes clear to me in the pleasant silence that follows how meaningful that statement is; I can practically hear Marti grinning on the other end of the phone.

She asks: "If you could've, would you have stayed with her?"

"I don't know. I like it here. It was good to reset myself."

"I fantasize about that sometimes," Marti says. The treble quality of her voice is amplified, oscillating. She must be lying in the empty bathtub; she does this sometimes (or so she tells me). "I imagine going to a new place where no one really knows me and being whoever I want to be. Like, just erasing everything about myself. Forgetting everything and everyone and becoming someone totally brand new."

"Yeah," I say. "But I'm pretty much still me."

"That's good," Marti says. "I like who you pretty much still are."

Me, I like *this*, and this, and *this*—our fifty-seventh, fifty-eighth, fifty-ninth kisses. We're here on that lakeside bench, freezing cold, kissing and clinging, cold cheek to cold cheek; my fingers dare passage between blouse buttons, find the seam between silk cup and flesh, slither inside in search of the stiff little prize. Almost midnight, and the cold breeze is asserting itself. It's a wind, now. Kissing, kissing, napes and necks, blowing foggy spumes to fight the gooseflesh—

Sorry, sorry, my sincerest apologies. I don't mean to show you yet another sloppy make-out session, my love. It's the conversation that follows our foggy spume-blowing that is relevant to what I'm trying to tell you.

"I'm going to ask you a question," Marti says. "But the answer doesn't really matter. Okay?"

"Okay."

"It's *the* question."

"Okay."

"Ready?"

"Ready."

"So …?"

"So what?"

"*Have* you …"

"Have I what?"

"You know what I mean. How *far* have you gone?"

"I went to Hawaii, once. When I was nine."

"Be serious," she scolds, smiling.

"Be more specific," I say. "How far have I gone with what? Say it out loud."

How did I play it so cool? How can I have failed to remember how charming I was in moments like this? The memories that have stayed clearest in my head are the self-sabotaging non sequiturs, the bone-marrow embarrassments. But the notion I have of myself as a tongue-tied teenager is decimated with the recovery and restoration of these archaeological treasures. Apparently I sometimes said the right thing.

She insists: "You *know* what I mean."

"But I want you to say it."

"Fine ... have you ever *fucked*?"

She lets loose this word to defy my light-heartedness, and the hard consonants, spit forth in her angel's voice, turn a pleasant loop deep in my gut.

"Well ..."

I fake reticence, but I'm really thinking of a lie. The truth, that I have gone only as far as we have gone together — kissing her mouth and neck and breasts, and twice offered relief by her generous lips and tongue — for some reason feels wrong, as if she has assumed, all this time, that I am her sexual superior, and, learning otherwise, she'll stand up, walk away, and never talk to me again.

"I've never had sex — technically. But I've done ... other things. With other people."

"Other things like what?"

"Like, everything *but* sex. Same sort of things we've done." I am secretly pleased with myself for misrepresenting my sophistication with such aplomb.

"Okay," she says.

"So, what about you?"

All innocent: "What about me?"

"Same question," I say, and it occurs to me that her answer to this question has been the point all along.

"Um, well, so ... so last summer, when I was staying with my dad in Cornwall, I kind of had this boyfriend. His name was Tyler, and we did it. We *fucked*..."

Again, that word, and that feeling in my gut, like I've been gently punched. But this time I can hear how uncomfortably it trips over her lips.

"... only once, though. And it was good to get it over with, because the first time, for girls, always sucks. But listen, though ... I'm totally glad that you've never done it before. Seriously. Don't think that I think less of you or anything. It's the opposite."

It fills me with unspeakable joy that she thinks I'd ever had a chance.

That she's more experienced than I am doesn't bother me in the least. Like I said, the issue of sex isn't something I give much practical thought to (impractically, abstractly, I am thinking about it all the time). I'm grateful for the time I've been given to touch and taste her body, and even more grateful for those hazy moments of ecstasy in which she has touched and tasted mine, but as for that grand procreative act, which in my mind stands far apart from the innocent fiddling we've already performed, I am rather terrified. The following week, when Marti says to me, "I think we should sleep together," I am indeed too terrified to spit out what should be an obvious answer, and instead say: "Really?"

We discuss our plans in great detail. Clever, we think, to skip the clumsy spontaneity of first sex, give ourselves ample time for preparation. Get those candles lit, hang that soft gossamer fabric from the canopy of the bed; pick a bright moonlit night so that our skin, in the darkness, glows blue like sunlight dying in an ocean abyss; study the suggestions in the illustrated sex manuals our parents keep hidden in the drawers of their bedside tables; make a mix-tape soundtrack that will forever link this historic moment to a suite of popular tunes. As our friends eagerly spoil their innocence with drunken humping in the backseats of cars, or in their parents' beds after school, or on camping trips, in tents, while just a few feet away their friends listen and giggle, Marti and I have decided to do it the old-fashioned way, the *right* way. This, we imagine, is a courtship worthy of Victorian mores. She is eighteen, legally able to smoke and vote and rent hotel rooms without the consent of a parent or guardian. So that's our plan: to find a hotel room, and, as Marti says, having now abandoned her brutish locution, *make love*.

There's a painting hanging above the bed: a landscape in pastel colours, depicting mesa formations and tri-pronged cacti raising their arms in surrender. The bedspread, too, bears a chaotic geographic pattern of intersecting squares and triangles in the same impartial colour scheme. Grey carpet, yellow bathroom tiles, pressboard closet doors printed in woodgrain. Everywhere, the false comfort of a dentist's waiting room, and yet the room feels, to my young self, elegant and sterile and perfectly like the place where such an other-worldly undertaking as *sexual intercourse* should occur. This standard queen room at the luxurious Prairie River Inn is the romantic setting we have chosen for our great metamorphic adventure.

Marti enters cautiously, as if into the private chambers of a stranger. I flop onto the bed and flip aimlessly from channel to channel while she tests the density of the mattress with her palm, twists the knob on the bedside lamp through three rising iterations of brightness, pulls open the drapes to assess our view of the highway. She appraises the room as if she's leasing it for a year rather than a single night. I'm focused on the television screen but can hear her opening drawers, clicking on the desk lamp, squeaking the springs in the midget armchair beneath the window.

"Come sit down," I tell her.

"Mmm-hmm," is all she says. She opens her backpack and removes two fat candles, digs the wicks out with her fingernails and places the fattest, dynamite-red, thick as my forearm, soon to stink of apple and cinnamon, on the bedside table, and the other, thin and beige and of indeterminate scent (such is the fragrant potency of the former), on the desk across from the bed. She lights them both with her Zippo, and, as if sensing a sudden anxiousness in the way I'm cycling madly from station to station, letting just stuttering blips of audio burp out, she says, "I just want to see what it looks like." She lowers the dimmer switch and scrutinizes the ambience evoked by soft flickering flamelight against creamy walls and dun-coloured drapes. With an imperceptible tightening of her eyes and mouth, she declares it unsatisfactory; she moves the candle from the desk to the opposite bedside table, and makes of the bed, with flames now dancing on each side, an altar.

"How about that?" she says. "That's nice, right?"

So, candles lit, ambience approved, nothing now lies between us and the grand deed. We lie together, watching TV. Some real-life medical drama that neither of us is really watching. Tense minutes stitch together into an entire anxious hour, until finally she asks: "Do you want to go to bed now?" Trying not to sound eager, for some reason thinking that eagerness, in this matter, would be uncouth, I say: "Yes."

Her bra and panties, red and edged with lace and thick with an ornate weave, are brand new. She bought them for tonight. I can smell that sterile new-clothes smell. I can taste the newness when I lick her nipple through the silk surface of her bra. Her legs are smooth. Her pubic mound, too, is smooth; in one direction it's as glossy-slick as porcelain, and in the other as scabrous as a man's cheek. Her shoulders and the channel between her breasts are aglitter with gold specks that smell of vanilla. Everywhere else she smells like something dark and sweet: like molasses, like something caramelized and slightly burnt.

We are in bed, now, beneath the coarse hotel blankets. We test the strange sensation of our naked bodies pressed against one another: from head to toe, naked skin against naked skin, like being turned inside out. She kisses me with dramatic flourish, in a way that seems a profit lazily earned from the investments of that other kid (that "Tyler") but which, refracted by what I now know, is clearly an attempt by Marti to load this moment with a passion and enormity that would make that other experience meaningless.

She pulls my hand away from her breast, where it has been busy clutching and cupping and caressing, and puts it behind her neck so that I'm cradling her like a ballroom dancer. She takes my other hand and presses it to her cheek and sets a distinct three-quarter rhythm with her tongue. She works me like a puppet. I'm holding her head with both hands, now, bracing my weight against her pelvic bone, which she curls against my mashed genitals in little upward swoops of her hips. Amazing to recognize in a creature as magical and unknowable as a Girl the same animal compulsion to rub and hump and persuade pleasure from friction and pressure.

Now she takes my hand away from her cheek, guides it down between our bodies, and there casts it free to do what she assumes it knows how to do. She is conducting, quite consciously, a new movement of her personal mythology: a Scherzo of Virginity Lost and Found and Lost Again!

This ecstasy of closeness, soon to be supplanted by increasingly deviant stuff, is so pure, here, I can hardly stand it. The soft parts of women previously hidden by denim and cotton are now open to me. I explore moist, alien terrain. It's invisible. I grope blindly, reading bumps and crevasses like Braille. It's a wholly tactile experience, my hands gaining knowledge while my eyes remain closed. After a while— before I even realize it has happened (which therefore leaves me unable to mark, for posterity, the exact nanosecond of my graduation from boyhood to manhood) — the parts of us forged by nature to connect in the exact right way connect in that exact right way.

Sorry, my love.
This part is just for Marti and me.

And so, after our exact right way of connecting, still slick in some places (and, where not slick, encrusted with whitish flakes where the slickness has dried), we are lying together with the blanket pulled to our chins, humbled (both of us, I think) by how much of ourselves we've revealed. I expected to feel different after such a momentous accomplishment, and I *do* feel different, but not different in the manner I'd hoped. I don't feel more of a man. I don't feel enlightened. The difference in me is cosmetic. I have learned something, but it's impractical book-knowledge, not a universe-shattering, curtain-pulling revelation.

Disappointed? No, not really.

Underwhelmed? Not under- or overwhelmed. Perhaps just *whelmed*.

Marti slides out from beneath the covers to use the bathroom. Hearing the plinking dribble as she pees is almost a more thrilling intimacy than the previous hour's sexual apprenticeship. She comes back, is about to climb into bed, but as she throws back the covers—

"Oh, God!" she snaps.

There is a comet-streak of brownish blood on the sheets.

"Are you okay?" I ask.

"Don't look!"

"Are you hurt?"

"Oh, God, that's *so* gross, I'm *so* sorry."

She pulls at the sheets. Futilely, because they are locked beneath the corners of the mattress by the secret bedsheet-origami known only to hotel maids.

"This is so disgusting. I'm so sorry."

"Don't worry about it," I tell her. Pulled along by her panic, I join her in the tug-of-war.

"Don't look!" she yells.

I turn away and stare at the wall as she heaves at the soiled coverings and levers the mattress up from the box spring. She lets go, the frames clap together, and the noise of it dislodges a sob that has been stuck in her throat—it bursts out with a *pop* and trails behind it a soft squealing. She's standing here, naked, crying, covering her face with her hands and instinctually, with her elbows, covering her breasts. I am compelled, too, by instinct. I slide across the bed, wrap my arms around her and coo: "It's fine, it's fine, it's fine. Seriously! Hey, come on. Here, I'll clean it up, okay?"

"Don't touch it!"

"It's just blood. I used to have bleeding noses all the time when I was a kid. I used to bleed in bed all the time." My voice sings. Where did this tenderness come from? It surprises my younger self, too; this sudden drawing away of all pretension and caution is as sensational as the act of sex itself, as weirdly blissful as hearing her pee.

"No big thing," I say to her. "Hey, you're being silly. It's not like you crapped the bed or anything, right?" She doesn't laugh, just sobs harder. "No? Not funny? Okay, come on." I draw her back into the bed, over onto my side. We lie for a while like this, and I continue to sing at her. It's my mother's voice, I now realize, that I'm mimicking—the *hey*s and the *come on*s are her consolatory tics.

She moans: "I lied to you."

"About what?"

"I never did it before."

Oh, relief! We are sexual dilettantes of the same rank. The truth spills out of me:

"That's funny. You know why? Because I lied, too. Yeah, I lied, I swear! I've never done anything before. Not even what I said I did...I just—I lied. I felt like a loser, so I lied, so it's totally cool. It's sort of funny, right? We lied about the same thing. It, like, cancels each other out. We're both a couple of liars. That makes this more special, right? Because it's the first time for both of us. I don't know why you're so upset. You're not mad at me, are you? For lying? Because I'm not mad at you. I don't care. I think it's funny. We were both embarrassed about the same thing, and we both told little lies about it."

"It's not my first time..." she sobs.

"But..."

"I didn't. But I *did*."

"What are you talking about?"

"I did, but I *didn't*."

"But...so, you did it already?"

"I did. But I didn't want to."

And finally her confusing syntax makes sense.

Of the story she told me that night, additional bits and pieces were later revealed to me. We didn't talk about it often, but when we did there was always some new detail to make my imaginings more terribly vivid, some minor footnote or citation that never failed to swell the primary text with deeper, more monstrous meaning: a spoken phrase, a poster on the wall, the ankle strap of a sandal. She sometimes spoke about it with a sort of scientific detachment, sometimes in tears, sometimes in a strangely satirical timbre. But she never spoke of it with an anger that seemed equal to the weight she was trying, by sharing all these sad words with me, to lift off her heart.

Give me a second to gather up all these narrative fragments and glue them together into a story with a beginning, middle, and end (just to prove to you that I can operate under such linear restraints). I will summarize for you the events in question, just as Marti described them to me that night, and subsequent nights and mornings and afternoons, when, for whatever reason, the topic came up.

Okay, all right, here it is, Marti's story:

• • •

It's the summer of 1997.

Marti, quintessential migrant child of divorced parents, was staying that summer with her father and stepmother and stepsister, indulging in long days of nothing-to-do, submerged in her boredom as if in a tub of pleasantly tepid water, fantasizing in the hours between waking up and rolling out of bed about the possibilities of the coming school year: her new pupal self now growing in this cocoon of hot afternoons, the new social contract she'd sign in September with her bright new wings. She was on a diet, eating only cottage cheese and cucumbers. She was teaching herself to sew: a girl who made her own clothes—that's who she was going to be. A summer like most other summers, swollen with unrealized potential, with ghostly thoughts of doing great things, but building inevitably to anticlimax, to sombre days of back-to-school. A summer like all the others, except that she met Tyler Madden at a barbecue. He was a relative of her stepmother's: the son of her sister's husband's brother. And what struck Marti most upon meeting him? Not that he was tall and broad-shouldered and, in the manner of most tall broad-shouldered boys, handsome despite the primordial largeness of his features. Not that he was older than her by three years, that he drove a silver IROC, that he was studying to be a paramedic at the local community college. Not even that he had his own place, a bachelor suite in his aunt's basement with a separate entrance, for which he paid a hundred and fifty dollars (an incalculable sum!) in rent. No, what struck Marti most on that sunny afternoon, as he slotted his legs into the picnic table across from her, set down his sagging paper plate of homemade potato salad, and inserted himself everlastingly into the folklore of her youth, was that he *introduced himself.* He held out his hand and said, "Hi, I'm Tyler." Just that simple human act, and Marti immediately knew that he was different than other boys, that he was a citizen of the grown-up world, that he was *mature*, that he was, if not yet a *man*, then the closest thing to it she had known in this context—that is, the context of being a girl and meeting a boy who seemed, like Marti herself had once seemed to me, unreachable, from the nadir of being sixteen and inexperienced and, generally, an unexceptional teenage specimen. It wasn't his confidence or candour or friendliness, but what seemed to Marti, who was herself still living through the theatrics and deceit of the Teenage Experience, an unfamiliar and exhilarating *trueness*, and she reacted to it in kind. As they talked that afternoon, she was confident and candid and friendly in a way that she'd never been. He paid attention to her, he was interested in her; he incanted, with every question and agreement and compliment, a spell of *opening up*—and she did, my beloved Marti...she opened herself up to him. She opened up, and the tepidity of the summer was superheated, came to boiling; her boredom turned to steam. The blurry possibilities of the new school year were now blotted out by the looming, definite possibilities of the next few days. It was her father's birthday, the following weekend. There was a party. The party was to be held at Tyler's aunt's house, where Tyler lived.

So a few days later Marti borrowed her stepsister's bike and rode to the mall with a mission to find an outfit that might further buttress her wobbly (but suddenly existent!) self-assuredness. She came home with a blue and white paisley-print dress, loose around the waist like those baby-doll dresses Courtney Love wore, but classier, fitted at the shoulders, open around the collar. Sexy, maybe. Sexy in a *grown-up* way. Sandals, too: so thin and flat you hardly knew they were there except for the swan's neck craning up the back of the heel and lassoing the ankle with a thin strap of leather buckled in the middle with a plastic daisy (and it occurs to me that despite her protestations she knew *exactly* what was sexy about her sylphic body).

"It was one of those nights," she explained to me two hundred and sixty-six days after we first walked home together in the snow, "that you memorize everything that happens because you know it's going to be this significant moment — somehow you know something important is happening, and the whole time I was *hyper-aware*, like my eyes and ears and everything grew *bigger*, could absorb more of it, could *hold* more of it."

She was telling the truth, too: of that night, she could recite entire conversations word for word, account for every sip of beer stolen beneath her father's watchful eye, could conjure, simply by closing her eyes and focusing, the smell of smouldering mosquito coils and five-dollar steaks wrinkling over propane heat. She could relive, just as I'm reliving her description of it, the sudden dread of seeing Tyler again, the hot shame of her too-obvious new dress, then the rising nauseous clench of defeat when he finally showed up and greeted her coldly (but how could any greeting live up to the swelling strings she had been hoping for?), then the sudden oxygenating relief when he found her in the back hallway and told her she looked amazing, that he was so happy to see her, then the steady erosion of her doubts as his attention once again fixed eagerly upon her. Yes, she could relive all of that at will, even without her life flashing before her eyes — that distinct sense of Tyler being there *for her. Only* for her. Again, it was the small things he did. When he leaned past her to drop something in the kitchen trash, he put his hand on the small of her back. When he addressed her in conversation, he touched her elbow. Each utterance of "you" (as in, "*you* should see that movie, *Face/Off*, it's dumb but kind of fun,") was emphasized by a pointing finger floating near her deltoid, then, as the revelry continued, by four fingers hovering just above her clavicle, then by his palm in the same place, but with his thumb outstretched and almost touching the divot between her neck's tendons. "You know who *you* look like?" he said. "You look just like the singer from the Cardigans." And his thumb made a little tick-tock motion against her throat.

Far, far away from them, as a distant ambient blur, the party passed through a familiar tidal timetable: high seas at eleven-thirty, the kitchen a conundrum of drunken voices talking over each other, and from there a steady declination, bodies coming to rest below sea level, on couches and loungers and the carpeted living room floor. At one o'clock, Tyler offered Marti a can of Coors Light from his private collection in the garage. He took her by the hand and pulled her outside to see his car. They kissed in the driveway, beneath the kitchen window, hidden from curious eyes. He invited her down to his room. She followed. Down the creaking basement steps, through a hinged closet door in the furnace room: a secret back entrance to his small, windowless, wood-panelled apartment. Posters were pinned to the wall: glistening bikini models splayed over sports cars, a skier in mid-flight tracing a powder contrail, the members of Metallica glowering in a back alley, Baz Luhrmann's *Romeo + Juliet*.

She said to him, oh my God, I *love* that movie.

All of a sudden: his lips, his tongue, his hot beer-can breath.

It was intimidating the way he went right for her, not

bothering, here in private, to go through the motions of seduction (as if by earlier flirting back she'd made clear her will to submit). But it was thrilling, too. This! ... *this* was passion and lust, the real *grown-up* version of what the eighth-grade boys who had previously pawed her blooming body didn't even bother to *pretend* to know. She thought to herself: don't be afraid.

The kissing was prologue, though. Just when she was getting used to it, matching his wild slimy rhythm, he leant his considerable weight against her, pushed her back onto the bed. She got nervous. No longer could she concentrate on matching the shoves of his tongue, no longer were her hands moving in willing circles over his impossibly broad shoulders. His kissing was getting sloppier. She felt like she was about to gag on a mouthful of spit. She disengaged, turned her head away, but his mouth stayed on her neck; he seemed intent on swallowing her whole in the manner of some large jungle snake. He bit her tentatively, testing the tenderness of her flesh, and yes, it delighted her, it didn't hurt, it scared her a bit, but the fear triggered a piston-like throb of pleasure, and she wanted him, against all rational instinct, to bite her again. But she also didn't want him to.

So she told him: wait a second.

Too much, too fast. She wanted it slower; she couldn't reconcile the disparity between the way it was happening and the way she had wanted it to happen, had always imagined it would happen (if *this*, indeed, was really happening). She just needed a little break to catch her breath, to think.

She told him: seriously, wait, hold on a second.

She laughed, because she was flattered by how badly he

seemed to want her, burrowing with this childlike single-mindedness. She laughed, too, because she felt swollen with confidence, singularly responsible for his stupor. She felt strangely in control, even as control was eluding her. She laughed, but while she laughed she was pushing him away and telling him, once again: okay, wait, just wait, just give me a minute.

But instead of waiting he let his considerable weight seep into his fingertips and gripped her wrists. She tried to pull her hands away, but they were locked there. He bit her neck again. This time with less reluctance. This time *harder*.

Okay, come on, stop for a second.

Being beneath him was like being encased in a block of lead; there was no room to move, barely room to breathe.

What could she do? Could she scream? No, it wasn't like that. What an idiot she would seem, screaming for no reason, causing a commotion in the middle of this party, ruining her father's birthday. It wasn't like *that*.

By now his breath was hoarse, a growl, the hard cartilage tip of his nose was stabbed against her breastplate, his whole face mashed against her chest, his jaws opening and closing on the flesh above her nipple, and a sickle-shaped pinch of pain surprised a cry out of her, but even then she caught it halfway, choked it, swallowed it, worried that someone might hear. Instead, she told him again to wait, told him to stop, just for a minute, I need a break, let me get a glass of water, let me take off my socks, but instead of stopping he lowered his barrel-chest against hers, a mass of hard iron that pushed the breath out of her lungs, and one of his hands disengaged from her wrist and disappeared down below, where, in the course of all the writing, her dress had bunched above her waist, and all that separated her from him was a hymen-like layer of thin cotton, which he tugged and yanked and tore away.

Wheezing, because she could hardly draw a breath with his whole upper body pressed down on her, she said: okay, okay, okay, stop for a second, please. She even let a tremulous note slip into her voice. She let him know that she was now in a panic.

Please stop, okay? Please, just stop.

But when she lifted her leg to kick him away, she opened herself, and with a swift settling of his weight he penetrated her and it was done.

—5—

Right there, floating above my head: the mobile phone that once belonged to the stern Scandinavian girl in yoga pants. I've been straining for weeks to reach it; a little game I play to keep my consciousness anchored for a while in the present—

No. It's more than a game. It's mental aerobics. It's emotional analgesic. I'm starting to feel suffocated by this ambient silence, and I'm hoping I might find some spark of life remaining in the phone's delicate digital innards. Maybe enough for me to shuffle through a few albums, discover some new tunes. Sure, there is music to be found in my past, tens of thousands of songs, each linked to specific surges of emotion, specific people and places, but as much perceptive exercise as I get inside my own head, here, in the sky, I am starving for new sensory input. I refuse to accept that every book and film and song that I haven't read or seen or heard is now lost to me. I am desperate to feel new things. Just to pluck the phone from its stationary spot and alter the topography, just to *touch* the sleek silver casing, would mean that I have not yet lost the ability to add fresh sensation to my stalled memory banks.

I should give it up, though. Even standing tiptoe on the armrest, there remains too much space between my fingertips and the corkscrewed loop of earphone cord nearest to me. I have even stripped off my jeans, tied them at the ankles, and swung them like a net to try to capture the elusive gadget. But no luck.

I was doing this, recently, whipping my pants around like a lasso, and briefly lost my balance, grabbed at the flap of fabric draped over the headrest, tore it loose, pitched it into the sky, and watched it fall away through the dead air, which is empty, now, of air currents and pressure waves and other atmospheric forces of resistance, so there was no fluttering or thrashing or swishing, the headrest-flap just plummeted like it was made of solid steel. I can only presume that it's now in the ocean (or perhaps *upon* it). So, clearly: gravity still exists.

I'll admit, I was beset by dread after this happened. I've been taking this state of stasis so lightly, thoughtlessly performing all sorts of high-wire tricks, sitting on the edge of the headrest, kicking my feet, leaning casually over to stare into the abyss, never quite sensing that I was in danger. But I am. The whole goddamn stratosphere is open beneath me. And what of the not-roiling water way, way below? Have the molecules maintained their distance, or are they all packed together? If I fell, would my body just explode against the solidified surface?

And, if gravity is still operational, what other common functions of the physical world remain intact? The sun, though half-extinguished, a dull yellow disc that I can stare at directly without even squinting, still casts shadows, which means particles of light are still colliding correctly. I suck oxygen into my lungs, and, though it tastes sort of sterile, like the fake fresh air they pumped into the cabin of the plane as we ascended to these unlivable heights, my cells are still metabolizing all that good biochemical energy; I am still conscious, I am still alive.

To this end, I recently carried out an experiment. With my pants around my ankles, standing tall above the petrified Pacific, I plunged my consciousness into that awful fifth-grade afternoon when Shawn Wong locked me in the library study room and whispered through the door a spot-on reenactment of the entire Matt Foley sketch from the previous week's *Saturday Night Live* until my convulsions of laughter sapped enough strength from my bladder to loosen its clenched-tight seal. Lying on the floor, curled and clutching my sides, I peed. I peed so hard that I could practically hear the whistle of escaping air—

—and from that horrible and orgasmic moment of release, I emerged into the present and looked down to see a solid stream of urine arcing into the abyss! Triumph! I was peeing. Here, in the present, in real life. My bladder felt hard as a rock, like I could pee forever. With my free hand I pressed a finger against my foreskin to control the flow. I swayed my hips and made wavy patterns, turned the solid stream into a rainlike spray. I shook my penis and made postmodern graffiti art.

One thing, though: my urine was dark and yellow, suggesting dehydration. Does this mean my body continues, in some secret way, to react to the empty environment? Am I actually starving to death, or suffocating, and rendered unaware by these constant expeditions into my past, where

I breathe old air and fill my stomach on already-digested meals? What substance is this? Am I pissing the water I drank before boarding the plane, or the water I sipped from a junior high school drinking fountain over a decade ago? Is this more than just a supersensory experience? Am I actually *travelling through time*? If my long-ago past can directly influence my present state, maybe it could work the other way, too—

All of this has given me an idea. Another experiment.

Let's try something:

The airport, the departures gate, the minutes before I'm airborne and carried irrevocably into the sky. Look at all these familiar faces: over there, the American dude, peeking over the pages of *The Beach* to eyeball the Scandinavian girl in yoga pants, who is sitting across from him, lost in her tunes, practising her evasion; and over there, the Japanese boy and his mother (she has her hand on his knee in premonition of her approaching contest of strength); and over there, the fortyish Thai fellow, head already tipped back, already napping, soft palate already rattling.

And then there's this guy: the Thai with the missing incisor, seated at an inconspicuous two-seat distance to my left, pretending to read the *Bangkok Post*. No ticket, no bags. The plastic card hanging on the lanyard around his neck says: *Ministry of Immigration*. He drove me here in a white van, just the two of us, and followed me through security, through customs, and into the bathroom, where he lingered near the far wall while I stood at the sink and choked back a fistful of painkillers, vomited them into the sink, then choked back another double dose. All of this without a single word of condemnation or concession.

You'd think this memory, just a few hours old in the traditional manner of timekeeping, would feel, I don't know, *fresher* somehow. Yet it's as shocking to behold (and besmell and betaste) as that earlier bit when, fresh from gestation, I first met my grandfather. It feels just as much like I'm hiding inside the unfamiliar sensory terrain of some other sentient being. Yes, these are someone else's mistakes I'm watching! These are foreign thoughts I'm thinking! This muddled, hysterical train of logic, this is the fever dream of an idiot stranger!

I have no idea where Carrie is, right now. The last time I saw her was yesterday afternoon, shortly before the Merciless Beating at Phrom Phong. The last time I spoke to her was while I waited blurry-brained in the Sala Daeng Police Station to be interrogated about my citizenship; she finally answered my fourth consecutive phone call with a quick admonition that was equal parts angry and beseeching. "*Please* leave me *alone*!" she said, and the signal was cut.

I have continued calling, though. In fact, I'm calling her right now. My desperation is well-documented in the memory banks of her phone (this is my nineteenth attempt), so there is no reason to stop calling, even though all this calling seems a concession of defeat, an apology, and the only way to counteract it will be to get through, to talk to her, to say that *one thing* (whatever it might be). But, just like the eighteen previous times, the lisping murmur of the spacebound signal is interrupted (without even the courtesy of a ring) by her voice: "Hi, this is Carrie's phone, I can't talk now, but leave a message, thanks."

So I fold up my phone and open my backpack, and here protrudes the upper edge of that *Suicide Squad* comic—a strip of blue sky, the crowns of yellow letters. My thumb and forefinger pinch it, I'm pulling it out, I want to look at what's inside, just take a peek, but I stop myself. I won't make this worse than it already is. Instead, I slump into the plastic bucket chair, steeple my fingers over my belly, and think of Erin Seeley:

We pass each other on the street, it hits us, that gape-mouthed moment of recognition (played over and over, with subtle changes to timing and choreography), oh my God, you look great, so do you, let's get a drink, sure, cool. Paris, Mumbai, rock-hard abs, etc.—

And then the woman at the security desk picks up her phone, presses a button, and a single musical note plays throughout the terminal. Her mouth moves, but she's being dubbed over by a giant female robot hiding somewhere in the rafters. "At this time we'd like to call all passengers requiring assistance to report to Gate 23 for pre-boarding…"

A matter of hours, now, until we find ourselves floating here.

I stand up and sling my bag and scuffle towards the desk with the other scuffling ticketholders. The immigration official (he's now standing a few paces behind me with his arms crossed) scolds me with his expressionless gaze; I give my documentation to the attendant at the front of the line, and when I turn back he's peering into his folded arms to examine his watch.

Oh, how boring this is for him, expelling me from paradise.

Now, let's try that again:

I scuffle with the other scuffling ticketholders. I give my documentation to the attendant. The immigration official scolds me, peers into his folded arms to examine his watch. Oh, how boring, expelling me from paradise.

As I scuffle down the grey gullet of the jetway, I invoke future memories of that wheezing warming-up-orchestra sound and the taste of jet fuel and the feeling of my stomach squished to the size of a coin. I whisper urgent warnings to myself. There must be a moment of structural weakness, a penetrable little moment of doubt through which I might smuggle back a little bit of foreknowledge and change my trajectory.

Come on, me! Fake an epileptic seizure. Scream a bomb threat. Tackle the Persian-looking woman scuffling ahead of you, throw a wild punch at the old Korean guy pressed up behind you, crack open his stippled bald head like a wren's egg, get dragged back into the terminal, get arrested, get re-booked on a slightly more reliable flight.

Can you hear me?

Can you feel this?

Stop yourself, Daniel!

Goddammit—*stop!*

Okay, let's try again:

Scuffling, scuffling, documentation, scolding, watch-checking, boredom.

If I can just (*nnrgh!*) wrench away motor control from this stupid scuffling version of myself. If I can just save up all my psychic might for a single blitzkrieg attack on a specific muscle group—let's say, yes, these thin fillets responsible for dorsiflexion of the foot, and, right when I'm about to step into the jetway, I'll unleash it, I'll redirect my footsteps (*nnh!*) in a planar curve (*ggh!*) back towards the bustling heart (*rrh!*) of the terminal, where (*ngrh!*) some other less fantastic fate awaits me—

Wait, yes, it's working, it's working!—

But.

But.

No—

—no, I just fucking scuffle.

Down the jetway, into the plane. It's all I can do. Even as my momentum seems to shift, even as my booming voice seems, within my head, inescapable, impossible to ignore, I'm nonetheless carried along with the other intercontinental commuters into this oblivion.

It was worth a try, though, right?

Gravity might still be exerting its inexhaustible will, and my present body's biological mechanisms might still be influenced by subjective suggestion, but the past, as vibrantly as it exists for me, is still made of immovable stuff. It's a backwards paradox of fate: I am doomed to always do what I did, there's no changing it.

–6–

Do I sound out of breath?

I'm just doing a bit of calisthenics. Some jumping jacks, some sit-ups, some hamstring stretches. A little cross-training. No, not for anything in particular; I spend so much time lounging around while my life flashes before my eyes that I'm beginning to worry about bedsores. I have to knead these mushy muscles, keep them functioning — who's to say they won't atrophy up here? So: a little bit of cardio, a few yoga poses. But, no, I'm not training for anything in particular. Ha! Where could I possibly go?

Count these push-ups for me, won't you, my love?

Hundred seventy-seven, hundred seventy-eight, hundred seventy-nine —

Just kidding!

Four.

Fiiiiiiiiive.

Hey, can I tell you something? I'm so glad that I'm able to talk to you like this. I'm so grateful that I have this chance to explain myself. We've always had such great conversations. I never struggle to explain myself, never worry what you might misinterpret or find fault with. You're the only person on earth

I want to talk to, right now, even if all my eloquent talking is just dissipating in the atmosphere—

—but, no, I *know* that you can hear me. We've always had that kind of special connection, my love. Wherever you are, right now, I know that you're close enough to hear my voice.

But, so, after the initial shock of finding myself stranded up here, I spent most of those first hours/days/weeks submerged in mix-tape loops of intimate interpersonal moments. With Marti, with Carrie, with others. Where else was there to go for comfort? Sure, there were some childhood birthday parties on my playlist; a few drunken teenage jags; some of my favourite films first experienced; some of my favourite songs first heard; a routine of my most well-received comedic barbs; and, of course, my lone athletic triumph, scoring that penalty-kick goal in that gym class scrimmage. But it pains me to say (to you, in particular) that most of my warmest triumphs have occurred between the sheets, between the legs, between consenting adults—or at least as prologue or epilogue to those in-between acts. Don't get me wrong, that period of convalescence wasn't all anatomical close-ups and spurting crescendos. I personally find fulfilled crushes and first dates and hands tentatively held far more stimulating than any sexual feat. But that sexy stuff—it's just the first place you think of to go. That's the Y-chromosome's dirtiest secret: the breadth and depth of its dirty secrets. But the novelty of seeing and smelling and touching those lost people and places and things quickly wore thin. Statistical analysis (which was, for a while, a fun hobby: tallying the precise number of cola-flavoured slushes I have consumed throughout my lifetime; the total number of comic books I have read; calculating a slush-to-comic-book ratio [1:4.26]) became as tedious to me as the high school math classes I revisited in order to train myself to do it. And, yes, even my erotic archives grew boring.

What luck to deduce that I could communicate with you, so that I could recount for you how it all happened, give you my million alibis and excuses and explanations, show you how fate carried me here, cruel twist after cruel twist, and describe for you what the wreckage looks like from my special perspective. Here in this depthless, directionless space, you have once again given me purpose.

I suppose I just want to tell you that I'm so very glad that you're listening.

Wherever you are.

—but let's forget all this sentimental stuff and get back to the facts. And, more importantly, how the facts fit together. I spent thirteen years in Catholic school and developed excellent skills in accounting for causality. You learn, from all those parables about prodigal sons and Samaritans, that everything is essentially your own fault; like the arithmetic operations taught in math class, those Bible stories teach you the deductive process that traces all sins back to the individual. The trick is to figure out, in the knotted wires of cause and effect, what you've done wrong. Vanity, pride, gluttony? Which of your mortal weaknesses betrayed you in the end? Don't forget: the Good Samaritan was preceded by a Priest and a Levite who twiddled their thumbs and whistled and looked off to the sky as if there weren't some poor naked bastard bleeding to death by the side of the road. A Catholic education doesn't prepare you to practise compassion; it prepares you to recognize a *lack* of it and compels you to judge that lack accordingly (*especially* if that whistling thumb-twiddler happens to be *you*).

Sure, yeah, I've sinned a bit — but no more than your average twenty-something North American white male. Less, probably. The opportunities presented to me for deep, sacrilegious transgression were few and far between. I was a pretty tame teenager, if you must know. And a pretty good kid.

Most of the time.

I confess: I did a bad thing, once. It was, oh, like ... a *medium-sized* bad thing. No minor infraction, but not a mortal sin. If I hadn't done it, I never would have been sent away, and I never would have met Marti, which means, yes, I'll admit it, I'm partly to blame for my present quantum conundrum; I have, to some degree, done this to myself. Which mortal weakness broke my will? Not greed, not envy; I was too young to for those things. Mine was the only sin a child is really capable of:

Wrath.

But it was justified, my love. I'll show you. I can go all the way back to the very beginning, the very first year of my life, and lay out the chain of circumstance that led to it (and *from* it) and you'll see, once and for all, that I shouldn't be here, I don't deserve this. No, not *this*, anything but *this*.

Hey, look, there I am!

I can see myself in the mirror.

I'm folding the flaps of a cardboard box in that special sequence that locks them together. I'm wearing worn jeans, my dad's old Soul Carnival Players T-shirt, white sneakers scuffed and stained with grass. Hanging from my neck is the gold cross pendant my dad gave to me when I graduated from high school, the one he used to wear, that I lost just a few months after graduation during a drunken swim across Walsh Lake.

But there's something amiss about my reflection. When was I ever this skinny? I don't remember the sinews on my forearms ever pulsing with such confidence. My stubble has never been so proportionate. If this is a mirror, how is it possible that I can see myself when my eyes are looking down at the box like that?

Oh, right.

I get it.

No mirror, just the same greenish-brown eyes, same small ears, same dunnish hair swept over the ear like a warbler's wing, same upper lip pinching to a point like a horizontal Nance bracket. How old is he, here—twenty-two, twenty-three? Yes, about that. Subtract the elements of my mother's genetics, and my father, at twenty-three years old, might well be my identical twin.

This apartment: I don't recognize it; there's no address for it in my memory palace. But I know it. This is my home. It must be the old place in Grovington my parents always talk(ed) about.

All afternoon my father has been browsing through it, assembling his books of Irish poetry, his horror paperbacks, his collection of German beer steins, his framed print of the poster from *Casablanca*, his typewriter, his stereo and speakers, his disassembled drafting desk, his easel, the red metal toolbox filled with capsules of oil paint, his dumbbells,

PART I

his sleeveless T-shirts, his ointments and sprays and foams from the bathroom, packing them in boxes and bags, and now, beside the front door, sits the modest accumulation of everything he owns.

(I am not one of those things.)

Today must be the day he moves out, which makes me about ... ten months old, and explains why I'm having such trouble focusing. Being ten months old, apparently, is like being drunk: the world is crisp and bright and swollen and heaving; colour and time and sound seep outside the lines, layers of reality are imprecisely aligned.

"Haybdeeshoodwnthair?"

What?

My father's enormous face has filled the plane of my vision, his enormous eyes like twin suns thick with gravity, his enormous voice tinny and dissonant and hard to make out, howling like wind out of his enormous mouth. I have to go back and listen again to hear what he's saying:

"Hey, buddy, what are you doing there? What's that? Sinker-ball? Knuckleball?"

Oh, this. An orange foam ball pinched in my fist, little concave dimples beneath each of my fingers, a dark blotch where it's soaked through with my saliva. The resistance of it—there's something pleasant about it. The weight, the texture. Like something poured into my open palm. Like something liquid and solid at the same time. A steam of sugar and ivory? Reminds me of something I love.

I'm compelled, lately, to put things in my mouth: chunks of potting soil from houseplants, cork coasters, record sleeves, the thin plastic sheaths from the ends of shoelaces, rock-hard dust-stubbled macaronis fished out from between the stove and cupboard, mouthfuls of wool blanket that blot dry my tongue, then, after a while, get heavy and moist and seep pleasantly when I bite down.

My father stands (my God, launched up into the sky like that, I can't even see him anymore!) and dips down (oh, here he is!) and slips his spaded hands beneath my armpits and (*oh my God I can't breathe!*) I'm plucked up and shockingly immersed into the sky and he carries me across the room, swinging me gently forward and back, and drops me back down onto my fat feet, and when he lifts his hands away my knees spasm, I try to jump, I want back up, I want to swing, *I want more flying, I want more of it*, but, no, he sits down on the couch, picks up a yellow legal pad, and begins writing.

What's different about him? He moves a fraction faster, like frames of film imperceptibly sped up. He seems brighter, too — the whites of his eyes, his fingernails, the pink in his gums. It's youth, I guess. But something more than that. He occupies space differently. He's *present*. Even today, which must be one of the least pleasant days of his life, he seems happier and more comfortably himself than he will be later in life, when I'm old enough to observe and account for such things as another person's happiness and comfort. Even the way he's scribbling on that pad, the veins in his hand bulging, the pen twitching madly, the nib scratching all seismographic, seems a more passionate act than any other I've seen him perform. It's hard to imagine this energetic young dude is the same man I presently know as my father. Twelve years from now, when I go to live with him, he'll have fully metamorphosed, his brightness will have dulled, his solidity will go all spectral and gauzy, he'll be worn out by the odd jobs he takes to enact his month-to-month survival plan: the ones that affront his dignity (door-to-door knife salesman, department store cashier, paperboy), the ones that appeal to his sense of whimsy (typesetter, letter-carrier, florist), the ones I have trouble believing actually exist (seniors' centre librarian, receptionist for a septic-tank inspection service, humane society corpse-removal engineer). In exile from husbandhood and fatherhood, he will embrace the moral rectitude surreptitiously instilled by his humourless churchgoing father and become the sort of local do-gooder/troublemaker who writes epic angry letters to municipal legislators, who organizes rallies to oppose the displacement of local songbird populations, who canvasses fervently on behalf of hopeless fringe party candidates. He will make a hobby of supporting small, futile causes simply because they are small and futile; perhaps because he feels small and futile himself and knows the existential sting of being passed over for your smallness and futility.

What is he writing, right now? Could it be a progenitor of his infamous angry letters? I'm beside him on the floor, but all I can see of the notepad are the folded-back pages vandalized with euchre scores and phone numbers and doodles of flying saucers. He is contemplating some locution, and as I look away, the pen takes off again, scratching against the pad.

How much time is passing? Minutes, hours? My father writes and writes, and I suck on the orange foam ball and squish it and it pops out of my grip and rolls away, so I scamper after it on all fours and pounce on it and pick it up with my teeth and feel a pleasant grainy tingle in the tips of my incisors, so I bite harder, and harder, and tear away a small segment of foam, which I swallow and feel scraping down my throat. Aeons have passed; it feels like weeks since he picked me up and carried me across the room.

My father stands up. He has torn a sheet from the legal pad and is folding it into small squares and walks off towards the bedroom with it. I try to stand up, but—

My head! Good Lord! My head weighs a ton! My whole body is thrown off balance by this iron block wobbling at the end of my noodle-neck! My locomotive reflexes have adjusted to account for it, though. I roll onto my shoulder and use the momentum to heave myself upwards. Balance is tricky, my short arms are poor counterweights, but I find my feet and step (no, *stomp*) after him. From the doorway of the bedroom I watch as, after a moment of consideration, he tucks the note beneath the blanket on my mother's side of the bed. He stands back and examines the topography of the bedclothes, flattens a few creases with his palm, and, satisfied, claps and rubs his hands in a nervous gesture I recognize as one of my own future affectations—

Did you hear that? From the living room: the click of a deadbolt, the whisper of the front door swinging open.

Mama!

I tumble to meet her. Just need to touch her leg, refresh that physical contact, absorb a little of the motherly vibe that resonates from the tuning fork in her chest. There she is! I signal with my spastic swatting hands and she drops her grocery bags and lifts me up and the sudden altitude winches my guts, the roar of flight fills my ears.

"Well, hello!" she says, and delivers a thousand quick

kisses to the cavity of my collarbone, each of which sends a vibration through my body like a harp's plucked string. Kiss, kiss, *kisskisskiss*!

Look at her! Unblemished, wiry-thin, angles sharp with girlishness where in later years they're round with age. So young! So stunningly young! She's just a girl! She's my age! No, she's *younger than I am now*! She is tall and thin and blond and beautiful and, in remaining thin and beautiful like this, has made clear her disdain for her peers in maternity: those girls who, post-pregnancy, cut their hair short and wear comfortable shoes and become *ladies*; those cake-bakers and lunch-packers and scraped-knee-smoochers — my mother wants no part of their gossipy gang. In the coming years, she'll live her life as a single mother as if she's single and not a mother, keeping company with her childless friends, bringing me along on Saturday nights to sit quietly at the periphery as they drink wine and watch TV shows recorded on VHS cassettes. She'll approach child-rearing with the same analytic method she applies to her fast-growing real estate business, subscribing to child psychology magazines, attending seminars on self-actualization for pre-teens, evaluating the stages of my junior high depression with a microchemist's attention to subatomic detail.

After a few more ticklish kisses to the neck, to the armpits, the belly, the toes, my mother carries me to the bedroom, where my father, playing it cool, is sweeping a constellation of coins off the dresser and into his cupped hand.

"Did you get the stuff from beneath the sink in the bathroom?" she asks him. "That grimy block of shaving soap is under there."

"Don't worry," my father says. "My grimy soap is gone."

My mother bounces me into the crook of her other arm. "Sorry I'm home already. I didn't think you'd still be here. I can leave, if you'd like."

Her patient civility treads perilously close to condescension, but my father seems to recognize that it doesn't quite cross the line. "No, I'm done," he says. "Just a few more things to take down to the truck."

"Did you take the griddle? You can have the griddle, I don't mind. I'll probably never use it."

"Keep the griddle," my dad says. "I'll get my own griddle." He pinches a few stray pennies between his fingers and slides the whole jangling puddle of change into his pocket.

How did my mother end up with this shy geek, this late-blooming libertine, this fragile former momma's boy? How did my father end up marrying a girl who shaped herself gladly by the erosive pressure of achievement and success? Only high school sweethearts could make such a mismatched couple. Only the resonance of teenage affections carried forward could maintain this tenuous connection. (Should I count myself among those ligaments?) No surprise that their marriage hasn't lasted. The real surprise is that they've stayed together long enough to create me.

With a quick glance back at the bed to judge satisfactory the undisturbed appearance of the pillows and covers and the letter hidden beneath them, my father hefts his remaining boxes and carries them downstairs. He returns just long enough to squeeze my toes between his thumb and forefinger (like being kissed by the fat, dry lips of a horse) and say: "See you later."

I suppose this is how it all ends.

There he goes, he's walking out the door, he's gone, he's banished. It is, finally, as it was always meant to be: my mother and me, just the two of us, and I realize now, by some paranormal umbilical connection with my future self, that I have sensed since birth the unavoidable conclusion of this family unit.

My mom says: "You getting hungry? You want a snack? How about a cigarette? Your mom wants a cigarette. You want a cigarette? No, yuck! *Yuck*, cigarettes! Let's have some peas, instead."

Peas!? I fucking *love* peas.

This promise of peas is the most exciting moment of my life!

Later that night, after suppertime and bath-time and story-time, the familiar evening sequence which is now a duet, my mother lays me in my crib with a bottle. I watch as she busies herself around the bedroom, gathering armfuls of laundry from the wicker hamper and organizing them into piles on the floor. I'm growing more confident in my dexterity: I'm one-handing this bottle, reaching out with my other hand to slap my moist fingertips against the vertical slats. I've finally gotten this three-dimensional thing down. Until recently I was aware of the world as a two-dimensional surface; simple shapes and colours hammered flat on a panoramic plane; all around me were shrunken objects floating at eye level, and when I reached out to grab them, my fingers closed on air.

But now, when I move towards them, they swell up to normal size, and, magically, I can put my hands on them. Depth! Very cool.

As my mother sorts through the clothing, she finds an errant pair of my father's pants. She shakes them out and holds them pinched between her fingers. After studying the patterns of worn-smooth denim, she presses the crotch to her face and takes a deep breath. Tossing them quickly aside, she then demonstrates the earliest reflex of a habit she will carry with her for years to come: she speaks aloud in a sort of crooning voice, to no one in particular, "Just checking to see if they're dirty."

She then leans over the bed, swats the pillows to the floor, and, using the fitted sheet like a bindle, pulls the bedclothes off the mattress as a single mass. She ties a knot with all four corners and drops the neatly enfolded package into the laundry hamper.

The letter!

As if taking orders from my current consciousness, the rubber nipple of the bottle pops out of my mouth. Am I going to warn her? Is this some valiant impulse in my clever baby-brain? Maybe — but my attention is now drifting downwards. I've notice that the hem of my shirt has rolled up to reveal my tiny belly and the wrinkled ampersand of flesh at its centre. My belly button hasn't yet sunk into a pillow of paunch; it's still flush with the soft surface, a Braille symbol that I can read by running my fingers over it, that I can trace, define, and scrutinize with my clumsy tactility; a fascinating, otherworldly imperfection on the otherwise perfect, silken, curvilinear front of my abdomen. With my heavy head leaned forward and my fingers hooked into and pulling up on the supple skin that skirts the fleshy knot, I can gaze directly at it. Just look at it! There is a significance to it, even to these toddler's eyes. The coiled crinkle represents the miraculous organic math of a logarithmic spiral. I sense it. I sense this thing's cosmic importance. Or maybe it's simply an innate understanding of the sealed aperture's vital role in my gestation, the same instinctual, animalistic sense I have of my mother, my towering mother, as the catalyst of my survival. Entire volumes could be written about the way this little vortex of skin is as unique as a fingerprint, how it contains, from my vantage point, all the depth and potential of a spiral galaxy. I press a finger against the shrivelled orifice. The feeling is strange: a sensory prologue to nausea. And it's *clean*, this new information. What do I mean by clean? Think of it like this: if the information one accumulates throughout a lifetime is constantly being written and rewritten and struck out and revised and erased and annotated and condensed and elaborated and erased again, then the psychic parchment upon which that information is recorded must be smeared and smudged and scuffed by the progress of one's intellectual development. But the surface upon which I am documenting these impressions of my belly button is blaringly white and clean. Belly button: this is new stuff, not yet footnoted by an accrued knowledge of human physiology, not yet rubbed out and replaced by the word *navel*, which has not yet been associated with the scientific term *umbilicus*, which has not yet been joined to the pubertal force that will later diversify my idea of the belly button/navel/umbilicus as an arousing detail of the opposite sex—

Whoa!

Suddenly my mother is *right here*, hovering over me. She reaches down to pick up the bottle. "You can't possibly be finished! Look how much is left."

She takes the bottle away.

I feel, deep in my narrow sinuses, the heat of approaching tears. I draw breath to speak, but my throat is blocked by a dribble of warmish milk that has been hiding, this whole time, in the seam between my bottom lip and the ridge of my gums. There's no voice there, anyway. Just noise, which comes out of me in coughs and gurgles and whimpers.

"Okay, fine," my mother says. She puts the bottle back in my hands.

What was I upset about?

I can't remember.

The mad half-hour my father spent summarizing three years of thought and feeling was for nothing; whatever apologies he offered, whatever ultimatums he proposed, were erased from the historical record during the spin cycle, and my mother slept for years on the diluted ink in which they were briefly documented.

What might that imply, my love, about this altitudinous conference of ours? What do words mean, if no one hears them? And how might those words have changed history? If a butterfly's beating wings can change the weather in China, or, say, stir a few molecules of hydrogen into a saboteur dewdrop capable of infiltrating a bundle of wires deep in the belly of a jet aircraft, surely that note would have calmed a few storms, altered a few particles, revised a few flight plans. Don't you think? If my mother had found that note, maybe my parents would have stayed together. Maybe, without anywhere else for me to go, she wouldn't have sent me away. Maybe I would right now be hovering above Madagascar or Baffin Island or the Tuamotu Archipelago instead. Who knows where else I might have ended up besides—

—the school office, thick with the bouquet of photocopy toner and old coffee, an astringent stink which has been brewed and burnt into the thick brown carpets and wood-panelled walls and the dust-covered leaves of plastic jungle plants and the yellow corduroy fabric of the couch I'm slumped upon, arms crossed, head hung low to hide my swelled-up eyes from the teachers and secretaries who are strolling past. I'm still blind with the brine of dried-up tears. On the other side of the door, I can hear their voices: my mother's matter-of-fact intonations and, right now, Principal Naidoo's trilling West Indian alto:

"... must acknowledge how serious, really, this situation is. The other boy, Justin Sloan, I understand that he's somewhat of a troublemaker (trouble-*maaayk*-ah), and I will, yes, take into account that he is probably the instigator (eensti-*gay*-tor) in this case, but you must understand, Missus Solomon, that this goes far beyond the realm of teenage misbehaviour, and is therefore beyond the disciplinary jurisdiction of the school, and, yes, even the school board. This, really, is a criminal (criiiiiimin-*al*) matter. I cannot *not* inform the police of this."

"Do *you* understand how out of character this is? My son isn't a violent boy."

"Again, I'm sorry, but I have no choice. A happening of this sort, I must report it to the school board and to the authorities, which will be, I hope, just a matter of procedure and will not result in any sort of legal action. Unfortunately, it is not my place to decide whether or not your son's actions were justified."

"And what exactly do you intend to do, as far your own authority extends? I don't want that other boy around my son."

Listen, you can hear the sly smile in Mr. Naidoo's voice: "Frankly, Missus Solomon, I don't think that boy wants to be around your son, either. As far as the consideration of the school board goes, the question unfortunately will be whether or not Daniel poses a danger to other students."

"Danger? That's absurd."

"Is it?"

Silence.

Mr. Naidoo continues: "I understand your resistance. But again, in my position, I cannot assign guilt or innocence or deal in hypotheticals. I must address what actually occurred."

My mother's turn to speak through a smirk: "And what is the outcome, then? If he is determined by the school board to be *dangerous*."

The school office is indifferent to my misery. Can you hear it? The glossy clatter of an electric typewriter. The buttery jingle of a ringing phone. Kids' voices in the hallway beyond; grade-sixers returning from the gym, probably. It's almost afternoon recess.

"I know that Francis has spoken with you about Daniel's academics, and I wonder if these two issues are not mutually exclusive. I will speak honestly with you, Missus Solomon, and tell you that I see no bright future for Justin Sloan, and whether or not he leaves my charge as a better young boy than he currently is, really, I don't care. But I do care for the future of your son, because, like you, I see that he is not a bad boy but just a boy going through a difficult (d*eeeh*-feecult) time."

I am, on the one hand, relieved to hear that my difficult time is being acknowledged; it has been d*eeeh*-feecult indeed. The invisible pressure on my rib cage rises enough that another sob (a sob of gratitude, this time) almost sneaks through. But, on the other hand, it's clear that they know nothing of my difficulty, its origins, its expense, and so the sob is stifled and resentment replaces gratitude.

My mother, in the dispassionate voice she wields on evening business calls, says: "And what do you suggest?"

Principal Naidoo says: "Sometimes, really, a change of environment can do wonders."

(W*aaaahn*-dahs.)

Eighty-three minutes previous:

I'm on my back in the hard-packed snow, the wind knocked out of me. A cloud descends: the stale reek of tobacco permeating his jacket, the damp attic-stink exhaled by his unwashed jeans, the weird vegetable smell of his slush-soaked sneakers. A weight descends, too, right on my chest, and the true terror finally comes when, looking up from this low angle, I see that his face, which even in moments of levity seems to be in the grip of some fantastical rage, is clenched like a fist. There's real madness in his eyes, the fog of a wild animal submitting to instinctual programming, and, as obscenities pour from his ridiculous mouth ("You want to fucking *die*, fuck!?") and his forearm crushes my throat, I'm worried more about the gathering spectators than I am about how hard it is, suddenly, to breathe. I hope that no one is seeing this (even though I know that *everyone* is seeing this).

Laughter from somewhere in the gallery.

I suppose it *is* kind of funny, the way my legs are desperately, hopelessly cycling. I suppose the cartoonish keening involuntarily broadcast through my clamped teeth *is* kind of hilarious.

"Fuck, don't start crying for Christ's sake ..." he says.

One lone voice from the back of the crowd: "Just leave him alone."

I'd join in the protest, but my small-mammal's survivalist vigour is squeezed out of me, cubic centimetre by cubic centimetre. He's still straddling me; he pins my wrists, and, leaning forward, looms, aligns his face over mine, lips pursed. A bubble of yellow spit blossoms.

My right hand crawls away, reaching, exploring spider-like the moon-surface of Precambrian detritus revealed beneath the powder of snow by my slithering, struggling body. What does it feel? Earth, dust, dirt, shale—

The loogie gains weight, slowly descends.

The congregation responds to the call by singing: "*Gross!*"

My hand keeps searching.

Pebbles, arrowheads, skipping stones—

Justin Sloan can't keep his puckered lips from smiling, and grunts a series of soft guffaws as the bubble of spit swings like a pendulum just inches above my nose.

Gravel, gravel, gravel —

It's the eighth grade, and I'm sitting on the edge of the bathroom counter, legs swinging, in a dharmic state of half-consciousness, reciting in an incantatory whisper the lyrics to "Let Your Backbone Slide." It's a Wednesday morning. Weiner Wednesday, when the cafeteria serves hot dogs. How do I know? Because even here, cloistered in the first-floor boys' washroom, I can smell the porky smell breezing through the halls.

I hide like this every recess. I put on my boots and jacket and trudge downstairs with the mass of playground-bound kids, and then, at the last minute, as everyone turns right towards the exit, I turn left, and, with casual purpose (*casual purpose* making me invisible to the patrolling eyes of the supervising teachers), stroll off in the opposite direction, to the boys' bathroom near the gymnasium, where I duck through the door and sit on the counter and wait out the twenty minutes of recess by fantasizing about, say, becoming a school celebrity by rapping onstage at the annual Christmas pageant.

I'm hiding in here to avoid the playground, the mood of which, particularly in recent weeks, has taken a turn for the treacherous. Escalating political instability has led to threats of violence. Non-interventionist allies protect their own interests by standing silent with their hands in their pockets, pretending not to see. World-governing bodies practise neutral observation, benumbed to alternating undercurrents of détente and hostility on the playground, having forgotten their days, not so long ago, of being scared little self-determined territories themselves. Yes, a state of emergency has been declared in the nation-state of Daniel Solomon. This hiding in the bathroom? This is my isolationist strategy.

Justin Sloan has declared war.

He torments me in countless ways, but do you want to know the very worst part? He's *a year younger* than I am. A sixth-grader, actually, held back for a second attempt to clear the bar, and so, on the socio-academic scale upon which we measure our worth, he's *two years* my junior. Double the shame! Is there consolation to be found in the fact that he's bigger than I am? Not much, no — though he is, at twelve, an absolute goliath: almost six feet tall, built like a racehorse, muscle and tendon like wrung-dry washcloths twisted around bone. His limbs are too long for his body, his locomotion is a limping gait, a mountain gorilla's lazy shuffle, a giraffe's stilted gallop. And, besides that, he's hideously ugly. And not just in my fog of my memory, which, I admit, is liable to twist his face into grotesque shapes. You gotta believe me, this kid is a real ogre. Didn't you get a good look while he was sitting on my chest, spitting in my face? No? Let me find a better angle:

See! Right there! Standing with his huddled coterie of sycophants and underlings. The tall one. On the left, with the kidney-bean-shaped head, the concave face, the small black eyes, like a shark's eyes, like a *doll's* eyes. You don't get a sense of it from this distance, but he has such a prominent under-bite that his crooked bottom teeth, when he thrusts his jaw in anger or shuts it to mimic a smile, almost touch his upturned bat's nose.

"Hey, fag!" he says.

I can pick him out from miles away. My vision, with the acuity of a field mouse scanning the sky for circling hawks, is attuned to the bright red beacon of his backwards (always backwards) Detroit Red Wings cap. Just this vision of him from the relative safety of a hundred feet ties my stomach into exotic sailor's knots.

"I said *hey*, faggot!"

Yeah, he's definitely talking to me.

He no longer asks for sips of my Coke or teaches me the etiquette of slurping up my leftovers; I've already proven my faggoty acquiescence, there is no longer any need for such formalities. While his name, spoken aloud or just phonologically considered, pumps hot columns of bile into my throat, it's entirely possible that he doesn't even know mine. The disparity between his presence in my life and my presence in his can't be measured; not even in light years, not even by the decay of carbon. Weeks pass, his attentions wander, he disappears, and just when it seems that the world had finally righted itself, the innate superiority of an eighth-grader over a sixth-grader effortlessly asserted, he'll call out to me through the mingling crowd:

"Hellooooo? Faaaaag?"

I turn around when I hear his voice (because I have learned the hard way that the tactic preached by parents and teachers and Saturday-morning public service announcements — to ignore the harsh words, to pretend like you can't hear — is even more dangerous than fighting back), and Justin Sloan goes into hysterics.

"See?" he says to Dave Brewster. "He answers to his name! Fuckin' faggot!"

Dave pushes a dismissive *psshhh* out the side of his mouth and turns away, disgusted. You should be disgusted, too. *I* certainly am. Disgusted at how relieved I feel, here in front of my peers, my friends, the girls I like, *just* to be called a faggot, that I don't have to run away, that this isn't one of those days that —

— he has me trapped at the edge of the playground. I'm knee-deep in a drift of snow, boots stuck, blubbering aloud that common call of the pathetic and abused ("Just leave me alone!") while he threatens to fucking kill me, for real, no joke, until finally the recess bell hums its B-flat warning and draws towards the doors the few curious onlookers who followed the elliptical wolf-and-rabbit chase that came to a climax way out here at the far border of school property. Justin Sloan waits and waits and waits, spitting intimidations, feinting fisticuffs, until we are three, five, ten minutes late for class, until finally, spent of his derangement, his point proven, he heads for the doors. When I finally return to class, no one bothers to ask, because it's winter, because it's cold outside, why my face is so red and why my eyes are so swollen and wet. But that's not really why they don't ask. They know. They saw.

What can I do? I'm a boy who has never thrown a punch, who has never even seen a real punch thrown! To be pushed to the ground, to be kicked, even in the strangely jocular way that Justin Sloan pushes and kicks when he's in his gentlest mood, as if bruising my shins with his Air Jordans is a game he has invented and is earnestly teaching me how to play, is terrifying to me. And this fear, it's crippling! It's stupendous! How did I get through all these years of fearing? How did I bear feeling this powerless, this vulnerable, this ashamed of my powerlessness and vulnerability? Here's something you forget: the shame follows you home, to the supper table, to your bedroom, to your bed, to all the places you're supposed to be safe. To my bedroom, even, where —

— I sit on my bed, looking through an old picture album I found while rummaging through my mom's closet for a sweater to borrow (it was briefly in fashion, I swear, for boys to wear oversized feminine sweaters). It's late, past my bedtime, and I've already been through it twice, but I keep flipping the fat pages: there I am, a shapeless, snow-suited amoeba smiling up from a bank of snow; there I am, on that spring-suspended rocking horse, the concave plastic nostrils of which I loved to poke my thumbs into; there I am, posing proudly in front of a far-off Rocky mountain in a Batman T-shirt and Batman shorts (the summer of 1989, the summer of *Batman*); there I am, proudly holding my grandmother's porcelain horse figurine in my open palm; there I am, in my grandmother's backyard, crouching over a plank of wood with the child-sized saw that was a gift from my mountainous great-grandfather. Look at that sweet kid. Shame he turned out to be such a coward.

This feeling will become familiar to me. This intense love for another, younger, guiltless self; a self that seems so separate for who you are *now* that you are capable of loving it the way you'd love another person: with a bit of pity, with a bit of jealousy, with a bit of longing, with a bit of embarrassment. The memory of that miniature woodworking set, the tiny hammer, the tiny plane, the tiny square-rule, brings heat to my eyes, a trickle of snot into my throat, soreness to my flexing cheeks. A lump of sorrow lurches up from my stomach and pushes past my lips.

—*sob!*

I look at myself in the mirror: my crying face.

Oh, how I hate my face. I hate it all: my thin blondish hair, like the downy hair of a toddler; my eyes, unevenly spaced and the appalling greenish-brown of mouldy bread; the dark circles beneath my eyes, like bad horror movie makeup; my nose (too round) and my lips (too angular) and my teeth (bucked and yellow-tinted) and my chin (recessed and dotted with acne and looking altogether like a small, rotting plum). Slowly the turrets turn inward. Justin Sloan could never hate me as much as I hate myself.

Just look at me. Pathetic baby. Little faggot.

Can you really blame my mother for not wanting me anymore?

"I suppose I really ought to explain," my mother says. "I think it's a good idea for you to go live with your dad. Because I think you need a change. And sometimes a change of environment can do wonders."

I'm still staring at my reflection, but now in the side mirror of our parked car, which, with its weird parabolic reflective properties, distorts my stupid features even further. I watch myself pinch a french fry by its tip and push it past my incisors, which *chomp, chomp, chomp* it until my fingers meet my lips and draw away. Inside my mouth the chopped-up segments of potato are mashed into a salty wad by my molars, and immediately my fingers have brought another fry to the precipice and start pushing it in, and so on and so forth, *chomp chomp chomp*, while my mother tells me that I'm going to go live with my father.

"This isn't about your grades, and it's not about what happened with the other boy, and it's not about how much I love you. It would be selfish of me to keep you here just because I like having you around, don't you think? Don't you? How selfish, right? What this is about is that you're getting to that age where you have to decide what kind of person you're going to be. And maybe it will be good for you to make those choices in a new place."

My mother pauses to sip her Diet Coke. Most of these words she speaks to the windshield, turning to me in the beats between conjunctions to measure my reaction. We're in the parking lot of the fast food joint from which these delicious fries came, and I'm aware that this meal, the burger and fries and melting sundae in the dashboard cup-holder, is an inducement. Which is why I'm scarfing it with such contempt (I'm thirteen; concession is purchased this easily). My parents, united now in discipline after a decade of wielding separate authority, have a plan for me. And it's a shock to hear my mother say it aloud. A shock for countless reasons, not the least of which is that my presence in her life has been (or so I thought) her greatest point of pride: she defines herself by not failing, and raising a smart and sensible and normal child (or so she thought) has been a triumph over failure.

No, this doesn't make sense. This must be my fault.

"We'll take it slowly," she says. "We'll try it for the first half of grade nine. It will be good for you, and maybe it will be good for me. I'm going to keep doing what I'm doing. You don't have to worry about me. I'll stay here and work, and maybe it will be good for me, too, to change things up. I was very young when you were born. I'm still very young. Sometimes I feel like I haven't started living my life yet. So we're in the same boat. We're both trying to figure out who we are. It's time to search for the call. Have you ever heard that expression before? Don't you think that's exciting? Don't you feel like this could be the beginning of the rest of your life? I know you're upset. But you'll see what I mean! I promise. You'll be happy. There's a great school in your dad's neighbourhood, and you can go there and be whoever you want to be. You don't have to worry about Justin Sloan or anyone like that. How do you feel about that?"

I shrug.

"It might be hard, at first. Sure. But I think you'll be much happier. I *promise* you'll be much happier. How's that? I'm making a promise. And you and your dad—you two are like peas in a pod. Think of how much fun it will be. Your dad isn't the most excitable guy, but, honestly, I don't think I've *ever* heard him sound so excited. Isn't that cool?"

I shrug again.

"A change of environment can do wonders, you know. Don't you sometimes want to go somewhere, anywhere, away from this place to a place that isn't this place?"

What she doesn't realize is that I've *already* been seeking a place that isn't this place. That's why I've been spending so much time here in the downstairs boys' bathroom, passing recess after recess in this meditative state, feet swinging over the edge of the counter, leaning forward, planning for the future, memorizing these lyrics, reciting them over and over in my head, imagining (shamefully) that Justin Sloan and I might become friends, that all the enmity and aggression might turn suddenly to admiration, that I might be allowed to join his huddled gang, and that it all might start when I'm onstage and these verses start spilling from my mouth with urgent, authoritative clarity.

Yes, such delusions work wonderfully to keep me safe from harm.

Until, of course—

—*today*, when I'm stopped by the gym teacher, Mr. Fraser, as, with my much-practiced *casual purpose*, I shuffle leftwards at the crucial intersection while the recessward crowd goes right. "Mr. Solomon?" He calls out. "Where would you say you're going?"

Why there's something embarrassing about saying "to the bathroom" I can't quite explain, but there is, especially with all these other kids around, so I say nothing, I just turn around, rejoin the flock, and am shepherded out into the cold afternoon.

And, of course, it's today of all days that I should step through the heavy steel doors into the crystalline chill, and, pupils squeezing to account for the sudden blaze of winter whiteness, ready to scan the landscape for that red beacon, ready to map a safe path to a quiet corner of the playground, that Justin Sloan should be *right there*, loitering near the doors, blowing into his fists, pressing his palms against his ears (this, back in the days when toques were worn only by dorks and geeks and wimpy little faggots). The shock of seeing him *right there* arrests my eyes. I'm mesmerized, unable to look away, even as Justin Sloan says, "What the fuck are you staring at?" But I don't know what I'm fucking staring at. So I can't think of what to say. And, as previously noted, such rhetorical queries are the most dangerous to ignore.

I'm able to take only three strides before a sweeping kick to my boots tangles my heels and toes and—

PART I

"Bumper caaarrrrrrs!"

On long-ago recesses we run in random circles with our arms crossed over our chests, seeking head-on collisions with other kids, and even though I'm the smallest of all the grade-one kids, I find the contact thrilling: having the wind knocked out of me, that sucking sensation in my chest as if the delicate little sacs in my lungs are all at once yanked inside out, that moment of being airborne, touching nothing, and the ticklish shockwave up your spine as you land and—

Now Justin Sloan is on top of me, sitting hard on my stomach, the globule of spit swinging from his mouth about to break free from its stretched-thin tail. My hand continues its survey of the local topography, finger-walking in a wide arc, feeling, slapping, grasping.

Earth, dust, dirt, shale—

His lips, still expertly pursed, curl in a smirk and almost pinch off the filament. Grunts of laughter backfire in his chest. The glutinous bulb swings ever closer.

Pebbles, arrowheads, skipping stones—

A girl's voice ("Oh my God, Justin, you're a *pig*!") which might have consoled me had it not been delivered with such unconcealed appreciation for his piggishness.

Gravel, gravel, gravel—

The pendulum is about to strike.

—a *rock*.

My fingers grip it and the wound-tight hinge within me snaps, tension travels from chest to shoulder to arm to wrist to fingers to the heavy chunk of stone held in my hand, which *blasts* into Justin Sloan's mouth, across his jaw, through his lips, through his teeth, and the pulse of the impact ripples back through my fingers and wrist and arm and shoulder and vibrates in the middle of my chest.

Oh, the *noise* of it!

The noise is the really terrifying thing: the deep, moist *fwack* of mineral against human face. It sounds like an unsucked gumball cracking between your molars. It sounds like a crowbar swung axe-like onto someone's femur.

A collective *gasp* from the gallery.

Credit to Justin Sloan, though: he doesn't panic, doesn't make a sound. He pauses to assess, puts a hand up to his mouth (but doesn't touch it), and then, staring right at me (which feels, in this moment, like it's the first time we've ever made direct eye contact), he tips over, hits the ground, and lies there dazed and dumb and literally slack-jawed.

The crowding kids have retreated, but not far—they continue to observe this latest recess calamity from a safe distance. Curious, now, about the size and shape and colour of the rock, I lift my hand—but find it empty. I suppose I've dropped it. I stand up, turn circles, peer about my feet, searching it out. You know, for posterity's sake.

On his hands and knees, with his hand cupped beneath his chin, Justin Sloan dribbles stringy blood, spits out bits of white. He still hasn't made a sound.

Oh, here it is — a softball-sized asteroid of sedimentary rock, notched and nicked, speckled with flakes of ancient ash and long-dead bugs and maybe a few spatters of dark blood.

I bend to pick it up —

And suddenly an arm swallows my neck and shoulders and lifts me into the air. One of Justin Sloan's friends? No, it's Mr. Fraser, the on-duty teacher, conveniently late to the proceedings. He pulls me to my feet, drags me inside the school, and, wordlessly, just huffing excited breaths, pushes me down the empty, echoing hallway towards the school office, where I'll cry on the couch outside Principal Naidoo's door until my mother arrives to give me a hug.

Crying, yes. Always crying. From fear, from guilt — but I'll tell you a secret, my love: the fear and the guilt are a thin, nacreous layer pearling around a grain of pride. Already it feels like that heavy rock was a good idea. Like the best idea I've ever had.

Is it really such a bad idea to go live with my father?

I am considering this question while crashed on the floor in front of the television. My tongue strums the steel scaffolding of my braces; I'm still finding pockets of mushed-up french-fry residue hidden among them. I'm supposed to be doing homework, but I can't lift myself up from this spread-eagled state of rest. I'm paralyzed, I swear: gravity is so much heavier here at the dawn of puberty; being thirteen is like living on the surface of Jupiter. I haven't been back to school since the

Incident, but academia, like Time (traditionally, I mean), is relentless, so Jenny Pritchett from down the street has been dropping off worksheets and reading assignments every day after school. They are spread out on the floor around me, packages of paper stapled at the corner, reflecting the blue light of whatever dumb sitcom I'm watching.

Will things really be so different somewhere else? I know Saskatoon pretty well. With the traditional domestic progression of his life abruptly suspended, defeated by marriage, dismissed as a parent, my father relocated there, and I've spent the last ten summers learning the geography, the borders, acclimating to the atmospheric perfume of manure. My parents have always shared me well. They've never argued, as far as I know, over the length and frequency of my visits, or my availability during Christmases and spring breaks. I'll still see my mother on holidays and special occasions, the same way I used to see my dad. They've simply swapped places on the depth chart.

And maybe my mother is right, too, about this being the beginning of the rest of my life. About going to Saskatoon and being whoever I want. That's the dream of all teenagers, isn't it? You occupy this state of perpetual self-loathing, and the only escape is your fantasy-gaze into the near future, when things might be different, when one's commitment to coolness might finally solidify and produce results: popularity, admiration, French kissing. This new city, this new school, this new life — indeed, a blank page upon which I can sketch whatever self-portrait I wish. That I am cowardly and dangerous are aspects of myself I can shrug off and replace with confidence, with charisma, with the suggestion of a different kind of dangerousness: the kind that sets girls aflutter.

Yes, I will spend the summer plotting to reinvent myself. I will lift weights every day, thicken my girlish arms; I will grow out my hair so that it hangs in my face; every morning, in the bathroom mirror, I will study the patches of blondish stubble that grow on the precipice of my chin and in front of my ears, and if it doesn't thicken by the start of the school year, I'll darken it with a shoplifted mascara brush; I will acquire a new wardrobe, a collection of expensive T-shirts from the vintage record store at the mall—Lynyrd Skynyrd, Misfits, the Exploited—groups I know nothing about, but whose silkscreened presence on my chest will suggest just the right permutation of irony and intelligence and good taste. I will weave myself a friendship bracelet and attach to it an arresting backstory (a gift from my girlfriend, who, in coming here, I'd been forced to leave behind, who was so racked with heartsickness over my departure that she considered moving here herself!). I will hoard cigarettes, steal them one at a time from my father's packs, and hide them in a cassette case. I will reinvent my character, too: I will act less goofy, be more aloof, more elegantly depressive. At night, I will dream of girls with dark lipstick and coffee-breath leaning close and whispering secrets in my ear, the kind of secrets you can only tell someone you love, who you'll never leave.

Because what it the alternative to all of this? To remain in quarantine? To finish the school year here at home, segregated, filling in these sheets to the cheers and jeers of a live studio audience? Should I wait and return to the eighth grade next year, where I can watch all my former friends indulge in the perks and profits of being ninth-graders while I float spectre-like through the hallways, half-seen, addressed indirectly in whispered asides, forever to be known as the Kid Who Did That Thing?

My mother is right: it's time to search for the call.

What, really, am I giving up by leaving?

Being held in my mother's arms, a baby, but too young to *know* that I'm a baby, too young to know anything more than this internal map of physical sensations, and still small enough to rest my head in the crook of one of her elbows and tuck my toes into the crook of the other, deep in the heat of her body, which is like the heat of the sun, but brighter, softer, hotter, cooler, and even though my eyes and nose and cheek are pressed into the fatty flesh of her breast, there is actually no such thing as my eye or my nose or cheek or her breast, because ours is a closeness so heavily concentrated that it doesn't exist, there is no need for the measurement of proximity between us, we are the same living thing, limbs protruding from the same central point, just us, just me and my mom. A baby, but not too young to know that I never want to leave this place.

EPIC DOMESTICATIONS

—7—

Hey!

Hello?

I'm still here!

Can you hear me?

Does my voice sound different?

Louder, clearer, closer?

Is there an echo, now that I'm up here?

Yeah, up *here*!

Way, way, *way* up here.

I'm standing on top of an emergency door floating horizontal near the tail section.

Yeah, I *climbed*! The whole way.

And, believe me, despite what I've long suspected about the whimsical physics of this place, it was no easy feat. Swinging and hopping and climbing and crawling through the dead air ten thousand feet above the sea wasn't as simple as I'd hoped. Strange currents blow. Or don't. The wind has died completely, and in its absence there is a reverse physical effect: the atmosphere sucks at me from all directions.

The exertion of climbing has disoriented me, too. I am breathing fresh air, but it's not the fresh air circulating in the troposphere above the Japanese coast. It's a sense-memory of fresh air. It's all the fresh air I've accumulated over the last twenty-three years, a whole conundrum of seasonal smells: the ozone tingle that preceded prairie thunderstorms; the clean, harsh aroma of winter afternoons; the florid exhalation of a million-year-old jungle, which, itself, is a million different fragrances of a million different plants and flowers. But it doesn't fill my lungs the same way *real* air does. It doesn't energize those little alveoli like it's supposed to. Every breath is a half-breath. I've been panting and gasping for weeks, years, decades.

Still, it feels good to be in the present. To be moving. I have a bit of life left in me yet, it seems; I am more than just the sum of scenes projected onto the surface of my brain; I am still a citizen of the waking world (however strange that world might be), and I have important places to go, important people to see.

The important place I'm going is the main section of the plane, the gutted abdomen, the wingless metal tube, eighty feet long, still aimed at the Japanese coastline as if hoping, upon Time's reclamation of the skies, that momentum might carry it to a belly-first scrapedown on the tarmac at Fukuoka Airport.

The important person I'm going to see is *you*.

I spotted you hiding up there, and began to plot a course. I spent months surveying, mapping, planning, sitting through geometry classes from the third grade to the twelfth to calculate angles of approach, skimming through museum trips to learn nineteenth-century mariner's tricks, scanning books to learn that one-eyed thumb-thing that landscape artists do. And, using these skills, I began to map a path. At first, through the isthmus of electronic offal trailing behind the plunging nose, where, by dancing across tatters of the fuselage (conveniently the size of stepping stones), I could reach an atoll of plastic cargo crates. But this particular approach proved too treacherous. Above the crates was another section of seats, six of them together in two rows, but tipped hard to starboard, headrests pointed earthward, cushions upside down, legs in the air. Forget whether or not I could grip the headrest with enough leverage to somehow pull myself up (definitely *not*), there was still a person strapped into one of the chairs, upside down like a bat, and I couldn't bear the thought of having to look as his/her contorted face as I grappled past. So instead I charted a path in the opposite direction, towards the tumbling tail—but at a crucial juncture that route would have required me to climb up the prostrate corpse of a skinny Thai fella frozen in a spiderlike crouch, and I found myself repulsed by the thought of touching him. His shirt was blown up over his face, and his brown belly, exposed to the rough wind, was rippled like wet paper. The cuffs of his pants were frilled around his knees, and I wondered: if I grabbed his bare calf to hoist myself up, would his flesh compress under my fingers? Would the cessation of internal combustion have cooled his body off? Would it be like trying to grip a slippery uncooked chicken breast fresh from the refrigerator, or would his leg be warm and hard and smooth, like a plastic prosthetic? Just another solid foothold in this landscape of footholds?

There seemed no other way. I would have to risk an implausible feat of acrobatics, or get intimate with the half-dead guy.

But as I prepared to depart for the atoll of crates, I happened to look behind me, back towards Thailand and all the people and places I left behind, and noticed, amongst all the avionic viscera trapped like flecks of dust in amber, hovering at the lower periphery of my vision, a panel from the top of the wing (a *spoileron*, it's called, slightly narrower than a surfboard, about the same length) and realized it might be close enough for me to jump. And if I could make the jump, my route to the main section of the fuselage would be unobstructed.

But to make that jump I had to forget what I'd learned about gravity's lurking presence (namely, that it was present and lurking). I had to remind myself that there was no wind resistance. I had to convince myself that, yeah, totally, the atmosphere *does* feel thinner, and yeah, *for sure*, that thinness will probably add a few inches to my maximum leaping distance. I had to conjure a bit of that ignorance that earlier had allowed me to pirouette fearlessly on the armrests, whipping my pants in the air.

So I girded myself and, with the seat belt wrapped around my forearm, slipped off the edge of the seat. I lowered myself until I could grab hold of the U-shaped steel bracket that had once anchored my Throne to the floor of the plane. Slowly, gently, the weight of gravity settled in my ankles and drew me earthward. Hanging there, I flipped my grip and turned my body to face the spoileron and, beyond it, the indistinguishable smear of horizon in the southwest. I breathed deeply, steeled my nerve, bit down hard on my wigglish, wormy doubt, and began swinging my legs, building momentum. I swung forward, back, employing the same kick-tuck-thrust method I mastered as an elementary school swing-set dynamo (the great triumph, in those days, was to get *bar level*—to make the taut chains go suddenly and thrillingly limp, to achieve a split-second moment of outer-space weightlessness). Swinging, swinging, I achieved terminal velocity, I opened my hands, I let go, I flung myself forward, I launched myself from my Throne to the spoileron—

Fingers of momentum brush back my hair.

Unanchored, touching nothing.

I feel my body pass through an electrical field, all my sleeping sensors stunned awake, all at once, rushing and bumping in a half-conscious panic. My stomach sucks into itself like a black hole and explodes in rippling waves of television static and—

( ).

( ).

( ).

—*BRNRGH!*

I landed sternum-first against the edge of the spoileron, which, as if it were still attached to the wing, as if the wing were still attached to the plane, as if the plane were safely and solidly on the ground, held its place, hacking my chest like a swung sword. My feet pitched out, sucking me down into the billion square miles of open space, but I scrabbled,

scrabbled, scrabbled like a cockroach, arms spasmodic, scratching, slapping, fighting a quarter-second crusade for friction, and my fingers found firm purchase on the far edge. I pulled myself onto my stomach, rested like that for a moment, like a castaway adrift in the sea, then pushed myself up, got one knee aboard the spoileron, then the other, and waited there for my breath to slip back into my ribcage and out of my lower colon, where, in terror, it was hiding. A stabbing pain lingered in my side, suggesting another broken rib or two or three—but what a victory to prove the continuing breakability of my ribs!

After the spoileron, the route became simpler. First, I scaled shreds of the burst nacelle, which were sickle-shaped, like God's clipped fingernails; I avoided the ones with their slippery humps skyward, stirruped my feet into the ones with friendly U-shaped concavities, and climbed up through the middle of them like climbing out of a well. From there, onto an engine pylon; I shuffled its length in a prostrate-scraping straddle to bring myself within reach of a panel of fuselage with the aluminum latticework still intact. I scampered up it like a ladder, and above it found a swirl of debris, bolts and pins and scraps large enough and close enough together that I could distribute my weight without being run through like I'd stepped on a nail. Remember what I said about this place being more dangerous than I thought? There are tiny immovable bits everywhere: ball-bearings, razor-sharp flakes of shrapnel—running into them would be like getting shot, a tunnel bored through your body.

From that cloud of effluvium, moving with a deep-sea diver's methodical steps, it took just a hop, a skip, a jump, a pull-up, a monkey-bar knee-hold, and I found myself balanced on the round rubber edge of a landing gear tire (they're absolutely gigantic when you see them up close!), close enough to touch the dive-bombing jet engine, peeled open like a tulip bulb to reveal the intricate inner machinery, a big blossoming tree of smoke grown up from it. A few metres above me hung the leaden potato-chip cradle I am temporarily calling home. It was just a matter, then, of finding among the clutter a firm ledge and comfortable handhold, and base camp would be reached. There, I'd have a little rest (perhaps a swaddled nap from my babyhood, the deepest of deep sleeps), a little hydration (maybe numb my throat with a long suck of sickly-sweet cola-flavoured slush), and I'd be ready to continue on.

But that column of smoke: arcing into the dull sun, so black, so *soft-looking*, like a lei of oil-soaked cotton. Desperate for a new tactile experience, I swept my hand into it and watched the speckled mass yield, each finger digging a deep groove, curling tendrils following them into open space, and when stretched to their limit, like some ethereal elastic substance, they retracted and settled gently back into the puffy trunk. It was like stroking lustrous black hair. It was so captivating that I hardly felt the skin of my fingers broil and burst open.

Just look at my hand, now! *Look at it!* It's horribly burnt!

But the skin on my fingers isn't blistering. It remains blackened and mottled pink, no signs yet of the anaesthetic squirt of pus or protective binding-up of the outer epidermal layer. My hand is a boxing mitt filled with boiling water. My lazy cells refuse to help out, so I've had to mimic a protective membrane with my boxer shorts, which I've wrapped and

PART II

knotted quite cleverly into a sort of mitten. Yes, I'm going
commando, now, and considering I've been wearing it for, oh,
a few centuries now, my underwear is in surprisingly good
shape.

Not far from the main compartment, now. A hop, skip,
death-defying jump, and I'll be up there with you. But first
I need to take a little break. My legs are aching. My hand
refuses to heal. To bear the pain, I'll spend a bit of time in
memories of washing up in cold lake water, making snowballs
with my bare hands, sipping from cold cans and bottles,
speeding down the highway with my hand stretched out the
window of my father's Lada, palm pushing back against the
passing landscape. I'll spend a bit of time, too, contemplating
the disturbing metaphysical inconsistencies that have become
apparent in the last little while. Like: why did the cushions
of my seat still compress, the armrests still tilt up and down,
the headrest-flaps still flap (one of them all the way down
into the ocean), but those screws and scraps, when I climbed
them, stay stuck in place? Pretty convenient, don't you think?
The same way it's pretty convenient that I can control these
scenes and snippets as they flash before my eyes. Yes, how
convenient that I'm able to dictate the pace and sequence of
my life's story, and therefore don't have to suffer through some
Higher Power's perception of its most important moments and
their eschatological meaning.

What purpose do these conveniences serve? To help me do
something? To help me *see* something? What more should I
be trying to accomplish, besides this meandering attempt to
explain myself to you?

I don't know.

That's why I'm trying to reach you. That's why I'm risking a fatal plunge onto the cement-hard surface of the ocean. That's why I'm suffocating on this fake-ass oxygen, breaking my ribs, incinerating my limbs. Not for exercise, not for kicks, not to pass the time (there's no time to pass, remember), but because I want to know why I'm here and what I'm supposed to do. And I think you might be able to help me.

Also, I'd love to see your face again.

It might seem like I'm being rather glib about all this, but over the years I've become somewhat immune to the shock of these kinds of volatile situations. It's a fact: the world has rules, they seem to make sense, and suddenly they don't. Mothers love their sons, then they don't. Sex is for pleasure, then it isn't. This latest revocation of physical law is not an unfamiliar experience. Which is perhaps why I'm dealing with it so well. Exploding planes and petrified human bodies and psychosomatic time travel—it's nothing compared to the cataclysmic change that occurred between Marti and me four years after we met, while we were living together in that one-room apartment near the freeway, in poverty, madly in love, performing, as a duet, our farcical imitation of the Domestic Life.

—8—

We are performing our duet, tonight, on the bedroom floor.

Technically, though, the bedroom is the living room.

And our bed is this thin, naked mattress.

And our bedside table is actually an overturned cardboard box, wrapped like a Christmas present in a hospital-blue bedsheet. We are fucking beside it, Marti on her back, legs elastically folded back (oh, pliable youth!) with a hand up above her head like her arm is the curlicue of a question mark and her dark areola is the dot, and the other hand reaching down to perform, as always, that secret code-breaking beckon at the juncture of our intercourse. I am rocking against her at a thoughtful, medium pace, and to maintain this pace and prevent my thoughtfulness from becoming thoughtless reflex, I am examining the top of our bedside box, which is caving in from the weight of the lamp; a random collection of round things have rolled to the centre and collected around the base of the lamp—a pearl earring, some peanut M&Ms, a plastic beach-ball keychain; a glass of water is perched on the slanted surface, in danger, with every spasm of satisfaction, of being tipped and spilled; a candle is burning beside the glass, a bubble of wax threatening to unreel itself at the edge of the thinning parapet. Marti loves candles, if you haven't yet noticed. There are swirling galaxies of hardened wax woven into the carpet all through the apartment. We tried, the first time a candle spilled, to scratch the wax out with our fingernails, and then to scrape it out with a knife, but we tore up the carpet in the process, so, with nothing to lose, we go on destroying it with vanilla-scented effluence. We have not yet learned the beginner's economic lesson of the Damage Deposit, and, after three years of reckless life in this small apartment, scraping chairs across the linoleum, allowing leaks to leak, letting the wax fall where it may, we'll be lucky if we don't owe money to cover the repairs.

Still, it feels like we're living some version of a grown-up life. We're not kids anymore. We're not students. We have jobs (occasionally). We pay bills (sometimes). As high school hurtled to its conclusion, I applied to university like everyone else, and was accepted here and there as an undergraduate of moderate academic capability but unlimited potential. My mother, canny comptroller that she was, had been saving money since those early days of a thousand collarbone-kisses, and even my father managed to hide a couple bucks. I was offered a scholarship or two; modest sums that, to my middle-class grasp, seemed negligible, but certainly would have turned some Third World immigrant kid's head to spinning. I could have gone anywhere. The east coast. The west coast. One of those rowdy places in between. Youth's Great Adventure lay before me: weed-reeking dorm rooms and sybaritic frosh week festivities; booze and booze's easy consequence — easy fun, easy sex, the easy pressure of self-discipline (that friendly inverted version of the discipline we fight against for the first seventeen years of our lives). So why not off into the wild blue yonder with my friends and peers? Why not off to indulge in the manufactured novelty of the gap year, to behold Doric columns in the flesh, to smooth my hands over art deco monuments, to climb the stone steps of Mughal mausoleums? Why didn't I drift away, like everyone else, after the Pangaean crack-up of high school?

Marti, that's why.

I stayed for Marti. To the wild blue yonder, I said: no thanks. Marti was my Great Adventure of Youth. My fleshy column was beholden to her Doric beauty; her decorous body was the only monument of art I yearned to smooth my hands over. I stayed because she needed me. She told me so. She made grand dramatic statements I'd only ever heard on bad television dramas:

"You're the best thing that's ever happened to me!"

"I can't live without you!"

"You make me feel so safe!"

Me! Daniel Solomon! Bullied and beaten by a sixth-grader, sent away by his mortified mom, succumbing and crumbling time and again to every violent pressure, now, suddenly, in the role of protector! To be *needed*! To be, at seventeen, the *best thing that's ever happened* to someone! It made me giddy with strength. I felt irradiated with responsibility.

Who was I, before Marti? A thing made of vaporous thought and idea and opinion but without mass or substance, lacking the nickel-iron core around which swirling gases might gather to form a life-supporting sublunary body. Marti was all nickel, all iron. She offered me the remaining half of her virginity in exchange for my protection, offered me her body so that I could partly bear the burden of its abuse, offered me some of her heavy, hard substance, and with it I began to forge a core and mantle and crust. Seventeen years old, when I met her. How could I not feel fully and finally a *man*?

So, as my cohort's post-secondary exodus began, I enrolled at the local city college whose name was the punchline to every derisive joke we told about the lower-class kids who pushed us around in high school. I got a part-time job with campus security and used all that saved-up money to move out of my dad's basement and rent a one-room apartment at the waistline of an exurban high-rise not far from campus. Meanwhile, Marti's mother was transferred to another bank branch and moved to the commuter community of a nearby city's exurb. Marti stayed behind, at first in the guest bedroom of a family friend, but I begged her to move in with me, and she begged her mother to let her, and by the end of September my apartment had become *our* apartment, where, right now, three years later, we are on the floor.

"Faster!" she urges me.

My thoughtful pace picks up.

Her voice, in this rough low tone, is just like the sound my knees are making as they chaff against the carpet. To my ears, though, her words are just another domestic sound, like the humming of the microwave or the trilling of the phone; a task announcing itself, demanding to be done. So I go faster. At this increased tempo, the insides of my thighs are slapping against the backs of hers. Ridiculous, this clap-clap-clapping, but in the moment (even here, *out* of the moment) it intimates something animal and erotic, and I like it. Marti grabs a nearby discarded T-shirt (*Soul Carnival Players*, it says) and throws it over her face and head; it's like an eyeless executioner's hood, but also, because in the dim light it's the same ashy colour as the carpet, it's now like I'm fucking a headless mannequin. With each inhalation Marti draws more and more of the T-shirt into her mouth, until it seems she will choke on it; the inside of her wide open mouth, palate and tongue and uvula, all modelled in cotton. When she bites down, I can see the outline of her teeth. With her free hand she wedges my wrist out from beneath me and guides it over her mouth, presses it there for a moment, and then, unsatisfied, moves it to her eyes, holds it there. Balanced with one arm, my rhythm corrects for this new oblique angle of engagement. I cover her already-covered eyes with my palm. Satisfied, she sprawls her arm back above her head.

We fuck like this every day. In the morning, in the afternoon; before dinner, after dinner; before brushing our teeth, *while* brushing our teeth; in the middle of the night, practically in our sleep; in the bed, on the floor, in the kitchen, in the shower, on our second-floor balcony, in a restaurant bathroom, in the staff room of the shoe store where Marti works. Since we've been living together: eight-hundred ninety-nine times (not including the additional one hundred and eighty instances of fellatio).

Marti is the master of our coital experiments. Just like she set the scene for our very first encounter in the hotel room, she now directs the various interconnections of protrusions and perforations, which include, besides the obvious, our ears and elbows and assholes, the cleft behind her knee, the arches of her feet, my pointless yet sensitive nipples, complicated mountaineering knots, lever mechanics, asphyxiation, and so forth. She is an empiricist, and she is using my eager, efficient eighteen-year-old dick as a constant variable. I am no reluctant participant, of course. How strictly I obey her commands! "Fuck me harder/slower/softer/faster." "Pull my hair; harder/ not so hard." "Not so deep." "Slap my ass." I respond to her nonverbal instructions without hesitation.

For example: look how quickly I close my hand around her throat when she says, "Put your hand on my throat."

It's not thrilling to choke her. But it *is* thrilling that she *wants* to be choked. It's thrilling that it thrills her. It's thrilling to improvise — to pull the cord of the clock radio out of the electrical outlet in the wall behind the bed, to wrap it around her neck, to softly hold it there, to be met with the exact right reaction: a sudden upward grind of her pelvis that traps her flicking fingers between our bodies; her spine locked straight like the blade of pocket knife; the tightness of her abdomen and thighs and shoulders and the corresponding rigidity of her interior muscles, sucked in like inhaling cheeks; the uncontrollable loudness that I sometimes stifle with my palm. And while she tests and discards and elaborates upon this variety of perversions (in search of something I secretly hope she never finds), I am, instead, collecting and cataloguing and erecting explicatory plaques in my museum of memory in honour of these perversions. Each new experience, each domination and submission and mutual mechanical ministration, seems to expand my manhood. Each time I come (*in* or *on* or *around* her) I am drawn further away, invisibly, as if by the current of a gushing river, from that stupid boy who had, that first night, stumbled his way into this goddess's world and could, when faced with her painful confessions, reply only with stupid, stupid silence.

I take my hand away from her throat, now, and brace myself with both arms. Am I merely tired? Unable to spare a hand to indulge Marti's artistic whims? Concerned, perhaps, with my own climax, against which I have lost ground now that her face is veiled? Or is this a moral crisis? I *do* feel a strange and sudden childish terror. I *do* want this so badly to be over. But I'm also a healthy young man beholden only to my own virility and conscious of not wanting to ruin (not even for the sake of this wonderful girl's psychic fitness) this rather wonderful arrangement I've made with her darker urges.

Anyways, I'm pumping faster, now, but still losing ground. Her breath is coming quicker, long whooshing breaths like a child's impression of the ocean echo in a seashell, and I feel her pelvic curl, her spinal uncurl, she's getting close, I'm not sure if I'm going to make it, but I do, I go all thoughtless, and with a final terrific plunge I blow my load into the pocket of chemical air at the end of the condom, and it feels like a cold and sugary milkshake sucked through a warm straw. It feels great.

And I'm still feeling great later that night when I venture out of our apartment and into the residential labyrinth that surrounds it, in search of post-calisthenic sustenance: dill-pickle chips and Diet Pepsi and peanut M&Ms.

Perfect nighttime ambience, out here; cool outer-space air descending and mixing with the absorbed afternoon heat still radiating from the asphalt and concrete. Down the curving laneways, through the tunnel of foliage formed by high-fiving elms, on my way to the twenty-four-hour corner store Marti and I refer to as "our store" — as if having a store is a symbol of status for a young urban couple, like having a dog, owning a condo, vacationing in Jamaica. All the houses, here in this gently snoozing neighbourhood, are single-storey wartime bungalows with narrow backyards; through dim windows I catch turquoise flashes of lightning as late-night TV introduces and dismisses its guests in descending order of esteem.

Sometimes I like to imagine that *he* lives here. Tyler Madden. Somewhere in this neighbourhood, somewhere on this street. Sometimes I like to imagine that, say, *this* is his house. Yes, this yellow one here. And I like to imagine, sometimes, that if he really *did* live here, in this yellow house, I would have the courage to—

○○○

—take a sudden right turn and march up the driveway, into the backyard, where he's hanging with his crew (he's the kind of dude, I've decided, who refers to himself as a dude and his friends as a crew), sitting in lawn chairs, drinking beers, smoking, snickering, all wearing their red baseball caps backwards, all braying in the retarded baritone of bullies, no idea that I'm there until I come around the corner, walking like a colossus, twenty feet in two strides, suddenly right beside him, appearing so quickly, so suddenly, that he's still in the midst of sipping from his beer bottle, his lips still touching the tip of it, and when he sees me he's about to lower the bottle, but, like I said, there's no time, already my hands are in the air, already this terrible instrument is raised over my head (what is it? A hockey stick, a baseball bat? A policeman's baton? No, some kind of steel bar. A tire iron? No, no, a *crowbar*, with its cobra-like curving head and forked tongue) and already I'm turning at the waist, wrists loose, swinging a beautiful smooth arc, the sound of it like the bass whisper of tires rolling on asphalt, every T-ball swing, every atom-league slapshot, every self-mutilating masturbatory stroke, every muscle twitch since birth now fulfilling its purpose, to crush this guy's fucking face, and, yes, here we go, *whoosh*, the heavy metal cudgel *blasts* through the beer bottle in front of his pursed lips, cuts it at the neck, dragging in its wake a comet's tail of broken brown pebbles, *blasts* into his mouth, through his teeth, and, at full speed, all you can see is the blur of the crowbar and an explosion of brown and white specks and the sound of calcified enamel tinkling on the cement.

(Back at our apartment, Marti soaking in the bathtub, looking down at herself, amazed as the half-moon scar on her breast puckers and folds and disappears.)

Ah, yes, it feels wonderful to take my revenge on Tyler Madden. But something is missing. What is it? The colour of his eyes. The fetid smell of his unwashed flannel shirt. His preferred brand of beer. In these fantasies, he has a mannequin's smoothed-flat features, a nothing-face. You'll recall from my anaesthetic reveries of Erin Seeley and her busy fist that objective detail is essential to such flights of fancy. He's in the details, right? And when you act as God, it's not your mandate to sweat over the physical framework of the cosmos, to draft all those far-reaching rules and regulations (no, science will take care of all that). It's your job to arrange each blade of grass so that it catches the breeze in diagonal waves, to draw fractals of frost on the windows of a parked cars, to put a mole right *there* (not over there) so that it appears above her collar each time she leans forward to read from her book. It's all proof that profundity isn't exclusively astronomic. It's proof that we're real, that we're consequential. If He cares about blades of grass, He must certainly care about us.

I need to know Tyler Madden like she knows him. My compulsion to learn is virtuous: I want to experience it in real-time, to slip on her consciousness, to live it, and, by living it, own part of it and help her carry the burden. I want to wear her first-person prose like a pair of goggles and peer backwards into her past. I want to know *everything* and, by possessing her knowledge, tighten my grip and make my possession of *her* more complete (still a coddling gardener, perpetually fearing drought).

I'm greedy for God's ennobling minutiae, I'm greedy for Marti, and that's why I do what I'm about to do.

Forgive me —

— but, come on, is this *really* such a despicable breach of trust?

She *lets* me read them. You've seen it for yourself! She picks out certain passages, certain funny phrases, and reads them aloud to me like bedtime fairy tales. Only a few pages are forbidden to me; Marti would scan through and flip past and explain that it was just embarrassing stuff: expired crushes, family fights, depressant poetry; feelings she felt but didn't feel anymore — no point in revisiting those deserted passions, right?

I've never kept a diary, but I understand the appeal: a compilation of empirical data from which might be deduced a rationalist answer to the question of who you are, why you're here. And much of the thrill, I imagine, must come from the possibility that your anecdotal record-keeping isn't just a primal cry into the void or a rhetorical conversation with oneself, but rather an artefact to be unearthed at some later date by an audience that might finally appreciate the true consequence of your thoughts and experiences.

With me, Marti had found her audience. I was the unknown ideal reader that, for all those years, she'd been writing for.

So what I'm doing, right now, can't be *that* traitorous. My conscience raises no complaints when I slide open the mirrored closet doors and go digging through her box of girlish miscellanea (widowed earrings, plastic-wrapped tampons, phone bills and prescriptions and, yes, the complete multi-volume document of her first nineteen years). I feel no reluctance to begin my research when I find the furtive edition — no, it's not this puffy plastic booklet, not this spiral-bound notepad, not this stack of loose-leaf secured with staples. No, *this* is the one I'm looking for: this classic ribbon-tailed leather codex.

Let's read together. Sit with me, right here on the floor, on the carpet, between the closet and the mattress, amongst these islets of polished-smooth candle wax. We'll start at the three-quarter mark of page thirty-six: a new entry in black ballpoint, dots and periods blobby and palm-smeared (a fresh pen still working out its internal pressure?), two concise stripes of written text between every faint blue ruled line, a whirlwind scribble in the bottom margin and beside it Don Martin–style googly-eyes shooting lightning bolts:

July 7 – Monday

Mood: happy, nervous, excited, doubtful, happy again.

I will try to explain what happened yesterday without making myself sound completely desperate and certifiably insane. I don't want to say anything corny and clichéd like "it was meant to be" but it is kind of funny since I really didn't want to go to the barbecue (the one at Derrick and Janice's) and all morning it seemed like I'd gotten out of it because no one said anything to me about it while they were packing up and getting ready to go. I was excited to have the place to myself and maybe watch a movie or something but then right before they leave Dad calls me down and asks me if I'm ready to go. I didn't say anything (I know better) and just went along despite feeling pretty annoyed by the whole thing knowing that I'd probably get stuck as usual with the C.O.D. (I think it's already pretty obvious how I feel about Kandice and Kory and my desire to stay away from them if I don't have the freedom to reprimand). Luckily the barbecue was a lot busier than I thought since a bunch of Derrick's family is in town and I was able to hang out without having to make a lot of small talk or answer a lot of questions or pretend like I'm having a good time so that I don't get that wide-eyed look from Dad that means "quit moping" and sometimes also "you're embarrassing me". There were lots of people I didn't know and who I didn't know how I might be related to through some weird connection of divorces and remarriages. One of the people I didn't know was this tall blond guy and something happened when I saw him because he looked right at me and we had a moment of eye contact that was longer than normal. Not long in a weird way like we were staring at each other but just an extra second of lingering before we looked away. I would probably think that I was reading too much into things except that almost right away he came over and sat down at the picnic table with me and introduced himself. My first reaction was that he was a bit older but he's actually only twenty, he's just very mature and we had a great conversation about skiing of all things because he had just gotten back from a trip to Banff with his friends (and he also made a little wisecrack about Cheryl so right away he's in my good books). It's hard to explain but I just really loved talking to him. He's really smart and charming and funny and I felt like I was being all those things too which for me is a pretty big deal considering that I feel the complete opposite of that about 99.9999 percent of the time. I sound like I'm thirteen again talking about "maturity" and acting "mature" but I can't think of another word for it. We had a great chat and it made me feel like I was coming up from underwater to where I can breathe more easily. It actually made me really want school to be over. So now maybe that's why I don't mind that song anymore. Before it seemed like a melancholy break-up song but now when I hear it it sounds hopeful like the beginning of something instead of the end. I guess for the record I should describe what he looks like: a bit like the guy who plays Blane in *Pretty in Pink* but without the stoner eyes and little bit better dressed and definitely more handsome. He's handsome instead of cute and that sums up what I mean about him being mature. His name is Tyler.

Now we're at the top of page thirty-nine, text in felt-tip pink, in the upper-right corner (in same pink) a woman's eye fringed with daisy petals, and hanging from it, filling the margin, a long curling stem with ribbed leaves and fish-hook thorns that opens up and encircles, at the end of the lower paragraph, the words "my fat face and greasy skin":

July 10 – Thursday

Mood: happy and slightly annoyed at my inability to let myself just be happy.

So here I go being a girly-girl which I will admit just this once is kind of fun and makes me realize why Kandice and Kory have so much fun cruising through the mall and trying on slutty dresses and getting their makeup done at the perfume counter at the department store. There's something in my DNA that responds to it all (against my will). Which is annoying but I guess I've been conditioned after living my whole life in a house full of girls and using a bathroom all summer that's full of old wrinkled copies of Cosmo and Glamour. I actually hate being all giddy and positive like this and I hate myself even more for hating it but I went to the mall with Kandice anyways and we shopped and tried on summer dresses and shoes and had lunch at the food court which I immediately regretted for obvious reasons such as my fat face and greasy skin. I found a couple nice dresses. I'll go back tomorrow and get one of them and probably some shoes which will break the bank for me as far as my summer allowance is concerned. [Seven words struck out here, but discernible beneath wavelength scribbles: "But hopefully it will be worth it."] I'm trying not to make too big a deal of this whole thing and I suppose it just goes to show how desperate I am that all I can think about is the party on Saturday and it makes me realize what a complete and total waste this summer has been. Which reminds me, I got a letter from Jenny yesterday and she has apparently found a summer boyfriend on the island and basically regaled me with tales of all the fun and amazing things they're doing and it sounds like something from a bad teenage novel with bonfires on the beach and flag football. Except that she already has slept with him twice which isn't much of a surprise since her virginity is a thing of the ancient past. But I hope everything goes well on Saturday even though the hoping makes me feel ridiculous. What is it that I can't even let myself be excited? Like being excited or hopeful is a bad thing. I guess I just don't want to be disappointed. I really just want to be happy. Then again that's what everyone says isn't it? Okay so I'm going to just be a girl and admit everything. I have a crush on a boy and I hope he likes me back.

9:05 p.m.

I just got off the phone with Tyler. He called to see if I was going to Dad's thing on Saturday night. He must have gotten our number from Derrick and Janice or else from his aunt. We actually chatted for about twenty minutes though unfortunately I was on the phone in the kitchen and the portable was out of batteries so I had to sit there with Cheryl listening to everything I was saying which made me self-conscious and cautious about everything I was saying. So I probably sounded like a complete imbecile. But at the same time it was just such an easy conversation. I even told him about going shopping for a dress today and he said (jokingly of course) that he had been shopping for a dress today too and that he hoped we didn't show up wearing the same thing.

Haw-haw. But it was actually pretty funny the way he said it. For now I feel foolish going on about this so I'm going to leave it alone and wait out this last forty-eight hours and maybe I'll look back on all this and laugh and cringe.

Follow my finger—now we're at the top of page forty-three. There is a row of paper teeth hidden in the seam between pages where a page has been removed. What follows is a second draft, such is the clarity and carefulness of her prose. The handwriting, in this passage, loses some of its thoughtful precision; loopier loops, spaced-out spaces, forward cant canted further forward. It's hurried, harried, excited, ecstatic. She was eager to get this all down.

July 17 – Thursday

On Saturday night everything changed. It wasn't at all like I thought it would be. It happened out of the blue and the world feels like a different place now. I feel like I've finally been let in on a big secret about human nature. I showed up in my new dress and new shoes and right away I felt self-conscious when I saw what everyone else was wearing which was basically T-shirts and shorts (it was a barbecue after all). I let Kandice do my hair and she actually did a great job by making it sort of wavy but not too curly. She wanted to do makeup too but I thought that the dress and the hair was probably too much already and that it was probably best to go

au naturel. I saw Tyler right away when we came in because he
was in the kitchen with Derrick and Jesse and I tried to play
it cool by chatting with Cheryl for a while before I talked to
him and when I did get a chance finally to say hi he just gave
me a quick smile and said hey and then just ignored me. I
was feeling pretty [inserted here with a caret: "ridiculously"]
crushed and justified in all the doubts I've been having all
week. But I came out of the bathroom about five minutes
later and bumped into him in the hallway and he seemed so
happy to see me and said to me "I wanted to tell you earlier,
you look totally amazing!" And isn't that what every girl wants
to hear? Even me sometimes. From that point on we just kept
bouncing off each other back and forth into the party and
back to each other and at some point we just stuck together.
He even chatted with my dad for a while and weirdly they
seemed to get along even though if you had asked me I never
would have guessed it. He made Dad laugh a few times too
which is no small accomplishment [the end of this sentence
is redacted by circular squiggles: "even though he had had a
few drinks by then"]. He obviously had had a few drinks too
(Tyler) and kept giving me these gentle little touches which
if it was anyone else would have been creepy I think but was
somehow charming because it was him and because he was
doing it almost nervously, like he was afraid I was going to
get away from him or something. He told me he thought I
looked just like the lead singer of this band but he couldn't
remember the name of it. It took us about half an hour to
figure out he was talking about the Cardigans. I told him he
was crazy but he was insistent that if I cut my hair short and

dyed it blond I would look just like her (so maybe I'll do that one day when I'm feeling brave). I have to admit that I had a few drinks too but it served to make me more relaxed like booze is apparently supposed to. Dad was basically passed out at midnight. He was sitting on the couch and his eyes kept closing and everyone was laughing at him and making jokes about how he's an old man now. Tyler took me outside to show me his car and that's when he kissed me [a note in the margin is connected to this line by an arrow: "That's right my life has become an old Motown song!"]. It wasn't like you'd expect between two drunk people. It wasn't sloppy or anything. It was very tender and slow and it filled me up like I was an empty glass. It gave me butterflies. There were still people milling around so we went back inside and played it cool for a little while. Dad was asleep. Cheryl and Aunt Kathy decided that they were going to walk down to the strip and get a pizza or something and it was kind of funny the way they were all giggling and acting like crazy teenagers. Tyler took me down into the basement and through the furnace room to where his apartment was and we lay on his bed for a while just talking and for some reason it felt so natural to be laying there like that on my side with my face just inches from his. Like we had known each other forever, since the beginning of time. He told me that it had been almost a year since he was with anyone and I told him that it was sixteen years and I had never been with anyone which totally surprised him because he said I seemed so mature and worldly and he couldn't believe that I didn't have a whole bunch of "pimply teenage punks" chasing me around. I regretted telling him that [caret insertion: "my virginity"] because it seemed after like nothing was going to happen. He told me he didn't want to hurt me, that he'd never want to hurt me, so I told him he could never hurt me, and I honestly never thought moments like that existed in real life. It was probably the most profound exchange I've ever had with another human being and it's this [the original "boy" is struck-out and replaced with "man"] I just met a week earlier.

[Should we stop here, my love? I can hardly breathe, all these little concrete half-cursives piled up on my diaphragm. She stopped here, too, you know. Same pen, same intense stenographic session, but her precision returns for the next paragraph, the letters are no longer leaning so far forward, no longer racing towards the climax.]

It all happened so naturally after that. It was like I suddenly knew exactly what I was doing. We were kissing passionately and I took his hand and put it on my breast and I took his other hand and put it between my legs. My whole body from head to toe was tingling like it was charged by an electrical current. He squeezed my breasts and very gently pinched my nipple and asked me if I liked it and I told him I did (it felt amazing) and told him so and he did it again except this time a little bit harder. I reached down and unbuckled his belt for him which was such a bold thing for me to do but I did it without a second of hesitation. I stroked his penis and he burrowed his face in my neck and bit my earlobe. He also did this other incredibly sexy thing where instead of pulling off my panties he just sort of pulled them aside with his hand and I could feel him right there pushing against me and I think he was about to ask me if I was sure I wanted to do this, but I didn't let him hesitate and used my heels to pull him towards me. It was so much softer than I imagined. We made love and I completely understand now the difference between having sex and making love. It lasted almost an hour even though it seemed like only a few minutes and also seemed like it lasted for days. We finished at the same time. And I came too. It was different from coming by touching myself. It was deeper and felt like electricity that started in the middle of me and radiated out to my fingers and toes.

It was amazing.

My eyes lift from the page, my hands lose their strength, the book tips towards the bright bedroom window. I'm sick to my stomach, thrilled by despair, not quite able to make sense of the words, so I read them again, and again, and again, trying to decode it all in phonetic chunks, the way you might teach yourself a foreign phrase.

I should stop reading—

No, I must go on to the end!

Keep reading, yes, what difference does it make, now, to know half the story or the whole thing? The horror, the titillation, this martyr's satisfying agony—these are fixed quantities. Reading the rest will make them no more or less powerful, so, yes, let's keep going.

July 26 – Saturday

Mood: ♥♥♥♥♥♥♥♥♥

Yesterday Tyler and I went to the Camden Locks and had a picnic under that old tree at the top of the hill. The tall grass was moving in waves. We drove there in his Mustang and the whole way I just lay with my head leaning against the edge of the open window and my hair was blowing in my face and it felt like something out of a music video. We made love under a willow tree. It was magical. It was all just so perfect. I really can't believe the way things have turned out. I slept over at his place last night and he told me all about his little nephew and how much he loves spending time with him and I could just see in his eyes how much he loves kids and when I told him so it seemed for a second like he might cry and my heart just about broke in half. We made love twice and I came both times. Today we didn't do anything. We just lay in bed all day and made love a few more times and I smoked a cigarette afterwards and felt like a European sexpot. I told Tyler that I would remember this moment like it was a black-and-white photo from the sixties and he told me that he would remember this moment in full colour like it was an old Renaissance painting except with a skinnier and sexier girl. And the weird thing was that I kind of believed him. He makes me believe that I'm all of the things he thinks I am. He might be the best thing that's ever happened to me. I don't know if I could live without him. He just makes me feel so safe.

Just hours after reading those words for the first time, I am stumbling through the door into Kyle Sutendra's parents' house. It's the big summer reunion party, and I must admit, it's a pretty decent counterfeit. I can almost believe that I'm still sixteen and just beginning to learn the art of adolescent alcoholism, faking the slurs and stumbles that later in life I'll try to suppress.

But you can see that something is wrong, can't you? Kyle says it himself when he greets me at the front door:

"Look at this morose motherfucker right here!"

Tonight I'm a seabird slick with spilled oil. I muck through the door with my bottle-shaped paper bag and croak hello. I muck through a gauntlet of former friends who take breaks from their tales of collegiate adventure to ask, "What you been up to?" It's our second summer as grown-ups, and everyone has returned to the nest to revitalize themselves on regurgitated parental comfort. Not yet twenty, most of us, and already we're steeped to bitterness in our own boiling hot nostalgia, attempting to recreate, here in these years of unrestraint, the outlaw house parties of our high school glory years, now only a year behind us. We play the same music: the cult classics, the anthems, the goofy pop hits that, in our blind love for our fading era of reigning supreme, we have learned finally to appreciate. We drink the same boozy drinks, drink them the same daredevilish way. It's still a common tic to count one's beverages throughout the night; the tally, we feel, proves something important about ourselves; "handling one's liquor," here at the dawn of our third decade is still an important personal achievement.

(I am not here to "handle my liquor." I have been reading and rereading Marti's blasphemous volume all week, searching for something, some form of encryption, some simple substitution cipher that reveals this all to be a joke, *anything* that might prove it false, a delusion, a hilarious semantic misunderstanding.)

I wander from the kitchen with a plastic *Jurassic Park* collector's cup filled to the razor rim with a half-half mixture of ginger ale and rye whiskey, down into the split-level living room, where a yelling and laughing crowd sits around the coffee table playing a card game called bullshit!, a version of gin rummy in which the earned points are drinks to be given away. I crash back into an armchair, Kyle's father's evening aerie, and take a long, jarring swallow. The poison I am hoping to purge from my body is a chemical compound composed of three primary elements, three handwritten words: *it*, *was*, and *amazing*. That's what I'm thinking, sitting alone in the corner, mustering a smile for the performing card players: it was amazing, it was amazing, it was amazing.

The card game before me has degenerated, as it's supposed to, into a drinking contest between Jimmy Boychuk and Karen Parenteau (that's her with the whale-tail of crimson thong surfacing above the waist of her jeans). A crescendo of encouragement from the crowd, a burst of cheers as they slam their cups on the table. From my periphery, a porcelain mug swings into the picture and taps with a hollow tock against my plastic cup.

"Hey, man! What's up?"

Looming over me is *this* guy: Thomas Zavacky, the ginger-headed kid who, despite his broad mollusc face and gnarly long hair and messy motif of dark freckles all across his entire body and the everlastingly damp and corn-smelling flannel shirt he wore for weeks without changing, possessed enough skill with a guitar to lure girls into his parents' Jeep Cherokee for Saturday night drives out to the sand pits. (But, no, why am I thinking this? He was always so kind to me: he drove me home from school, sometimes; he shared jugs of home-brewed beer he stole from his father; he recorded all his Pearl Jam CDs onto cassette tapes for me. Why do I right now feel so resentful towards him?)

"Hey, man," I say.

"You just get back?" he says.

"No, I…"

"Where are you going to school, again?"

"No, actually, I was at Riverwood for a while, but I'm taking a year off to … you know, I'm still around here."

"Oh, cool, yeah."

In sympathy he tips back the dregs of whatever was in his mug, exhales dramatically with his tongue wagging, and looks left and right at the gossiping crowd around us. "Have you seen Phil? I heard Phil was here tonight. He's moving to Venezuela or something, eh? Or Portugal. Or something. Have you talked to him?"

I haven't seen Phil, no, and I haven't kept in touch with him, just like I haven't kept in touch with anybody, but here comes Kyle, just in time to obstruct my non-answer with a slow-motion jab to Thomas's jaw, which Thomas accepts with a slow-motion whipping back of his chin, both of them pushing whooshing slow-motion noises through their teeth.

Wsssh, dsssh!

For a while I listen to them talk about a bunch of things they've done, the knowledge they've accumulated.

Wow, that was fast! My *Jurassic Park* cup is already empty. And, wow, it's already full again, and already empty again. I'm in the upstairs half of the living room, now. Lens flares and manual focus adjustments give the scene a jittery speed, and my head is once again an iron block wobbling at the end of a noodle-neck.

I know that girl: that's one of the Jennifers.

I know that guy, too.

I'm now the silent circumferential segment in a roundtable discussion about the excesses of university life, a clockwise game of one-upmanship. They don't converse or debate; they prefer to communicate through personal fables. They don't listen, they wait restlessly to speak. They've never learned the art of segue. Instead, they fight through the din, bully each other with interruptions of increasing volume, share, by brute force, their personal folklore. A table full of Aesops, here, but no one is interested in learning any morals. Our lives are *anecdota*, not *rhetorica*. Just listen to us:

"That's like this one time I ..."

"I remember once I ..."

"When I was a kid I ..."

"That reminds me of when I ..."

It's a genre-bending anthology: police dramas, gross-out comedies, drug frenzies, soft-core pornography, political thrillers, coming-of-age quests, art-house altruism, quirky romances. I laugh at the funny parts, gasp at plot twists, but all the while the mutant offspring of Resentment and Disappointment worms inside me like a length of electrified wire pushed deeper by each sip of fizzy bitterness. In my stomach, it coils into a heavy ball. And, three, two, one: here I go. I jump up from the couch and walk straight-spined upstairs, find the master bedroom, find the adjoining bathroom, and shut the door behind me. It begins with that hot preparatory grimace, then it breaks, and I'm sobbing, from the top of the scale to the bottom, *mi, re, do*, and sucking in air through a stretched and spit-thick mouth. I force it out. I sing my sobs instead of stifling them.

Oh, Daniel, you fucking baby. Always crying in the mirror. Snap out of it. Come on.

I stumble out, red-eyed, back into the heart of the party, back to my place on the couch. Where's my cup? The one with the T. Rex chasing the jeep? Oh, it's gone. Okay, I'll have this beer. I'll take this shot. That one, too. I'll chug this drink that someone has left behind on the table, and . . . oh, that's funny, it's my cup from before — see, that red cavity of dagger-teeth about to swallow screaming Laura Dern! All this alcohol, it's seeping into my bloodstream up here in the sky, and I can show you only these murky streaks of movement and inaudible clips of conversation to connect my couch-sitting with my stair-sitting. Yes, back at the top of the stairs again. And — well, well, look who's now sitting beside me: Karen Parenteau, beer-chug runner-up, blowing vomit-flavoured breath up my nose.

She's gained weight, you know, since high school. Her

arms are thick where her shoulders connect to her trunk, she's developed those wrinkly vaginal folds in her armpits. She hunches over on her haunches and a tessellated ring of chub squishes out over her jeans. She's telling me about this one time, it was so funny, this guy said this thing, and then she was, like, *oh my God*, and they were all so fucking *wasted*.

It's not my fault. I turn around and her face is right there, descending, eclipsing, I don't even have to move, her wet lips are on mine, our tongues are furiously twisting and licking. With her new meaty breasts heaved against me she stage-whispers into my neck that I should go with her. *Yes*, I think, *I should*. And I do, and now we're in the off-suite bathroom, my secret refuge, and her shirt is bunched up beneath her chin to reveal the veiny pale plane of her bust and my pants are bunched down to reveal the pale pocked meat of my inner thighs, and I'm thinking:

You know what's amazing? *This*.

This is amazing.

Do you hear that? Her key is in the lock. Marti is home from work.

I keep my eyes fixed on the television:

She enters. Behind me, out of sight, the zipping and swishing and thwapping of clothes coming off, then the thunderous shush of the shower. Vigorous hairwashing (you can tell from the heavy drumbeat on the tub as water is wrung and flung out of her hair). A long and thoughtful rinse, then some lower note of the bellowing water pipes fades away and, along with it, the hot water. The shower knob slams shut and everything is quiet.

Things have not been well between us, this past week. I have been employing the classical masculine methodology: silence, disinterest, sarcasm, absence, condescension, callousness. Marti has said that my mind seems to be elsewhere, and she's right: I've been composing, in my head, a devastating oration about my hurt feelings, about the oily contamination seeping backwards to taint my memories of the last four years, about the myriad mental illnesses such a deep and drawnout falsehood suggests, about all the poor women out there, legitimately groped, authentically molested, certifiably raped, and how would they feel to know that you've co-opted their pain and used it for personal gain, huh?

I'm also testing an alternate ending in which, to save face, to win a real shutout victory, I don't admit to having read her diaries but instead claim that the truth has dawned on me through a superhuman act of psychological deduction. However, to omit the content of her diaries from my polemic poses problems. It will expunge one of my sharpest arguments; specifically, the epic hurt caused to me in knowing that she was consciously attempting to recreate, with picnic lunches and carefully placed candles and a certain style of lovemaking, her favourite memories of Tyler. Has this all been a sham from the very start, since we were seventeen and just beginning (so I believed) our lay education in boy-girl affairs? And what of Tyler? This poor friendly chap you've been secretly slandering? He seems, in your descriptions of him, to be a rather nice fellow, a real cool dude, a real family man, a real clavicle-licker, a real *catch*.

As Marti emerges from the bathroom in a steamy exhalation and stands silently in the kitchen, I'm still arranging these topics into a winning sequence, it's still a work in progress, but I know how I'm going to end it. Here's the *coup de grâce*, the final line, delivered (I imagine) with such compassion, such magnanimity, that when I say it Marti will collapse, fetally curled, choking on her tears. I will say: "I would have loved you, anyways. I would have been with you, anyways."

That repetition is powerful, isn't it? Yep, it's a real toe-curler, this speech of mine.

A cupboard clicks open, a mug sings from its ceramic lips as Marti drags it off the shelf. The tap is on, a deepening gush, the tap is off. Silent sips. Eventually she sits down at the kitchen table and speaks:

"Did you go to class today?"

Silence.

"Did you at least pick up toilet paper, like I asked?"

I shrug with disinterest.

"What's wrong with you?"

Callously, I refuse to answer.

"You seriously don't have anything to say to me?"

With as much condescension as I can muster, I say: "I seriously have nothing to say."

"Really?" My continuing silence confirms that I'm telling the truth. "So you're just being a dick for no reason, then?"

"I guess so."

"Don't do this sarcastic asshole thing, it doesn't suit you. You're not like this. You're more respectful of me than this. At least talk to me. Like you care about me. Like we're grown-ups. At least say *something*. Don't do this silent sarcastic asshole thing."

"You know what?" I begin. But I've already forgotten what my first broadside volley was supposed to be. I think something ominous, like, *Do you have something to tell me?* But cleverer, subtler, with more context. She's stolen that line, anyways. Nonetheless, the whistle is blown, the game has begun, the clock is counting down, and now, face to face with her, I find my confidence inverted, now a lack. This opponent isn't a stranger, it's not the scheming doppelgänger I've been sparring with in my head. It's her. It's Marti. *My* Marti. I didn't count on that. What comes out of my mouth, instead of the tactical stabs I've choreographed, is:

"Listen, just … what*ever*."

Oh, boy, that dismissive addendum really sets her off! Otherwise shy, otherwise restrained, otherwise passive, Marti, when she must, can expand her indignation like some unfolding deep-sea jellyfish. She can fill an entire room with it. Which she is doing right now. Her whole body opens up: her stance widens, her neck stretches, her arms spread. Marti angry is Marti in full bloom. My Thronebound heart heaves with love; she has never been more beautiful than she is right now, furious and murderous and trying to cleave me with the cords of her neck. What vigor she has. What vitality she brings to her disappointment:

"I've been putting up with this for, like, almost a week, and I thought maybe it was just a pissy mood, like every other pissy mood, and, fine, I'll put up with your pissy moods, I've done it before, I'll do it again, but it's *disrespectful*. Seriously? Fine.

Whatever. I don't care. But this is so out of the blue. This is *so* unlike you. What's happening that you're suddenly going to be like this and not even have the decency to apologize, or explain, or even tell me what's wrong? You're not even trying to explain it, it's like you're doing it just to spite me. It's scary. It scares me. You're scaring me. You're acting like a different person. I don't like it. Don't do this. Don't act like this. Please, please, don't just sit there not saying anything. Say something! Tell me! If there's something that I'm doing, or something that I'm not doing—I'll do anything, just tell me what it is. What are you thinking? Why are you mad? Don't be mad at me, please, I need you. I feel like you're mad at me, like you hate me all of a sudden, and all I want is for you to tell me you don't hate me and that you still love me."

All my words have fled for dark corners. Silence is my only weapon, and I maintain it.

"Fine! *Fine*, fuck you! You dick! You fuck! Who are you? Who are you supposed to be right now? You're an asshole! Fuck you! You think you're cool, sitting there? You're torturing me, right now, and I know—this isn't you, because I know that you love me and you'd never be this much of a *fucking asshole* to me. This is ... this is just ... *so* fucked up, you're acting like a child, you're being a little fucking baby. I don't even care anymore. I don't care. You had your chance. So, whatever, keep sitting there, you can't even be enough of a man to *look me in the eyes*."

She's right, I'm not looking her in the eyes; I haven't looked at her once since she arrived home. The ceiling, the walls, the peninsulas of wax in the carpet—everywhere but her face.

Marti sobs: "Just tell me what I did. Tell me what I did. Tell me why you're being like this."

And here I go.

With a great guttural heave I push those four ferrous words over the precipice of my bottom lip:

"Because you're a liar!"

"What?" she says.

It comes a bit easier the second time: "You're a liar."

"What the fuck are you even talking about?"

But the weight of my accusation engages some pulley system and her eyes are drawn towards the closet. She catches them, though, and manages, with her corneas jittering, pupils contracting, lids shivering with anaerobic effort, to keep her gaze on me, but it's too late: I know that she knows. She sways for a second—

"What are you talking about?"

—but says it this time with no conviction, says it with the same slow force as the second half of a cleansing deep breath, the yogic expelling of bad fumes. And it's all bad fumes, now. She knows that I know, too, and shakes her head trying to shake into order the consequences of this knowledge. She's angry: I can see her assembling an accusatory sentence about how she can't believe I'd read her diaries without her permission, but I can see, too, that she knows the dauntless degree to which my transgression is dwarfed by hers. Her lashes are glued into isosceles chunks and the whites of her eyes have dimmed to sunset-orange; her lips are warped; she's wearing a shiny moustache of mucus.

"You don't understand—"

I should leave. But where can I go? Oh, what I wouldn't give to have a friend I could call, whose couch I could crash on, who could validate my cruel stoicism with a few *fuck yeah*s and *sure thing*s. But my only friend is Marti. I long ago closed the iris on everyone else, and kept her, only her, right there in the spotlight circle of my attention and affection and dedication. I haven't had time to be a buddy or pal to all my buddies and pals.

She's still pleading: "You don't *understand*."

"Understand what? How amazing it was?"

Whatever justification she is searching for is too insubstantial, just vapour, she can't get hold of it.

"Fuck, it wasn't—"

She pushes her fingers up through her hair and curls them into fistfuls, standing inverse akimbo with her elbows over her head, still shaking her head, perhaps unable to believe that it came this far, that the secret she thought buried forever was disinterred and dropped onto our apartment floor, upon which, for these three years, we have shared so much boredom and tenderness. This ugly thing, neither boring nor tender. It's quite obvious: she just doesn't know what to say. A grin, now. And in this moment the show seems to be over. Airs deflated, pretensions distended. Such sportsmanship, admitting defeat like this!

She says: "I didn't mean to lie, I just—"

But her grin stretches too wide, becomes a grimace, and in a machine-gun burst of blubbering she collapses spectacularly to her knees. In the fog of her wailing I catch an utterance or two; she's singing back-up harmonies behind the melody of her own ascending and descending sobs: "I didn't mean to."

Marti draws in a long, wet sniffle, rolls onto her knees, and crawls across the carpet towards me. Not in a lithe, shoulder-rolling, cheetah-like manner; in the manner of a toddler, for whom crawling is the unconscious solution to the problem of the distance between point A and point B. She crawls to my lap and puts her chin in the divot between my knees.

"I lied," she says to the inseam of my jeans. "I lied, I'm sorry, please believe me."

How pathetic and grotesque this is. All her crawling and bawling. I can see, now, that it's an affectation. Everything she's doing, everything she's done: a collection of gestures designed to draw out my sympathies. A grand performance, amazingly sustained: just think back to the beautiful tears she shed in the hotel bed, the dry-throated tale-telling delivered with such a raw and tragic vocabulary.

Still, this is how I like Marti: a spilled puddle, wrecked and ruined, nowhere to go and no one else to turn to. Just me. How long, I wonder, can I resist putting my hand on her head and stroking her hair, or rolling her soft little earlobe between my thumb and forefinger? But better, I think, to deny her the thing she wants?—which is a sound or gesture that suggests that we're not irrevocably severed, that there is still an *us*. Doesn't matter, though. She makes the gesture herself. She takes my hand and puts it on her head and guides it in a stroking motion through her hair. We sit like this for a while, until my lap is damp with guilty breath and expiatory tears.

We'll never speak of this night again, but the truth, now released into the open air like a toxic agent, will slowly poison us. First we'll suffocate; with no breath to speak words, a black silence will grow between us. Then we'll go blind, unable to look at one another, instead the floor, instead the ceiling, instead anything else. Then our skin will become irritated; even a glancing touch, even *proximity*, will ignite flutters of revulsion in our chests. After that, death; no feeling, no memory; we will cease to occupy the same mortal plane, and it'll be off to our individual afterlives, she'll move in with her mother, I'll move in with my father, and we'll relearn our basic bodily functions under new environmental conditions.

Already we've been changed by it. As Marti sits here half in my lap, all the heft she once held, the liquid density of victimhood that anchored her so heavily to the ground, that kept me a groundling, too — it's gone from her. It's been transferred over to me. Victimhood! I'm heavy with it. When I put my hand, finally, on her back, she arches her spine, cat-like, to feel the pressure, to make sure it's really there, and when I run my palm in circles, it's as if I'm drawing on her back some magical glyph of clemency, because she vomits out a chain of sobs so long it's almost a minute before she's able to draw in another breath. Still sitting kingly like this, I let her climb upon me and kiss my face and neck with her wet, desperate lips. She folds up my head in her arms and tries to absorb me by pressing the bridge of my nose through her sternum. I can't breathe; I have to push her away.

Why am I so angry? Not because the Lie has invalidated *her* but because it has invalidated *me*. I gave up my friends to make her feel safe, I gave up four thrilling years of youthful indulgence and accomplishment because she couldn't live without me, and it turns out she's not in danger, it turns out she has managed to live just fine without me. Who am I, now, if I'm not the best thing that ever happened to this girl? What am I worth? Nothing.

And suddenly, I'm thrilled. *This* thrills me. This tipping over of our world together, the big spill of affiliations and affinities we've spent years organizing into drawers and cubbies and plastic tubs. This new, unknown person, just inches away. I have no feelings for this stranger; I could do anything to her.

We tip forward onto the floor. A squall of hands, pulling at this, grabbing at that, bunching up and stretching, snapping off and yanking away. Her fingers fumble at my chest, but I knock them away. Her thighs vise my hips and try to pull me down, but I twist out of her grip. She lets her hands fall to the floor; they lie palm-up at her shoulders in a casual gesture of surrender. She's perfectly still, now, flat on the floor, chin dipped slightly to one side, looking down her nose at me. Her nipples are so pale that they've disappeared into the opaline landscape of her rising, falling breast.

All those things she asked me to do: I do them now without her guidance; I do them now with the force of purpose I could never before muster; I do them now as if I *want* to do them. And she lets it happen. A handful of hair in one fist, a gathered-up fistful of her small breast in the other. Her nipples, now knotted, indelicately pinched and twisted to the limits of resistance, pulled away like berries plucked from a branch, her whole breast distorted, conical, dropping droplet-like back into place. Her thin wrist in one hand. With the other, the taut wires in her throat are strummed, then plucked, then clutched like the stems of a bouquet. The pocket of air caught between my swung palm and the outside of her thigh cracks like gunpowder. An electric sting with each *smack!* against her legs, thighs, breasts. We seemed always to melt into each other, to become, at our meeting middles, even when those meeting middles were ends and edges, a single amorphous compulsion, a mixed-up swirl, an invisible entity like the blurry and oblong force that separates two opposing magnets. But I'm aware, as I drop my hips hard against hers, and lift, and drop, that there is nothing blurry or oblong or invisible about us; we are two hard, sharp objects, colliding; two magnets electrically drawn and clapping violently together. Again: *smack!* My fingers tingle with false sympathy.

So much air between us, getting caught in all these divots and hollows, pressed out in burps and smacks. The sound of it is so ridiculous; the ridiculousness makes me angry; so I do it harder. Everything, harder, faster. Just like she always wanted.

I loved Marti because she was broken. And now that I've discovered that she is unbroken, I am trying to break her. I am thinking: maybe if I do something terrible we can be united once again—this time by our terrible deeds.

Okay.

Okay, okay.

Hoo!

Hah!

I'm ready.

This is going to be easy.

What is this? Like, ten feet? *Maaaaybe* twelve.

Just have to hop across to that narrow metal rail, that floor beam half-extracted from its scabbard in the undercarriage, and dance down its length on my tippy-toes, then, with my built-up momentum, I'll heave myself across the open expanse and into the main cabin, the still-smouldering sun of this junk galaxy, which is generally level and has plenty of handholds and footrests with which I can safely clamber to within arm's length of my prize.

Yes, I'm going to do it.

But give me a second.

I have to steel myself.

I have to smuggle back a bit of courage from when I was—

—five years old, a Sunday morning daredevil in a blue flannel jumpsuit, and, while my mother sleeps late, I climb the back of the couch, swing a leg over the wooden railing that separates our split-level kitchen and living room, hoist myself up, and, balanced there, with my duck-footed feet sheathed in crinkly white plastic, race from one end to the other. I never fall; I never hurt myself. I have the dumb luck of the reckless.

—nine years old, and my long and lonely walks home from school are endured only by narcotizing myself with elaborate reveries. I walk, heel to toe, on the edge of the concrete curb, and, across the street, assembled on lawns and driveways, is a cheering crowd—my schoolmates, my family, my favourite television personalities, and a panel of blank-faced judges marking tens on scorecards. I am the best in the world at walking on curbs. Empirically, this is true. The sportscasters are saying it right now, as they analyze, in slow-motion instant replay, the impossible precision with which the toes of my sneakers roll and raise and reset, one in front of the other, over and over, for blocks and blocks and blocks.

—fourteen years old, in mid-air, bent at the waist, palms together, colluding with gravity to execute this perfect dive, now pushing the tips of my fingers through the flat surface of

Walsh Lake, now swallowed by the cold from chest to groin to calves to toes, now feeling that jolt in the middle of my chest, now blowing bursts of oxygen through my nostrils as with a single beatific stroke I turn myself sunward and emerge into the light and the heat. My father applauds from the dock and hollers: "Ohhh, the Ukrainian judge only gives him an 8.7, but, *yes*, can you *believe it*, a perfect ten from the Japanese, he's going home with *the gold medal*!"

—twenty-three years old, just months ago, I'm leaving my apartment, on my way to work, and I step out into the nuclear-bright sunshine, feel the atoms on the surface of my body shuffle apart (in the heat I'm minuscule fractions of a centimetre taller and wider), and breathe deep of the beautiful decaying-chlorophyll reek of downtown Bangkok in dry season. Have I ever been happier, more fully alive and in touch with my body and its relationship with the physical world, than I am right now?

( ).
( ).
( ).
Made it!
Ha!
I counted down from ten, and, with only a half-second pause after reaching minus-three, broke into a sprint and

crossed the hanging floor beam on the balls of my socked feet. I stepped lightly because I was worried that the railing, which, as you can see, is no thicker than my girlish wrist, might bend beneath my weight, but I'd stupidly forgotten that my ascent was thus far made using pins and screws and bolts as handholds and footholds, and navigating the skinny rail was really no more precarious than strolling heel to toe on the edge of that curb. The difficult manoeuvre came when I reached the end of the beam and faced the gap that separated it from the nearest jut of the main cabin's torn-up floor. But my body, despite these centuries of sloth, reacted with athletic grace. I landed skidding on my knees and almost skipped right through the centre aisle and out into oblivion. But I was able to grab one of the intact stanchions of the wall that once separated business class from commercial (the atmosphere's violent act of social justice has annihilated these distinctions of class).

The main cabin is frozen at a pretty perilous degree of declination. It's the largest remaining chunk, the thorax from which the head and tail of the plane were wrenched. The whole right side is missing where the erupting engine blasted it away, but the slanted floor is intact, and there are still a few rows of triplicate seats, just like my Throne, arranged in their marching formation. It's a picture book's cross-section diagram. On the other side, the curving half-pipe wall and ceiling remain whole, the overhead compartments still baffled, jaws agape, one mouth, in its terror, barfing up a dry-cleaning bag. Two breathing masks, clear plastic tendrils with yellow cone heads, are turned to face each other as if to say: seriously, can you fucking believe this?

Using the chair legs as rungs and hooking my burnt, underpant-wrapped hand around the seatbacks, I descend to the front of the tipped-forward cavern, where, with my foot wedged against the front wall of the cabin and my hand gripping the accordion flap of a seatback pocket, I can reach out and just about touch my prize.

You'd think it would have flapped farther away. But ... I don't know: pressure waves, surface tension, centrifugal force, the Will of God — they all must have conspired to bring it back to me. When I first spotted a corner of it shyly peeking out from the steel cadaver's cracked ribs, I could hardly believe what I was seeing. It must (I thought) just be one of those in-case-of-emergency instruction cards, or an inflight magazine, or maybe the pony-tailed guy's copy of *The Beach*.

But, no: that yellow gunshot type was unmistakable.

Suicide Squad. By John Ostrander, Luke McDonnell & Karl Kesel.

Issue #23, Jan 89, U.S. $1.00, CAN $1.35, U.K. 50p.

Approved by the Comics Code Authority.

After darting from my tray table into the sunny crevice, the comic, in its plastic slipcover, must have looped around for a while in the stratosphere, pushed and pulled by colliding currents of wind, then, in the vortex created by the plane's earthward thrust, was somehow sucked back in to the rocketing shell of the main cabin and dragged down with it until the precise moment all the atoms of earth refused to continue their vital vibrations.

(And let me take a moment to congratulate that little snatch of adhesive tape on the polyethylene bag, which, though frail with age and further weakened on its sticky side by a fur of dust-specks, prevented my comic and its contents from escaping into the sky.)

But now that I'm standing here in front of it, I'm hesitant to touch it. What if, like the slices and shreds and scraps I used as rungs to climb up here, it remains immovable? What if I can't open it? What if it's iron-hard, like a welded plate, and my ascent has been for nothing? What if—

—oh, Jesus, Daniel!

Of course it will move.

All these convenient new rules of physics have brought me this far—why would they now deny me the chance to see you again?

I'm just ... nervous, I guess.

During my first years on my Throne, when I soothed myself with all those reruns of sexual profligacy, I indulged, too, in revisiting the many long sessions I spent staring at your picture. Even before my sense-memory was super-powered, I could identify each perforation along its edge, each topographic crease. That lustrous square of paper, that colourless constellation of pixels, that internal account of sonic waves, that rough sketch of life, that blurry organic curlicue. You wanted to know, before, why I was weeping over the loss of this comic?

Because, my love, tucked inside the pages is a lovely little portrait of *you*.

That, the doctor pointed out, is the head.

That, he told us, is the left leg.

This, he announced, is your daughter.

—10—

"I'm pregnant," your mother says, and because I have
nothing more than stunned silence to contribute (seven whole
minutes of it), we mutually agree that I should take a few days
for the news to settle (*settle*, I imagine, much the same way
a hangover seems to be a cloud of swirling particles within
your body that only time and stillness can draw down to the
soles of your feet, allowing, at length, for sober consideration).
When we stand to say goodbye, now with the unfathomable
matter of human life between us, it feels right to embrace, or
even to make eye contact, but instead we mark the unfamiliar
ceremony with our eyes on the floor and a handshake that
feels just as foreign as that first handshake on the muddy
streets of Poipet (this time, though, the topography of her
hand feels right; soft where it should be soft, rough where it
should be rough).

Disappointment, disgust, dread; this is what I remember
of the three days that followed. But they weren't days of de-
liberation. No, I already knew what I was going to do. And
so, instead of reflecting judiciously upon the little cellular
circumstance in Carrie's womb, I passed the time until our
next meeting in gluttonous fashion. I spent an entire day at

the Paragon Cineplex, roving from movie to movie, lunching on popcorn, supping on chocolate, snacking on dried squid-strings, hiding between the four walls of the theatre, which, as far as I allowed myself to know, were the furthest borders of the universe, the dimensional barriers of space-time itself. I wandered through shopping malls, through minimalist stereo stores and barren clothing boutiques, ejecting crisp thousand-baht bills into cash registers as fast as they were ejected from the cash machine and into my wallet. I went alone to lonely pubs for lonely pints (for dramatic effect alone), and spent a lot of time with Erin Seeley, flexing my muscular fantasy form, watching her bend in supplication and lap cat-like at the trigger (then we'd go for a sunset coffee at a Viennese café). I rode the river taxi all the way up to Nonthaburi and back; a young Buddhist monk came aboard at the Bang Chak pier, and, convinced that he possessed some secret arcane knowledge learned in the monastic stillness of the wat, perhaps transferrable through some ingenious aphorism, I had to fight the urge to share with him my astronomical news. *Excuse me, sir, sorry to bother you, but can you tell me: does everything change, does nothing remain without change?* But I didn't bother the poor guy. Instead, I shrugged off the weight of responsibility onto the reliable shoulders of my love chum, Fate, and gave myself up to this epic domestication.

Yes, I decided that I would let your mother decide.

This, right now, is the meeting we've arranged to discuss our shared quandary. But just look at the location we've chosen: Summer/Winter, the award-winning restaurant, aglow in soft candlelight, ahum with ambient electronica, amok with French cheeses and erotic Eastern-fusion entrees. We've made the mistake of turning this arbitration into a date. Just look at how your mother is dressed for the occasion: a casual cotton beach dress rendered formal with a fat belt, shoes with heels and a hundred criss-crossing straps, makeup so adeptly applied that it appears she's not wearing makeup at all. Just look at the way I'm dressed: a Dolce shirt strategically unbuttoned, sleeves rolled up, feigning informality, feigning contemplation while I wait for her to tell me what we're going to do:

"I don't know how to feel," she says. "On one hand, it's a baby, it's a human life, it's a *huge* deal. It will change our lives completely. But, on the other hand, it's just a baby, and how many thousands of babies are born every day? You know what I mean?"

"Yeah, I guess people make it work, even when it's not... like, an *ideal* situation."

"But I don't want to just *make it work*. That's not how I want to start a family. That's just..." She shakes her head. "I have old-fashioned ideas about it, I guess."

"That's not old-fashioned," I tell her. "It's sensible."

"This whole thing, it has me thinking a lot about my family and how fucked up they are and how can you possibly control it, that passing along of your own family's fucked-upedness."

"Fucked up how?"

"The usual ways, I think. My mom and my older sister always at each other's throats, always stewing over some injustice or another, turning our house into this battleground. You know in the Civil War, how there'd be this fog, this mist from all the cannons? That's what it was like. A *fog* of anger. They'd recruit me to be a messenger, they'd pass notes and comments and warnings through me. Then I became their confidant. They'd both come to me to vent, they'd mine me for information under the pretext of asking my advice—should I do this, did she say that, where was she really?—and then they'd both end up pissed at me for selling them out. That was really the only time they got along: when they were angry at me for revealing their secrets and strategies."

Your mother is picking the tomatoes out of her salad, and I'm struggling right now to suppress my unpleasant habit of extrapolating from each tic and twitch a system of branching realities, trying not to imagine myself ten years from now, swatting away the stack of plucked-out tomato halves and screaming through the romantic quiet of the restaurant: *just don't order the goddamn salad with the goddamn tomatoes!*

"My dad and younger brother have this coach/player thing going on—their whole relationship was based on this cycle of instruction and encouragement and criticism and praise, over and over. It was completely predictable, like menstruation. Every year, according to the season, the sport, you could mark on a calendar when they'd be best pals, when they'd have their falling out, when they'd make up. He's in college, now—my brother, I mean. He's playing football in Florida, and my dad, whose whole life revolved around that kid, is suddenly empty. No more practices to go to, no more game film to examine.

He did that, you know. He bought an expensive camera and recorded all of Matt's games, then played them back and took notes. 'Look, the lineman's head comes up when they're about to blitz!' 'You'll never hit a curveball with your elbow so close to your body!' Hours and hours, every night, like fucking ESPN or something. And I can't help but wonder, what if he had pushed me like that? What if, when I was six and I sang a solo in the church choir, and everyone told me how beautiful my voice was, how I should be a singer, which, of course, is the kind of thing you'd say to a six-year-old, but, still, what if they'd redirected just a little bit of the energy they spent keeping my sister in check and building a pedestal for my brother and hired a vocal coach or sent me to music school or encouraged me in any sort of way? What then? I don't know. I was never brave enough to insist. I wasn't that type of kid. I did what I was told, I was obedient, I was good, I never asked for anything, and I was drowned out by all these screaming, pleading voices asking for *everything*, always, all the time."

Now she's spearing the plain arugula leaves, pushing them off to the side, excavating a foxhole where the hard-boiled quail's egg can hide, holding her fork loose and lazy like you'd hold a watercolour brush while stroking a wispy cloudscape.

"So, I grow up, I'm an adult, and I tell myself that I need to be more self-confident, I need to be proactive — when I want something, I should ask for it. And what happens then? Where does that get me? I end up pressuring some poor asshole to bring me along on his exotic overseas adventure, and he does, and now I'm alone. Which isn't so bad, I guess. My brother. He's not even a starter, you know. After all that work, he's a second-string player, a backup defensive back. He fucking *hates* football. You know what he loves to do? He loves to smoke weed and play video games. He could give a fuck. But he knows what he needs to do to make his father care about him, and so he does it. Me, I have no idea. I thought maybe *this* was it. This faraway place. But you know what? I've been here for almost six months, and they've called me twice. Six months, two phone calls. I left them behind and already they've forgotten that I exist."

She impales the egg, then leans her fork, still tine-deep in yolk, against the edge of her plate. She's finished, it seems.

"So I guess what I mean when I say I can't help thinking of my own fucked-up family and all the things that can go wrong, I'm wondering which of those mistakes I'm going to repeat, or, even worse, what horrible new mistakes I'm going to make by trying to correct theirs."

The waiter appears and gestures with a cupped palm to the disassembled salad in your mother's dish, and she nods for him to take it away.

"I'm not, like, *against* abortion," she says. "I have friends who have had abortions. I just don't take it lightly. I know the health care here, if you can afford it, is pretty amazing—but still, it's scary. I don't want to just decide, okay, I'm going to terminate it, and then wake up the next morning and feel like I made a terrible mistake. But I also don't want to have a baby without being a hundred million percent sure about it. Because I'm not ready to have a baby, yet."

"I'm not ready to have a kid yet, either," I say.

"But I feel like I *could*."

"I feel like *I* could, too."

"But *could* and *should* are two different things."

"Yes."

"I don't think I *should* have a baby."

"I don't think we should have a baby, either."

"But I also feel..."

She shrugs that amazing shrug.

"...I feel like I have everything I need here to survive. Like I'm a castaway on a lush tropical island. Did you ever watch *Swiss Family Robinson*? I was obsessed with that movie when I was a kid. I used to watch it over and over and have these elaborate fantasies about living in that big house on the beach with the elevator and all the gadgets built from coconuts. All alone, all by myself. We have everything we need, here. The hospitals are awesome. It's probably *way* cheaper to have a baby here, too. So what's the big rush to go home? It's not like I'm some pregnant runaway teenager, like I need to hold hands with my mom at Lamaze class, like I need some nurse to teach me how to burp a baby with a plastic doll. I'm twenty-two. When she had my sister, my mom was *younger* than I am right now. I'm not a kid. We're not kids. We don't have to run home, like we're in trouble or something. This is it, *right now*... this is what it's like to be *grown up*. I don't want to leave. I didn't leave when Chad left. Why should I leave now? Why should *we* leave? Why shouldn't we just stay and have a baby and forget what everyone else thinks and says and just do it the way *we* want to do it. Why not?"

Your mother is dressed for athletics, this morning. No cotton beach dress, no formal fat belt; she's swaddled in loose cotton shorts and a baggy T-shirt, hair tied messily back, again with those big sunglasses, which, in their versatile way, now seem an accessory of bereavement, some funerary flourish. Sneakers on her feet, too, and, yes, I've verified it, this is the first time I've seen her in sneakers: puffy white cross-trainers that reduce the proportions of her body back into childhood. She looks sixteen, fourteen, twelve. She looks like a kid, and I feel a paternal protective urge.

We arrive at Bumrungrad Hospital and check in at the front desk (all it takes is a passport, you know—these developing countries really know how to run a two-tier health care system). We wait for almost an hour in the expansive lobby. We leaf through the scattered newspapers, the indecipherable magazines. We stare at the wall. We say nothing. Your mother and I are both feeling self-conscious, I think. As if, in the shifting pH levels in the amniotic ocean, our little biological accident might sense the proximity of our bodies. So our hands move towards each other; my delicate, short fingers wrap around her mannish, knobby knuckles. By mimicking the language of a loving couple, we are hopefully assuaging your suspicions.

Eventually, a nurse appears. "You can come, for get ready," she says to your mother, and leads her away. With a tired twitch of his wrist, the doctor gestures for me to follow him into an examination room. He points at a chair. I sit. He sits down, too, in front of a computer, and moves the mouse around with the studious precision of a digital-illiterate. I rather despise small talk for the sake of making noise, but, right now, I'd welcome any banal comment about the weather or sports or politics (I never realized it until now, but look at him: square head, arrow eyes; he's a dead ringer for the deposed Prime Minister Thaksin!).

Soon your mother reappears, now wearing a knee-length green gown. Her arms are hidden, she's barefoot, and she looks even more like a child than she did in her sneakers. I try to restrain it, to recall those post-coital days, hiding, evading, what a hassle she seemed, what regret I felt about hooking up with her, but my heart nonetheless swells as she crawls up into the chair and looks over at me and exhales a nervous breath.

The chair hums and reclines and swings her waist and feet into the air. The stirrups slowly diverge and she is opened up to the cool air. She frowns and twists her lips into an absurd smirk and, I swear, if that expression had been on her face when I first met her in the streets of Poipet, it might very well have catalyzed something as unlikely and ridiculous as Love at First Sight.

Maybe it was.

Maybe it did.

As I sit here now, holding her hand, all my memories of us (the border, the hallways of Admissions America, her apartment) are cropped and coloured and texturized and sharpened and now seem to suggest that I have been or will soon be in love with her, even though, at this exact moment, I can't quite pull that feeling into focus.

The doctor squats on a low leather stool at your mother's side. The nurse opens a seam in the middle of the gown and farts clear jelly from a tube, makes a swirling cake-decoration all over your mother's flat stomach, while the doctor unholsters a plastic phaser gun with a tulip-bulb barrel; he uses it to smear the jelly, and the faint quake of your mother's stomach muscles sequentially clenching beneath the tool's touch is familiar in an utterly inappropriate way. Can you blame me for doubting there is anything at all to see? But the doctor, yawning, pausing once to sneeze into his collar, again to scratch a persistent itch on the inside of his thigh, manipulates the white plastic bulb and the image on the flatscreen monitor oscillates. A black mass expands in the sea of static. A grey archipelago surfaces in the dark sea. Black shadows reveal topographic features on the largest of the grey islands. Now a white blotch pulses to the forefront. The doctor taps the screen, identifies the bright star in the messy midst of these swirling black and grey tones.

"Right here." His fingers drum sonorous bass notes from the picture tube. "Right here, right here. You see?"

There you are: a tiny human form in profile, curled up on itself, tadpolesque. "Is only this big," Doc says and holds his thumb and finger less than an inch apart.

"Crazy," your mother says.

"You want picture?" the nurse asks.

I nod my head.

Your mother's warm bed. Your mother's cold apartment. Of course we spend that night together; we're still improvising happy couplehood for your benefit. We even make love (in consideration of you, our little budding bulb, we do it gently, slowly, with the lights off and the blanket shoulder-high, with a lot of soft caresses and eye contact and close-mouthed kissing). Reclined and pressed shoulder to shoulder in the narrow breadth of her bed, emitting heat like a switched-off lightbulb, she asks me:

"What are your parents going to think? Happy? Fake-happy? Sad? Happy-sad?"

"I don't know," I say. "Happy, I think. Or flawlessly fake-happy. My dad will wish I were back home. He'll offer us a place to stay, money, babysitting services, undying devotion."

"Not your mom?"

"She'll be fake-happy, too."

"But not one of those baby-crazy grandmas?"

"She wasn't even a baby-crazy mom, so ..."

Your mother lets that last syllable die with dignity.

"What about yours?" I ask. "Happy-sad? Their daughter-in-exile, so far away. Do you think they'll want you to come home? I mean, they will, won't they?"

"Maybe."

"It'll be hard for them to be so far away."

"Maybe, yeah."

"But not for you?"

She shrugs; a distant, deformed cousin of that cute, self-aware shrug I remember from our first meeting. "I just don't feel that connection that I think you're supposed to feel. I never have. I feel completely detached from everyone — my parents, my brother and sister. It makes me kind of scared. For this one, I mean." She pats her still-flat abdomen.

I shimmy down the bed, lean close to your mother's tummy,

and with my lips hovering beneath her belly button, where I imagine you might be floating, say: "But you'll love us. Won't you, my love?"

"She'd better," your mother says.

"We're very worldly and cool and good-looking," I tell you. Your mother laughs.

"And you're going to be worldly and cool and good-looking, too."

It seems that your mother and I have found a solution to our respective dilemmas. Didn't find it — created it. We created it, and your mother is keeping it locked safe and simmering to thickness in her womb. What seemed at first to be a grave mistake is instead ingenious. I'm giddy with this realization! Placed in my hands is a life that, even before it begins, is a trillion times more fascinating than my own. A life, in genetic terms, that *is* my own. A duplicate little me to ponder! What is a child if not a physical manifestation of our innate human narcissism? A little piece of ourselves to love. Don't you hear that all the time? That fathers see themselves in their sons? That mothers see themselves in their daughters?

As you, in your unthinking chrysalis stage, are stitching together the organic material that will help you survive this planet's peculiar trials of chemistry and physics, a funny thing happens: I feel, in the shadow of the colossal responsibility that looms over me, strangely *unburdened* of all responsibility. Something familiar takes the place of my manic, phobic, my-opic self-interest: the blithe childhood feeling of nothingness all around me; all tangents of worry and censure swallowed up by cosmic matters like the Creation of Life and the Eternal Responsibility of Parenthood.

But perhaps *nothingness* is the wrong word to use. The sensation I'm trying to describe is quite the opposite; a consciousness not rooted in *nothing*... rather, in *everything*. So, a *blithe feeling of everything*, eternity, the infinite expanse of life. Finally, a chance to make corrections, to live through it all again and, this time, to do it right! The great casting off of my useless, fruitless past! The great big brutal edit! The unburdening, the unfurling, the maturing of Daniel Solomon! Yes, for a while it's all fine, it's all dandy, it's all just wonderful. Our prodigious little tadpole each day grows in million-molecule iterations, steadily becoming just like me and just like Carrie.

And your mother feels it, too. I'm sure of it. The unfurling and unburdening. She even lunches, one afternoon, with Chad Billings, and tells him our good news, to which, from her reports, he reacted with a satisfying blend of genuine gladness and suppressed envy (and though my interrogation about the deeper mood of their meeting is cunning, I can tell, from her equivocal half-answers, that there are still secrets she keeps from me, that the sentient entity that was Carrie-and-Chad maintains a consciousness closed off from mine). She sends a giddy mass email to her friends: the former members of her high school clique, the loyal and loving hair salon colleagues, and the few distant acquaintances she's collected during her abbreviated term at university. The replies are unanimously enthusiastic, all exclamation marks and smiley-faced emoticons, and come with queries about due

PART II

dates and sexes and the mysterious virile chap responsible (tell
them I'm the son of an Eastern European dictator, I suggest,
living in exile, obscenely rich, above the law). Many want
to know when your mother is coming back to Columbus to
have her baby, but she eludes these questions by remarking
on the scarcity of flattering maternity wear and her struggle
to survive, in her variable state, the stunning summer heat.

I thought it was a cruel twist of fate that your mother
rescued me on that first sun-scorched afternoon. My self-
seeking journey felt threatened; I worried that I wouldn't be
able to resist that department-store catalogue beauty. And I
suppose I couldn't. But what I didn't see in her then I can see
in her now: that she's the one who needs to be rescued, to
be protected: from her dumb family, her dumb friends, the
sad fate awaiting her back in suburban America. I am worth
something to her. And she is worth something to me — an
anchor keeping me moored here in Paradise.

We're a happy couple, these days. We embark on ambitious
shopping trips to appease the savage materialism of her nesting
instinct, stroll through the soft jazz and hard fluorescence
of Paragon Mall, through myriad stores, arms hooked
in shopping bags, smiling wide smiles. I stay over at her
apartment, or she stays over at mine, and we lie awake deep
into the night, discussing the particulars of our accidental
family unit: the details of childhood most vital to future
confidence and contentment. Phone calls with her mother and
father and sister have become more frequent, and with each
carefully plotted conversation she is less and less embittered
and cynical by the very notion of parents and children and
the abiding, impossible bond between them.

Yes, our perfect future is taking shape, and for the first time in a long time, since I stupidly gave everything up to be the best thing that had ever happened to a person, there feels to be a path beneath my feet, and I have a vision, however indistinct, however chopped up by the horizon's stratified glimmer, of where I will be tomorrow, and a week from now, and a year from now (the days and weeks and years had begun to compress themselves even back then).

A thousand miles from home, bound up by the collapsing star in her cervix, your mother and I are building a path towards our happy ending.

But, then—

The middle of the night.

Darkness.

I'm standing in a doorway. My eyes quickly adjust.

She's sitting on the closed toilet, recovering from what was, if duration and intensity can be derived from the circumference of the wadded-up toilet tissue in her fist, a pretty torrential cry. I flip on the bathroom light and her complexion blossoms, blotchy bursts in her cheeks and forehead. Her eyes, usually blue, are dimmed a dreary grey and shrunk to three-quarter scale. I sit across from her on the edge of the bathtub and use the heels of my hands to stroke hard circles on her upper back. But when she leans her forehead into the crook of my neck, she keeps her arms folded over her belly.

"Are you okay?" I ask.

"It's just hormones," she tells me. "It's just nothing."
But it's not, because then—

We're walking through Benjasiri Park on a Saturday afternoon, on the shady path that follows the perimeter, past the basketball courts, past the fountain. We weave between old shuffling couples, juke around kids chasing pigeons, sidestep joggers running sweaty circuits. On our way to the mall (again!) because your mother wants new sheets, new curtains, a rocking chair (no, not that one, the *nice* one, the glider with the upholstered back—*no*, the *black* one). She seems to have a very clear vision for this yet-to-exist nursery, but lately, when I suggest that we look at new apartments (like, maybe a Western-style condo with a real kitchen, with separate rooms, with space for all three of us) she responds with a medley of thoughtful nods and considerate squints and deliberative *hmm*s, as if the very concept of living together is just now metastasizing... then she quickly changes the subject:

"I would love to walk, like, ten feet without bumping into someone or getting bumped into. I could scream. I constantly feel on the verge of a panic attack."

"Maybe claustrophobia is a thing you can develop when you're pregnant."

She sneers, scoffs, shakes her head in disbelief.

"I'm serious. You keep telling me that your body feels all fucked up. Food tastes different, you get crazy motion sickness on elevators. Maybe it's one of those weird pregnancy things."

"It's always been like this, though. I could never spend more than an hour in Chatuchak without losing my mind."

"I thought you used to go to Chatuchak almost every weekend?"

"Don't you find it overwhelming sometimes?" she asks, and flips her palm to indicate the hundreds of miles around us.

"Here?"

"Yeah."

"This beautiful park? This beautiful, idyllic park?"

"This park full of concrete and exhaust fumes and diseased birds?"

"Is it that bad?"

"And, *God*, the *heat*!"

The purring electric motor is blowing ice-cold exhalations that swirl in circles on the ceiling. Sticky heat beneath the sheets. Your mother's sleeping body, back turned, is beside me. I am awake, despite my best efforts. I've been studying the stucco ceiling for hours, considering the perfectness of our perfect future. Here, among her things, her photographs and lotions and books and pillows and stuffed animals and colourful cotton undergarments curled on the floor like living things in the throes of death, the lurking sense of disconnection I've had since we first met is amplified: we are two ill-fitting puzzle pieces; we lack interlocking tabs and slots. Just as quickly as she once converted me with her sweet speech about being a castaway on a lush island, about being grown up and fighting the urge to run home, she has lately begun to reflect aloud on the obverse—at first in the rhetorical mode, asking questions that she quickly answers with a dismissive head-shake, then proposing tricky logic problems that press the most vulnerable pressure-points of our exile's life: among them, the overpowering nostalgia of youth, and the desire to recreate that specific experience. We have figured this out almost immediately: that a parent wants only to (1) replicate exactly his or her own childhood, and (2) correct with severity all the fatal mistakes of that childhood. But I'm worried now about the truce we've established. The fragility of it is evident to me only during these anxious, wakeful nights.

Those little girls there: no older than ten, in their school uniforms, sitting on the concrete steps of the pedestrian overpass, sharing a roti with alternating stabs of toothpicks. They chatter like birds; that magical, animal language. We pass them on our way to the office (for weeks we've been arriving and leaving together; Rob Sangran and P'Milk and the others haven't had to make inquiries; our status as proximate, parallel entities is clear). Your mother is drinking a smoothie, this morning, and draws on her straw until the silent sucking-up sound turns to roaring static. "To me, childhood is all about riding bikes and playing in parks and being out in the open—you know, making mud pies in someone's backyard, building a fort in the woods. Living in a neighbourhood. Having a community of people around you.

I can't imagine being a kid in a place like this. I can't imagine not having this whole open world around you to explore."

We descend the stairs on the opposite side of the overpass, out onto a precarious slab of sidewalk barely wide enough for both of us. An armless beggar is slumped against the concrete wall, his knees folded tight, practically tucked into his armpits. Your mother manages to step around him, and, with her back to me, with her fists planted in the small of her back (she's not even showing yet and already she's appropriated this child-bearing posture), watches the oncoming crawl of traffic.

I add, jauntily, cloyingly, with needles hidden in all the vowels: "I think it would be amazing to grow up in a place like this."

She sees a cab in the distance, swirls her hand at waist-level to flag it down.

"Of course you would."

I guess it should have been apparent to me, huh? Having lived for a second time through those contemplative first weeks, I can't believe I didn't hear the utter lack of conviction in your mother's voice when she said things like "I've always wanted to run away," and "I feel like I have everything I need here to survive." The timbre of it. The pitch. The vocal fry and upturned end-syllables. Eighty percent of everything she said back then was false bravado, and the other fifth was a commixture of blind hope, subjective assumption, and good, old-fashioned delusion. Not quite the elaborations of a bad liar — the elaborations, rather, of someone who isn't quite persuaded by their own subliminal coaxing. I am willing to believe that she wasn't conscious of doing it—of stringing me along, of building this bad case, of presenting this circumstantial evidence. But I'm not willing, yet, to forgive her. Because look where I ended up: separated from you by hundreds of horizontal miles, thousands of vertical feet, and one or one million immeasurable units of Time. After all those brave statements about forgetting what everyone else would think, about doing it the way we wanted, about building something from scratch, it turned out that all she wanted was to take you away from me. And that's exactly what she tried to do. That's exactly what she *did*:

A sweltering afternoon. A cloudless eggshell sky. A light mist of rain. A depressing non-day filled with difficult traffic and passive cabbies, sidewalk bottlenecks and dawdling pedestrians, baleful stray dogs and braying pop songs, slow internet connections and obtuse autocorrections, off-centre sips of soda that dribble down my chin and asymmetrical forkfuls of food that fall in my lap, a thigh-thumping lump of coins in my pocket and not a single purchase cheap enough for me to use any of them. This is pure existential frustration, the spinning earth is out of sync, I'm a step ahead or behind of where I should be. If I could just, ha-ha!, *stop time!*

At this hateful arrhythmic pace, I stomp to your mother's apartment. I have a few hours to kill before I'm supposed to meet Benz for dinner later in the evening (he has finally convinced me to go out for chicken and rice, to learn the secret cipher that will reveal to me why he's uniquely qualified to attend MIT in the fall) and have been trying all afternoon to call her but can connect only to her voicemail, and now I'm in a dangerous cool state, prepared to exert my coolness with severity. But I should cut myself some slack: out of the rain, in the elevator, my temperament warms up, a half-day of hoarded irritation turns to steam and wafts harmlessly out of my collar and cuffs and waistband. I'm eager to see her. I'm eager to rub her belly and say hey, hello, how's it going in there?

Down the hallway. I stop at your mother's door. Through the door I can hear her voice. She's talking to someone. I stand with my back against the adjoining wall and lean forward, line up my ear with the edge of the door frame and listen. It doesn't sound like your mother's voice. Not her normal speaking voice. It's a baby-talk drawl, a squish-lipped coo. She's saying:

"I know.

"Yeeeeeah.

"*Yeeeeeah.*

"But it's just that I miss you guys, too.

"Yes, totally.

"He said that? Oh my *God*, that's *so* cute that he'd say that!

"I miss him, too! I miss my baby bruvver.

"Yeeeeeah, my *baby bruvver.*

"I know.

"Oh, I know, I know.

"I want to …

"Yeah, I totally want tooooo …"

The projected humiliation of catching her unawares subsumes my curiosity; to atone for my stealth, I backtrack a few steps so I can make a plodding racket as I approach the door.

When I knock, she's already saying goodbye in her natural inflection, which now sounds awkwardly formal. I push the door open without waiting; waiting would be strange; waiting would imply that I'd been listening.

"Hello?" I say.

Your mother is sitting on the bed, head down, examining her phone.

"Hey," she says. "I didn't think you were coming over."

"I tried to call, but your cell was busy."

She doesn't look up at me when she says: "I was talking to my sister. She called and so I called her back and the connection kept breaking up so I had to call her again and again."

"What did she want?"

"She didn't *want* anything. She just wants to know what's going on. But, anyways, that's why I was on the phone for so long."

They've been chatting a lot, lately, your mother and her sister. After months and months of neglect, those sprained familial tendons are regaining their tension. Where in the summaries of their conversations there used to be a lot of contempt and dark mockery (the word *cunt* was tossed around pretty liberally), there is now a lot of silence, a lot of furtive vagaries. And I'm about to find out why:

"She really wants me to come home," your mother says. There's such manufactured casualness in her voice that it crackles on the high notes; she's practically singing when she says it.

"Oh yeah?" I say.

Hear that? My manufactured casualness is much more artful.

"She wants me to have the baby in Columbus."

"Why?"

"She thinks this is a Third World country. She's worried about the medical care."

"...so you told her that she's a retard, because the hallways at Bumrungrad are filled with sheikhs in white robes because they fly here from Dubai and Saudi Arabia because the hospitals here are like five-star resorts?"

"She means well. I think she's worried that I don't have anyone here."

"*I'm* here."

"Like, friends and family."

"*I'm* here."

"I *know*," she says. "God, *relax*!"

Propelled by that last axe-chop syllable, your mother hops off the bed, crosses the room, and begins digging through her dresser. She opens the lowermost drawer, scatters the rolled-up T-shirts fastidiously arranged within. "I guess we can't even have a conversation about it without you jumping down my throat."

"A conversation about what?" I ask.

She ignores the question. "Or without you calling my sister a retard."

Your mother swims out of her ill-fitting souvenir T-shirt that says *Same Same* on the chest and *But Different* on the back and pulls on a tank top. She stomps out of her shorts and, as she bends to pull on a pair of jeans, I examine the inverted arches of tan flesh beneath the cotton hemline of her white underpants to see if, indeed, as she has been mournfully claiming these last few weeks, her ass is getting bigger (it is, I think).

I say to her: "A week ago, you said she was the worst person you know. Those were your exact words. 'My sister is the worst person I know.' You can't constantly be telling me what a cunt she is, all the shitty things she's done to you, and expect me to be sympathetic. Especially if she's trying to convince you to leave."

"She's not trying to convince me of anything."

I follow her into the bathroom, narrowly evading the still-open dresser drawer and the spilled-everywhere viscera of cotton shirts, and find your mother bent over the sink and washing her face. Months ago I was bent over this same sink, and she was massaging my temples with her thumbs and saying—

"Why did you stay? For a girl?"

"Of course."

"Why does anyone go anywhere or do anything?—"

Another vibration from inside my pocket.

"—you're either chasing or escaping."

"What are you trying to escape from?" I say.

"It's not escaping. *This*—" she makes an expansive gesture with her wet hands "—this is an escape. I'm *done* escaping."

"So you *do* you want to go home?"

She buys some time to think about her answer with a long breath and a drawn out shrug and an exasperated shake of the head, but all she comes up with is: "I don't know."

"Come on. Yes you do."

The surety in her voice is nowhere to be found in her gaze; the whites of her eyes are too dim. "Maybe," she says. "It might be nice."

"What might be nice?"

"It might be nice to have my baby back home."

"*Your* baby?"

"*Our* baby, I mean. It might be nice to have *our* baby back home, where I'm comfortable and know people and have family to help me out, oh my *God*, isn't that *crazy*, isn't that *impossible* to fathom!" She pushes past me, out of the bathroom, and I can feel myself trapped on the edge of a steep precipice, helplessly hanging on as squalls blast through and threaten to loosen my grip. Between gusts I gather enough calm to say:

"We agreed that we were going to, you know, figure things out and forget what everyone else thinks, and just—"

"We never agreed that we'd stay here. You just *assumed*—"

"You're right, we've never talked about this, and now you're suddenly making this huge massive decision without even asking me or telling me or—"

"Oh, right, *fuck me* for missing home! *Fuck* me for having an opinion about where I raise my child."

Sternly, now: "*Our* child."

"*My* body."

"*Our* baby."

"What do you want me to say? I miss boring Columbus. I hated it, but now I *miss* it."

How dare she doubt this place! She planted this idea in my head: that we could stay here, that this place was big enough for the three of us to be happy. It's just (I think to myself) your mother's recovered capacity for brutal, supercilious criticism. This (I convince myself) is just her nature. If she stopped complaining, if she stopped finding fault, she'd probably asphyxiate and die.

Her arms are crossed, now. "I'm sorry. I want to go back. I'm *going* back."

This is the Carrie I'm afraid of. The unpredictable Carrie lurking behind the bright banter and cute cooing: beholden to no logic, loyal only to her own shifting whims, suddenly dead certain of the very thing she was lately dead against, and with no hindsight to appreciate the contradiction.

With eerie composure, she adds: "And I love that you're arguing against me being close to my family. After everything I've had to go through with them—I thought you might be, like, *happy* for me or something, or proud of me, or supportive, but, I guess—" She has to catch her breath, here. "—I guess that's maybe too much to expect from someone who's *so close* to his family that he moves to another country and never talks to his mom or dad. I guess that's the *totally healthy* and *normal* relationship I should be aspiring towards. I know that being here is basically *all* that you have going for you, and the idea of going back home and having to live a *real, grown-up* life, having to be *responsible*, it probably feels like the end of the world for you, but it's just a place, get over it, there's no difference, here or there, you're still *you*."

Her sarcasm, when she draws from it such precise notes of pomposity and derision, paralyzes me with anger. And yet, I have to admit, I admire her when she conjures it so expertly. I admire the way she can make me feel calcified, turned hard from the inside out; my mouth doesn't feel like it's even moving when I say: "I'm leaving now."

"No, you're not," Carrie says.

"What?"

"You can't leave."

"Why not?"

"Because you can't say *our* baby *our* baby *our* baby and then walk out in the middle of this discussion like it doesn't matter."

"This is a discussion?"

"It's *supposed* to be, but you're not *listening*."

And here her secret is revealed:

I still matter. I am still vital to her vision of the future.

She refused to be cowed by her boyfriend's preference for exotic docility, she refused to flee weeping for home when she was abandoned, she refused to abandon the yield of our reckless night together because she saw that it could be something wonderful. And she refuses, now, to be defeated, and returning to Columbus alone and pregnant and resigned to single-motherhood would, for her, be a defeat. But to make that defeat brutally clear, I have to go, I have to go *right now* and force her to suffer the hot shame of being once again abandoned. I have to leave. Just like Chad Billings left. So I pull my best manoeuvre — a dismissive shake of the head, a smirk, a snicker, and I step towards the door.

"Fuck this," I say.

But your mother sidesteps, mirrors my movement, blocks my way.

I take another step.

She backs up against the door and stands with her fists stabbed into her hips, and I can see, now, how the few extra ounces you've added to her frame has given her posture a maternal denseness; she appears an immovable object.

"You're not leaving!" she says.

"You're totally right. Being here is all that I have. So I'm going to stay here. Have a good flight home."

I reach for the doorknob and she slaps my hand away. Through gritting teeth she emits a high-pitched animal noise that coalesces to form the words:

"You're *not* leaving!"

I reach for the doorknob again and she clutches my forearm with a falcon's overhand grip. "You're *not* leaving!"

But I do. She tries to close the door on me, really digs in with her heels, really yanks, but I manage to squeeze through, and when I'm on the other side I let the door slam shut with a violent *crack*.

I ignore the commotion. I march down the hallway. I am getting in the elevator. I am going to leave the building. I will get on the Skytrain. I will go to my apartment. I will disappear, I will become the void, and I'll prove to her that she needs me, that I am invaluable to her, that, in fact, she *cannot* leave me, and therefore cannot ever leave this place.

Hours later, I'm sitting in the passenger seat of Benz's Benz, speeding smoothly through the neon-streaked night. The tinted windows are set to a too-slow shutter speed; the city outside is a vibrant blur, a series of flashing images, dioramic mini-vistas of subtropical street life: barefoot ladies in yellow polo shirts incessantly sweeping, flower-choked gold statues beneath bejewelled porticos, vendors stirring red-hot alien goop in steel troughs, all inside a black cave of wires and arches and awnings and crumbling tenements, and the ceiling of the cave sparkling with signage, *Thai Massage, Coca-Cola, Tom Yum Restaurant, Kodak, British Pub, True Mobile, Hotel, Restaurant, Hotel, Coca-Cola, ID Photo, Restaurant, Guest House*, amongst all those indecipherable others with their elegant Khmer-ish curves.

Benz and I have just stammered and paused and politely laughed our way through another fruitless meeting. The little restaurant he chose was a stretch of slanted sidewalk occupied by little kindergarten stools, little plastic tables, each with its ration of chili sauce and pink napkins; the laminate menu featured various curryies, french freids, freid crap, fragrance rice, muscle chicken, and banal Sundays, but Benz insisted on ordering for me, and of course it was the chicken and rice.

"When I'm young," he told me. "My dad take me to this place, just me, not my sister or mum, and we have *khao gai.* But when I'm young, we don't have many money, so chicken and rice, for us, is very expensive. Right now, for us to have a big steak, is same same. My dad make thirty baht, one week. *One week*, only thirty baht. But we take bus for six baht and we have chicken and rice for twenty baht, and then we take bus home again for six baht, which is *thirty-two* baht, more than one whole week! For me, chicken and rice is food for poor people. Chicken and rice is for when I'm bored or when I'm hurry. But I come here and remember what is like for my dad, with no money. And it make me, uh … it make me stronger, to do harder work. I come here and it feel like before. Not now. I feel the same as when I'm young and with my dad, the same day. When I'm outside and is smell of cars and smoke, is like doing it again. This is why I go to school. This is why I go away for school. So I remember what is like to be my father. To, uh … to do the same thing as him, but better. But different. To be somewhere different, but make it the same. Understand?"

I nodded and ate my rice and made a half-decent show of being struck by the profound realization he was hoping to extort. I'm paid by the project, not by the hour, and my commission is stretched thin between all his tics and twitches and intonations. All I ever get are these impressions of his self-determined self—they mean nothing, they're not real. It's all a convenient arrangement of cherry-picked facts, the sum of which, he hopes, is the place he thinks he deserves to be.

The whole time we're driving, a dactylic double-bleat has been pleading for my attention: missed calls from your mother's number. Three of them. But I let her wait. Thrilling to be so cold, to deny a person something only you can give them. I feel, finally, the satisfaction that eluded me earlier, when it seemed nothing I said could convince her of the profound wrongness of what she was proposing. And all I had to do was leave. I left her apartment, and already her boldness, her brashness, her imperious proclamations about how things were going to be, about how it was *her* body, *her* decision—it's all gone. Employing just my absence, I've reduced all her bluster to this: despairing, conciliatory phone calls.

Now Benz is slipping through the gridlock, clipping a rambling bicycle cart, shooting out to join a phalanx of taxicabs on the main drag and eluding them with a series of wheel-spinning Indy-car manoeuvres that choke me with the shoulder belt. Approaching a barrier of brake lights, he makes a preposterous pair of near-perpendicular turns and swings into the inside lane; with a half-second to spare, a stray dog sniffing along the divider levitates sideways to avoid the Beamer's cruising front tire.

"Where you go?" Benz asks.

I give him the address of your mother's apartment. I am feeling magnanimous (must be the magical chicken and rice) and so have decided to check in on her, to accept whatever apologies she might offer.

Benz repeats my direction, "Sukhumvit Soi *sip-song*!" He laughs. "Your Thai sound good more than my English."

Soon we reach a puzzle of idling vehicles that even Benz's aggressive wheelwork can't solve. We're at the Asok intersection, and all ten lanes of the thoroughfare are crammed up, bumper to bumper, mirror to mirror. I roll down my window and stick out my head. Fat drops of rain drum my skull. Ahead of us, on the far side of the empty intersection, a wall of vehicles: cars and trucks lined up brick-like, police *motocy* clustered between them like mortar. A single policeman in a white helmet and yellow slicker stands in the centre square of crosswalk ladders, arms reaching, pressing with the power of Moses against the held waves of traffic. I look to Benz for an answer, but all he can give me is the universal pantomime of ignorance: a shrug, a hooked lip, a tented eyebrow. He leans out himself and appraises the situation. When he plops back into his seat, he has a big smile on his face. "Is King," he tells me over his shoulder. "Or maybe not King. Maybe Prince. Maybe Princess."

Of course, I think. The Royal Family. They own this very road, why shouldn't they reclaim it at will? This is paradise, after all, where the amazing is mundane: the divine appearance of a King or Queen, of an heir or heiress, is really just a minor traffic delay, a commuter annoyance.

A few minutes more and a black sedan fires through the intersection, followed by a sextet of speeding *motocy* cops in parallel formation, another black sedan, another, then a white truck that draws cheers from the gallery of pedestrians and vendors watching from the concreted walkway above us. Two more sedan-shaped bullets, and now the policemen scatter to their parked bikes. Moses drops his arms with a weightlifter's relief, and they all race off together after the convoy.

The Thursday evening honk-and-lunge resumes on Sukhumvit. We drive on.

What a fantasyland this place still seems, with its Kings and Queens, with its T-shirt-hawking peasants and their unconditional fealty, with tree roots breaking through the paving stones and creeping vines tying nooses around stone posts. The ancient jungle still lurks beneath the industrial cityscape. Before I was up here on the Throne, time had stopped, time had compressed, the future and past were all crashed together in the sleek and crumbling streets of Krung Thep. I never, ever, ever want to leave. I'll do whatever it takes to stay. This is the place I deserve to be.

Ten minutes later, I'm knocking on the door to your mother's apartment. No answer. I wait. My shoulders are wet with rain, my sneakers are soaked through and squelching. I knock again, and again there's no sound from inside, no croaking bedsprings, no approach of footfalls, so I try the door and find it unlocked. My first step inside almost takes me asswards to the floor, but my hand finds the door frame and my feet find their balance. A puddle of rainwater at the threshold; she must have just come home. I enter the room in squeaky baby-steps. All the lights are off, but the AC is hissing, the room is morgue-cold, the way your mother likes it when she sleeps.

"Hello?"

I see her, now: on the floor at the foot of the bed. Casual, it seems. Gently to one side, leaning on an elbow, legs crooked at the knee and enfolded beneath her; she's still in possession of that child's athletic facility to find comfort in the most awkward sitting positions. Did she fall asleep watching TV? Is this sexy slump prelude to another seduction? But it's an illusion cast by the shadows. She's not comfortably sprawled. As my eyes adjust to the dark, I can see that her shoulders are stiff, her torso awkwardly inclined, her legs not loosely bent but clenched together, toes pulling tight the tendons in her heels, whole lower body taut and shaking with exertion. Her free hand is flat between her thighs. The other, the one she's leaning on, is clutched in some strange yogic salute: thumb tucked, pinkie and ring-finger perfectly straight, pointer curled, middle finger folded flat and almost touching her wrist.

I sit on the floor next to her and brush back her hair. Her pallor is ghostly. "Are you okay?" She draws in a quivering breath. Her bottom lip sucks against her teeth and rattles there. This breath becomes a sort of moan, deep in her chest, like she's steeling herself to speak, and when she speaks she says: "I think I need to go to the hospital."

Here's the hot flood of fear I've been waiting for.

I ask: "Are you okay? Is it the baby?"

She shakes her head in a sidewise manner I can interpret neither as affirmative nor negative; she keeps shaking, no, yes, no, and now she's swivelling her head wildly, and so I grab her wrist and try to pull her hand out from between her thighs.

"Let me see," I say to her.

"No," she bellows. "Not yet, not yet."

My eyes, having reconciled with the dimness, can now see the dark bruises on your mother's legs. "What happened?" Blackish bruises like a fantasy map's imaginary continents. Bruises? Not bruises. Blood. Blood on her legs and puddled beneath her, beneath me, smeared by my shoes as I crossed the room, soaking now into the knees of my jeans.

The second deluge, my veins and capillaries flushed with a thicker form of dread, and I feel, from head to toe, like a mud-sculpted golem, jointless, muscleless, airless, inert: "Fucking Christ!"

"Not yet," your mother cries.

With my golem's lumbering dexterity I grab for my phone but in my panic I can't find the seam of my pocket and yank at the square protrusion on my hip as if I trying to wrench it through the fabric of my jeans. Pulling it out, finally, I freeze with my finger poised to strike the first note of alarm. What's the equivalent of 911 in Thailand? I have no idea. Your mother's incantation continues: "Not yet, not yet, not yet..."

So much blood. My knees are sticky with it. Polka-dot patterns on the keypad of my phone as I punch numbers.

Speeding, riding shotgun in the *songthaew*-style ambulance, I have my back to the windshield, I'm hurtling backwards through the city, watching through the rear porthole window as they do the usual things: press a mask to her face, apply clear tape to IV needles and absorbent pads. At every sudden stop I crack my back against the dash. A quick left turn sends me into the driver's lap. He tells me to turn around, but I pretend not to speak English; I keep my face pressed to that little window, just in case she looks up, just so that she'll know that I'm there, that I came when she called me.

No turmoil of lights and sirens when we arrive. It's all quiet and calm, just the jiggle-click of stretcher legs falling, just the friendly whisper of the electric doors sliding open. Doctors walk briskly but don't run, paramedics talk quickly but don't yell, patients in the waiting room don't moan and groan and clutch bloody stumps, they just glance up from their gossip magazines and, when they see how serenely we float about the slow-rolling bed, return to reading. A few technical pleasantries are exchanged, then her entourage sneaks discreetly into an elevator, the doors close, and now I am alone.

Anything, anything, anything to distract me! A heavy stack of coins still in my pocket. I count them out and march to the hospital café, where I wait in line behind a dashiki-draped man-mountain in deep contemplation of the breakfast menu. Can he get hash browns *and* boiled rice, he wants to know. I wait patiently, and when my turn comes, I order a sweet mocha variant of coffee. After a few syrupy sips, though, I'm racing to bathroom and—

Hgg!-huuuuh, nnnh!

—chucking it back up. But this doesn't feel like the familiar physical process of vomiting. It feels like choking, rather. It feels like I'll never be able to eat or drink again. I can hardly breathe. My entire internal self, all the fleshy netting and organ-hunks and coiled tubing, has spilled out, and in my desperation, without thinking, I've crammed it back inside myself in squishy fistfuls, but now it's all mixed up, the hoses don't connect, the pipes are in knots, my liver is in my throat, my throat is in my leg, I've reassembled it all wrong.

Look at your mother, now. Except for the white plastic band around her wrist and the tube in the back of her hand, she might just be taking an afternoon nap. Her face, sunken-eyed and cadaverous just a few hours ago, is once again flushed: pink bands tinted orange by the sun, a portrait painted with a sunlit sky-hue palette. I love the purplish pockets beneath her eyes, those tattoos of fatigue, those elegant imperfections where once her perfect complexion too plainly reigned.

The doctor checks in. He's young (though perhaps only young-looking; he wears, on the front pocket of his white coat, a button with a photograph of two school-aged children). He's conscientious, too. The specificity with which he offers every explanation, the consideration with which he delivers every question—his concern for your wellbeing seems genuine.

"It's called *placental abruption*," he says. His tongue is dexterous when it's pronouncing these medical terms; that melodious *R*, that steady *L*. All his conjunctions and modifiers are still spongy, though. "The placenta separates from the uterus." He presses his palms together in a *wai*, then curls them apart. "This cause bleeding, and also a danger of no oxygen going to fetus. Understand? Very serious condition. Can be caused by trauma. Like car accident, or fall down stairs, or things like that. But luckily the separation is not very big." His hands come back together, praying again, fingertips floating a centimetre apart. "Just minor. But still, very serious. Understand?"

"Is the baby okay?" I ask.

"We are monitoring fetus. Still things look okay. Heart rate is okay, fluid is okay. May require medication for helping the fetus's lungs to mature, but that is something for later to decide. Wife is okay but lost a lot of blood, and so we are monitoring, too."

I don't bother correcting his categorical error.

Your mother's hand is folded in mine, and I draw lines with my fingertip from knuckle to knuckle to knuckle. How could these hands have been the source of so much trepidation, attached, as they are, to such fine forearms? Fillets of aerodynamic muscle dressed in magnetic silk and rolled in fine shavings of sunlight.

"Only sixteen week, *na*?" the doctor says. He thumbs the corner of the form clipped to his clipboard as if he's going to turn the page, but he never does, he's not even reading, he's staring at the same spot, then he looks up, says softly: "Very rare this happens so early. It's important for her to stay here so we can make sure everything, uh ... stabilized. She will stay here, okay? Understand?"

He seems hesitant to leave, but he does. When we're finally alone, I touch your mother's face, stroke her hand, her hair, her arm. The steady whoosh and tick of her breathing isn't quite enough to convince me that she's okay; I'm secretly hoping to wake her up. I draw her bangs back from her forehead by running the tip of my finger along her hairline, where I know, from that first night and my first exploratory touches, she is most ticklish. Finally she stirs. Her thighs flex against the pillow, her eyes flutter open.

"Hi," I say.

She has the vacant eyes of a newborn.

"How are you feeling?"

Her voice comes from somewhere deep in her chest; only the trailing end of each word makes it past her teeth. "What are you doing here?"

"Where else would I be?" I tell her.

She settles back into her half-sleeping state.

"Everything's okay," I say. "It's all okay, it's okay—"

"—it's okay, it's okay."

I'm telling this to Marti, who, now finished with her tale, now spent of tears, is breathing steady breaths into the centre of my chest. The hotel room has become unbearably hot, so we've kicked the pastel-print comforter to the floor and lie naked on the sheets. I can see, over the top of her head, my shrivelled member hidden in a thicket of still-blondish curls, the terrible instrument deflated and edgeless and somehow remorseless. With the exception of my mother and grand-mother, this is the first time a girl has seen it.

Marti's warm breath rolls down my stomach, brushes against an expectant nerve. The nesting predator twitches.

My heart is hammering. Can she feel it, I wonder? She must—it's hammering against her temple; it's hammering just for her.

"I'm sorry," she says.

"For what?"

"For ruining our night."

"It's okay," I say.

Do I feel pity? Yes. Sympathetic? Yes. Protective and venge-ful? Yes and yes. I feel injured, too. She has shared her hurt with me, and now a little bit of it is mine. This thing she couldn't bear alone, I can bear some of it, I can be hurt, too, and here's the thing you'd never expect about this kind of second-hand hurt—it feels so good, it makes you feel *whole*, it makes you feel *necessary*, and even if you don't realize it right away, you'll find, as time passes, as the bearing of the hurt further intoxicates you, makes you more fully hers and she more fully yours, that you'll do anything to keep it; you'll say anything, you'll believe anything, you'll compromise any-thing, you'll build your self-worth around that tiny grain of hurt she lent you, and in return you'll hold her chin in your hand and run your thumb over the corner of her mouth and tickle the back of her earlobé with your finger and whisper to her over and over and over that "it's okay, it's okay, it's okay—"

"—it's okay, it's okay."

But.

Wait.

Where is this?

A grassy backyard. A single adolescent tree. A play struc-ture, a swing set, a sandbox, and everywhere between there are toys stomped into the soil: plastic pirate cutlasses and armless Playmobil traffic cops. Above it all hovers the discordant cloud of noise that only a group of playing children can produce.

And ... what's this?

A baby in my arms. A crying baby.

It's coming to me, now. This is the daycare I go to after school. That woman there, in the pink frock, bent at the waist to mediate an agreement between those two bawling toddlers, we call her Aunt Cindy. This is her house. She is our caretaker.

This baby I'm holding is really screaming, isn't he?

I am five. No, I am six, I am attending full days of school, now, and I am one of the oldest kids here. I'm being very helpful, holding this crying baby.

But this kid's wailing is more than just a baby's instinctual alarm of hunger or fatigue; his cries carry that treble note of true anguish. He buries his hot little snot-smeared face into my shoulder. Actually, he's *writhing*. He's trying to get free of my grip. He's crying because I'm digging my fingernails into his soft shoulders. I'm pinching him with one hand and gently caressing his heaving back with the other. I'm making him cry.

But, wow, there's something captivating about the way he's squalling, I just love the sound of it. I can feel it resonate in my chest; the alto undertone, the scribbling overtone. His crying makes me helpful. His crying gives me a reason to hold him. Aunt Cindy is busy with the other squawking imps, and my ability to hold this crying baby makes me an important boy. In a minute, she'll turn around and see.

I am a good boy.

I am the kind of good boy who takes care of crying babies.

That is who I am.

I'm opening the door to your mother's apartment, and when I do it lets loose a hot chlorine belch right in my face. All those friendly cosmetic scents that before distinguished this place as a site of fine-smelling feminine activity, the balms and salves and soaps, have been chemically eradicated by the paramedic clean-up crew. Even the woody smell of your mother's body, which those perfumes and deodorants were meant to conceal, has been burnt away. It smells inorganic, dead. It smells like the hospital room. Her place is otherwise as we left it, though. Blankets and sheets are still braided together and hanging over the edge of the bed. The desk chair is still tipped over. The dresser drawer is still open.

Your mother is scheduled to be discharged this afternoon. I can tell that she's eager to be out of the hospital, away from all the dinging machines and inquisitive rubber-wrapped fingers. But she doesn't want to come back here (understandably). And she doesn't want to stay at my apartment (for some reason). So I've done the chivalrous thing and booked us a room at the Sukhothai, which is her second-favourite local hotel, and the only one I can (barely) afford. She has sent me here, to her apartment, to pack up a few things—you know, the essentials: shirts and sweatpants and underpants and lotions and hair elastics. Her mood over the past couple days has been like the rainy-season sky, continuous cloud cover every so often pierced by intense columns of sun, but I am optimistic that her spirits will improve once we're checked in and lounging by the pool (bed rest is the prescription, and, to show my support, I plan to rest in beds and beach chairs alongside her).

With great care I begin to fill up the pockets and pouches of your mother's orange-striped backpack, which seemed, when I first saw her rifling through it on the bus to Poipet, such a boast, so out of place, but now appears to me something Holy, a talisman of everything optimistic and ignorant and good in her. From the cairn of socks in the corner I pick out a few cozy-looking pairs. From the ceramic dish on her vanity I snatch a pair of cubic zirconia studs and the gold ring her father gave her when she turned sixteen. These thigh-length khakis are favourites of hers. So is this pair of cut-off sweatpants with *FALCONS* stitched across the backside — they're a relic from her high school days; she sleeps in them almost every night. And *this* shirt: it's huge, practically a bedsheet, the collar and sleeves cut wide with scissor-snips. And this shirt, too: I bought it for her at Suan Lum, it has an illustration of plastic army men, but instead of holding rifles and flame-throwers, they're playing guitars. Before I stuff it into her backpack, I hold it up and press it to my face and take a deep draft; the chlorinated air is filtered out, and I swallow the smell of laundry detergent and faint tastes of her skin and sweat.

On the little desk she uses as a vanity, a chess match of small glass bottles has stalemated. Nail polish, lip gloss, lotions, toners — who knows. As I sweep them into the backpack, one of the little phials tips onto the floor and spins over the linoleum to the foot of the bed. It's only now, as I stoop to pick it up, that I notice the cloudy brown smudge that has been polished, with counter-clockwise wipes, into the tile floor. It could almost be a trick of the light, an afterimage, but it's not, it's a nuclear shadow.

I won't tell your mother about this. I'll tell her that the place is spotless. That it looks the same, smells the same. That the bed is made, the sheets and blankets laundered, the floors pristine. I'll take a break from my sympathy bed rest, come back here, clean it myself, and when she finally returns I'll say, see, I told you so, just like it always was—

—but when I get back to the hospital, your mother isn't there.

I double back to verify the number on the door.

Yes, this *is* the room where we've spent the last few days. But it's now occupied by a young Thai woman in a crescent-shaped double-cast, holding both her broken arms curled in front of her as if she is perpetually accepting an embrace from an invisible pal. When I poke my head through the door, the woman rolls her shoulders to look at me, her torso tilts, her plastered palms reach like claws. She seems excited to see me, or maybe I'm misinterpreting her ossified body language.

"*Sawatdee*—" I say.

A nurse sidles past me into the room. I recognize her as one of the legion of austere nurses who, with their ointments and sensors and trays of gourmet food, have expedited your recovery. But before I can ask her where your mother has disappeared to, she turns back to me and says: "You come back?"

I ask: "I'm looking for the girl who was in this room."

Just a blank stare from the nurse.

"Did she go somewhere?

"You go home," the nurse says, nodding. It's not a command, more a statement of fact, or maybe a confirmation.

"Do you know where she went?" I ask.

The nurse laughs, like it's a joke. "*Mai kao jai,*" she says. *I don't understand.* "You go home. She go home. You take her away already, *na.*"

"But when I left, she was still here."

She's confused, now, and says: "Yes. Before. When you come here."

I shake my head.

She's annoyed, now, and says. "She go home already, *you* take her—"

This surreal exchange makes me doubt my recall. Was she really in room 407? So I check the floor above, and the floor below, and return once again to the fourth floor to verify that, yes, that broken-armed girl is still waiting for her hug, and your mother is still nowhere to be found. I go to the administration desk and ask the nurse behind the counter what room Carrie Franklin is in.

The nurse doesn't even bother to look it up on the computer. "She discharge," she says. "This morning."

I call your mother, but there's no answer. I call again and leave a message. I text. I text again. No answer.

Your mother has disappeared.

And she has taken you with her.

—11—

But, so, here I am, risen, Lazarus-like, shed of grave-cloths, up, up, up and away from my Throne, ascended in spectacular acrobatic fashion into the upper levels of wreckage, imperilled by every leap, threatened by every immovable metal edge, up, up, up, to find myself here in the hollowed-out skin of the passenger cabin, face to face with my *Suicide Squad* comic, an arm's length from the prize within, and still, hmm, no, I can't quite bring myself to touch it.

Do you see, now, why I'm so anxious? I almost lost you once. A treacherous batch of unstable cells tried to set you adrift inside your mother's womb, but you played it cool, you held on tight when the atmosphere turned perilous, just like your dad, and now you're being patient, waiting for time to pass, slowly gaining strength until you're ready for what comes next.

Can you see, too, why I don't trust these subatomic particles anymore? They care nothing for our safety; they just do whatever they want. I don't trust myself, either. What if I've remembered wrongly the last gesture I made before descending into that drowsy fantasy of Erin Seeley? What if I tucked your ultrasound photo, instead, into the seatback pocket, or between the seats, or beneath my leg?

But I didn't. I *know* I didn't. I'm no longer capable of remembering wrongly. The plastic slipcover is still sealed. The comic is still inside. Your portrait is still inside. *Of course* I'm going to touch it!

Okay.

Okay, okay—

I'm going to *(here we go)* pinch the upper corner of the slipcover with my thumb and middle finger *(just like this)* and feel the glassy texture, but it's not glass, no, because *(do you hear that?)* there's the familiar hiss and crackle of plastic flexing *(a real, brand-new sound!)* and the comic is, yes, it's curling away from the wall, it's moving, it's not solid, not affixed! I am touching it and by touching it have made it like me: a free-willed thing in this world of quantum calm.

I peel the upper half away from the wall and the comic seems to lose its magnetism. It flops into my hands. Isn't it beautiful, this sound? *Crinkle, crack.*

If I roll it into a bullhorn and put it to my lips I can go:

Hello!?

Hellooooo!?

An object! A real, tangible, palpable, physical fucking object, *right here in my hands!*

Okay, let's open the flap. *Ffffflick* goes the tape. *Shhhhhwish* goes the cover as I slide the comic book out of the plastic.

Now let's open the comic. Let's find the right page. Paper corners flick against my thumb, and *(there!)* it falls open to the exact right place.

There it is!

Oh, darling! Here's what I've been looking for, tucked into the stapled seam. Your portrait, as glossy to my touch as ...

Wait, do you hear that?

No, not that. *That.*

It sounds like ...

It sounds like a *sound*!

It's getting louder. It's filling the sky. Is that you? Are you doing this?

Jesus! Did you feel that? A breeze? No — a wind! It almost snatched your picture right out of my pinched fingers. Look at this: the comic is quivering, shivering, rattling, trying to flap away again. It's getting stronger. You feel that, right?

So loud. Can you still hear me? *Hellooo!?*

I feel *wet!*

You don't think — it can't possibly be ... !

( ).

( ).

( ).

( ).

( ).

( ).

( ).

( ).

( ).

( ).

( ).

( ).

( ).

( ).

( ).

( ).
( ).
( ).
( ).
( ).
( ).
( ).
( ).
( ).
( ).
( ).
( ).
( ).
( ).
( ).
( ).
( ).
( ).
( ).
( ).
( ).
( ).
( ).
( ).
( ).
This is—
( ).
I'm—
( ).
( ).

Oh, God!
( ).
( ).
( ).
Help!
( ).
( ).
( ).
( ).
( ).
( ).
( ).
( ).
The speed—
( ).
( ).
( ).
( ).
I can't
hear
anything!
( ).
It's too
( ).
loud!
( ).
( ).
( ).
( ).
Wait!

Waitwaitwaitwait!

Have an idea!

( ).

( ).

( ).

Grab something.

Go anywhere.

( ).

Anywhere, please!

( ).

Back, anywhere, now!

( ).

( ).

( ).

Now!

( ).

( ).

( ).

NOW!

( ).

( ).

( ).

Okay.

Okay.

Okay—

The scratched surface of a window.

My eyes are finding focus.

The city passing by outside is a confusion of horizontal smears.

Landscape ruined by strokes of an eraser.

I'm on the Skytrain, back inside my memory. My reflection in the opposite window, projected over the eradicated city blocks, reveals the slackness in my face; all the ligaments have been snipped with scissors, my expression is melting, my demeanour is enfeebled. A female voice gently announces each stop as if she's tapping us awake from a catnap. *Ratchadamri. Mo Chit. Chid Lom. Siam. Asok.*

Yes, let's rest here for a second. Must collect myself—
What just happened!?
I *fell*.
I was *falling!*
For real, here, in the present—falling!
All of a sudden gravity just … *switched back on*.

The arrow of time has resumed its flight, it seems. And so have I. Everything—all those bits of avionic business hung in the sky, they just started to move. Slowly at first, then accelerating, then—I don't know. I barely managed to jump free of the plunging main cabin. But, no, no, it wasn't much of a *jump*. The floor dropped out from beneath me and in that half-second of slowness before the pipe of fuselage tilted and began to dive, I could only take a single step towards the open end, the breach, the sky, but the purchase I felt through my socks was just an illusion of leverage, there was no surface to step from, the cabin simply plummeted past me and it was dumb luck that I wasn't drawn down with it.

It seems that I'm safe inside my memories, though. Yet more quantum principles introduced for my convenience: as time unfolds at pace within these recollections, only nano-seconds pass on the outside.

And this particular memory? I dodged into it without

thinking. I needed to stop the falling and was willing, of course, to go wherever my unconscious might take me.

Where is this? The Skytrain, yes, of course. But when?

Oh, right — this is a few days after my argument with Carrie, after everything that ensued. I'm carrying her orange-striped backpack on my lap. Sitting across from me is a girl in canvas shorts just slightly more modest than underwear, in a shirt of such diaphanous material that it seems less a

physical object than

an effect of —

( ).

Oh, no!

( ).

( ).

I'm being *(ungh!)* pulled away!

My fingers are being tugged out of these sensory gloves.

My ears are plugged with wind.

I'm staring out the Skytrain window, at my own face —

— but the panorama is pulled out of focus, fluctuates, fades, is superimposed with a fuzzy cloudscape,

falling debris,

fire —

( ).

Ack!

Gnng!

Gnnnnng!

( ).

( ).

( ).

( ).

Slipped out.
Falling again.
( ).
( ).
( ).
Stop!
( ).
Can't hear myself
think.
Concentrate!
( ).
( ).
Flock of stuff.
Garbage!
Baggage!
Look out for that bag!
( ).
( ).
( ).
Somewhereelsequick!
( ).
Okay. Back on the Skytrain.
Focus, Daniel.
Be *present.*
Focus:
Sitting across from me is a girl in canvas shorts just slightly more modest than underwear, in a shirt of such diaphanous material that it seems less a physical object than an effect of light, with delicate stubby toes banded by jewelled sandal straps, with a face of blown glass and a finger of polished ivory

poking at a flipped-open phone. When she thinks I'm not looking, she studies me, and when I glance back and catch her, she shrugs back behind her phone and resumes her timid clicking—

It's taking an immense amount of concentration to keep from sliding out of this memory. As I perceive each of these perceptual echoes, the million threads attached to my million nerves are tugged by external gravitation. I can still feel the steel tension of my tongue pressed in mortal terror against the roof of my mouth; I can still taste the fumes of acid drawn up from my gastric depths by the rapid change in altitude; I can still feel my eyelashes pushed flat by the pressure of velocity, even as I stare at the light above the sliding doors and watch it turn from red to green.

The Phrom Phong stop is announced. I stand up and sling the backpack and jostle for a place in front of the sliding doors. Commuters encroach on all sides as our momentum slows; forearms graze, hips bump, toes and heels tap and retreat. Some safety instinct from way back in my hunting/gathering days raises an alarm, but I'm too busy brooding over your mother's decampment to look over my shoulder, and—

( ).

( ).

Stop!

( ).

( ).

( ).

( ).

Go to here instead.

( ).

Go to there.

( ).

No.

( ).

( ).

Not working—

( ).

Back to—

( ).

Phrom Phong station, where I'm headed for the exit.

This backpack, stuffed with the comforts of home that I've collected for your mother, is making it difficult for me to sidle through the crowd; it's pummelled by elbows, collides with other bags, gets stuck when I attempt to sneak through a narrow corridor of shoulders.

There's that instinctual tickle, that warning, but I think nothing of it.

At the top of the stairs leading down to the street, a woman sits with a sleeping child, a baby, but the baby isn't comfortably curled, not bundled up, rather flung naked across the woman's splayed legs, hairless head tipped back, toothless mouth drawn open, little fists spread in surrender, little bump of a penis pointing at the ceiling. The woman pleads as I walk past. I've been told by Rob Sangran that they drug their babies, these beggars—that most of the time the dead-asleep infants aren't even theirs, just passed-around props, and I use these bit of hearsay as armour against the arrows of my conscience. I pass by the woman without acknowledging her. Her open palm brushes my leg and—

( ).

( ).
Whoop—
( ).
( ).
( ).
My skin is
roaring
radio static.
( ).
Can't feel—
( ).
( ).
( ).
( ).
Weird.
( ).
( ).
Get back in.
Find the next—
Find—
( ).
( ).
( ).
( ).
( ).

I'm trying to find a taxicab. When I reach the bottom of the stairs, I survey the oncoming traffic, scan the lower corners of windshields for the bright red digital character that will tell me which taxis are free. There's one. There's another. But before I'm able to lift my hand to call one over, I feel that whisper of suspicion burst into a scream, but it's too late, because—

****!

No time to absorb the momentum of the blow with a backward shrug. No time to flex my neck against the onrushing force. No time to even blink my eye as a pinkie or thumb or possibly that fortune-cookie-shaped fold of skin at the outer edge of his clenched fist touches my cornea. What this blow to the side of my head lacks in power it certainly makes up for in abruptness. I turn away. I duck. My arms fly up and make an X in front of my face, and through the cross I catch a glimpse of his face. A white paste of churned saliva bubbles between his clenched-tight teeth; he's literally foaming at the mouth. He swings his fist again, this time square on my forehead, but, because I'm falling backwards, the force is absorbed, the touch is gentle, almost affectionate.

What am I going to do?

I'm dying. I'm about to die. I'm dead.

No, not from that blow.

From *this*.

From the falling.

( ).

Don't

( ).

( ).

Let me.

( ).

Okay.

( ).

( ).

( ).
( ).
A bit of control now.
Finding a rhythm now.
( ).
( ).
Some open space.
Legs out arms out.
( ).
( ).
Yes this is better!
Skydiving pose!
( ).
( ).
( ).
Okay yes
and then—
( ).

—I land hard on my ass and here starts the fury of kicks, to my legs and butt and open flank. The round rubber toe of his sneaker plays a melody across my ribs *(thud, thwack, thwang, thud, thud)*, then his knee is on my stomach and his fists are flying around my face, hammering the top of my head, slapping my cheeks, jarring my jaw, chopping my shoulders. I curl up beneath him like a piece of paper set aflame. It's like he has eight arms. It's like there are four of him. Can't stop the storm of knuckles, so to shield myself from this preposterous assault, I do the one thing I'm able to do:

I laugh.

But this just makes him angrier. "Fuck you, fucking pig!" he screams, then some more gibberish distorted by the buildup of bilious spit in his cheeks. He grabs the backpack, lifts me, bodily, and with the snap of a canvas strap I land back on the cement. Balled-up socks bounce beside me. A tube of hand cream rolls off the edge of the sidewalk and into the street. He clutches the backpack to his chest and growls. "This is hers, motherfucker!"

I'm up on my elbows, now concerned with crawling away, perhaps to that cozy garbage-strewn alcove beneath the stairs, when his foot finds an unplayed note on my ribcage, *thrung*, and—

Wait.

What did he just say?

( ).

( ).

Steady.

( ).

( ).

Steady.

( ).

( ).

Down hard on my ass, *thud, thwack, thwang, thud, thud,* fists flying at my face, hammering, slapping. This guy. I said I didn't recognize him, but it's not true. Beneath his screwed-up expression there's something familiar about the proportion and arrangement of his facial features.

"Fuck you, fucking pig!" he screams.

No, not his voice. Definitely never heard that voice before. But his face, yes, even in this anamorphic state, all purplish and rippling with hatred and hissing this invective that sounds, now that I'm hearing it again, something like: "Fucking ever touch her again I'll fucking *kill you*!"

He looks like —

Who does he look like?

( ).

( ).

( ).

( ).

FNGH!

Ow!

( ).

( ).

Ooooooowwwwwwwgoddamit!

What was that!

( ).

( ).

At your mother's apartment, a cold Singha sweating in my hand, a fresh swallow of beer still bubbling in the back of my throat, I'm inspecting the photographs tucked into the frame of the mirror while she spreads sheets of the *Bangkok Post* on the tile floor: your mother and her friends from home, posed poolside in bathing suits, in prom dresses as bridesmaids; a Jack Russell terrier, asleep on a corduroy couch; a raisin-faced newborn swaddled in yellow. And then there's *this* guy. He's standing at the end of a dock, shirtless, in board shorts, wearing a baseball cap that casts a shadow over his face. Still, I can see it clearly enough. Crease his brow a bit, pinch the skin where his eyebrows meet, widen his eyes and flare his nostrils, give it a fluorescent glow, and, yes, this is definitely him, this is the guy who is—

( ).

( ).

My leg!

Fucking—

GAH!

( ).

right through my—

( ).

( ).

Lifting me bodily, snatching the backpack, growling, "This is hers, motherfucker!" And then, as columns of hot blood plug my nostrils and fill my cheeks with the taste of pennies, as the light behind my eyes flickers and fades and I'm drawn down into the darkness, the Rapture arrives.

Chad Billings is lifted off me, straight up, enwrapped in the arms of angels, those three beefy Brits, up, up, up into heaven's blinding light.

( ).

( ).

My leg!

Oh, my leg—

is broken.

is burning.

( ).

Can't control this spin—

( ).

( ).

( ).
( ).
Falling so fast!
( ).
( ).
( ).
It hurts—
( ).
I feel everything!
I can't feel anything!
( ).
( ).
Oh God look how close I am!
( ).
( ).
( ).
Oh God I can almost see the—
( ).
( ).
( ).
( ).
Oh God how can there
still be
so far
to go—
( ).
( ).
( ).
( ).

( ).
( ).
( ).
( ).
( ).
( ).
( ).
( ).
( ).
( ).
( ).
( ).
( ).
( ).
( ).
( ).
( ).
( ).
( ).

REASON, RECOLLECTED

—12—

Hello?

It's me.

Yes, *me*, your father.

Remember me?

I'm still here.

Still alive.

(Sort of.)

I know—It *has* been a long, long time.

As soon as I touched your photograph, the Gears of Time re-engaged, the plane (in portions) resumed its doomed flight, and I found myself once again skydiving among the fiery chunks, kidneys shrivelled, stomach stuck in my throat, the approaching ocean oscillating, etc., etc. I tried to stop myself. I tried to remember. I remembered as hard as I could. I remembered *like my life depended on it*, but I just couldn't stay inside my memory of Chad Billings's merciless beating, and it appeared, when I was pulled out of my recollection that final time, that it was all over —

But then a violent gust of the awakened atmosphere yanked your sonogram picture out of my hand, and as soon as it left my fingers, the whole scene began to slow down again.

Time's Arrow lost momentum. The expansion of the universe puttered to a stop. Like before, everything froze in place.

Everything but *me*. I kept falling, gliding, somersaulting, down, down, down, down through the quiet sky, down through all the hung-up junk. I was fortunate, though, to collide with that aileron over there, which, at the very moment of time's arrest, had connected with an unhinged lavatory door, and together they formed a sort of spout down which I slid, slowing me just enough that I regained my impression of up and down and kicked out my leg to catch the edge of that suitcase over there. I was spun in a tight spiral, like a finger-flicked coin, but sidewise, luckily, towards my new Throne: this cargo crate, a big burnished-steel cube all bound up in canvas straps like a ribbon-wrapped gift, which caught me mid-cartwheel, thundered with the impact, knocked the wind out of me, but stopped my fall and is now my permanent isle of residence.

Caught, yes, and safe—but I awoke to a new injury.

At first I thought I'd simply strained a muscle in my leg, but it turned out to be a dead-straight tunnel bored through the fatty part of my thigh. I must have been run through by a tiny fleck of metal suspended by the re-stiffened atmosphere. It went right through me, like being impaled on a hair-width needle. I plugged up each end of the wound with wads of paper I chewed into a pasty salve (shipping forms I found taped to this crate's eastern face), but the bleeding still, even after all this time, won't stop.

First I burn my hand. Then I hurt my leg. Funny to think that I've been beaten up in limbo as badly as I was in life. "If only these wounds would heal," I used to say. But then realized: Isn't that what they all say? These bummed-out autobiographers, moaning into the sky: *if only these wounds would heal!*

This pseudo-bullethole, however, is the least of the damage. It was the violation of my senses that really laid me out. It was agony. It was like being born. There I was, happily floating in the quiet and cozy void, then it all contracted and throbbed and I was pushed out into the hard, loud, cold, bright, and savage physical world. My five senses, atrophied except for the false responses they so accurately simulate during my recollection, were obliterated. The wind hacked at my eardrums and lashed my bare skin. Particles of light accelerated from zero to a hundred thousand miles per second and collided with my fragile corneas. My sense of touch fainted dead away and my hearing died instantly of an overdose. Even my tongue was set ablaze by the spicy sting of burning jet fuel.

My recovery has been slow. There's still an angel of orange light burnt at the centre of my vision, still a digital alarm whining beneath the ambience. But I'm alive. I survived.

So, why didn't I call out to you after I landed safely?

Well —

See —

Hmm —

During my long rehabilitation, I spent a lot of time in the past. The pain was duller there, and I was occasionally able to subsume it completely with reiterated stimuli. At first, sure, I went looking for comfort in many of the mnemonic joints I frequented during in my early days on the Throne — you know, the stuff that "occurred between the sheets, between the legs, between consenting adults" (in my defence, orgasms are extremely effective painkillers, better than aspirin, better than oxy, better than a whole hospital full of caring professionals). But as I regained my strength, as my senses slowly healed, as all the sexy bits grew dull, I began to meditate about this long lecture of mine, and it occurred to me just how much I have misunderstood, misread, and suppressed.

For example: how did I manage to live through the assault at Phrom Phong *three times* before I recognized Chad Billings's face? I have gone back to verify it, and, yes, sure enough, he had been following me all afternoon:

There he is, reflected in shop windows, in the windshields of parked cars, stalking a half-block behind me as I make my way to the Skytrain station.

There he is, in the blurry periphery of my vision as I twist my head back and forth before crossing the street.

There he is, on the Skytrain, sitting just a few seats away as I stare out the window of the speeding train and formulate the new accusations I'm going to make against your mother.

I didn't recognize him. And I *still* didn't recognize him when we returned together to that memory of the street fight so I could show you how I received my "much-celebrated hip-bruise and canonical elbow-scrape."

You'd think that this perfect recollection would allow me to see the world perfectly. But senses aren't objective. An ear picks up a single voice chatting in a cacophony, an eye twitches from here to there and bends light in different directions; I have chosen to observe one thing, not another, and the thing called *truth*, which seems absolute, but which is experienced conditionally, is defined by all those small sensory adjustments. I used to think that everything I told you was fact because I could alter nothing, conceal nothing. But everything I described to you was altered. Peripheral matter was concealed. I couldn't help it.

Marti said to me, once: "You can choose to remember it however you want. I choose to remember it another way."

She was right. Consciously or not, we choose. As our neurons are firing, recording perceptions, encoding emotions, we're choosing what to remember, which details to make phosphorescent, which to obscure in murk and shadow, and over time, as we accumulate these details, they get heavy. You collect enough of them and they can create their own gravitational field; you can get stuck in the orbit, you can spin around them for years, for decades, for your whole life.

So I asked myself: what facts did I misconstrue? What empirical information did I omit? What incidents and explanations did I arrange in the manner most likely to earn your sympathy? It occurred to me that the real value of this experience isn't the amazing ability to gratuitously relive all my favourite moments (though that's pretty cool), or to gather anecdotal evidence that supports the explanations and alibis with which I am trying to convince you that I'm deserving of your love (have I done an adequate job?), but rather to correct those angles of approach, to observe the unobserved; listen for different voices, focus on different things.

So I embarked on an archaeological mission. I ventured deep into the long-ago present, far into the unmapped territories of Daniel Solomon. I observed, I hypothesized, I refined and recalibrated. I sifted and sorted and restored and reinterpreted. I theorized, I investigated, I disproved, dismissed. I searched out those hidden details, those mistakes of interpretation, and sought to make sense of the question I initially hoped to answer for you: why you have to grow up without your father.

And now, after weeks/months/decades of study, I have finally figured out how I ended up here in the sky.

Would you like to see where it all started?

I'm born, yes, it's true, that's how it begins.

In the beginning, it's just *us*, just me and my mother, just the heat of our bodies, which is one body, and the roaring rush of our blood, which is the same blood. Just this smell: my mother. All other smells are derivatives of this smell. All other love is derivative of this love. In babyhood, I plunge into hysterics when she is beyond the range of my vision. In toddlerhood, I feel a fraction of a whole when she drops me off at daycare. In childhood, there is so much sweet touching. So, so much. I press my cheek into the corner of my mother's neck. I fall asleep with my mouth open on her skin. I hide behind her legs and nervously rub the rubbery pocket behind her knee. I sit in the nest of her cross-legged lap and absently stroke her calves with the heel of my foot. I crawl into her bed on weekend mornings and wriggle worm-like into her loose arms. I twist my fists into her hair and munch big mouthfuls of it. I suck on her knuckles. I suckle at her breast.

And then I'm weaned from the breast. Wet kisses become dry smooches, and then there's no smooching at all. Our mouths are forever separated. It continues with the onset of puberty, when my androgynous form takes on mannish qualities. My shoulders grow broader and harder to enfold. I get heavy and harder to heave. I no longer fit in her cross-legged divot. I grow past the backs of her knees. And still no kisses. I was eight years old the last time my mother kissed me on the lips. From then on, that bit of tenderness would be the domain of other women.

How can they stand it, these loving moms, these women who would kiss you forever if they could, giving up the lips of their charming little boys to this pantheon of girlfriends and hook-ups and wives and mistresses and their ten thousand new kisses?

How can they stand it that their kids are so eager to escape them?

But that's the way it goes; the inevitable progression of things.

"I suppose I really ought to explain," my mother says.

I chose to remember this conversation as my mother's attempt to exempt herself from the daily responsibility of motherhood, to choose autonomy over obligation, to send me away and sate herself with the excuse that it was all for my own good. And maybe it was. It certainly sounds that way, doesn't it? How else to interpret the words she's speaking to me as I stare at my reflection in the side mirror and jam french fries into my mouth.

"This isn't about your grades," she claims, "and it's not

about what happened with the other boy, and it's not about how much I love you."

I won't look at her, just at myself, or out the window, or into my lap, where my finger is digging for crumbs in the grease-blotched cardboard container. But I can hear her voice, and in her voice there are clues:

A fuzzy hum in the back of her throat when she says, "It would be selfish of me to keep you here just because I like having you around."

A bracing deep breath before she says, "We'll take it slowly, we'll try it for the first half of grade nine."

She can barely get her mouth around the words, "You don't have to worry about me. I'll stay here and work and maybe it will be good for me, too, to change things up."

(Do these equivocations sound familiar, my love?)

In remembering this moment, I have chosen to dismiss just how heavily her discomfort fills the car, but I can feel it, right now, it's real, it's a tangible thing, like smoke seeping from a lit cigarette, it's stinging my eyes, I can smell it, the stink is soaked into our clothing, oily whorls have collected against the roof.

Still, this is the only explanation she will ever give me. In the ensuing decade, as we let diminish the biotic closeness that (I can only assume) most mothers and sons enjoy, we'll make up for it by becoming good friends, close pals, chums, buddies, and we'll reminisce fondly about the silly things I did as a kid, the famous quotations I uttered, the trips we took, the accidents I survived, and she'll remind me often that she loves me, that she misses me, that she can't wait to see me the next time we see each other, whenever and wherever that might be. But she will never elaborate further on what she says here in the car. And I'll never ask. When she says to me, "sometimes I feel like I haven't started living my life yet," it's all I'll ever know about why we can't be together.

But —

You have to wonder, don't you —?

In the moments before she dies, when everything is frozen solid and she's shuffling through all her most meaningful recollections, will she be addressing me? Will she be narrating in meticulous detail all the essential episodes that led up to this moment, right now, here in the car? Will she find a way to tell me all the things she can't quite find a way to tell me right now, and finally explain *why*?

Maybe.

But by then it will be too late.

"Fine! *Fine*, fuck you! You dick! You fuck! Who are you? Who are you supposed to be right now? You're an asshole! Fuck you!"

Marti has never been more beautiful than she is right now, all furious and murderous and pleading and pained. And I have never felt more righteous. I know her secret, and her secret is a weapon; I'm hiding it in my pocket, waiting for the right moment to wield it —

"Just tell me what I did. Tell me what I did. Tell me why you're being like this."

— *now*.

With a great guttural heave I push those four ferrous words over the precipice of my bottom lip: "Because you're a liar!"

She's hugging herself, and I can remember remembering memories of this, and in them she was smoking, holding a half-smoked cigarette down by her hip, pinched casually between two fingers, intricate ribbons of smoke rising up and suggesting effluent metaphors about how she is *smoking mad* or *steaming under the pressure*. But she's not smoking. She never smoked in our apartment. That was another time. Or a different time. And she's not angry, either. That was a different time, too. She's scared. She knows. She looks towards the closet, where the incriminating diary is within, then looks back at me, and I can see in her eyes that she knows that I know what she knows.

"You don't *understand*," she says.

She's right, I don't. Why she lied to me, why she *kept* lying to me, why she thought I wouldn't be desperately in love with her anyways—I don't understand any of it. But why ask questions when I can score easy points?

"Understand what? How amazing it was?"

It always bothered me that she didn't bother to explain herself. Or even to elaborate further on the lies she'd already told. Keeping this farce alive required years of diligent maintenance. Screechy hinges oiled with offhand references, cracks in the foundation spackled with crocodile tears, drooping roof abutted with the burlesque of bad moods—and now she's content to let it all collapse. Why isn't she making excuses? Why isn't she begging for my forgiveness? Why is she just rambling on:

"I didn't mean to lie, I just … I didn't mean to —"

What does she mean when she says she didn't mean it? What does she mean when she says I don't understand?

A woman is offering a hunk of pink meat to a comatose alligator, just casually dangling it above its snout like she's feeding a pigeon in a park, and when she turns around to make sure that this incredible feat is, indeed, being caught on tape, the gator lunges, clamps down on her forearm, she's suddenly wearing it like a glove.

Freeze frame. Rewind. Here it comes again.

I'm only half-listening when Marti, on the other end of the phone, says to me:

"Remember I'd read to you from my mom's romance novels? I don't think I've ever laughed so hard. I was thinking of that because I was thinking of how much I liked the name Claire, and I think I read it in one of those books. What was that one part? Oh, oh, oh, that one part about 'his fleshy horn.' How did it go?"

"He could restrain himself no longer," Marti reads aloud. "He didn't bother removing her panties, he just pulled them aside with his hooked finger and pressed himself against her."

It's a Tuesday. Our subtle scheming has won us an evening alone together; her mother is working the late shift at the hospital; my father thinks I'm stocking shelves at the grocery store. But I'm not stocking shelves, I'm coolly reclined on this leather couch in the dimly lit living room, the round weight of Marti's head on my left leg and a half-erection restrained against pulled-tight pant-fabric of my right. She's reading aloud from a worn paperback called *A Flame Simmers to Rise*:

"This was more than making love, it was sex in its most primal, animalistic form. It might have been days instead of hours, Claire had lost all sense of time. As Eric thrust against her, stretching her *wet hole* with his *fleshy horn*, she felt an electric sensation grow at her core and radiate outward to her fingers and toes, a rushing ocean of pleasure that crashed like a wave against every nerve. Her orgasm came *hot* and *hard* just as Eric's gleaming body *spasmed* and he *filled her with his milky essence*."

We both laugh.

"The warm tickle of his *seed* spilling out over her thighs gave her a *rapturous* shiver. The tall grass moved in waves. All around them the remains of their abandoned picnic were scattered in the grass beneath the willow tree."

Our apartment, three years later.

I am sitting on the edge of the mattress, withered, breathless, buoyed, flayed, heartsick, engaged in my manic examination of Marti's diary:

"I stroked his penis and he burrowed his face in my neck and bit my earlobe," Marti has written. "He also did this other incredibly sexy thing where instead of pulling off my panties he just sort of pulled them aside with his hand and I could feel him right there pushing against me."

And further down the page:

"We finished at the same time and I came too. It was different from coming by touching myself. It was deeper and felt like electricity that started in the middle of me and radiated out to my fingers and toes. It was amazing."

And a few pages later, in prose which seems lovingly printed, but which now appears an exaggeration of affection, the elaborations of a bad liar:

"Yesterday Tyler and I went to the Camden Locks and had a picnic under that old tree at the top of the hill. The tall grass was moving in waves. We drove there in his Mustang and the whole way I just lay with my head leaning against the edge of the open window and my hair was blowing in my face and it felt like something out of a music video. We made love under a willow tree."

It's true: Marti was a liar.

But not how I thought.

Do you remember, when I was reading to you from her diaries, the redaction I dismissed as a failed first draft of her exaltation of Tyler Madden? Remember I described the "row of paper teeth . . . where a page has been removed"? That missing passage should have struck me as more significant, but I was too busy trying to show you how badly I'd been tricked, how blameless I was for finding myself here on the precipice of death, that I skipped right past it, went straight into the really heavy stuff, and didn't give it a second thought.

Why would she remove a page? What could she have

composed in that "failed first draft" that she would immediately want to forget? My mission, remember, was to observe the unobserved, to learn the truth. But the *absence* of a thing was no good to me; I can't escape the confines of my own life experience. Like every song I've never heard, every person I've never met, every experience I've never experienced, the words Marti scrawled were beyond my reach; only she could know what was written on that page, and she destroyed it long before we met. Not even my omnipotent memory could retrieve it—

But memory is not the only tool at my disposal.

What else, besides memory, do I possess in an infinite abundance?

Time!

Yes, Time! I've been blessed with it. Endless Time. Nothing but Time. And there is no riddle that Time cannot solve; it has cured every plague and conquered every empire. So I used Time and all its atomic fragments to search for clues. I lived over and over through those hours spent alone with Marti's diaries—but instead of focusing on the words, I turned down the volume on my inner voice and set loose my other senses to investigate. I assessed every mote of dust and appraised each vague scent, and finally, in the most obvious place, *right there* on the page, I found what I was looking for.

Our apartment, again.

I am sitting on the edge of the mattress, scanning, skimming, retreating, rereading. Her diary is open in my lap and

I'm unconsciously pressing the spine of it against the erection that has, like an uninvited guest drawn to a party by the clamour of music and voices, arrived on the scene. I turn past the torn-out page and continue reading:

"He told me he didn't want to hurt me, that he'd never want to hurt me, so I told him he could never hurt me, and I honestly never thought moments like that existed in real life."

And with that sequence of words unspooling their terrible meaning inside my brain, I once again suffer that moment in which "my hands lose their strength and the book tips towards the bright bedroom window" — but in my doubled consciousness something caught my eye: a faint reflection of light on the paper's flat surface. Crescents and segments glinted. Imperfections in the paper's texture. Indentations.

The missing page was written upon with a ballpoint pen, and it made these impressions on the page beneath.

Having spent so much time studying the delicate patterns of ocean waves from up high on my Throne, my eyes were well-trained for such a fastidious task. But after much intensive examination, I still couldn't make out whole letters. This glimmering revealed only small strokes.

I was sure there were more clues. So I put my other senses to work.

Our apartment, sitting on the edge of the mattress, back again, back again, back again, a million-and-a-half times more, until —

—here we go, just sixteen seconds after my despairing hands lose their strength and accidentally catch that stray flash of sun, as I'm reading for the thirteenth time the paragraph that begins "We were kissing passionately...":

I move my hand absently over the surface of the paper, and, in doing so, record on the sensitive tips of my fingers the minute impressions pressed into it by the compositions of the previous page.

I saw it, then *touched* it: forensic evidence of what Marti wrote and threw away. It was raw material, yes, just microscopic fractions of pen-strokes, but remember, I had almighty Time on my side. I had nowhere to be, and nothing more important to do than solve this puzzle —

—and I did.

I assembled those fractions and turned them into letters; I engineered those letters into words; I uncovered the phrases that were the sum of those words. Some segments took me days of careful concentration to pick out. Some words took months to spell. Some phrases years to write. Nonetheless, in this careful manner, cycling through that three-hundred second span for the last three decades, I recovered the missing verses of Marti's diary and reproduced them here in the frozen present.

It's all right here: these hieroglyphs that cover the crate upon which I'm marooned. Draft upon draft, crossed-out, corrected, and when I ran out of space, I lay down on my stomach and composed upside-down on each of the four sides of the metal box, around the hinges, overtop the bands and straps. To transcribe, I used a narrow steel rod I found floating just within my grasp, some subsidiary tendon from one of the plane's long limbs, and plucked a few short hairs from the side of my head. Then, with a strip of the adhesive tape that I peeled off the cargo manifest on the side of the crate, bound them together to make a brush. And the ink? Well, what seemed at first to be an unlucky physiological peccadillo has turned out to be a blessing: I dip the end of my brush into the wound on my leg, which, lo these hundred years, hasn't yet scabbed up and stopped bleeding. I have jotted these excerpts in blood.

It's all here, now. Everything that I missed.

Where the passage that described her encounter with Tyler is too perfectly declared and out of sync with her journal's unconscious conversational tone, Marti's writing, in this lost passage, is sloppy. The verb tense slips back and forth from present to past; her penmanship (or the suggestions of it that I have been able to recover) is an indifferent, disorderly likeness of her usual orbicular style. There is no date, no heart-scale record of mood, no quoted pop song. There is no clear notation of time. It simply says:

"I go downstairs and Dad was passed out on Derrick and Janice's couch and I can't even bear to look at him or wake him up or ask for a ride home but I have to get out of there right away so I walked home even though it's more than an hour but I walked anyway and what I remember is my thighs sticking together when I'm walking because the blood there is all dried up and sticky and it was like I couldn't even walk because my skin is tearing with every step. But I kept walking with my brain completely turned off and I made it home eventually I don't know how. I showered forever. I showered until there was no hot water left just this tepid water and I might have fallen asleep because I woke up suddenly and didn't know where I was and for a moment I'm thinking that I'm still there at that house and I couldn't it was I just [the sentence trails off here]. I slept in. Surprisingly I slept surprisingly easy. I slept in until surprisingly late. When I finally came out of my room I was in the kitchen pouring a glass of juice and Cheryl is there and she has this stupid grin on her face and she says to me in this teasing way so how was last night and whatever I looked like she thought was something else because she laughs and gives me a hug and says don't worry I won't let your dad find out. So I guess that means that he told everyone that he fucked me. But maybe I would have done it anyways. I probably would have if he just gave me a chance to get relaxed so I guess it's really not that big of a deal and I should just relax relax relax relax relax. Today I watched about three hours of Pokémon with Kandice and then me and Dad played cards for a little while in the kitchen and it's almost like nothing happened so maybe it really is like nothing happened. Except for the part that I found out for sure that everyone knows we slept together and they think that I lost my virginity to him in his shitty basement bedroom while everyone else was upstairs and it's this funny joke to everyone and it's all even weirder because I just keep waiting for him to call me like as if by calling me it will all somehow be okay like a regular relationship or something and all the time everyone keeps saying to me isn't Tyler such a nice boy, why haven't you called Tyler, do you want me to invite Tyler over for supper. But how can I be mad because I keep thinking about how all night in front of everyone I'm following him around like a little puppy and laughing at every stupid thing he says and how I go downstairs with him and let him kiss me and lay down in his bed in fact was excited to lie down in his bed and so maybe I really am just some drunk teenage slut who changed her mind after the fact which is exactly what he will be telling everyone. I'm already remembering it differently. I'm already thinking about if it was as bad as I thought. I kissed him back and so maybe he thought it was okay to do what he did. Or little details like when he bit me what if it was a soft bite meant to be sexy but then I look at myself in the mirror and I see the mark on my breast and it doesn't look like it was a soft bite and besides it still hurts but then maybe it's supposed to hurt and all I can do is think maybe if I can try to remember it all in the best way possible then it will make everything okay again."

Her chin is in the divot between my knees and she says to the inseam of my jeans. "I lied, I'm sorry, please believe me."

That's it, that's all. She doesn't explain. She doesn't tell me what she lied about, what she's sorry for, what she wants me to believe.

Instead, she climbs into my lap and tries to kiss me. Instead, she goes limp and lets me push her to the floor, take handfuls of hair, fistfuls of breast. Instead, she endures me.

The same way she endured the long walk home. The same way she endured, for the rest of that summer, the sidelong glances and whispered quips of her family, the humiliation of being associated, in such an innocuous way, with the person who had violated her. The same way she endured his most sadistic gesture — to pretend like they were genuine lovers, to lie next to her afterwards as if it had been a casual, consensual encounter, and offer her a drink of water. Because she didn't scream for help, because she gave up her protests once he'd broken her, she must have believed that she was in some way responsible for what happened. She'd flirted too recklessly, she'd said yes too many times before finally saying no. And she must have hated herself for it. So she did what she could to change history: she falsified her records.

She corrected her memories of that evening and fabricated a whole happy ending to make it seem more real. And then I showed up, and under her meticulous direction (in snowy alleyways, on long walks home, in set-dressed hotel rooms, in our cramped little apartment, on a mattress where I graciously followed her explicit instructions) we spent the next four years making that happy ending real.

I'm an idiot.

I'm a fool.

How did I not see it? The proof that she was telling the truth was right there in front of my face the entire time:

Above her right nipple, that sickle-shaped impression, that lustrous curve of re-knit skin, a little pink scar the width and thickness of a man's tooth.

"Sorry," Marti says. "I'm just tired. Tired and a bit wasted. I shouldn't be calling you this late. What is it, there? Two in the morning? Seriously, I don't know what I was thinking. I had that weird baby dream, and it was so *real*, it was like time travel, it was like I was back there. Remember how much our apartment reeked? Remember we left that half-eaten Christmas turkey out on the balcony until, like, the middle of February? Remember how fucked up all the carpet got from candle wax? I miss it sometimes. I get homesick for it."

Prone before the TV as another snowboarding stunt goes terribly wrong, I pry the heel of my boot with my toe, I tongue the groove between my teeth and cheek to clean out the starchy paste of bread and cheese, and I say with as much disaffection as I can muster:

"Was it really that great?"

All the hurt I've caused her is compressed into an electric pulse and fired through a hundred miles of buried and suspended wires.

"You can choose to remember it however you want," she says. "I choose to remember it another way."

"Iz *dvukh zol vybi — vbyi, vbyi … uhhh, vbyi*rayut *men'sheye.*"

The clock on the wall reads 2:02 p.m.

"It's a famous old Russian saying," your great-grandmother explains. "Which means that when all the choices are bad, you, uhhh ... you choose the one that is ... you know—the one that ... *hurts* the least."

She is about to die. Just like me. What luck that she isn't marooned in some inescapable place. In the early days of my altitudinous captivity, idling on my Throne, all cramped up and bed-sore from trying to tuck myself between the metal armrests, I would have killed for the comfort of a bed and pillow and blanket. But I suppose my grandmother and I are the lucky ones; just think of those poor folks who are crushed in collapsed buildings, or burnt in house fires, or mauled by grizzly bears—what scenery do they get to enjoy?

"It's okay," she says. "He's drunk, he's asleep. He won't hear a thing."

I wonder if she was able to stand up and move around the room. Could she walk out the door, out of the building, into the streets? Did she spend a millennium wandering the empty earth? Or, like me, did her physical injuries and afflictions follow her into that in-between place? Was she bedridden the entire time, memorizing the family photos pinned to the wall, the angle of the sun, the position of the bumblebee bouncing against the window? Did she map the landmarks of her room the same way I've made maps from ailerons and spoilerons and nacelles and wing flaps? Was she plotting, too, to convince someone that the mistakes she made were the fault of indiscriminate Fate?

"I'm grabbing your hand, and, oh, hell, stop, leave that behind—yes, *that*, you don't need that, Masha, come with me."

She's been talking nonsense like this all afternoon, accusing the nurses of stealing her things, mixing English with Russian, her Russian with English, forgetting the grammatical rules of both midway through sentences, so of course, when she says —

"It's such an easy thing to do. Look how easy it is. You just —there we go, like this."

—I take it to be just another synapse misfiring in her brain, another note of her cadenza misplayed. But for some strange reason (yes, I remember this part) I find myself thinking of:

The hot tropical sun.

The sound of the ocean.

Ah, this lovely heat!

Oh, the slow lisping drum of the salty surf!

Warm winds are blowing napkins off our table. The sand kicked up by all this soft gusting is stinging our ankles. My mother and I are sitting at this beachside café, waiting for our greasy lunches, sipping icy fruit drinks. I'm visiting her here in Florida for March break; she had business in Sarasota last week, then stuck around for a few days to visit her cousin in Fort Myers, and now has flown me down so that we might make a vacation of her remaining week on the Gulf Coast.

"You should see their place," my mother says. "They've turned the backyard into a par-three. You can tee off from the back deck. You remember Edith, don't you? She's Aunt Masha's and Uncle Bill's daughter."

I am holding the puka-shell necklace I just bought at the hotel gift shop, fingering the sharp edges, imagining how cool I'll look when I stroll through the hallways at school,

contemplating how much closer it might bring me to becoming the coolest iteration of myself it is possible to be and,
consequently, that much closer to being worthy of some cool
girl's attention.

"You know," my mother says. "Before your Aunt Masha
was married to your Uncle Bill, she was married to someone
else—a man named Eugene Grimes. But he died not long
after they were married. Maybe just a year. Maybe even
less than that. He died in a fire. Their farmhouse outside
Washegin burned down, and it was a miracle your aunt wasn't
home when it happened. I never knew any of this until Aunt
Masha told me. And she was very matter-of-fact about the
whole thing. She said it was a good, because if the fire hadn't
killed Eugene, Eugene probably would have killed her. Isn't
that nuts? I'm not even sure Edith knows. I was going to ask
her while I was down there visiting, but —"

Here's the waitress, balancing our beige meals on her upturned palms.

"—I never quite built up the nerve."

"Oh, it's so hot!" your great-grandmother says. "Even from
far away. We're so far away and it's still so hot! Can you feel
how hot it is? I can feel it on my skin."

"Are you too hot, Grandma? Do you want me to take off
the blanket?"

She shakes her head: "I say to you, he's asleep, he's drunk,
I promise—he won't feel a thing."

"I think you're just having a bad dream."

"Yes, you're right. Don't look, Masha. This is just a bad dream. You'll wake up soon and it will all be over."

And here comes that peaceful clarity, that drawing in of a cold draft, that normalizing sigh after a bout of deep laughter. A skipped beat. But not just one—a thousand, a million, a *googol*. Your great-grandmother feels it, too. Suddenly energetic, shockingly agile, remarkably fast, she reaches over and picks up the bauble sitting beside her bed, turns it over in her hands, examines the foal's shiny forehead, runs her thumb over the ridges of grass. She looks up at me and says:

"Oh, hello. It was on purpose, you know. And I'm only sorry that I'm not sorry."

This clarity lasts just a second, though; then it's gone, and the room fills once again with its sad ambience: the smell of diapers, the smell of harsh medicines, the smell of elderly sweat, which is the smell of browning bananas.

She looks like she has fallen asleep. Her eyelids don't close, they wilt; they're like curtains cut too long, all bunched up on the floor. The pink inner corner of her eye, that little pebble there: I can still see it, even though her eyes are closed. But they're not closed. She's not sleeping. For a second I thought she was. But she's not.

How long did it take for her to figure out that she all she had to do was touch that little porcelain horse? It took me a millennium to figure out that your sonogram picture was my way out, but in my defence, I had much further to go to get my hands on it.

And further still.

Yes, there is more I must tell you.

There is worse.

Back in my Catholic school days, in the early grades, on Ash Wednesdays, with our foreheads all coal-smeared, we'd line up outside the guidance counsellor's office, along a wall decorated with construction paper eggs and coloured bunnies, and when our turn came up, we'd step inside to sit on a folding chair beside a black sheet hung from the ceiling, and on the other side there'd be some soft-spoken old guy, or maybe some bearded young guy, and you'd tell him the bad things you'd done: the homework you didn't finish, the candy you'd eaten on the sly, the mean things you'd said on the playground (or, if you were a real arch-criminal, the cans of pop you'd shoplifted from the convenience store, the cash you'd stolen from your parents' wallets), and these guys would offer you the standard package of forgiveness, delivered on behalf of the Father and the Son, and that would be that, back to class, back to ignoring homework and sneaking candy and all the rest.

This is all I know of confession. The whole notion of forgiveness always seemed so frivolous to me. You stub your toe and take the Lord's name in vain, you obey your primal genetic directives and covet your neighbour's sexy significant other, you're a genocidal dictator famous for his bad paintings and historic inhumanity—all you have to do is ask: forgiven! It's too automatic, too easy.

But I'll ask you to forgive me anyways. I'll confess what I've done. That's the point of purgatory, right? To come to some internal consensus about your moral shortcomings, to recognize them, to speak them aloud. No qualifications, no excuses.

Okay —

Here it is, then.

Here is the reason we can't be together.

****!

Stars!

Agkch!

Fttt!

"Fuck you, fucking pig!" Chad Billings screams.

Thud!

This is when I finally recognize him. But it's not his face that I find familiar. It's his righteous fury — I owned a similar slice of it, once upon a time. It's not the dispassionate madness of a mugger or meth-head, or the temporary insanity of some defamed and vengeful stranger. No —

Thwack!

— this guy knows me.

Thwang!

He's coming after me the same way I went after Tyler Madden in my silly fantasies of crowbar beatings, every muscle twitch since his birth fulfilling its purpose, to crush my fucking face.

Thud!

"Fucking ever touch her again I'll fucking *kill you*!"

Thud!

But why me?

Oh, he has good reason.

"I'm leaving now," I say.

"No, you're not," your mother says.

I am infected by her idiocy, shivering with anger, vomiting forth invective, harsh thoughts half-formed and sloppily delivered, and your mother is spitting back at me with the same black vigour.

"You can't leave."

"Why not?"

"Because you can't say *our* baby *our* baby *our* baby and then walk out in the middle of this discussion like it doesn't matter."

"This is a discussion?"

"It's *supposed* to be, but you're not *listening*."

It's not fair. My plan all along was to do whatever she said, to be whoever she wanted me to be, as long as I could do it and be it here, as long as she didn't make me go somewhere else.

"Fuck this," I say.

"You're not leaving."

"You're totally right. Being here is all that I have. So I'm going to stay here. Have a good flight home."

I move towards the door.

"You're not leaving!"

Already I know that I have no hope of convincing her to stay. Already I know she is going to take you away, and that my choice is binary: stay behind, or renounce Paradise to be with you.

"No!" she barks, and tugs on my forearm.

I try for the doorknob, grab it, turn it, but there's masculine power in her masculine talons, she's pushing my arm down, trying to push me back into the room, but I'm able, just barely, to pry the door open behind her, and despite those few extra ounces, despite the illusion of density, she's still just a five-foot-something girl, still just a hundred-something pounds, and she moves easily when I lever the door against her back, opening a gap that's wide enough for me to slide through, out into the hallway, and now our tug-of-war has reversed, I'm trying to pull the door shut, she's trying to pull it back open, and this entire time there's a slight smile on my face, as if acknowledging the absurdity of this childlike wrestling might make it less absurd, might make me feel like less of a child, and I swear, I swear on your *life*, that I haven't once during this struggle remarked or remembered that the bottom drawer of the dresser is still open, that it's right behind your mother's feet.

But I could pull away right now —

—or right now —

—or right *now* —

—but I'm sick and tired of being taken advantage of and having my sympathy preyed upon and sick of being tricked and manipulated and forced to compromise myself for the convenience of others and tired of giving up my will to make everyone else comfortable —

—or right now —

—or right … *now* —

—but what I *really* want is to see her wrecked and ruined and crying, crawling on the floor, begging, pleading, admitting that she lied, that she didn't mean it, that she's sorry —

—or now —

—or now —

—please, let go *now* —

—but, no, I don't, I wait for her to lean back, to roll her weight back on her heels, to really plant herself for another good yank, and when she does I take my hand away, and the metal knob thrums as my gripping fingers slip, the door slams shut, the cheap laminate wood crackles and splinters, and a hollow *fwump* announces the meeting of your mother's tailbone with the hard tile floor.

−13−

Oh, my love!

My sweet Annabelle! Darling Charlotte! Gentle, brooding Beatrice, with your mother's fine patrician nose! Emma, my angel, inheritor of my grandmother's careful idealism, my careless sentimentalism. Oh, Dorothy! Oh, Penelope! I won't be around to correct all the errors of behaviour and belief that your mother might inflict (or, likewise, to inflict any of my own), so we'll have to rely on genetics to make sure that you carry forward a bit of my mother's quick precision and my father's dreamy looseness (of which I am the loosely precise product). By the time you're born, will your mother have forgiven me? I'll be dead, after all, and the great thing about being dead is that everyone forgets your shortcomings, they inflate your virtues, they canonize you. Especially when you're taken so young. Especially when you're taken in such dramatic fashion. I'm pretty lucky, if you think about it.

You'll grow up in Columbus, probably. But maybe you'll stay in Bangkok. Maybe Chad Billings can craft a more compelling argument for your mother to stick around. Maybe *he'll* be your father. Maybe his affection for your mother will be reignited by this drama. Or maybe it will it be some other fella, some rugged Ohioan, some callous-fingered builder, some simple guy who mutters in monosyllables but has a big ol' heart, who will cry only once in his entire life, when he sees you onstage accepting a diploma or at the altar exchanging vows.

Who will it be? Who will you call Da-Da, then Daddy, then Dad, then Father? Say it once for me? Call me that name just once so I can die happy!

While my body and consciousness have hurtled forward, you have remained, down there on the surface of the earth, in your second trimester, still another five months until your little lungs will be ready to wrangle earth's brutal oxygen. Just like these clouds and aluminum panels and turbines and flocks of footless shoes, you're stuck in place, waiting for me to get on with it.

So I will.

I won't delay your sweet sprouting with any more vain-glorious time travel. You've probably grown tired of my first-person anthropologist's accounts (I'll admit it: even *I'm* exhausted by the present tense).

I wish that I could offer you some oracular piece of advice before I go. Something that will help you avoid the mistakes I've made. I suppose the closest I can come is to tell you that mistakes are inevitable, you'll someday make them, and so will others.

Or how about this:

Don't take my absence too personally. Let it be your strength, not your weakness.

(That's kind of nice, right? The sort of selfless thing a good father might say.)

It might seem absurd, all these dumb trivialities and their cumulative power. But just you wait and see—it will all be same for you, too. You will write Homeric epics about the contents of your grade-school lunchbox; you will write operas about your Saturday morning fugues in front of the television; you will expend a billion breaths trying to describe the brightness that another person's smile can ignite in the dim depths of your belly. That's the great paradox of being alive: even though it doesn't matter, it *does* matter, it *will* matter, it *has* mattered, every single crumb and twitch and exhalation.

And now it's your turn. Your turn to paint nostalgia on the flat surface of your memories to give them the illusion of a fathoms-deep magnitude. Your turn to build a golden idol of yourself to worship. Your turn to hurt and be hurt by others.

I've had my chance.

Now *you* try —

∘ ○ ○

—try this soft segment of orange, which you know, instinctively, from its juicy texture and moist weight, is food and goes in your mouth. So you put it there. It slips a bit from your fingers, but, there!, you wedge it in with the heel of your hand and press together the itchy bands of muscle behind your lips (just now growing these flat enamel scales) and the fleshy resistance tautens and pops and your mouth is flooded with a feeling you've never felt before. It's some amalgamation of the tickle in your bladder when you pee, the surprise of a cool breeze in your wet ears after bathtime, the sweetness and slipperiness of milk from the breast. All those things, but with a hundred unfamiliar sensory allusions, too. Your lips suck into your mouth, tears grow on your lashes, your whole face is doing something instinctual to suppress the intensity of the taste, and, oh, how your mother laughs! Her big floating head, the sun, the moon; swirling spots invert, flat lines curve, it all means happiness. An orange, in your mouth, to your ears and eyes: happiness. Oranges are the only thing that matter, and all you want to do is —

∘∘○

—play this game forever, this version of catch you and your father have invented in which you bounce a rubber ball against the pavement, watch it rise high into the cloudless sky, turn to a speck of dust, then wait, wait, wait for it to fall and attempt to trap it in your cupped hands before it touches the ground. You've devised an elaborate scoring system, because what's the point of playing if there's no winner? Your father never plays casually, never holds back: he winds up and fires the ball against the ground, the momentum almost carries him off his feet, and it disappears into the blue sky. You wait with your neck craned, hands above your head to block the sun, sure that the ball is going to come down right between your eyes, right down your throat, but afraid to look away, waiting, waiting so long that you're sure it has fallen already, ready to lower your hands, give up, but then you hear it *thwack* against the sidewalk a few yards behind you, and your father starts counting.

"One! Yes, ha! Better get it! Two! Better *get it*! Oh, so close … that's three!"

It's the number of bounces, you see, that count against you. "That's forty-three for me. Seven more points and I win. Crunch time, little lady. Can you do it? The seconds are ticking away. Last chance, this is *it*, for the *win*!"

So, so, so fun. The *most* fun. When have you ever had this much fun? Never. This is the only place you'll ever want to be, here on the street with your father. You'll never want to leave. You'll only ever want to be right here —

∘ ∘ ○

—on the floor, flat on your stomach, wedged up on your elbows, toes tight and bouncing in alternating, unconscious strokes. *Bleh!* This stickiness! Your tongue is swollen with sugar. Your teeth are velveteen-glazed. You're chewing the purple spoon-straw through which you just sucked up forty-four ounces of Coke-flavoured slush. Now you're absently scratching the wax off the empty cup. Somewhere a television drones. Where are you? What house, what room, what city? Ah, yes, of course: New York! You're in the Big Apple, in the blown-open vault of the First Metropolitan Bank. Hydro-Man turns into a tidal wave and surges out the door, sweeping Spider-Man up and carrying him outside. Do you hear that? The spelled-out *WHOOSH!*? Look at the way Sal Buscema details the wrinkling metal beneath the Beetle's fingertips as he uses his bionic carapace to tear open a solid-steel door: it's the sort of profound confluence of lines and shapes that might describe the epic, cross-continental path of an emigrating flock of swallows, or the heartbeat of a million-year-old volcano stoked and cooled and kept in rhythm by the dilation and constriction of deep-crust arteries. This comic book panel is a thing of such consequence. To be nine years old is to trust unequivocally in such things, to have faith that you will someday be —

o o O

—walking down the street in early September, sneakers snapping against the concrete sidewalk, crunching over fallen maple leaves, sloshing through shallow puddles left behind by the previous night's rain. It's cloudy, cool, the air still smells of ozone. That post-rain freshness fills you up, and with each deep breath it feels as if every cell in your body has been cleansed of your lame, girlish history. And your cells react accordingly: you walk differently, now, striding rather than stepping, marching rather than ambling. This is the first day of ninth grade, your first day at a new school, and there is such purpose to your pace that you cross whole blocks with a single step! You float past the houses and wonder which ones you'll see from the inside. Which of these houses will your friends live in? Will you sneak cigarettes behind that garage? Will you discuss crushes in that living room? Will you glue together science projects in that kitchen? Will you make out with a boy behind that upstairs bedroom window? You're already giddy with memories of things that haven't yet happened. You're excited to become the person built from those memories. You're so happy that you chose to be here. You're so happy that you'll have the chance to —

∘∘○

— watch this long-haired boy take the stage, hefting an acoustic guitar, holding it like a machine gun, like it's liable, at first stroke, to recoil in a death-spraying epileptic fit. His hand trembles against the strings and (here he goes!) he picks the first progression of notes but (oh, no!) they trick his long fingers. He stumbles through to the power chords, and now he starts strumming, which, for him, is a bodily endeavour, but bless his heart, he's really going for it, like he's paddling a canoe, and he leans close to the microphone. There's music in there somewhere. You can almost hear it. Despite his inaudible, atonal muttering. Despite the gymnasium acoustics. Despite all this theatrical swaying, all this silly, shut-eyed intensity. Despite it all your heart will spill over with love for this boy, and in the months that follow you'll expend the bulk of your mental energy hoping that one day you'll have the chance to be —

∘∘○

— in bed with this tattooed girl, still naked and tangled in the blankets and refusing to acknowledge the sunny weekend unspooling, minute by minute, hour by hour, before you. Stinky and slothful and thoroughly euphoric, even though you're down to your last twenty dollars and struggling to reconcile your limited monetary resources with the desire to do something more significant with your time than watch TV behind the gloomy veil of bedsheets hung over the living room window or take the bus downtown to wander through the air-conditioned mall and make lists of things you'll buy when you're rich. "Let's go for a walk," you say, and you do that thing where you press your forehead against her arm and chest and the side of her head, roll it back and forth like you're shaking your head no, then bounce it in gentle head-butt fashion. And along with your baby animal's urging, you coo, "Come on come on come on," and her breath smells terrible in the most wonderful way. You could probably just stay here forever. Why would you ever leave? Why would you ever find yourself —

∘ ∘ ◯

— suddenly awake in a strange bed, stinking of boozy sweat, joints gummed up, neck shellacked with some person's dried saliva. Triplet digital numbers afloat in the blackness inform you that it's almost noon. You roll off the bed, out of the room, down the stairs. You tiptoe through the post-apocalyptic wasteland, evade beer-bottle booby traps, creep past couch-sprawled corpses, step outside into the blinding light, down the street to the transit station, but after waiting half an hour for a nonexistent express bus, you give up and walk the rest of the way to the apartment you share with two other girls who are maybe still passed out at the party, or at home sleeping, or away for the weekend visiting boyfriends, aunts, grandmothers, high school friends. Your hangover is grievous; this hour-and-a-quarter cross-town hike is doing nothing to bleed from your bloodstream the poisonous remnants of the previous night's excess. You stop twice to vomit in the bushes, but each time can hack up only a few gluey strings of lemony spit.

But it's worth it, isn't it? Because somehow you know that this is the prologue, and the prologue is where you introduce the problems that the rest of your story will solve, and the funny brew of regret and pride and contentment and fear now swirling around with the alcoholic concoction in your stomach will be distilled, reduced, clarified when you finally arrive —

○ ○ ○

— in this foreign land, where, standing in the taxi queue outside the airport, you suck up the milk-thick equatorial air for the very first time. Soon you will be coasting towards the blooming fluorescence of the city skyline, descending into it, smelling the curious smells, hearing the enchanting sounds. You're next in line. A taxi pulls up.

"Um, downtown," you tell the driver.

He roars off without a question.

Inside the cab, a pointillist rendering of what appears to be a rocket ship is finger-painted on the ceiling; the dash is cluttered with statuettes and amulets and tiny gold-framed photos; hanging from the rear-view mirror is a brace of coloured beads and a die-cut air-freshener with a cherubic grinning Buddha swinging a flaming sword.

You have arrived.

You're finally here, where you're meant to be.

Do all that, won't you?

Do it for your dear old dad.

In the meantime I'll be right here, just trying to —

Rrngh.

—just trying to, you know, get to where I'm going. Like always.

This?

Oh, *this*?

Don't worry, I know what I'm doing.

Trust me.

I can —

Rrrngh.

I can *alllllllmost* reach the bottom corner. Just have to make sure I get a good grip; I'd hate for a glancing touch to drop me another five feet.

Fnngh.

Got really close that time!

It can't possibly be coincidence that in the turmoil of Time chugging back to life your sonogram picture blew back to me like this. Another impossibility made conveniently possible by the weird quantum laws of this place. You're sitting right there, just inches out of my reach, all curled and caught kite-like mid-gust. Probably the same gust that snatched you away from my fingers in the first place.

You wonderful girl, you darling angel — you've been searching for me, the same way I've been searching for you! And I'm so glad that you found me. What would I do without you? I'd be trapped here forever. I'd have to chuck myself into the Pacific and hope for the best. But I almost have you, now, and you're my ticket out of here. You can help me kick things back into gear, the same way that little porcelain foal asleep on his patch of grass helped my grandmother get things going.

And now —

Okay —

Hoo!

Just exhale, Daniel, come on ... reach *farther*, make yourself *longer*, gently pull apart each atom in the bones and muscles between your wrist and heel, and —

There we go.

Juuuust a little bit farther.

Just about have it —

Just a few centimetres, and —

You know, I've often wondered: what if all this wreckage were reassembled?

Fluttering wing panels arranged flat edge to flat edge and bolted back onto the long aluminum skeleton, newspapers and magazines uncrumpled and folded flat and slipped gently into seatback pockets, shoes returned to the feet of the passengers thrust jarringly back into their chairs—all these torn portions of fuselage sewn together with rivets, jagged wounds scabbed over and eventually, through some microscopic binding process, healed. There it would be, unmistakably, irrevocably: a jet airplane! Yes! How nice to travel backwards, to heal my face and ribs by throwing them against Chad Billings's fists and kicks, to see the military dictatorship pushed out of power by a corrupt government content to maintain a friendly border. It would be hard, I suppose, to suffer through the sad years that follow: your mother and I would reabsorb you back into our bodies, we'd part ways in the streets of Poipet and I'd return home all bummed out. But then Marti and I would slowly drift together, we would move in together and I would read Chinese-style through her diaries and forget everything I know. Oh, blissful ignorance! Oh, ensuing happiness! Backwards through puberty, through droughts that decimate acne-pocked plains, coarse hairs growing feathery as they're absorbed back into my pores. On and on through youth, as my sense of the world narrows in scope, as my capacity for astonishment and awe grows and grows. That's how it should be, don't you think? A great swelling of contentment, then stripped of sensation, then back into the cozy void.

Yes, that's where I'd like to go, I think:

Back into the cozy void.

It's okay, my love. I'm ready.

I've been ready for years/decades/centuries.

Hggh.

Almost.

Try again.

Hggh.

Yeah.

Almost.

Yes.

Got it!

And

here

( ).

we

( ).

( ).

go!
( ).
( ).
( ).
( ).
( ).
( ).
( ).
( ).
( ).
( ).
( ).
( ).
( ).
( ).
( ).
( ).

Acknowledgements

This notion of an author toiling away in darkness, alone, isolated, removed from the world, is not entirely inaccurate. But it overlooks those mechanisms that enable his/her solitude and discounts all those people who sacrifice their happiness to maintain that solitude, not to mention the people who enter the picture after that stretch of solitude is complete; those exceptional folks who nurture and amplify and improve the jumbled mess that is the product of that solitude. So an author doesn't *really* work in solitude, and is never *really* alone, and certainly isn't the sole arbiter of the work to which he/she often receives sole credit (there is only one name on the cover of this book).

— and, yeah, yeah, yeah, I know: you hear this sort of thing all the time. But to *experience* it is an entirely different thing. It feels impossible, frankly, to acknowledge, in this brief addendum, the true existential meaning of what these caretakers have done for me, and how much their contributions have shaped the book you have (hopefully) just finished reading. But I'm going to try anyways. And hopefully succeed. Because each of these people have tried and succeeded on my behalf.

Early Days

The manuscript was incomprehensible mush when it ended up in the hands of early readers Alan Neal and Janet Slavin. That they managed to provide rational, thoughtful feedback was an act of such colossal generosity that they should be presented with humanitarian medals in a lavish garden ceremony attended by world leaders and celebrities.

My solitude wasn't really all that solitary, because I was able to commiserate and complain and pontificate and boast and generally pretend to be a real-life writer with *actual* real-life writers like Christine Fischer Guy and Megan Findlay, both of whom were very kind and patient and wise, listened to my complaints/pontifications/boasts, and continuously assured me that it was all good, don't sweat it, chill out (no, seriously, *chill out*).

The Wider World

Marilyn Biderman, whom I am proud to call my agent (and not just because of how cool it sounds to say "my agent" in casual conversation), was the first person who took me seriously as a writer and has invested much time and energy into transforming me from some guy you've never heard of to some guy you've never heard of whose rambling acknowledgements you're currently ~~reading~~ enraptured by. I am indebted to her for everything that has happened (and will happen) in my writing life.

One of Marilyn's countless terrific ideas was to involve Lara Hinchberger, who somehow managed to find the real story buried deep within the aforementioned incomprehensible mush, and who provided such deft and discerning guidance that I *still* think all her brilliant ideas were my own.

The remarkable folks at Goose Lane Editions — Peter Norman, Martin Ainsley, Julie Scriver, and Susanne Alexander — are the architects and engineers and craftspeople who built this thing you're holding in your hands. Thanks to them, some of my favourite memories of writing this book have been discussions about the hierarchy of parentheses, debates about em-dashes vs. en-dashes, and deliberations over cloudscapes and arrow shapes. That I was included at all in these discussions/debates/deliberations is just one of the many kindnesses they have shown me.

Bethany Gibson should probably have her name on the cover of this book. Above mine. In bolder type. She is as responsible for its presence in your hands as whatever chopped-down tree was pulped and flattened to print it. That's a pretty bad metaphor, actually, the kind she would have had me rethink or refine or remove. I have come to trust her opinions and instincts more than my own. She has been an advocate and a guardian angel and has made me believe all those unbelievable things you hear about the quintessence of author/editor relationships.

Practical (But Very Important) Matters

The Ontario Arts Council, the Canada Council for the Arts, and the Banff Centre all assisted in the creation of this book. I am proud to live in a country that supports artists (especially artists still early in their development) the way Canada does.

Even Earlier Days

Jeanne Madore was my humanities teacher at St. Patrick's High School in Yellowknife and did the thing that great teachers do, which was to make me feel, for the two years I was lucky enough to be her student, like I was her favourite. I am, to this day, still fuelled by the enthusiasms and approvals that she scribbled in the margins of my essays and stories.

Those Closest

My dad taught me about the magic of telling stories, and my mom taught me about the discipline of hard work. The result is this book. For the record, they are far, far better parents than the parents you've read about in these pages (or any pages, for that matter). They have been, since the very start, my most enthusiastic fans, and now, having become a parent myself and finally able to see all the great things they did for me, I am theirs.

And of course, throughout all the solitude, the person closest to you suffers your suffering and is elated by your elation, but receives his/her accolades (if ever) only in private. My wife, Emma-Leigh, has tolerated living in a house where things don't get fixed, has spent sunny weekends hanging out by herself, has endured my absent-mindedness and distraction, and has too often gone to bed alone while in another room I stared forlornly at some uncompliant phrase. These are no small sacrifices. And she has made them without complaint. From her I have received the two great gifts of my life — the time to write this book, and our daughter, Penelope Leigh — and for that I can never repay her.

(Oh, And One Last Thing)

I have always been a poor student, and have resisted, stubbornly, wastefully, all attempts by schools and institutions to educate me. For many, many, many years, throughout the long adolescence of my writing life, my only teacher was John Updike, and though our conversation was one-sided, and though it took place over a distance of decades, he remains, to this day, the person/entity/influence to whom I owe whatever writing skill I possess.

photo © 2016 by Dwayne Brown Studio

Jared Young's writing has appeared in places like *Maisonneuve*, the *Millions*, the *Toronto Star*, the *Bangkok Post*, and the *Ottawa Citizen* and has been anthologized by *McSweeney's*. He is also a co-founder and contributor at the film-writing website Dear Cast and Crew. He grew up in Yellowknife, and currently resides in Ottawa.